MY SISTER SARAH

Sisters Beattie and Sarah Melford have never understood each other, and a rift is caused when Beattie begins an affair with Edward, the young naval officer Sarah hoped to marry. Beattie's reputation is destroyed when it is discovered she is carrying Edward's child.

In the devastation of London after the Great War, the two sisters face very different lives, but will their paths cross again?

Spanning two World Wars, this warm-hearted and absorbing story shows how hurt may turn to healing.

MY SISTER SARAH

MY SISTER SARAH

by

Victor Pemberton

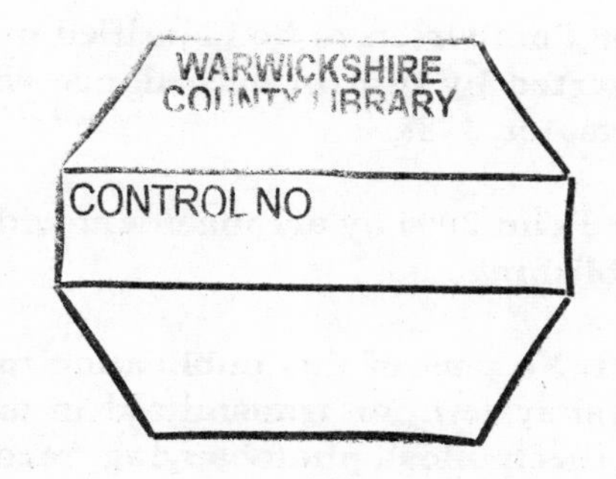

Magna Large Print Books
Long Preston, North Yorkshire,
BD23 4ND, England.

British Library Cataloguing in Publication Data.

Pemberton, Victor
My sister Sarah.

A catalogue record of this book is
available from the British Library

ISBN 0-7505-1547-3

First published in Great Britain by
Headline Book Publishing, 1999

Published in Large Print 2000 by arrangement with
Headline Book Publishing

Magna Large Print is an imprint of Library Magna Books Ltd.

Printed and bound in Great Britain by
T.J. (International) Ltd., Cornwall, PL28 8RW

For Ruth Messina, my dear friend,
and in memory of her husband, Cedric,
who gave me so much encouragement

Author's note:

The incident in Campbell Road, mentioned in this book, is a fictional account based on true events.

PART 1

1917 – 1921

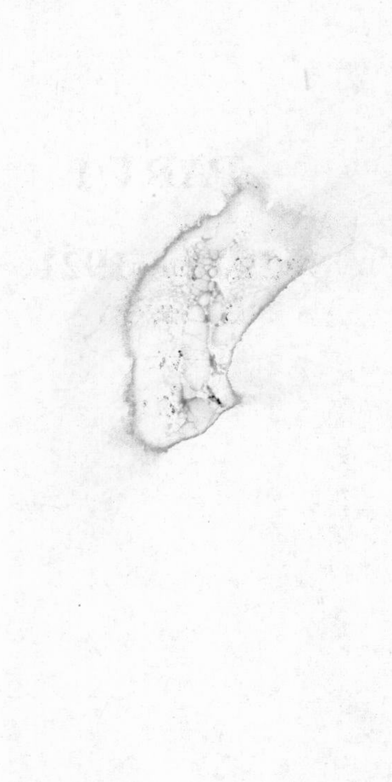

CHAPTER 1

The Eaglet was Beattie's favourite pub. There was something about the place that appealed to her, the friendly atmosphere with the gang of regular customers who were always good for a laugh, and the warm welcome she always got from the landlord and his missus, who, unlike plenty of other publicans in the area, didn't object to an unaccompanied young girl propping up the counter of the public bar every Friday and Saturday night. Besides, these were the people she liked, not the stuck-up old buggers from her own part of Islington, up 'the Cally', but real flesh-and-blood working men, who knew how to give a girl a good time. Yes, The Eaglet's customers were the salt of the earth all right, or at least those remaining of them who had managed to get home on leave from the hellhole trenches of France after three years of savage hand-to-hand fighting with the army of Kaiser Bill.

Beattie was always popular with the male customers, especially the Tommies. To them, she was 'one of the lads', for she could join in with any bawdy song they sang, down a glass of bitter, smoke a fag, and play a game of darts with the best of them. One or two of them had enjoyed her company in more ways than one, for with her full bosom, rose complexion, shapely thighs and flashing blue-green eyes, she was more often than not the best-looking female customer in either the public or the saloon bar.

'Looks like the fleet's in port.'

The young bloke in naval uniform wasn't in the least surprised when Beattie approached him; they'd been eyeing each other up across the bar all evening through the thick haze of blue fag smoke.

'Anchor's down, and here I stay,' he replied with a knowing grin, and in an accent that was more public school than Islington. 'What'll you have to drink?'

Beattie sat down on the wooden bench seat he had vacated for her. 'Shandy,' she replied.

The young bloke pulled a face. 'Wasn't that a bitter you were drinking with the boys over there?'

Beattie smiled. 'They're my mates,' she replied, her accent an unnatural cockney. 'I only drink alcohol with people I know.'

'Then we'll have to do something about that, won't we?' The naval bloke offered her his hand. 'Edward. You can call me Ted.'

Beattie hesitated a brief moment, allowing herself time to look directly into his eyes, which were a bright, glowing pale blue. 'Beattie,' she replied, shaking his hand. 'You can call me Beattie.'

Edward laughed. He liked her. He liked her a lot. He had no way of knowing that he was not at all her type, for he was too clean-cut, too good-looking, and far too much like the family she had been born into.

'So you're an officer then?' she asked.
'Non-commissioned,' he replied.
Beattie looked puzzled.
'I'm a petty officer. A bit like a sergeant major in the army.'
'In other words, you're not just any old Jack Tar,' joked Beattie, picking up his cap from the bench beside her, and trying it on. 'Nice uniform, though.' She watched him closely as he adjusted the cap on her head to a cocky angle.
Whilst he was making his way to the bar to order their drinks, Patch, a black and white mongrel dog, who was a firm favourite with The Eaglet's customers, was on his hind legs, swirling round and round in a dance, to the sound of 'See Me Dance the Polka' played on the pub upright piano by his loving owner, old Tubby Layton, a local rag-and-bone man. By the time Edward got back with the drinks, the customers were laughing, applauding, and cheering, which meant that Tubby's well-worn flat cap, placed on the piano lid, was soon tinkling with the sound of coins being dropped into it and pints were being lined up beside it.
'Beattie?' Edward said, once the noise had died down. 'Must be short for Beatrice?'
Beattie, sipping her shandy, eyed him flirtatiously over the rim of her half-pint glass. 'You could be right.'
He drew closer, and stared straight into her eyes. 'But why do I think I've seen you somewhere before?'
'Oh, I get around,' was Beattie's only reply. For the time being, she had no intention of telling

him that although they had never met, she knew Edward Lacey well. In fact she knew quite a lot about him.

A few minutes later, Patch had to sit guard on old Tubby, who was now the worse for all the booze that had been pumped into him by his fellow customers. A little later, everyone was reminded that there was a war on when the gaslamps on the walls began to flicker and lose their glow, plunging the pub into a gloomy half-light.

Beattie left The Eaglet with her petty officer. Behind them, with the blackout blinds firmly drawn, the pub, which nestled comfortably on the corner of the main Seven Sisters Road and Hornsey Road, was nothing but a dark three-storey shape on a chilly late September evening. But from inside, they could hear the start of what promised to be a rowdy singsong, clearly intended to raise spirits and defy the war.

Beattie and her petty officer strolled hand in hand along the darkened Seven Sisters Road, heading in the direction of Finsbury Park, where Edward had lodgings. Apart from a tram with no interior lights, which clattered past them, the road was quiet.

A short time later, an eerie silence descended on the area. Even The Eaglet's customers had calmed down, exhausted by booze and song. Then a strange sound approached, whirring and throbbing.

In the distance maroons exploded into the air, giving a belated warning that an enemy aircraft was approaching.

A moment or so later, a barrage of anti-aircraft guns opened fire, sending out a profusion of shells with great puffs of white smoke into the low-lying clouds. This was followed by a crisscross of two searchlights, which scoured the sky for the intruder. Unfortunately, they were too late, for by the time they had picked up the great silver cigar-shaped Zeppelin in their beams, the deadly German war machine had deposited its high-explosive bomb on to the road below.

The bomb landed directly on the roof of The Eaglet, tearing straight down three floors into the saloon bar, before exploding with a deafening blast in the cellar below.

In the sky, the great silver cigar disappeared into the protection of the dark evening clouds, engines whirring at full speed, heading back towards the Channel coast and home.

It was some hours later that they dug out those who had perished in the devastating explosion at The Eaglet.

The only survivor appeared to be a black and white mongrel with a black patch over one eye. He was scraping frantically in the dust and debris of the ruined pub.

Sarah Melford polished the brass letterbox plate on the front door until she could see her face in it. This being a Tuesday, it was cleaning brass and silver day, and by the time she had got around to doing the letterbox, everything in the house, from the silver condiment set in the dining room to the brass fireguard and companion set in front of the sitting-room fireplace, had been restored to pristine condition. There was, of course, no need for her to do all this, nor in fact any of the house cleaning, for the Melford family could easily afford servants if they had wanted them. But Sarah hated servants, or at least the idea of them. Why should her father spend good money on getting people to clean the place when she herself had a perfectly good pair of hands, two good legs, and a healthy body that was perfectly capable of keeping the house in tiptop condition? And to Sarah, the family house, on Thornhill Road in the Barnsbury ward of Islington, was worth looking after. It was where she had been born nearly twenty-three years before, and she loved every single yellow brick it was built of, every window, and every room on all three floors. For that reason alone, she was perfectly happy to devote her daily life to its upkeep.

Once she had finished the letterbox, Sarah made her way to the closet room, where she tucked away the Brasso and cleaning cloths, and poured some water from a china jug into the washbasin. Whilst she was washing her hands, she took a passing glance at herself in the mirror above the washstand. Although she would never admit it, she was a lovely-looking girl, with a slightly pallid complexion, grey-green eyes, and long flaxen hair that was pinned up into a full bun behind her head. She looked more like her father than her mother, for her face was marginally narrow, with a dimple right in the middle of a finely shaped chin. But because she was rather set in her ways, Sarah wore no makeup, and her daily wear usually consisted of a plain white blouse and a skirt that never rose up above her ankles. Her only concession to current fashion was the Royal Worcester Kidfitting corset she wore on special occasions, which helped to accentuate her already slender figure.

The smells of cooking that were coming from the kitchen at the back of the house finally persuaded her to join her mother. But not before she had wiped the washbasin round with a clean cloth, and tidied the few straggly hairs that had fallen over her forehead.

'Smells good,' Sarah called, as she joined her mother at the hob, where she was stirring a rabbit and onion stew. 'I can see why it's Father's favourite.'

'Well it won't be for much longer,' croaked her mother, Geraldine Melford, who was still recovering from one of her regular bouts of laryngitis. 'It says in *The Times* today the Government's going to ration meat and butter. But only in London and Southern England.'

'What?' snorted Sarah, outraged. The prospect of doing without meat stews, meat pies or the Sunday roast was, to her, quite unacceptable. 'Why should it always have to be us in the south who take the brunt of the war? We not only get bombed by Zeppelins and war planes, we also have to have our food on the ration.' Even though she was well-spoken, her voice, like her mother's, was often quite sharp. 'I tell you it's not fair. It's about time they picked on them up north for a change.'

'North, south – what does it matter? We're all the same country, Sarah. If we're going to bring this hateful war to an end, we're all going to have to do our bit.'

Sarah wasn't convinced. For a girl only in her twenties, she was curiously autocratic. She frowned on anything that hindered her own style of living. But she knew she'd been relatively lucky.

'I still can't stop thinking about those poor devils who got killed in the bomb blast at that public house a few months ago. How can their families ever recover from something like that?'

Geraldine sighed. 'I don't know, Sarah,' she said, going to the kitchen table to finish peeling potatoes. 'This war has been so ugly, so unnecessary. We've lost so many of our boys, young men who haven't even been given the chance to know what life is all about. Lord Kitchener has an awful lot to answer for.' She put on her rimless spectacles and picked up the peeler. Geraldine had a similar build to her daughter – tall, well-proportioned, and quite slender, especially for a middle-aged woman – but there the resemblance ended, for Geraldine had a full, rounded bust, and her face was rosy with high-boned cheeks. Like her daughter, she dressed older than her age, wearing a black lace bodice over a white blouse, lace cap to match, and a long dull grey skirt. 'Anyway, we must stop being so gloomy,' she said, as Sarah joined her at the table to start on the carrots. 'Now you've got a young man, you've got a whole exciting new life ahead of you.'

Sarah flinched. 'Oh, Mother,' she said, embarrassed. 'I've told you, I hardly know him.'

Geraldine looked up over her spectacles. 'You've been walking out for months now. It's time he asked your father if he can marry you.'

Sarah abruptly stopped peeling carrots. 'Mother! That's an absurd thing to say. How long was it before Father proposed to you? Three, four years?'

'That was different,' replied Geraldine, with just a hint of mischief in her voice. 'I was the only lady friend your father ever had. He was never sure whether I wanted him.'

Sarah felt a little reticent. 'This is the only man *I've* ever walked out with.'

Geraldine leaned across, and covered Sarah's hand with her own. 'All the more reason why you should grab the chance whilst it's there.' She continued with her peeling. 'So – when are you going to bring him home to meet us?'

'Oh, Mother!'

'For goodness' sake, child, why are you keeping so shy about him? You haven't even told us his name.'

Sarah put down her peeling knife, and smiled gently at her mother with a pleading look in her eyes. 'When I'm ready, Mother,' she said. 'When I'm ready.'

Samuel Melford was a lucky man. In fact, he told himself so every single day of his life. Samuel was never a person to take things for granted, and he was always grateful to the good Lord for giving him a loving wife and family, a well-paid job, and a home he could be proud of. Why then, he asked himself, as he made his way home on foot through the darkened streets of Barnsbury, was his mind these days so ill at ease?

'Evenin', guv'nor.'

On his way home on a Tuesday evening, Samuel never failed to make his ritual stop at Sid Perkins' hot chestnut stall on the corner of Richmond Avenue, where the warm glow of burning embers helped to soften the chill of a raw February evening. 'Good evening, Sid,' he replied, savouring the sweet woody smells that were wafting up from the hot chestnuts, whose hard brown skins had already split open over the intense heat. 'They smell good tonight.'

'That they do, sir,' sniffed Sid, who seemed to have a perpetual runny nose, which he only ever wiped on the cuff of his frayed jacket. 'Fresh from the Cally Market this mornin'. Same as usual, sir?'

'Two bags, please, Sid.'

Sid scooped up the blackened chestnuts, and filled two small paper bags with them. Then he wrapped them up in an old page of the *Islington Gazette*.

'Saw your youngest terday, sir,' he said, handing over the chestnuts. 'Reckon she was 'avin' 'erself a real good time.'

Samuel looked up with a start. 'Oh, really,' he said, guardedly. 'Where was that?'

'Up the Cattle Market. She was wiv a 'ole bunch of geezers. They was 'avin' a right ol' knees-up round Fred Kiley's barrel organ. Laugh a minute, it was. She's quite a gel. Chalk and cheese to your eldest.'

Samuel paid the twopence for the two bags of

chestnuts, and after thanking Sid, went on his way. It was too dark for Sid to have noticed the pained expression on his customer's face.

After he left Gamages Department Store in Holborn each evening, where he was the General Manager, for Samuel the journey home seemed interminable. However, he always quickened his pace when he walked home to Thornhill Road from the tram stop in Liverpool Road, for the prospect of supper with the family, a pipe of good tobacco in front of a warm fire, and a chance to settle down with either *The Times* or *The Illustrated London News* was one of his few real pleasures in life. But tonight was different. Tonight, he walked slower than usual, for his mind was now preoccupied. '*Saw yer youngest terday, sir. Reckon she was 'avin' 'erself a real good time.*' Those words echoed through Samuel's mind as he strolled past the access to Lonsdale Square on his right, clutching the two bags of hot chestnuts in one hand and his briefcase in the other. At the corner of Richmond Avenue, he paused a moment or so before completing the last few steps home. Not a light was to be seen at the windows of any of the fine Georgian and Victorian houses, for the blackout regulations were strict, despite the fact that there had been no Zeppelin or aeroplane raids over the area for weeks. But the moon tantalised the rooftops as it sneaked in and out of the dark night clouds, enabling Samuel to take a lingering look at his own home, a sprawling Victorian building on three floors, and standing apart from all the other houses along Thornhill Road.

As he stood there, Sid's words were still ringing in his ears. *'Reckon she was 'avin' 'erself a real good time.'* What was it about his younger daughter that made her stand apart from the rest of the family? Why *was* she so different from her elder sister, who loved her parents, her home, and all the good things in life? Samuel rested his briefcase on the ground for a moment whilst he adjusted his homburg hat. Aware of its German origins, he had often felt guilty about wearing such a hat during wartime, but it was more comfortable and warmer than his usual trilbies.

At that moment, the moon emerged from behind the clouds again, and flooded the Melford house in a bright white glow. It also brought a warm, affectionate smile to Samuel's face. In some strange way, it encouraged him to think positive. Both his daughters were still very young, he said to himself. Both had a lot to learn about life and how to live it. Chalk and cheese they may be, but when it came to knowing what was right and wrong, neither would let her parents down. Not Sarah. Not even Beattie.

'They say the Bolsheviks are going to put the Tsar and his family on trial. I really think Mr Lloyd George should protest. It would be terrible if they tried to excuse them or something.'

As she talked, Geraldine Melford set the large china casserole dish on the kitchen table, where it joined other hot dishes containing boiled potatoes, spiced white cabbage, and baby beetroot with chopped parsley. It was an odd custom that prompted the Melfords to use the kitchen for family meals, while the dining room was only used on high days and holidays.

'Well, it's their own fault,' sniffed Beattie, indifferently. 'They should have looked after their people more, the *real* people!'

'Beattie!' Her mother looked at her aghast. 'That's an awful thing to say. You can't blame the entire Russian royal family for all the things that have gone wrong in their country.'

'Well, it's true,' replied Beattie, provocatively. 'A royal family is no different to anyone else. They should be made to work for their livin'.'

'Just like you,' added Sarah, cuttingly, as she handed her mother a supper plate.

Beattie flicked a contemptuous glance at her elder sister, but decided to ignore her. 'If you ask me, I reckon our own King and Queen could do with a few lessons on what's goin' on in Russia.'

Samuel Melford broke his silence. 'King George and Queen Mary are only figureheads, Beattie,' he said gruffly. 'They have nothing to do with politics.'

Beattie took the first plateful of rabbit stew her mother had served, and handed it to her father. 'Then I don't see the point of having them,' she said, determined to have the last word.

Samuel saw no point in discussing the topic any further with his younger daughter. They had been down that road before, monarchy versus a republic, and as long as he lived, he would never understand how a girl from Beattie's privileged background could be such a champion of the working class, particularly when she herself had never done a day's work in her life. 'Please pass the potatoes,' he said to her vacantly. It was the safest way out of the conversation.

Once Geraldine had finished serving everyone with their share of the rabbit stew, supper continued in the same way that it did most evenings – in total silence. For almost an hour, the only sounds were of eating, knives and forks working hard on china plates, and the sipping of water from fine cut-crystal tumblers. To an outsider, it would seem hard to believe that this was a close-knit, middle-class family gathered around the kitchen table for their evening meal. Occasionally Geraldine could be heard cooing, 'My angel!' to one of four cats, who ritually lined up on the floor beside her, waiting for a titbit of anything that might accidentally fall their way. The furry quartet were all strays that Geraldine had collected over the years and she adored them, much to the intense irritation of Beattie, who did not hesitate to give them a surreptitious sharp kick beneath the table.

Samuel Melford waited until the apple pudding had been served before bringing the silence to an end. At the best of times he was a man of few words, and his shyness often gave the false impression that he was moody. But he was a very thoughtful person who would often spend long hours in quiet contemplation and no decisions were ever taken until he had first considered them carefully and at some length. That was why his courtship of Geraldine had been for nearly four years, and even when he proposed to her he insisted that the actual wedding should not take place for a further year.

'Beattie,' he said now without looking up at her, 'what was your business in the Cattle Market today?'

Beattie, clearly taken off guard, looked up with a start. She answered immediately, without swallowing the mouthful of apple pudding she had just taken. 'The market?' she replied, indignantly. 'Who told yer I was up the market?'

Her father glanced up at her. 'It doesn't matter who told me, Beattie,' he said gently. 'I merely ask what business you were engaged in.'

'Do I 'ave to 'ave business to go up the market?'

Samuel refused to be stonewalled. 'Yes, Beattie,' he replied, with quiet insistence. 'An unaccompanied young lady should only visit a market when she has a specific purpose for doing so.'

Beattie gave a bored sigh and slumped back into her chair. 'Oh really, Father. That's so old-fashioned.'

Samuel smiled politely at her. If it hadn't been for the fact that the only hair he had on his head was a thinly greying fringe over his ears, he and his youngest daughter were almost identical in appearance, with faces that were round and open, and blue-green eyes the colour of the glass lampshade dangling over the kitchen table. 'To be old-fashioned is no burden for me, my dear,' he said quietly, precisely. 'The welfare of my family is of far more importance to me than the fashion of the day.'

'I like the market, Father,' Beattie replied, irritated. 'I've got a lot of mates up there.'

'Ha!'

The sarcastic retort from Sarah only irritated Beattie even more. 'Oh yes,' she snapped, glaring at her sister. 'And what's it to you?'

Sarah wanted to answer, but an anxious look from her mother persuaded her otherwise.

'Listen to me, child,' said Samuel, distracting Beattie's attention from Sarah. 'No one is interrogating you. I just want you to be aware that some of the people in that market are not to be trusted.'

'That's not true!' Beattie snapped, sitting bolt upright in her chair. 'Costermongers are the salt of the earth. They're worth far more than some of the muvver's darlin's round this neck of the woods!'

Sarah was finding it hard to contain herself. Only her mother's hand covering her own on the table restrained her from speaking her mind. But she was heartily sick of hearing her young sister spouting on about her working-class 'mates'. She was sick to death of hearing her speak in an unnatural cockney accent, far removed from the way she had been brought up.

Beattie went on, 'It's not the officers who're fightin' this war, yer know. It's the Tommy, the poor old foot soldier. If it wasn't fer 'im, Kaiser Bill'd be sittin' in 10 Downing Street right now.'

'That's all I have to say on the matter, Beattie.' Samuel wiped his mouth on his damask napkin and rose from the table. Although he was only a moderately built man, he held himself straight, and his jacket, purchased at discount from the men's department of the store in which he worked, was well cut and styled. 'In future, if you have time to spare, use it wisely.' Samuel turned from the table, and quietly left the room.

As soon as he had gone, Beattie started again. 'It's ridiculous. He treats me like a child.' She got up from the table, folded her arms, and strode to the other side of the kitchen. 'People are important ter me, no matter where they come from. I want to mix wiv me own type.'

Her mother, still seated, clenched her fists angrily. 'Has it ever occurred to you, Beattie,' she said tersely, 'that *we* are your types – your own family?' Finding it difficult to control herself, she raised herself up from her chair, and glared at her youngest daughter, who watched her quite impassively from across the room. 'What happened to all the young people you used to know, your friends at school, in the Girl Guides, the church choir?'

'Oh please, Mother,' sighed Beattie, embarrassed and turning her back.

This only angered Geraldine even more. 'Don't you ever dismiss me, young lady!' she snapped, pointing her finger menacingly at the girl. 'Your father and I brought you into this world. You will *not* dismiss us!'

Sarah, already on her feet, quickly went to her mother. 'Don't be upset,' she said, putting a comforting arm around her. 'Beattie means no harm.' She said it unconvincingly, without so much as a glance at her sister. 'Why don't you go and join Father in the sitting room? I'll finish the washing-up, then bring you both a nice cup of tea.'

Her mother took a deep breath and, eager not

to increase her anger, smiled gratefully at Sarah, and left the kitchen, closely followed by three of the four cats.

Sarah, now alone with her sister, turned to her. 'Why do you have to upset them like that?' she asked calmly. 'It's not fair, Beattie.'

To her credit, Beattie looked concerned. 'I'm twenty-one years of age. I'm entitled to a life of me own.' She returned to her place at the table, picked up her dessertspoon, and aimlessly scraped at the remainder of her apple pudding. 'I don't want to be spied on every time I step outside this house.'

Sarah started to collect the dirty dishes. 'Mother and Father are not spying on you, Beattie. They're just concerned for your safety. There's a war on. There are so many dangerous people around.'

Beattie looked up with a start at her. 'Dangerous working-class people. Is that what you mean, Sarah?'

Sarah stopped what she was doing and looked at her young sister. In that brief moment, she thought she really didn't know her any more. Images of all their days of growing up together were flashing through her mind: their time at Barnsbury School just around the corner; sharing friends; outings to the seaside; the laughter, the tears, the disappointments. And yet, when she thought about those days carefully, she realised that even though she had always been Beattie's 'big' sister, they had never been close, and Beattie had never looked up to her. There were so many more memories of difficult times in their relationship than good ones. Why were their personalities so different in every conceivable way?

'Father goes to work, Beattie,' she said, without rising to her sister's bait. 'So do I, right here in this house. We're just as much working class as any of your friends in the Cattle Market.'

Beattie slammed her dish down on the table, and got up. 'I hate being told to do what's expected of me!' she growled, tossing back her straggly, unkempt auburn-coloured hair, like an unruly child.

Sarah said, 'Nobody expects you to do anything you don't want to do, Beattie.' She put down the pile of plates she was holding. 'Look, Beattie,' gently, she took hold of both her sister's hands, 'you're a beautiful girl. One day you'll find a man you want to settle down with.'

Beattie, irritated, tried to pull away, but Sarah held on to her.

'You'll have children of your own, children you care for, just like Mother and Father care for you and me.'

Beattie finally managed to break loose. 'I don't need anyone to care for me! I'm not a kid. I'm a grown woman!'

Sarah's expression hardened. 'Then start behaving like one, Beattie.'

Beattie smiled caustically, then made off towards the door. She paused briefly, and turned. 'Don't get too cocky, sister dear,' she said. 'You're not the only one with a classy boyfriend.'

Sarah watched her go. Beattie's remark had baffled her – in more ways than one.

The Islington Cattle Market positively bristled under the bright winter sun. Since the start of the war, the place had been used for many purposes other than the auction of cattle, for the costermongers down 'the Cally' had cashed in on the severe wartime shortages by setting up every type of stall from fruit and vegetables to household junk, and bric-a-brac concoctions of every shape and size. The air was filled with all kinds of sounds, from the vast crowd of chattering customers jammed around every market stall trying to bargain with the sharp local barrow boys, out-of-town farmers lining the cattle pens, inspecting the livestock before auction, the forlorn howls of domestic puppies and kittens waiting for sale, and, in the middle of it all, the whistling and chirping of hundreds of caged birds, resigned to their lifetime of captivity. Over the years, the old Cattle Market, situated between the main Caledonian Road and York Way, had gathered a reputation as a unique meeting place for rich and poor alike, and was nicknamed 'thieves market' by local residents. Many a rich farmer and well-to-do lady had been relieved of their wallet or purse, and so there was always a strong presence of 'foot bobbies'.

There had been a good inch of late February snow, which overnight had turned to ice, and it was so cold that many of the stall holders had lit braziers. This, of course, had the advantage of luring potential customers to the stall, to warm their hands over the fire, and view the goods on sale.

Despite her family's concerns, today Beattie was with her usual gang of 'roughs', most of them several years younger than herself and therefore not yet eligible for conscription. To her mother's despair, she had left the house that morning looking more like a gypsy than a girl from a well-heeled home in Barnsbury. Her cotton dress was more suitable for summer than winter, and much shorter than the austere fashion of the day allowed. Over her head she wore a brightly coloured shawl, which also covered her shoulders and body, and was her only concession to the cold. These days, Beattie was practically a fixture at the market; her raucous laugh alone was enough to turn heads. But despite this she was certainly not the queen of the castle in the market, for there were plenty around who could give as good as they got.

'Keep your bleedin' 'ands to yerself, Shiner, or you'll get my fist in yer face!'

Shiner was having none of this from no cut-glass moneybags from up Barnsbury. He was from the tough end of 'the Cally', and for most of his seventeen years he'd had to beg, borrow, and steal to survive. 'Don't give me no lip, Beat!' he croaked, his voice already hoarse from smoking too many nicked cheap fags. 'Yer gettin' too big fer yer boots these days.'

Beattie angrily shook off the tight clench of his hand from her arm. 'You touched me up, you dirty sod! Yer know yer did!'

Shiner, his ragged flat cap pushed back on his head, snapped back in a flash. 'So wot if I did? It's the first time *you've* ever complained!' He knew he was riling her, because he was a good-looking young bloke, and the rougher he was, the better she liked it. 'Wos up, Beat?' he said with a smirk, his dark mischievous eyes undressing her. 'Don't like the rough no more, is that it?'

Beattie, indignant, turned away from him.

'Prefer a bit of slap wiv the petty officer?' he called at her back. Beattie turned, and swung her fist at him. But he was there before her, and grabbed hold of her wrist. 'Wos 'e got that I ain't, Beat? Must be somefin' speshul?'

Although Beattie despised him, at the same time she was attracted to him. 'Why can't you leave me alone, Shine?' she said, pulling her arm away.

'D'yer want me to?' he replied, smiling. 'I mean – really?'

Beattie started to walk off. But he followed her.

'You've bin seein' this geezer for quite a time now,' he said, pursuing her. 'I fawt yer said la-di-das ain't yer type?'

She came to an abrupt halt, and turned to face him. 'Shine,' she said, completely ignoring what he had been saying to her, 'how can I get a job up here?'

Shiner looked taken aback. 'A job? You? In the market, yer mean?'

'That's what I mean,' she replied. 'I want ter do somethin'. I want to earn some money of me own.'

Shiner sized her up for a moment. 'Wot kind er job?'

'Anythin'.'

'You're not cut out fer – anyfin'.'

Beattie stared him straight in the eye. 'I reckon

I'm the best judge of that,' she said.

Shiner looked down at his filthy boots. 'I'll give it some fawt,' he said. At that moment, he caught sight of a couple of bobbies in the distance, slowly winding their way through the market crowds. He pulled his cap low over his forehead and was instantly gone.

Beattie turned back in the direction from which she had come. But as she did so, she came face to face with Nagger Mills, a young costermonger's daughter, who worked the tea urn for the farmers over in the cattle pen. 'Yer mustn't pay no 'eed ter Shiner, Beat,' she said. ''E's a stupid sod. Always puttin' people's backs up.' Nagger, whose real name was Lucy, but who got her nickname because she was always nagging her old man, took hold of Beattie's arm and gently strolled along with her. 'Did yer know, 'e's 'ad 'is call-up papers?'

Beattie turned with a start. 'Shiner?'

Nagger nodded. ''E burned 'em. Now 'e really will 'ave the bobbies after 'im.'

As they walked, Beattie thought about Shiner, and how, if only he knew, he would be far better off in the army; at least he would get a couple of decent meals in his stomach each day. But then she remembered all the young blokes from the market who had been dragged off to those blood-filled trenches with Kitchener's army, and she felt ashamed even to have thought of such a thing.

'I'm lookin' for a job, Nags,' she said, pulling the shawl closer around her head and shoulders. 'D'yer know anyone round the market I could ask?'

Nagger came to a halt. She was shorter than Beattie, and younger. 'A job?' she said incredulously, briefly taking off her flat cloth cap and scratching her short mop of brown hair. 'You?'

In the background, a crowd of market customers were joining in with Fred Kiley's barrel organ as it played 'I Wouldn't Leave My Little Wooden Hut For You'. The sound they made seemed to defy the intense cold of the morning, for it drifted right up above the coloured stall awnings, and disappeared into the crisp blue sky.

'I'm getting desperate, Nags,' said Beattie. 'If I don't get a job of some sort soon, I'm going to land in real trouble.'

Nagger was baffled. 'But yer don't need ter work, Beat,' she said. 'Yer've always said so. Not in your situation – I mean, comin' from a good family an' all that, a roof over yer 'ead, and food in yer stomach.'

Beattie turned to her, looking unusually anxious. 'The thing is, Nags, the way things are goin', I may not 'ave that roof over me 'ead for much longer.'

CHAPTER 2

Sarah Melford longed to be a married woman. Ever since she was a child she had fantasised about the day when she would stand at the church altar, gaze into the eyes of the man she loved, and say 'I will'. And that was what she intended it to be: love – love real, love from the heart. It was perhaps every young girl's romantic illusion that love was all that was needed as the foundation of a long and happy marriage. After all, that was how it had been for her own parents; Geraldine and Samuel Melford had never had relationships with anyone else before they met, and they had now been married for almost twenty-five years. So if it had worked for them, Sarah was convinced that it would work for her too. She wanted to be married, she wanted to be able to walk into shops and be addressed as Mrs this or that, and talk to the other married women about mutual things such as children, and the kind of food she cooked for her husband when he came home from work in the evenings.

The trouble was that despite the fact that she was now twenty-three years of age, until recently she had never actually made the attempt to go out and try to meet a potential husband. But then she had met the man of her dreams quite by chance.

It had happened during the previous summer

when she had paid a visit to a patriotic war exhibition which was being held in Gamages Department Store in Holborn. The exhibition, one of several organised by the War Ministry to bolster public confidence in the armed forces, was manned and operated by members of all three services. Months later, Sarah still could not believe how brazen she had been to ask the young naval officer questions about some photographs of warships she had been looking at on the display walls of the exhibition. But when she had overheard his well-spoken voice, so clear, articulate and manly, she felt compelled to speak to him. And when he called her 'miss' and she found herself staring straight into his pale blue eyes, she felt a strange surge flowing through her entire body, something that she had never experienced before. What's more, he was an officer and a gentleman, anyone could see that, even if he was only a noncommissioned officer.

'I'd better warn you,' said Sarah, as she clung on proudly to her petty officer's arm as they ambled along Whitehall, on a windswept Sunday afternoon, 'my mother's dropping hints that it's about time I brought you home to tea.'

Although the young petty officer had been expecting this sooner or later he was still taken off guard. This was what he had been dreading. It was a step towards formalising their relationship. After a brief hesitation he turned to her and, with a weak smile, asked, 'How d'you feel about that?'

As he was a good head taller than she, Sarah had to look up at him when she replied gauchely,

'That's what I was going to ask you.'

The petty officer thought carefully before answering. 'It's up to you, Sarah,' he said, fidgeting uneasily with his uniform cap.

Sarah stiffened a little. 'It's not compulsory,' she said, her smile rather fixed. 'I just thought – well, since we've been walking out together for some time now, you might be a bit curious to know what kind of a family I come from.'

The petty officer managed to give her a forced smile without actually answering.

'They're not bad, once you get to know them.' Sarah was doing her best to reassure him. 'Except for Beattie, of course – my sister. She's quite a handful.'

At that moment, a gust of wind almost prised Sarah's large brown felt hat from her head, and in her desperation to hold on to it, she crushed the peacock feather attached to it. Most of the other Sunday afternoon strollers had the same problem, for March was living up to its reputation with an endless stream of gales and cold early-spring rain. In a gallant effort to shield Sarah from the wind, the petty officer put his arm round her shoulders. Sarah stiffened and pulled away.

'Not in public, Edward!' she said, looking around to make sure that no one had noticed.

Every time Sarah did something like that, Edward felt like shrivelling up inside. This girl was so set in her ways, so determined not to present the wrong type of image to everyone around her, that, even if he loved her, which he didn't, he found it difficult to see how they could possibly spend their future life together. So why, he asked himself on so many such occasions, was he incapable of just walking away from her and calling it a day? In fact, Petty Officer Edward Lacey had no idea how he had become so involved with someone like Sarah in the first place. What she was looking for was companionship, and a place in society. What he wanted was a woman who would give herself to him, in every meaning of the word. After all, she was a beautiful-looking girl, whose pallid complexion only enhanced the sparkle in her grey-green eyes. Oh how he longed to see that bun removed from the back of her head. How he longed to see that massive heap of flaxen hair tumble down over her shoulders. He wanted to see her, to feel her, to hold her close to his own body. But it was impossible. Sarah was untouchable; they never even held hands, or embraced. Each time they met, he hoped he might see the other Sarah, the one that was longing to be released.

'Everyone says it's hard to believe we come from the same family.'

Edward, still deep in thought, hadn't heard what Sarah had said. 'Er, I'm sorry. What did you say?'

Sarah sighed. 'Beattie. My sister. We've never been friends. Not *real* friends. When we were small children, our parents bought us so many beautiful things, lovely dolls, and so much else. Beattie hated dolls; she preferred to play in the street outside with some of the rough children of the neighbourhood.' For a brief moment, there was a wistful look in her eyes. 'Beattie doesn't like nice things. She doesn't like nice people. She just wants to be different.'

Edward felt a tight feeling in his stomach. He was aware that Sarah had turned to look at him, but he was too riddled with guilt to respond.

'Your cap, Petty Officer!'

Edward turned with an abrupt start to find an army captain just passing by. He immediately straightened up, adjusted his cap, and with a smart salute croaked back, 'Sir!'

'You're wearing the King's uniform, Petty Officer,' barked the army captain, without stopping. 'Don't forget it!'

'Sir!'

Before saying anything, Sarah waited for the captain to disappear amongst the crowds strolling along Whitehall. 'He's an army officer,' she sniffed indignantly. 'What's he doing giving you orders?'

'A commissioned officer is superior to me in any of the services, Sarah,' Edward replied rather gawkishly.

Sarah remained indignant, and after one last glare over her shoulder towards the army captain, she grabbed hold of Edward's arm, and led him off. As they passed Downing Street, a large crowd of pacifist demonstrators were being herded on to the pavement opposite Number 10, shouting loud protests at Prime Minister Lloyd George's refusal to enter into a compromise peace settlement with Germany. Sarah and Edward quickly eased their way through the sea of placards, and made off towards Parliament Square.

On their way to the tram stop on the Victoria Embankment, Edward had to tell Sarah that their Sunday afternoons together would have to be curtailed for the foreseeable future, as he was about to be transferred from his administrative position at the Admiralty, and posted to a crew-training job on board a warship being prepared for active duty in Portsmouth.

Sarah took the news far better than he had expected. 'The war has to be won,' she said bravely. 'But when it's all over, we shall have our whole lifetime together to look forward to.'

Sarah's confidence in the future weighed on Edward's conscience like a heavy lump of metal. As he helped her on to the Number 38 tram, and watched it disappear into the dark recess of the new Kingsway tunnel, the only thing his mind could take in was the feeling of betrayal and deceit.

Bob Sluggins had known the Melford girls since they were kids. In those days, he and his missus, Vera, were, for a brief period, landlords of the White Conduit public house on the corner of Dewey Road in Barnsbury. Although it was not exactly the most salubrious of pubs, Bob was well liked in the district, and, because he was quite a nifty handyman, he was often called upon by some of the locals, including the Melfords, to do an odd job of plumbing, or furniture repair. Some said he was also quite a hand at crochet work, which left him wide open to some pretty cryptic comments from his regulars down the pub. However, the same amiable feelings were rarely accorded to his missus, for to most people she was considered to be a bit of a bossy old slag, who was well known for giving short measures at the counter, especially on the shorts. Vera Sluggins couldn't bear the Melford family, especially the females – 'stuck-up bunch of cows' she used to call them – which made poor old Bob feel uncomfortable, for whenever he went to do a job for them, he really enjoyed their company.

But even in those days, he could tell the difference between the two girls, Sarah and Beattie. He was amazed how 'chalk and cheese' they were, one relishing the security of a comfortable family environment, and the other a creature of the streets – and the rough part of the streets at that.

When, some years ago, Bob and Vera had given up the pub, they'd taken over a pawnbroker's business in the Holloway Road. Vera took to the work like a frog to water, but Bob found it depressing, dealing with the misery of folk from the highest to the low. But it did provide him and the 'old slag' with a respectable, if not lucrative, living, for there were many regular customers, including young Beattie Melford.

'One an' 'alf guineas, Miss Beattie. Top price.'

Beattie pulled a face. 'Come off it, Bob,' she groaned. 'My dad bought me that bracelet for my sixteenth. It's solid nine carat gold.'

Bob was still looking at Beattie's delicate, fine bracelet through his eyeglass. 'I can see wot it is, Miss Beattie. But ter me, it's only worf its true value.'

Beattie looked desperate. It was bad enough

having to come into such a tiny shop at all, with its oppressive smell of poverty, leather purses, belts, handbags, rolled gold, silver, brass, copper, threadbare fox furs riddled with moth-holes, second-hand boots and shoes, men's suits, women's dresses and coats, kid gloves, ships squeezed into bottles, stuffed animals and birds, and any amount of old pictures that might prove more valuable one day than they looked. 'Couldn't yer just make it a round two quid, Bob?' she pleaded. 'I've got ter get me 'ands on some ready cash – and soon. *Please!*'

Whilst Beattie was still pleading, Bob was shaking his prematurely grey head. 'I can't do it, Miss Beattie,' he insisted, removing his eyeglass and putting it in the lower pocket of his open waistcoat. 'Times in't good, yer know. There's no cash around 'cos of this ruddy war.'

Beattie's desperation was turning to irritation. 'Two quid ain't goin' ter break the bank, fer God's sake!'

'It may not break the bleedin' bank,' screamed Vera Sluggins from the back parlour, 'but it could break us!'

At the sight of the old slag approaching from the parlour, Beattie stiffened visibly.

'Let me see wot she's got there,' growled Vera, grabbing Beattie's bracelet from her old man's hand. She was a huge woman, with thinning hair dyed with henna, and a wisp of straggling hairs growing from her chin. 'Looks a bit of cheap old brass ter me,' she said provocatively. 'I fawt you Melfords was s'pposed ter be so loaded.'

'In case yer don't know, *Mrs* Sluggins,' snapped

Beattie, furiously, 'that's a valuable piece of jewellery. An' if you're not interested in it, I'll take it elsewhere.'

The old slag grinned, and held out the bracelet to her. 'As yer wish.'

Before Beattie had the chance to take it back, Bob retrieved it from his wife. 'Wot say I split the difference wiv yer, gel? Firty-five bob?'

'Wot!' His missus, outraged, grabbed the bracelet from him, and thrust it back at Beattie. 'Wot d'yer take us for? Bleedin' millionaires?'

For the first time, Bob showed his anger. Before Beattie had the chance to take back her bracelet, he grabbed hold of his wife's hand, and retrieved the jewellery. 'Fank yer, my dear,' he growled, through clenched teeth. 'I can manage this transaction on me own.'

The old slag glared at him as if she was about to hit him. But something told her that she had better not push her luck too far, so, with a haughty shrug of the shoulders, she retreated her back to the parlour whence she came, slamming the door behind her.

'So?' said Bob, undeterred. 'Do we 'ave a deal or not?'

Beattie sighed, and nodded.

Bob took the bracelet, and placed it carefully in one of his jewellery cases beneath the counter. 'I'll give yer a ticket,' he said, writing in his receipt book.

Whilst he was filling in the details, Beattie leaned across and, lowering her voice, said, 'I'm lookin' fer somewhere ter stay, Bob?'

Bob looked up with a start.

'Can yer 'elp me?'

Bob sized her up for a moment. 'You leavin' 'ome?'

'I – might be,' said Beattie cagily. 'It's possible.'

'Your folks know about it?'

As usual, Beattie reacted by flaring up. 'That's my business, Bob.' But then she suddenly remembered that he was one of the few people she knew who had always been kind to her. 'Yer see, I've got a few fings ter work out fer meself. I'm twenty-one now. I need me independence.'

Bob stared at her for another brief moment, then continued filling in the receipt. 'You're lookin' fer somewhere round 'ere? Round 'Olloway?'

'Anywhere. I'm not fussy. I just need a room, that's all.'

''Ow much can yer afford ter pay?'

Beattie hesitated. 'Not much.'

She waited whilst Bob finished filling in the receipt. His silence before he spoke again seemed an eternity, and she felt that all the stuffed animals and birds in the shop were watching her every move. In fact, she was unaware that they were not alone. In a cluttered corner of the shop a tall, well-built young man was waiting to be served. He'd felt obliged to keep out of sight whilst Beattie had been haggling a price for her pawned bracelet.

Bob tore off the bottom half of the receipt, and gave it to Beattie. 'That's yer ticket. Don't lose it.'

Beattie took the ticket, and waited for him to hand over the thirty-five bob from the cashtill. 'Will yer keep yer eyes open for me, Bob?' she said with difficulty. 'Ter find a room?'

'Can't promise,' he replied, flicking his eyes up only briefly to meet hers. 'It ain't easy.'

She took the money from him and smiled awkwardly. 'Fanks a lot, Bob. I'll keep in touch.'

A moment later, Beattie was out on the Holloway Road. There was still plenty of snow on the ground, but over the past few days the bitterly cold wind had dropped, and with the milder temperature, a thaw had set in. The road was as busy as ever, with trams and omnibuses with open staircases chugging to and from the Archway in one direction, and Upper Street, Rosebery Avenue, and the Thames Embankment in the other. People were wrapped up well against the cold – women in their long, ankle-length winter coats, and what men were left over from Lord Kitchener's army in woollen hats, heavy topcoats and mittens. As food was now more scarce than at any time since the war started, shop windows were pretty bleak, and there were queues outside every butcher's shop for even the most basic available food, such as penny pig's trotters and hot saveloys and pease pudding.

Beattie pulled her shawl around her shoulders, and dipped her hands in her dress pocket to keep warm. As she did so, she could feel the thirty-five bob she had just received for her bracelet, which she clasped tightly in her hand where it felt cold and heartless to the touch. She decided to return home to Barnsbury by the same route she had come. This meant crossing over the main Holloway Road, cutting through Madras Place into Liverpool Road, then straight along to

Barnsbury. On the way she passed by a terrace of Victorian houses which, earlier in the war, had been hit by a hand grenade, thrown from the control casket of a Zeppelin airship raider. Although there was little sign of any damage, she remembered reading in the *Islington Gazette* how an elderly man and his dog had both been killed when the small hand bomb had exploded right in front of them.

'If you're lookin' fer a place, I can 'elp yer.'

Beattie stopped dead. For a moment she resisted the temptation to turn and see who was addressing her, for, ever since crossing over the road from Bob's pawn shop, she had been aware that someone was following her. Finally, she turned around to find herself face to face with a tall young man, whose flat work cap was covering a head of ginger hair, and whose rough good looks were completely unsettling.

'Wot you after then, mate?' Beattie growled contemptuously.

'I'm not after nuffin', *mate,*' the man replied. 'But you are.'

Totally unafraid of the man, she strode right up to confront him. 'I never talk ter strange men,' she quipped.

The man grinned. 'Then 'ow yer goin' ter find this place you're lookin' for?'

Beattie's smirk became a look of steel. 'Where d'you 'ear that?' she demanded.

'The pawn shop does 'ave uvver customers, yer know.' He moved a step closer to her, and she could see that not only had he not shaved for a day or so, but the red choker tied around his throat was almost the same colour as his hair. 'Ever 'eard of the Bunk?' he asked.

'Who?'

'Yer mean yer don't know the Bunk – Campbell Road – up Finsbury Park, near Seven Sisters Road?' His face broke out into an even broader cheeky grin. 'Don't know much, do yer?'

'I don't know wot you're talkin' about.'

The man took a half-finished fag butt from behind his ear, fumbled around in his trousers pocket until he found a loose match, which he ignited by striking it against one of his fingernails, and then lit the fag. 'They got rooms up there,' he continued, after taking a deep puff. 'Goin' cheap.'

''Ow cheap?'

The man exhaled, then picked a strand of tobacco from the tip of his tongue. ''Alf a crown a week?'

Beattie's eyes widened. ''Alf a crown! Whose leg you pullin'?'

'If yer don't believe me, go an' ask fer yerself. Try Number 22. Yer can trust the ol' gel there. 'Art of gold.' He turned and started to stroll off.

Beattie was taken aback. 'Hey! Wait a minute!' she called.

The man stopped and, fag in mouth, turned to look back at her.

'Wot's in it fer you?'

The man took a deep pull of his fag, then exhaled. 'Nuffin' in it fer me, darlin'. I just don't like ter see a young gel taken fer a ride – if yer get my meanin'.' He turned and started to walk off again, calling back over his shoulder, 'Number

22. Tell 'er Jack Ridley sent yer.'

Beattie watched him disappear round the corner, back into Holloway Road. For a brief moment she couldn't believe the extraordinary encounter she had just had. Then she decided to take it all in her stride, shrugged her shoulders, and walked on.

But then, Beattie was like that.

CHAPTER 3

Sarah was sublimely happy. She had had the first letter from Edward since their last Sunday afternoon stroll together along Whitehall nearly three weeks ago, and although it was a short letter, it contained enough for Sarah to know that he missed her as much as she missed him. Or at least, that is what she read into his words: 'When I get back to London, we'll have a lot to talk over, about us, about the future.' For Sarah, those words were a declaration of Edward's intent. After all, he had always said that as soon as the war was over they would be able to spend so much more time together, and if the news coming out of the war each day was any indication, the end could not now be that far away.

With all this in mind, Sarah started to make plans. First on her list was an absolute determination that Edward should meet her parents, so she wrote straight back to him, inviting him to come to tea on the first Sunday afternoon he was able to get leave from his new posting down at Portsmouth. To her delight, Edward wrote back immediately, accepting her invitation, and giving her a firm date on which he would be able to come.

The days leading up to this important tea party were the most exciting and nerve-racking of Sarah's life. She wanted everything to go so well, for all of them to get on together. She wanted to impress Edward; she wanted to show him that she was the kind of girl who was going to make him the best wife he could ever hope for.

At least a week before the big day, she chose the dress she intended to wear: her blue silk with the large bow fixed behind, and a hemline that was cut just on her ankles. For this one occasion she would comb out her bun, and tie her hair with a blue ribbon behind her head. As always, she would not indulge in make-up, which she stubbornly insisted was only intended for women of the street, but before Edward arrived, she would pinch her cheeks to try to disguise her pallid complexion. During a shopping expedition in Holloway Road, she stopped at the main window of James Selby and Sons, the large department store, where she spent several minutes staring at a 'new season's' wedding dress displayed there with a confident, determined look in her eyes. As far as she was concerned, it was now only a matter of time before that wax model would become herself. The scene then was set. Everything was now prepared to make Edward's first meeting with his prospective in-laws as comfortable as possible. There was, however, one problem still remaining.

'Don't worry, sister dear,' gibed Beattie, in one of her mischievous moods. 'I wouldn't dream of barging in on your precious tea party. I've got better things to do with my time.'

Sarah was, as usual, having a hard time with her sister. It was only on very rare occasions that she ventured into Beattie's bedroom on the top floor of the house, but what she had to say to her was important enough for Sarah to risk being placed at a disadvantage. 'I don't think you understand, Beattie,' she said, refusing to rise to her sister's bait. 'I *want* you to be there at tea on Sunday, I *want* you to meet Edward. After all, you're my sister, you're part of the family.'

'Nice of you to say so,' replied Beattie, cuttingly. 'Sometimes I wonder.' She was sitting at her dressing table, which was so full of junk it was impossible to make out what anything was used for.

'You'll like him, Beattie, you really will.' Sarah moved behind her sister, and talked to her reflection in the mirror whilst Beattie gave an impression of trying to brush some sense into her tangled auburn locks. 'I've told him all about you, all sorts of things – like how when you and me were young, we used to chase the ducks in Finsbury Park. He thought that was hilarious!'

Beattie raised one eyebrow. 'I bet,' she said dryly.

In a desperate attempt to try to sell Edward to her, Sarah leaned over Beattie's shoulder, looking at both their faces in the mirror. 'I told him how you've always been the rebel in the family, but that it's never stopped us loving you.'

'Oh really?' was Beattie's bored response. 'And what about 'im?' she asked, carefully watching Sarah's reflection. ''Ow much d'yer know about 'im?'

'Oh, Edward comes from a very good family,' she said with mounting enthusiasm. 'They were in kitchen utensils.'

Beattie's face screwed up in disbelief.

'What I mean is, his mother ran a company that manufactured them. His father was in the navy. Unfortunately, he's a widower now. Mrs Lacey died several years ago.' In her enthusiasm, Sarah folded her arms around Beattie's shoulders and squeezed them. 'Edward lives with his father out in Suffolk. One day he's going to inherit a huge detached house.'

Beattie broke loose, got up, and moved away. 'Well 'e's got it all made for 'im, ain't 'e? You'll be able to clean 'is detached 'ouse till the cows come 'ome.'

Sarah waited a moment. She was trying so hard to make some kind of sisterly contact that she was prepared to compromise on anything Beattie said. 'I know he's not the kind of person you're interested in, Beattie,' she went on, knowing it was an uphill task trying to inject some kind of enthusiasm into her sister, 'but he's what I want. And I want him to like you too.'

'Well, you can but try,' Beattie said adroitly, as she sat down on the edge of her bed.

Sarah went across and sat beside her. 'You know, Beattie,' she said, 'things haven't always been – well – as they should be, between you and me. Somehow, we never seem to talk to each other, unless it's to criticise or squabble.' She put an arm around her sister's shoulders. 'I don't want to squabble with you, Beattie. You're my sister, my own flesh and blood. When I get married, I want us to be friends.'

Sitting so close to her young sister, Sarah could feel their two hearts beating, almost, it seemed, in unison. They were both from the same womb, they shared the same flesh and blood, and yet it was extraordinary that their hearts and souls were so different. She felt the urge to lean her head on Beattie's shoulder, and in one courageous move, that is what she did. It took all of Beattie's resilience not to react in the way that she really felt, so she just remained quite impassive.

Going through Sarah's mind were thoughts of what it had been like to have a young sister like Beattie. In those few quiet seconds she recalled times they had spent together as children – Beattie doing all the things they were told never to do, like trying to smoke one of their father's pipes whilst he was out, and feeling utterly sick as a result, and trying to get Sarah to play hookey from Sunday school, and go fishing down the Islington canal with some of the costermonger boys from the Cattle Market. And in one momentary flash, Sarah remembered the times when they used to go to the shop in Liverpool Road and buy their favourite sweet, sherbert powder with a liquorice bar bought for a penny, and served in a paper bag folded in the shape of a triangle. They were such vivid images, yet never seemed to reveal the true nature of the two sisters' relationship.

For her part, Beattie couldn't recall one single moment when she had actually enjoyed being in her sister's company. As far as she was concerned, Sarah was nothing more than a hindrance to her life, her freedom, her desperate attempts to express herself in her own abandoned way. Her sister's effort to create some type of bond between them only embarrassed her, making her feel hemmed in more than ever. To her mind, she and Sarah could never be friends. There never had been and never could be any kind of communication between them; to try would only end in tragedy. And yet, there *was* something that never ceased to trouble Beattie. What, she had asked herself on many occasions, would she feel if anything should ever happen to Sarah? What would she, Beattie, do? How would she react? She would never know that it was a question Sarah also had often asked herself about her young sister.

'What're yer afraid of, Sarah?'

Beattie's sudden question took Sarah by surprise. 'Afraid?'

Beattie got up, releasing Sarah's arm from around her shoulders. 'You didn't come up 'ere just ter tell me that yer want us ter be friends. Yer came 'ere because yer want ter make quite certain that I don't make a fool out of yer in front of yer fancy naval officer.'

Sarah, hurt, got up immediately. 'Beattie, that's not true. And in any case, Edward isn't an officer. He's–'

'I don't care wot 'e is!' snapped Beattie. 'I don't 'ave ter put on no airs an' graces for the likes of 'im!'

'No one's asking you to.'

Sarah used her handkerchief to wipe the small beads of perspiration that had formed on her forehead. Despite the cold outside, the room was stifling and smelled of soiled clothes, for Beattie would sooner die than open a window to let in some fresh air.

'Look, Beattie.' Sarah was determined not to be roused. 'I don't want – I don't expect you to be anything but what you are, not to me nor Mother and Father, nor anyone else. But I do want Edward to like my family. One day, you'll be doing exactly the same thing.'

Beattie threw her head back with a dismissive grunt. 'Ha!'

'Oh yes, you will,' persisted Sarah, as she watched her sister winding the handle of her one cherished possession, a gramophone. 'And when you bring *your* young man home, whoever he is, wherever he comes from, you'll want us to like him too.'

Beattie was shaking her head. 'Yer don't understand, do yer?' she said, with a fixed, unsmiling expression. 'As long as yer live, you'll never understand. My life ain't about gettin' married, settlin' down an' 'avin' kids. If that's wot you want ter do, then that's fine. But don't expect me ter be the same – 'cos I'm not.'

Sarah felt crushed.

Beattie turned her back on her, and placed a record on the gramophone turntable. 'Don't worry,' she said, with just the faintest hint of remorse, 'I won't disgrace yer on Sunday.'

Sarah felt there was nothing more she could say, so she turned and made for the door. She paused there then, without turning to look back, said, 'How can two people be so close and yet so far apart?'

Closing the door behind her, for a brief

moment she stood on the landing to recover from the stale air of Beattie's room. Then in deep despair, she started to make her way down the stairs.

As she did so, she heard the wail of Beattie's gramophone record as the house echoed to the sound of the popular singer Gus Elen, lamenting on a forlorn hope, 'If You Were the Only Girl in the World'.

The steeple of St Andrew's church in Thornhill Crescent reached right up towards the bright blue spring sky like a hand stretching out towards the Almighty. During this gruelling time of war, the steeple, topped by its small cross, appeared to the residents of Barnsbury as a symbol of hope and defiance. Flanked on one side by the elegant curve of Thornhill Crescent, and on the other side by the rich splendour of Thornhill Square, the church was actually situated on Bridgeman Road, a quiet and pleasant back road that eventually led into the main Caledonian Road. Built of large quarried stone bricks, with a series of grey tiled roofs, St Andrew's doors were open night and day for all who wished to pray for the safe return from the front of their loved ones, and a speedy end to the war that had destroyed so much of the nation's family life. And, like so many other parts of Islington and beyond, Barnsbury had had its fair share of tragedy, so much so that during the early days of the war, the residents had organised the Barnsbury War Fund, which was one practical way in which people could help to relieve the suffering of the countless victims' dependants.

Samuel and Geraldine Melford, who were on the committee of the Barnsbury War Fund, tried never to miss Sunday morning service at St Andrew's and today their presence was especially important, for two more names were to be added to the endless list of local men who had been 'killed in action'.

'Private Harry Turner, nineteen years of age, 11th Battalion, London Rifle Brigade. Beloved son of Joseph and Laura Turner, Offord Road, and younger brother of Susan and Lizzie. Killed in action, Western Front, 25th March 1918. Rest in peace. And Lance-Corporal Ben Travis, nineteen years of age, Royal Army Medical Corps, 8th Field Ambulance, 2nd Division, beloved husband of Mary, and father of twins, Michael and Davey, Brooksby Street. Killed in action, Western Front, 4th April 1918. Rest in peace.'

Together with a hushed and crowded congregation, Sarah and her parents listened as the Reverend Cyril Wheatcroft concluded his litany of tragic news from the front. Despite the fact that news of the war had been improving day by day, it was inevitable that the Reverend's address had been a sombre affair, for even if the war were to end that very day, it was too late to save these two young men, whose families would probably never fully recover from their loss.

It was a difficult service for Sarah to attend, for although her heart was aching from the news of so much death and misery, her stomach was churning with excitement. This was the day that she had dreamed of, had planned for, the day when her family would meet the man that she had firmly decided to marry. But as she looked around the sea of sad faces, and heard the quiet sound of sobbing from the bereaved families of those lost two young Barnsbury boys, she felt churlish for even thinking of her own happiness at such a time. Even at her tender age the Reverend's sermon had brought home how brutal the war really was: 'In life, death is never far away.'

After the service, Samuel and Geraldine Melford stayed behind to offer their condolences to the bereaved families, so Sarah made her own way home. On the way, she passed fine houses, many built during the Georgian and Victorian period, though the war had taken its toll on all the elegant squares and terraces. With the lack of money, and superficial damage caused by enemy Zeppelin and aeroplane attacks, many properties had fallen into a sad state of disrepair, and the whole area had taken on an uncomfortable, seedy appearance.

'Sarah! Wait for me!'

Sarah was halfway along the wide and tree-lined Hemingford Road when she heard her friend, Winnie Carter, calling to her. She stopped to let Winnie, in Sunday best, and with her own copy of the Bible held firmly in one hand, catch up with her.

'I saw you in church,' Winnie said, out of breath, but displaying her cheeky, glowing smile, her pure white teeth seeming far too big for her mouth. 'I wanted to wave, but I thought, under the circumstances…'

'I saw you too,' replied Sarah, who had known

Winnie since they were at Barnsbury School together. 'It was so sad.'

'I know,' said Winnie, her smile becoming more wistful. 'D'you remember Harry? Harry Turner? He used to walk me home from school. I can't bear to think what's happened to him. His poor mum and dad.'

As they walked, Winnie, who was much shorter than Sarah, had to take twice as many steps to keep up. 'You know,' she said, using one hand to hold on to her brown beret, 'when this war's over, there are going to be so many blokes we once knew who won't be coming home.' She sighed, but then broke into another of her huge smiles. 'I've got a terrible feeling I'm never going to find someone to marry me.'

'Don't be silly, Winnie,' said Sarah. 'It'll happen sooner or later, one day when you least expect it. There's always someone for someone.'

'It's all right for you,' Winnie said, quick as a flash. 'You've got someone for you already.'

Sarah came to a sudden halt. 'What do you mean?'

'Oh come off it, Sarah,' replied Winnie, cheekily. 'Everyone knows about you and your petty officer. Mr Wheatcroft was saying before the service that he was pretty sure he'd be putting up the banns for you any day now.'

Sarah was thunderstruck. Apart from her own mother and father, she hadn't told a soul about who she was walking out with. 'Just who told you all this, Winnie Carter?' she demanded.

Winnie's smile turned to a grin. 'Who d'you think?'

'Not – *Beattie?*'

'She stopped and talked to me in the Cattle Market the other day. She was with her usual gang, of course, so I didn't want to hang around for too long. But she told me all about your petty officer, what a good-looker he was.'

Sarah stiffened. How could Beattie possibly know what Edward Lacey looked like when she hadn't even met him?

Winnie was relishing every moment of the outrage she was causing. 'She said he was more your type than hers,' she continued mischievously. 'Speaks with too many plums in his mouth, *she* says.' Suddenly she became alarmed that Sarah was taking all this a bit too seriously. 'Oh, I wouldn't pay any heed to Beattie,' she said quickly. 'You know what she was like at school. Always making up things as she went along.'

Sarah was too deep in thought to respond.

Winnie's smile finally faded. 'It's nothing, Sarah,' she said, trying to reassure her friend. 'If you ask me, your sister's just jealous.'

Sarah perked up a little, and smiled weakly. She was determined to show Winnie that she was not nearly so concerned as she looked. But after Winnie had left her, as she made her way home her mind was racing.

Beattie had never cared for Seven Sisters Road. For one thing, it was too long, stretching all the way from the Nags Head in Holloway and carrying on right up to Tottenham in North London. The part of this big main road that she hated most was between Holloway Road and

Hornsey Road, for that was where all the shops were, and when she and Sarah were kids, their mother had dragged them around those shops, where they often had to spend what seemed like hours waiting for her whilst she dithered about how much cheese to buy, or take her place in a queue for two pounds of dried peas. No, if she had a preference for any part of that road, it was where it was flanked on one side by Finsbury Park, and on the other by a terrace of tall Edwardian houses, most of which were now used officially as cheap board-and-breakfast accommodation – and unofficially by servicemen for more dubious purposes. A typical 'pay-by-the-week-and-no-questions-asked' resident of one of these 'guest houses' was Petty Officer Edward Lacey.

'You're late.' After letting Beattie in the front door of the so-called Hazelville Hotel, he followed her up the stairs to his room on the third floor. 'I thought you said one o'clock?'

'I had fings ter do,' called Beattie, over her shoulder. 'I had ter go ter work.'

'Work!' called Lacey, his voice echoing down the well of the great barn of a house. 'Since when?'

'Needs must,' replied Beattie, breathless as they reached the second-floor landing. 'One of me mates got me a job up the Cattle Market. I'm goin' ter need all the cash I can get.'

As they made their way to the last flight of stairs, they passed another resident's door, which opened slightly. Watching them go, with a certain amount of titillation, were two pairs of eyes. It was that kind of establishment.

Once on the third floor, Beattie was relieved to be back inside Edward's room. She could never bear the smell of boiled cabbage and soiled underwear that hit her the moment she entered the downstairs hall.

'What do your parents think about all this?' Lacey asked, as he locked his bedroom door behind them.

Beattie threw off her shawl and swung around to look at him. 'About what?' she asked, puzzled.

'About you getting a job? Aren't they curious?'

Beattie ran her fingers through her rarely combed hair and shook it loose. 'What the eye doesn't see,' she said. 'But they'll know, sooner or later.'

Lacey, too impatient to wait any longer, went straight to her, threw his arms around her waist and pushed his lips against hers.

Beattie could tell he'd been drinking, for his breath smelled of whisky. 'Not so fast!' she snapped, prising him away. 'I've got a bone ter pick wiv you.'

Lacey looked at her in disbelief. This was the first time she had ever rejected his advances. Isn't this why she came here? 'What's up?' he asked.

'You didn't tell me yer'd written to 'er,' she said, her whole face bristling with irritation. 'Yer've said you'd come ter tea wiv 'er – back 'ome.' She pushed him away and looked him straight in the face. 'Wot's this all about?'

Lacey sighed, went across to the double bed, which was neatly made ready for the afternoon, and pulled out a Players Navy Cut cigarette from a packet on the small cupboard beside it. 'I've made up my mind, Beat,' he said, poking a cigar between his lips. 'I've decided to break it off with her.'

'Then why didn't yer tell 'er in the letter?' she said, watching him light his cigarette.

Lacey's face emerged from a cloud of smoke that drifted around the small, claustrophobic room and settled on the wash jug and basin nearby. 'It's best I tell her face to face,' he said, sitting down on the edge of the bed.

Beattie came across to him. 'But 'ow can yer tell 'er if you're 'avin' tea wiv 'er, an' Mum an' Dad?'

Lacey inhaled deeply before looking up at her. 'Beattie, I have no intention of having tea with Sarah, or your parents.'

For a moment, Beattie just stared at him. This was the first time that she had actually *seen* him, for in that face and voice was now all that she hated most in her life. Why then had she got herself involved with someone like this? Yes, it was true that she had enjoyed making love with him in that bed every weekend he had been home on leave from his new posting down at Portsmouth, but the more she was with him the more she was aware of her reasons for taking up with him, and she hated herself for it.

'Wot're yer playin' at, Ed?' she asked tersely.

'I'm not playing at anything, Beat,' he replied. He got up, went across to the window, and stared out through the grubby lace curtains. 'The fact is, since I wrote that letter, I've done quite a lot of thinking.' He turned back to look at her. 'I don't love Sarah. I never have done. I blame myself. I should never have let it go on as long as it has done.' He went to stand in front of her. 'It's all been a farce, Beat,' he said. 'Sarah doesn't know how to live. She doesn't know what the world is all about – not the *real* world.' He tried to take hold of her hands, but she pulled them out of his way.

'And what is your *real* world, Ed?' she said, moving away from him. For the first time, her eyes took in the tawdry surroundings: the poky little fireplace with only just a few pieces of coal there to keep the room from being ice-cold, the small, bare table with a chipped enamel kettle, brown china teapot, and a couple of stained white cups, and the two gas lamps on the wall that were never lit until it was almost dark. But most of all there was that double brass bedstead, where time and time again she had given herself to this man, not because he was what she wanted, but because she wanted to experience what Sarah wanted more than anything else in the whole wide world. 'If your world is all about tearin' somebody's life apart, then I don't want any part of you, mate.'

Lacey stiffened. 'You knew what you were getting into, Beat.'

For a brief moment, Beattie held her breath. Although she couldn't bear to agree with him, what he said was true. She turned, and slowly made for the door.

'I didn't mean it to be like this, Beat,' he said. 'I promise. I thought I loved her, but I was wrong. I want someone who doesn't flinch every time I touch her. I want someone who responds to me.' He finally went across to her, put his arms around her waist, and leaned his head on her shoulder. 'I want someone like you, Beat.'

It was a moment or so before Beattie spoke. When she did, she did not turn to look at him. 'You've got to meet her. You've got to tell her.' She turned around, and stared him straight in the eyes. 'If yer don't, I never want to see yer again.'

Lacey smiled at her with those pale blue eyes that had always so utterly defeated her. Then he nodded.

For the next hour they made love.

Sarah reached the tram stop in Liverpool Road almost half an hour early. She had made the arrangement to meet Edward there rather than have him come straight to the house because she wanted to arrive with him as a future married couple, arm in arm. Although it was only three thirty, the sky was so overcast it was obvious that it would soon be prematurely dark. Sarah didn't much like standing alone at a tram stop in a place like Liverpool Road, for there were many ruffians about, especially in the nearby Peabody Buildings, and as she was wearing her very best Sunday clothes, she worried that she might attract too much attention. Luckily, there weren't many people around.

By four o'clock, which was the time Sarah had arranged to meet Edward off the tram, her stomach was churning with a mixture of nerves and excitement. Her life was about to take on a whole new meaning; by the time the tea party at the house in Thornhill Road was over, her walking-out with Edward would be official, and her future assured.

As there was a Sunday service operating that day, only two trams came during the first half-hour that Sarah was standing there. Although she was well wrapped up against the cold, her thin kid gloves were not really warm enough, so every now and then she would rub her hands together to try to get the blood circulating. At one stage, an army Red Cross motorbus passed by, but she tried not to look at its passengers – young soldiers who had been injured at the front, on their way to the Army Hospital further along Liverpool Road.

Several times, Sarah looked at her watch pinned to the breast of her topcoat, but it was not until forty-five minutes had passed that she started to become anxious. Had she told Edward the right stop to get off? Was she sure it was four o'clock they had arranged to meet? Gradually, her mind was becoming tormented by the possibility of her own fallibility. So many times she craned her neck to look as far as she could along Liverpool Road towards Holloway. She knew he had to change from a bus on to the tram somewhere, but couldn't remember exactly where. But what did it matter. He knew where she lived. She *must* have given him the right time, the right place. It was inconceivable that she, practical Sarah, could have been so negligent. Trying to dispel all negative thoughts from her mind, she transferred her gaze across to the other side of the tramlines where, with dusk drawing close, the residents of the long terrace of Georgian houses were beginning to draw their blinds for the evening blackout.

By a quarter to six, the sky had darkened even more, and it threatened to rain. Sarah decided to wait for just one more tram, and when it arrived, her heart nearly missed a beat, for as the tram approached, the first thing she saw was a man in naval uniform sitting in the front seat on the top deck. She waved frantically but as the tram screeched to a halt, she realised that, although the man was in naval uniform, it certainly wasn't Edward.

She watched the tram leave the stop, but waited until it had finally disappeared into the darkening gloom of the old road to the north. Once she could see it no more, she moved on.

It took her far longer than usual to walk the few minutes home. Somehow the distance seemed like an eternity.

CHAPTER 4

Under normal circumstances, the death of somebody called Manfred von Richthofen would have meant absolutely nothing to the residents of Barnsbury, but mention the Red Baron and it was a completely different story. In April, the Baron, one of Germany's most feared and skilled flying aces, was shot down and killed during aerial combat over the Western Front. Most of the newspapers couldn't make up their minds whether it was a Canadian fighter pilot who had shot him down, or an Australian army machine gun unit in the Allied lines, but Samuel Melford was convinced that none of this was true, and that the commander of the 'flying circus', who was credited with shooting down more than eighty British aeroplanes in little more than a year, was in fact brought down by 'one of our own courageous young fellows'. Whatever the truth, Barnsbury, like the rest of the nation, celebrated the event with renewed conviction that the end of the war was now surely in sight.

Unfortunately, the final flight of the Red Baron meant little to Sarah. The fact that her petty officer had failed to turn up for afternoon tea with her family two weeks before had left her feeling dejected and humiliated. The only explanation she could offer to her parents was that Edward must have been called away suddenly on active service, and that he was not the sort of person to do such a thing unless there was a pressing reason. Even though her parents appeared to have accepted her hollow explanation, Sarah felt sick inside. She hated lying. In her heart of hearts she knew only too well that her petty officer could not be trusted, for the letter that she had written to him in Portsmouth had not been answered, which led her to the conclusion that he had jilted her.

But there was something more worrying her, something that had been nagging inside ever since Winnie Carter had suggested that Beattie knew more about Edward Lacey than she, Sarah, had imagined. Until she knew exactly what it was that Beattie knew, she would be unable to dismiss it from her mind. However, since the day of that ill-fated tea party, Beattie had spent a great deal of her time away from the house, and on the rare occasions that she was actually there, she had made a point of keeping herself to herself.

On the day of Geraldine and Samuel's Silver Wedding Anniversary, things came to a head. The event started well, with members of both families coming to stay in the house for the weekend, and, to everyone's surprise, Beattie even gave up her own bedroom for her mother's elder sister, Dixie, who, like Beattie herself, was a bit of an outcast in the family, mainly because of the succession of 'amours' she had gone through since the second of her two divorces. On the whole, everyone got on well with each other, especially with Geraldine's mother, Bella, who was the biggest chatterbox in the world, and made a point of finding out all she could about her fellow guests even before the first cup of tea had been served. Both she and her husband, Ronnie, who had spent his working life in an insurance company, were really quite young for their age, which was in marked contrast to Samuel's father, Benedict, a widower, who must have been old the day he was born, for he never stopped complaining about rheumatism, and smoked cigars nearly all weekend, much to the disdain of Aunt Dixie, who constantly drew attention to the old boy's vice by coughing dramatically every time he lit up. One of the real problem relatives, however, was Terry, who was married to Geraldine's younger sister, Myra. Terry, who was a good bit older than his wife, was well known for his roaming eye, and as the weekend progressed, he was clearly beginning to get on Beattie's nerves, for he never stopped leering at her and twitching his pencil-thin moustache, which was apparently meant to overwhelm her with desire.

Several young cousins also turned up, whom Sarah adored and Beattie loathed, but apart from them, other guests, who were mainly the Melfords' friends from St Andrew's church and the Barnsbury War Fund, popped in from time to time to offer congratulations, and to sample Geraldine's home-made apple wine, together with a piece of Silver Wedding fruit cake made specially for the occasion by their neighbour, Bertha Stevens. So, all in all, it was a happy day.

The real problem came towards the end of the celebratory dinner on Saturday evening, which Geraldine herself had cooked with the help of

Sarah, and Sarah's favourite cousin, Jenny, and which took place in the little-used dining room. Shortly after the speeches, in which various members of the family had praised the wonderful years of marriage of their hosts, Jenny's fourteen-year-old brother, Cecil, deliberately mocked his cousin Beattie by asking her when she was planning on getting married.

'If I was stupid enuff ter get married and 'ave a blockhead like you for a son,' snapped Beattie, vociferously, 'I'd go an' drown me bleedin' self!'

Aunt Dixie made no attempt to stifle her amusement, but the other guests showed their indignation by making up to Cecil, who clearly revelled in the mischief he had instigated.

'I must ask you not to use that kind of language in front of your family please, Beattie.' As usual, Samuel was convincing nobody how strict he was with his younger daughter, for even as he spoke the words he tried to soften their impact. 'I think it's fair to say that Beattie is no admirer of married life.'

Beattie was having none of this. 'I'm sorry, Farver,' she said, cuttingly, 'but marriage ter me ain't nothin' more than a 'ole lot er words on paper.'

'It takes more than words to make a marriage, dear,' said Geraldine's mother, Bella, doing her best to sound conciliatory.

'Marriage is an institution,' said Ronnie, her husband, who was already joining Samuel's father, Benedict, by smoking a cigar. 'It has to be worked at. But, my God–' he stretched out his hand to cover his wife's – 'it's worth it!'

Bella gave him an affectionate smile.

Nobody had noticed that two of Geraldine's cats were up on the sideboard, heads buried deep inside a large silver tureen, sipping the remains of the first-course vegetable soup.

Now it was Terry's turn to stir up some mischief. 'So what would it take for you to tread the path to the altar, Beattie?' he said, also puffing away at a cigar.

'A man,' retorted Beattie, without a blink. 'I mean – a *real* man.'

Terry nearly choked on his own cigar smoke.

'And what's *your* idea of a real man, Beattie?' It was the first time Sarah had said anything, but it carried far more significance than anyone at the table could have imagined.

Beattie paused for a moment before answering. Although she knew what her sister was getting at, she was going to take her time before she said what she really wanted to say. In some perverse way, she was glad. She *wanted* to talk about men, she *wanted* to tell Sarah that she had been having a relationship with her fancy man. This was the opportunity she had been waiting for, the chance to expose the kind of person Sarah had always admired so much, someone from the same side of the fence as herself, who spoke and behaved well, and knew how to do all the right things in company. Yes, Edward Lacey was that kind of person all right, but he was also a liar and a cheat. What kind of a superior being was it that tried to have a relationship with two sisters at the same time, who broke promises, and left someone standing at a tram stop for the best part of two hours? All this she wanted to say to her sister, but for some reason, the words stuck in her throat. 'A real man is someone I could trust,' was all she was prepared to say – for the time being.

Sarah's eyes were lowered. She resisted the temptation to look at her sister.

At this stage, the two cats had finished off the remains of the soup and were now starting on the scraps left over on the serving dishes.

Aunt Dixie, who had been bored out of her mind from the very first moment that she had arrived for the weekend party, was at last enjoying herself. Much to the disdain of the male members of the family, she had already helped herself twice to the decanter of claret, and now she was reaching out for it again. 'You know, Beattie,' she said, 'I can't help agreeing with you. Men are such fickle creatures. You never know what they're going to get up to next.'

'Well, you couldn't have won this war without 'em,' sniffed Benedict, indignantly.

'We haven't won it yet!' insisted Dixie, gulping down her claret.

'Women ain't stupid, Grandfather,' Beattie said, leaning forward in her seat so that she could see Benedict at the far end of the table. 'We've got brains, and we oughta be given the chance ter use 'em.'

'Brains!' Old Benedict leaned back in his chair, refusing to meet his granddaughter's gaze. 'You mean like that damned Pankhurst woman, blowing up Lloyd George's house down at Walton just before the war? If you call that brains, I'd rather be without 'em!'

Beattie's hackles were rising. ''E asked fer it, the stupid old goat!'

'Beattie!' said Samuel, his voice raised just enough to be firm. 'That's enough now.'

'Well, it's true!' snapped Beattie, refusing to be silenced. 'That's the trouble wiv women. We've let blokes 'ave their way wiv us fer too long. We've got the right ter be 'eard!'

To everyone's surprise, Samuel thumped his fist on the table. 'I said – that is quite enough!'

Once again, there was a hushed silence.

Beattie flopped back on her chair, exasperated. After a moment she got up and made for the door. She turned and looked back at the hushed gathering around the table. 'Times're changin',' she said, quietly defiant. 'It won't always be like it is now.' With that, she left the room.

Samuel waited a moment before speaking. 'I'm sorry about all that,' he said, embarrassed. 'I'm afraid Beattie has a mind of her own.'

'It's to be expected given the type of people she mixes with.' Old Benedict snatched the claret decanter away from Dixie and topped up his own glass. 'You've only got to listen to her. Can't even speak the King's English. She's got a problem, that girl, and no mistake.'

Sarah's eyes remained lowered. She quietly got up from the table, collected some of the dessert plates, and went out to the kitchen.

As she returned to the hall, Sarah noticed the sitting-room door partly open. Within, as she expected, she found Beattie stretched out on the sofa. Sarah closed the door quietly behind her. 'That was a pretty little scene,' she said icily.

Beattie flicked her eyes up only briefly. 'Don't know wot you're talkin' about,' she replied indifferently.

'This is their night, not yours.'

'Oh, do shut up!' snapped Beattie, getting up quickly from the sofa, and going to look at herself in the large, ornate oval mirror hanging above the fireplace. 'I didn't ask ter spend me 'ole weekend wiv all that lot.'

'For God's sake, Beattie,' sighed Sarah. 'They've been married for twenty-five years. You may not approve of that, but at least you can help your own mother and father to celebrate on just one day of their lives.'

Beattie tried to pretend that she wasn't listening. She turned away from the mirror, went to a card table at the back of the sofa, and started aimlessly shuffling a pack of playing cards there.

Refusing to give way to Beattie's apparent indifference, Sarah went across to her. 'What do you know about Edward Lacey?'

Beattie's reaction was totally blank. '*Who?*'

'Don't play games with me, Beattie,' said Sarah, firmly. 'You know who he is, you know what he looks like. How?'

Beattie looked up only briefly from the playing cards she was setting out on the table. 'Are you talking about your petty officer?' she asked coyly. 'The one who jilted you?'

Sarah knew only too well that Beattie was taunting her. But she had to get to the bottom of it. 'How?' she demanded.

Beattie finally looked up. 'Coincidence really. We met in a pub. He bought me a drink.'

Sarah was stony-faced.

From the dining room across the hall, they could hear the sound of laughter.

''E's quite a good looker,' continued Beattie, 'if yer like that kind of face. Can't say I do really.' She started to play Solo with the playing cards. ''E took a shine ter me. I couldn't do nuffin' about it, Sarah – honest.'

'I don't believe you.'

Beattie flicked her eyes up. They were as hard as steel. 'I'm not askin' yer to,' she said. 'I'm not asking you ter believe nuffin''. All I'm tellin' yer is that I've bin seein' 'im ever since.' She lined up a Jack of Diamonds. ''Is idea – not mine.'

On impulse, Sarah lunged forward, and with one hand swept the pack of carefully arranged cards on to the floor. 'You're a liar!'

'Oh yeah?' Beattie smirked and crossed her arms. She wasn't in the least bit intimidated. 'Why don't yer ask 'im? If yer can find 'im, of course.'

Sarah was much more unsure of herself than of Beattie. There was a time when she could tell whether Beattie was telling lies or not, but not any longer. Right from the time when she was a little girl, Beattie had loved to taunt people, to make them doubt themselves, to set one person against another. She had done it several times with their mother and father, and goodness knows how many times with Sarah herself. But this was different. It had to be a lie, it just had to be. How could it be possible that Beattie had been seeing a man who was so alien to the way she herself wanted to live? Now, face to face with Beattie, she was determined to find the truth.

'Where did you meet him?'
'I told yer, in a pub.'
'What pub? Where?'
'The Eaglet – in Seven Sisters Road.'
Sarah did a double take. 'The one that was bombed?'
Beattie smirked. 'The same night.'
'You're lying!'
Beattie shook her head slowly. 'It was a lucky escape, Sarah. A few minutes later an' I wouldn't've been standin' 'ere now.' She smirked again. 'Terrible fawt, ain't it?'
Sarah now had no intention of letting up. 'You've been seeing Edward ever since then?'
Beattie nodded.
'And in all that time, you never told him that I am your sister?'
Beattie did not answer. She seemed to be staring straight through her. 'I didn't 'ave ter tell 'im. 'E already knew.'
As she spoke, an old grandfather clock in the corner of the room chimed the hour.
Beattie waited for the chiming to stop, and then continued. 'It's me 'e wants, yer know – not you. And d'yer know why? Because I give 'im wot you never could, because you're incapable of it.' Sarah raised her hand as if to strike Beattie across the face, but Beattie quickly grabbed her wrist and held on to it. 'This is the kind of bloke you're dealin' wiv,' she said intensely. 'One of your *own* kind, who plays by the rules – providin' 'e's the one who makes 'em up.'
Sarah struggled to release her wrist, but Beattie's grip was hard and strong.

'D'yer know wot the joke is, Sarah?' said Beattie, her eyes making direct contact with Sarah's. 'The joke is, I can't bear the sight of your fancy man. He's wet an' weak an' everythin' I despise in a bloke. So as far as I'm concerned, yer can 'ave 'im. I 'ope I never set eyes on 'im again as long as I live.' She finally released Sarah's wrist.

Sarah felt quite empty inside. She turned and went to the large bow-shaped window, though the blackout curtains were already drawn. The shadow of her own image seemed to be dancing on the wall in the flickering of the gaslamps. So she just stood there, her back towards Beattie, not knowing what to do or say.

'If what you say is true,' she said eventually, her back still turned, her voice only barely audible, 'I want nothing more to do with you ever again.' She then turned to face Beattie. 'But I've known you too long, Beattie. I know how you like to hurt people. But you're not going to hurt me, because I don't believe a word you've said. Edward will write to me sooner or later, of that I'm sure. *He'll* tell me the truth, and then I'll never have to listen to any of your lies ever again.'

Sarah was about to turn and make her way to the door, when Beattie suddenly said, 'I'm pregnant, Sarah.'

Sarah stopped with a shocked start.

'Yes,' continued Beatrice. 'It's 'is kid. But I don't want it.'

Sarah was shaking her head in disbelief.

'Oh it's true all right,' said Beattie. 'If yer don't want ter believe me, go up ter the clinic up Wells Terrace. Ask fer Dr Brooks. 'E'll tell yer.'

Sarah could bear no more. But as she rushed to leave the room, she found her way blocked by someone standing in the open doorway. It was their father.

'I want you out of this house first thing in the morning,' said Samuel, directing his look straight across the room towards his younger daughter.

With that, he left the room, closing the door quietly behind him.

Aunt Dixie was fast asleep when Beattie slipped into her room. It had been a long supper party, one that Dixie had thought would never end. But her salvation had been that decanter of claret, and by the time everyone had completed their day of congratulations to Geraldine and Samuel, Dixie had only just enough strength left in her legs to climb the three flights of stairs to Beattie's room.

After her lively encounter in the sitting room with her sister and father, Beattie made herself scarce. The first thing she did was to walk the darkened streets to give herself breathing space before she did what she knew she had to do. Then she went back to her bedroom and packed a suitcase. She hadn't really any idea where she was going to spend the night, but it didn't matter. All she wanted was to get away from that house, that family, and everything that had stifled her for so many years.

One last look back at the sleeping beauty, snoring away in a drunken stupor in her bed, and Beattie was gone.

The way she felt, it was very doubtful if she would ever see the house again.

CHAPTER 5

The summer of 1918 brought mixed blessings to the war-weary British people. On the Western Front the Germans launched an offensive near Compiegne, which was later repulsed with a massive Allied counteroffensive. The Allies also halted the German advance towards Paris, which raised hopes that the war was at last near an end. The news from Russia, however, brought an air of dark gloom as it was announced that the new Bolshevik regime had executed the former Tsar Nicholas II, together with his entire family. The shock waves spread throughout the entire British political arena, and prompted angry clashes between monarchist supporters and disaffected radicals. At home, Prime Minister Lloyd George and his coalition government were accused of giving misleading statements about military manpower to the House of Commons, and also criticised for abandoning Home Rule and conscription for the increasingly belligerent Ireland.

Like her father, Sarah followed the news of the day with passionate interest, and each evening, they analysed the day's copy of *The Times* together. During recent years, they had usually found that, in general, they were very much in agreement about the way the country should be run. But as the summer progressed, both Samuel and Geraldine began to notice a change in Sarah's attitude to life in general.

It had now been over three months since the events of that terrible Saturday evening, when Beattie had left home in the middle of the night. The news that Beattie was pregnant by Edward Lacey had devastated Sarah's vision of her own future, and turned her against her sister more than she would have thought possible. And yet, in some ways, Beattie had opened Sarah's eyes, for with the painful realisation that marriage on her terms was not to be, she had learned a cruel lesson about the type of person that Edward Lacey really was, and that out there in the wider world, there were plenty more Edward Laceys, just waiting to betray and deceive.

However, to everyone's surprise, Sarah had recovered remarkably well from the trauma of her experience. Instead of bitterness, she had gained strength, and she was determined to show that from now on, she would never allow a man to rob her of her dignity, her happiness, or her independence. Sarah's strength was in her resolve, and this, she was determined, would sustain her through the coming years.

The effect of Beattie's departure was felt mainly by Geraldine Melford. When she heard that Samuel had ordered their daughter out of the house, it prompted the first real quarrel they had had in their twenty-five years of married life.

'Whatever she's done,' insisted Geraldine, to her husband, on more than one occasion, 'she's still our own flesh and blood. How can we turn our back on her when, whether we like it or not, she's going to give us our first grandchild?'

But Samuel would have none of it. Thoroughly entrenched in his view that Beattie had brought shame and disgrace on the family, he absolutely forbade any contact with her, and made it quite clear that the girl would not be receiving a penny's allowance from him. As each day passed, Geraldine felt more and more depressed that Beattie was out there alone in the world, disowned by her parents and with no one to support or guide her. The very thought was not only consuming Geraldine with guilt, it was making her ill.

The moment Beattie confronted her that fateful evening, Sarah made a conscious decision that she would never resume contact with her sister. But *never* was a long time, and when Sarah started to think more carefully about the situation, she wondered what she would do if she were to suddenly come across Beattie with her child walking along the pavement towards her. But that was still a long way off, at least another six months by Sarah's calculation.

In the meantime, one of the most difficult problems Sarah had to face during the summer months was her mother's persistent attempts to find a suitable replacement for Edward Lacey. Every time she and her parents went to church, her mother had carefully planned a chance meeting with a different young man. It was, of course, not only embarrassing for Sarah herself, but also for the intended suitors. Time and time again, Sarah tried to explain to her mother that she was no longer interested in finding someone to walk out with; as far as she was concerned, marriage in the foreseeable future was out of the question. But even though Geraldine had been just as shocked and outraged as her husband by Beattie's callous betrayal of her sister, she was convinced that it was her duty as a mother to stand by both of them. In her eyes, the real villain was Edward Lacey, who had brought such pain to her elder daughter, and shame to the Melford family. She was absolutely determined not to let this rogue destroy Sarah's life, so from now on she would concentrate all her efforts on helping Sarah to find the happiness the poor girl was entitled to.

At the end of July, however, Sarah's vision of a cosy future managing the day-to-day affairs of the family house in Thornhill Road began to feel worryingly insecure when, over supper one evening, her father had something to ask of her.

'Sarah, I want you and your mother to start looking round for a lodger.'

Sarah sat bolt upright in her chair. Was she hearing right? A stranger paying money to share the house with them, the Melfords' own house, which Sarah cherished more than anything else in the whole wide world? 'A lodger?'

Samuel, trying to make the announcement sound as unimportant as possible, continued eating whilst he talked. 'Both your mother and I feel that it is a waste to keep your sister's room vacant when it could be contributing to the expenses of running so large a house as this.'

Sarah swung a startled look at her mother, who was clearly doing her best to avert her gaze. 'A lodger? Here? In *this* house?' she asked. 'Is such a thing really necessary, Father?'

'Not necessary,' Samuel replied casually. 'But in the circumstances – appropriate.'

Sarah thought for a moment. She tried again to exchange a look with her mother, still without success. 'Do we need the money, Father?' she asked outright.

'This is wartime, my dear. Everything is expensive. We need to make as many savings as we can. And in any case, the running of a good household should always be backed with an adequate contingency.'

Adequate contingency? But here was the man who had always propounded the notion that 'the Englishman's home is his castle', and that it would be folly to bring strangers into such a place. The very idea of a lodger living in the house that she loved so much filled her with despair. She felt a sense of disquiet, and found it difficult to continue with her meal.

'Perhaps it would only need to be a temporary arrangement,' said Geraldine, rather feebly.

'That remains to be seen, my dear,' Samuel answered. 'We have the space, and we should put it to good use.'

Sarah looked straight across the table at her father. 'But what happens if Beattie comes home?'

Samuel quietly put down his knife and fork, and returned her gaze. 'That is not a situation that will arise, Sarah,' he replied calmly but firmly. 'Your sister has already decided which course she wishes her life to take.'

Sarah couldn't believe this conversation was

taking place. She sat back in her chair and glanced around the walls of the large kitchen, trying to imagine what it would be like if a lodger were to move in and use the place to cook his or her own meals. The whole idea offended her. This wasn't just a house, it was a home – the Melford home. One day it would belong to her, or Beattie, or both of them. It would be a sin to taint it with an outsider. But the more she thought about all this, the more anxious she became. Was her father experiencing some kind of money problems? If so, it was hard to believe, for not only did he have his well-paid job in the largest department store in London, but he owned one of the loveliest houses in Barnsbury. What *was* behind all this? 'Is there no other way, Father?' she asked.

Once again, Samuel briefly looked up from his plate. 'Needs must, my dear.'

'If there is a need, then why not let me help?'

'That's why I'm asking you to–'

'If it's money we need, then let me find a job.'

'Oh no, Sarah!' her mother said emphatically. 'Not you.'

Sarah was irritated. 'Why not?' she said sharply. 'I'm not a child. I've got a good pair of hands, and I can think for myself. If we need to bring in some money, I see no reason whatsoever why I can't contribute.'

Samuel was shaking his head.

'Oh for goodness' sake, Father – why not?'

'Because you are my daughter,' he replied, 'and I do not expect a daughter of mine to go out to earn a living.'

For a brief moment, Sarah thought of Beattie. 'Forgive me for saying, Father, but that's very old-fashioned. You've kept me long enough. I can't just go on being a millstone around your neck.'

'Don't be silly, Sarah,' said Geraldine, agitated.

'Well, it's true, Mother.' Sarah stretched across, and covered her mother's hand with her own. 'You and Father have always been so wonderful to me. I've lived a life of luxury since I was born. It's time I did something for you, for this house.'

'That question does not and will not arise,' said her father, rather forcefully. 'You know very well that when your mother and I have gone, this house will be yours.'

'I am glad to say that that question will not arise for a very long time,' she said spiritedly. 'I want to help, Father. If we have a problem, you *must* let me.'

Samuel put his knife and fork down on his plate, and dabbed his lips with his napkin. 'If you want to help, Sarah,' he said quietly, 'find a lodger.'

Gamages Department Store was quite an imposing building. Situated on the corner of Hatton Garden and Holborn Circus, the building reached up four floors, and overlooked a busy, bustling, and thriving community of newspaper offices, commercial buildings, and small shops that stretched all the way to the well-known half-timbered houses of Staple Inn on the main Gray's Inn Road. Although not in the same league as the more affluent Harrods in smart

Knightsbridge, Gamages was considered by many to be the ideal family store, and, like its nearest competitor, Selfridges in Oxford Street, busy on nearly every day of the week. However, like many similar establishments in London, Gamages' fortunes had been severely hit by the austerity of war, and for this reason stocks were kept to a minimum and only replaced on demand. But all who passed through its doors could not help but warm to its friendly, welcoming atmosphere.

Samuel Melford had been appointed General Manager just before the war, and amongst the innovations he brought to the store were eye-catching displays, good discounts on all shop-soiled items, and a cafeteria that was the envy of every other big store. Samuel was, on the whole, quite popular with the staff, though some thought he was a little too strict and severe, and if there were any complaint at all about his management style, it was that he always played everything by the book.

Sarah's decision to seek an appointment with the personnel officer at Gamages was taken after a great deal of heart-searching. She knew that her action was likely to incur the wrath of her father, for she had not told him what she was doing, but with so much at stake, she was prepared to take that risk. She was determined at all costs not to advertise for a lodger, as her father had instructed. In spite of the despicable way in which Beattie had behaved to Sarah, it somehow seemed wrong to turn her room over to a stranger. After all, it was still just conceivable that Beattie would one day try to come home. Also, ever since Sarah had been jilted, the house in Thornhill Road had taken on a hugely increased significance for her. She'd always had a deep affection for the place, but now it was as though it was a part of her very soul. She adored every nook and cranny of the place from the red brick facade under the constant summer shade of a tall plane tree, with its fussy, straggling branches, to the large rooms inside, with high ceilings edged with white stucco mouldings; the wide staircase from the entrance hall to Samuel and Geraldine's and Sarah's rooms on the first floor, and Beattie's at the top. Above that staircase on the ground floor was a small length of exposed modern timber beam, which Sarah touched every morning as she came down the stairs with a bright 'Good morning, beam!' To Sarah the Melford house was a living thing, and she had absolutely no intention of sharing it with any stranger.

'You're not by any chance related to our General Manager, are you, Miss Melford?'

Sarah was prepared for the first question she was asked by Mrs Hetherington, Gamages' personnel officer. 'Oh, goodness me, no,' she replied, without a trace of guilt. 'Is that his name too?'

Mrs Hetherington smiled. It was a warm smile, for she had a chubby face that looked as though it wouldn't know how to frown if it tried. 'A small world,' she said fleetingly.

The day had started well for Sarah, for on the way to Holborn, she had managed to find a front seat on the top of the open-air omnibus. It was now the first week in August and the weather was absolutely sweltering. As she passed along the sun-drenched streets, below her everyone was turned out in the minimum of clothing – women in short-sleeved dresses and summer bonnets, like herself, and she even saw men not wearing ties, although these were mainly manual workers. When she got to Gamages, the place was full, for she already knew that her father had supervised the August Bank Holiday week sales, which were clearly doing a roaring trade.

'I see on your application form that you've had no experience in selling.' Mrs Hetherington was peering at Sarah over the top of her pince-nez spectacles.

'No, I haven't,' replied Sarah, at her most businesslike. 'But I feel I have an aptitude for it, and I do learn very quickly.'

Mrs Hetherington smiled at Sarah's confidence, but it was obvious that she liked the girl. 'Well, to tell you the truth,' she said, 'if you'd applied for a job here just a couple of weeks ago I wouldn't have been able to help you. Things haven't been too good for the company of late. In fact we've had to lay off quite a lot of the staff, mainly in the storerooms. This war has taken its toll, I'm afraid. That, and all the troubles in the boardroom.'

Sarah was intrigued – and anxious. She wanted to ask more, but decided it was too risky to do so.

'Anyway,' said Mrs Hetherington, endorsing Sarah's application form in front of her, 'I'm sure we'll muddle through somehow. Once this war's over, things can only get better – *and* when we can get your namesake to pull himself together.'

Sarah was now really worried.

'Well, young lady,' said Mrs Hetherington, taking off her pince-nez and getting up from her desk, 'I'm going to try you out in Books. You've got a very nice speaking voice. You'll go down well with our reading customers.' She lowered her voice as though there was somebody else in the room listening. 'You can always tell breeding,' she said. 'Unlike some I could mention.'

A few minutes later, Sarah found herself being taken on a guided tour of the store. Mrs Hetherington was a very thorough guide, for she failed to omit one single department, from Ladies' Wear on the ground floor to the parlour games department on the top floor. For obvious reasons, Sarah couldn't tell her personnel officer that she had visited the store on many occasions, so she showed the necessary enthusiasm everywhere she was taken, though at any moment she quite expected to find herself confronted by her father. If this were to happen now Sarah knew it would be a disaster, for her whole plan depended on her getting the job on her own initiative, and not telling her father until he got home that evening. However, on every floor she was taken to, there was no sign of him.

'Heavens!' said Mr Lumley, who looked after the book department, and who had just been introduced to a Miss Melford, his new assistant. 'Not another one?'

Sarah and Mrs Hetherington laughed. 'No, Mr Lumley,' said Mrs Hetherington, reassuringly, 'you're quite safe. Miss Melford is no relation to our GM.'

Mr Lumley breathed a sigh of relief. 'Thank goodness for that,' he said. 'I couldn't cope with two of them.'

Sarah smiled weakly. 'Your General Manager sounds like a bit of a tartar,' she offered, trying to be as discreet as she could.

Mrs Hetherington answered, 'Not really. He's a bit too much to stomach, that's all. Poor man. He just can't seem to cope any more.'

Sarah felt all the hairs on her head bristling with concern. 'You mean he interferes a lot? He comes down here often?'

'Comes down here?' Mr Lumley exchanged a fairly cutting look with Mrs Hetherington. 'That'll be the day!'

Sarah looked puzzled.

'We don't see him at all, dear,' said Mrs Hetherington, again lowering her voice. 'No one sees him, not in any of the departments. In fact, Mr Melford hasn't been seen in the store, nor in his office, for six weeks.'

It was such a hot evening in Barnsbury that a lot of people were sitting at open windows or in their small front gardens, savouring the sweet, humid smells of summer. Samuel Melford had found it a stifling journey home on the tram. The lower deck had been jammed with people returning from work, and he had had to stand all the way. To make matters worse, the new starched collar that Geraldine had bought him for his previous birthday was cutting into his flesh and leaving a sore mark all the way round his neck, so he eagerly looked forward to removing it as soon as he possibly could.

He reached the corner of Richmond Road, where Sid Perkins' winter chestnut pitch had been taken over by Marco Rossini with his Italian water-ice van, which was little more than an ice box on wheels. As usual, there was a queue of small children and their mothers or fathers waiting there, for Marco's ice cream, which was made from flavoured frozen sugar syrup, had the reputation of being the best in Islington. Samuel shuffled past, for the humidity had slowed him down quite considerably, and made him look older than his years.

'Sorry to be late, dear,' Samuel said to his wife, who met him in the front hall. 'The heat seems to slow everyone down.'

After greeting him with a kiss on his cheek, Geraldine helped him off with his jacket. 'You poor thing,' she said, taking his briefcase and putting it down by the hall coat stand, 'you look exhausted. I'll go and pour you a nice glass of cool lemonade.'

As Geraldine dutifully rushed off into the kitchen, Samuel took his copy of the *Evening Standard,* and went into the sitting room. Sarah, who had been watching him from the top of the stairs, came down and followed him in.

Samuel went first to the mantelpiece and collected his favourite pipe. At the precise moment he was retrieving his jar of tobacco from the ornate, highly polished bookcase, he heard the sitting-room door close quietly behind him.

Standing there was Sarah.

'My dear,' he said, as brightly as he was capable, 'I trust you've had a good day?'

'I have, Father, thank you,' Sarah said. Then she slowly strolled to the middle of the room, and waited whilst he filled his pipe. 'And you?'

'Busy, as usual,' he replied, packing the tobacco as tightly as he could into his pipe. 'There were so many people in the store today, our staff were almost literally dying of the heat.'

Sarah said nothing as she watched him make his way back to his favourite leather armchair in front of the fireplace. She waited for him to be seated before asking, 'Were you in your office the whole day then, Father?'

Lighting his pipe took Samuel quite some time. 'Every minute,' he replied, between puffs. 'Except for forty-five minutes during the lunch-break. I took a stroll in the sun along Farringdon Road. From there, you get such a splendid view of St Paul's Cathedral. That great big dome was absolutely bathed in sunshine.'

Sarah found it impossible to look directly at her father whilst he was saying such things, but she sat down on the sofa opposite him as calmly as she could, and clasped her hands together on her lap. 'Father,' she said eventually, and with some difficulty, 'I paid a visit to Gamages today.'

To her absolute astonishment, her father did not budge an eyelid. 'Oh really, my dear?' he said. 'And did what you saw please you?'

Sarah stared hard at her father, finding his behaviour increasingly strange. 'I went there to get a job, and I've been offered a place in the book department.'

This time there was a long pause. After a moment or so, Samuel emerged from behind a cloud of thick pipe smoke. 'I wish you hadn't done that,' he said in a very downbeat way. 'You know my feelings on that matter.'

'Father. Why did you say you were in your office today?' Sarah had now gone too far to turn back. 'I heard it said that you haven't been to work for the past six weeks.'

Samuel remained silent, staring down at the Persian rug, his pipe clenched tightly between his teeth.

Sarah leaned forward. 'Father, I don't understand. You've been leaving this house at the same time every morning, and returning at the same time every night, and yet you haven't been near your office. What is happening?'

Samuel suddenly sat quite upright, a bright look on his face. 'Happening? What's happening? Why nothing, my dear. I've just felt a little under the weather, that's all. But I'm much better now. I shall be going back to work on Monday.' He stood up, went to the fireplace and tapped the ash from his pipe.

Something was terribly wrong with her father, Sarah thought. He was trying to give the impression that life was perfectly normal, and yet it clearly wasn't. Something had happened to him, but she couldn't, as yet, detect what. She went across and gently put her arm on his shoulder. 'Father–'

He suddenly swung round to face her. 'It's very exciting, my dear,' he said, his eyes fixed but glowing. 'Just you wait and see. This is just the start. Once the war's over, the Melfords are going to be right on top again. Oh yes.'

Sarah watched him relight his pipe. She was devastated.

CHAPTER 6

Campbell Road had quite a reputation. Not only was it just about the roughest backstreet in Islington, but its residents, young and old, were considered to be nothing more than a bunch of wild animals. 'The Bunk', as the street was known, was just a stone's throw from the Seven Sisters Road at Finsbury Park, and nobody in their right mind ventured down there unless they had to, especially after dark. Gangs of adolescent and teenage thugs hung about on every street corner, pitching dice and intimidating anyone who dared to pass by. Cats and dogs were sought out and, as a matter of routine, strung up by their necks from lampposts until someone with a spark of humanity cut them down, usually only in the nick of time. There were so many fights, so many break-ins, so much mayhem in this lawless corner of the borough that the local copper station down at Hornsey Road assigned one particular flatfoot full time to pound the beat. The unlucky police constable, who had in fact volunteered for the job, was named Ben Fodder, and known by the locals as Big Ben. Big Ben was a huge man, weighing fifteen stone, who had once been a star amateur wrestler, which gave him a certain amount of notoriety, not to say respect, amongst the local troublemakers.

Beattie Melford moved in to Number 22 within a few days of walking out on her family. For the first night, she'd slept out rough, kipping with some of the down-and-outs beneath the railway arch opposite Holloway underground station. Then her friend, Nagger Mills, put her up for a day or so, although that was a bit of an ordeal as Nagger and her dad lived at the back of a cattle shed up the market, and the smell of cow dung kept her awake at night. Her break finally came, however, when she remembered the bloke she'd met that day after she'd been to pawn her bracelet at Bob Sluggins' place. Jack Ridley was his name, and she remembered how he had suggested a place up the Bunk. When she got there, she was none too sure; Number 22 was just about as seedy as you can get, with lace curtains hanging up at the windows that looked as though they'd never been cleaned, and the rest of the house, like all the other two-up two-downs along the grubby, litter-strewn street, was a run-down mess. If it hadn't been for the fact that the landlady, Ma Briggs, was standing at the street door, Beattie might have turned her back and made off. But Jack Ridley was right: Bunk or no Bunk, this was one old lady who did have a heart of gold, and, in complete contrast to the outside of the house, inside, from top to bottom, was spotless.

'Think of this as yer own 'ome, dearie,' she said, when Beattie said she'd take the room. 'Ol' Ma Briggs'll look after yer.' Beattie moved in at once, and had not once regretted it.

Come October, Beattie was over the worst of

the morning sickness. Now it was just a question of waiting, which wasn't exactly easy, for she had had to take a job in a candle factory to help pay for her board and keep, and with a baby's feet now kicking quite regularly inside her stomach, working at a factory bench from seven in the morning to six in the evening was the type of initiation into working life that she had never anticipated.

As promised, Mrs Briggs looked after Beattie as if she were her own daughter, for apart from giving her the best room in the house, she often had a meal waiting for her when she got back home from her day's work. However, the old lady was very concerned that Beattie's baby would arrive in this world without a father. 'Yer should write to 'im, dearie,' she said. 'Make 'im face up to 'is responsibilities.'

But Beattie had no intention of writing to Edward Lacey. Since the day he'd promised to tell Sarah that he didn't want to carry on with their relationship, and had broken that promise, she'd vowed never to see him again. And she was determined that Lacey would never see his child either. The more time she had had to think about the prospect of motherhood, the more she realised just how much it meant to her. In some strange way, her instinct told her that giving birth to a child was the one way she could come to terms with her own life. When the child was born, it would be hers, and hers alone, and she would never allow Lacey to be involved in bringing it up.

During the second week of October, Jack

Ridley called to see Beattie. His visit was quite a surprise, for it was the first time she had seen him since the day he recommended Ma Briggs' place to her. She was immediately struck again by his flashing good looks, ginger hair and dark eyes, and thick, pouting lips. What she did remember from their previous meeting was the thick stubble on his cheeks and chin, but he had clearly recently shaved for his skin was now clear and smooth. However, for this initial meeting, Beattie did not yet feel confident enough to ask him up to her room, so she met him outside the house, where they perched side by side on the coping stone by the tiny front garden.

'I'm glad the old bird's takin' care of yer,' said Jack, who was picking his teeth with a matchstick whilst he talked. 'Just as well – wiv the way fings are wiv you.'

'I'm very grateful to yer, Jack,' Beattie replied. 'I don't know wot I'd 'ave done if you 'adn't told me about this place. If there's ever anyfin' I can do fer you, just let me know.'

Jack grinned but only inwardly. 'So, who give yer the bun then?'

'It's a long story.'

'Army? Navy? Flyin' Corps?'

'Could we talk about somefin' else?' said Beattie, irritated.

Jack shrugged his shoulders. 'Suits me. I wos just wondrin' 'ow you're goin' ter cope, that's all.'

'I'll manage.' Beattie turned away to look along the road where a group of rowdy teenagers were kicking a milk bottle as though it were a football. 'What about you?' she asked, suddenly, turning back to Jack.

'Me?'

'I don't know nuffin' about yer. Where d'yer come from? Wot d'yer do?'

Jack flicked his matchstick into the kerb and pushed his cap to the back of his head. 'I come from anywhere I put me 'ead down, and I do anyfin' I'm asked ter do – brickie, bit of plasterin', chippie...'

Beattie was intrigued by his laid-back style. 'So you make a livin'?'

Jack turned to look at her with a smile. 'You could say that. Wiv a bit on the side, of course.'

Beattie was puzzled. 'What does that mean?'

Jack's mouth was curled up at the sides in a weird grin. 'I nick,' he replied quite unashamedly.

Beattie fixed him with a suspicious look. 'Nick? Yer don't mean – yer steal fings?'

Jack was quite surprised by her reaction. 'Why not?' he asked.

''Cos it's wrong,' she said.

'Wrong ter eat, yer mean?'

'There're uvver ways.'

'Tell me.'

Both turned to look off in different directions. For a moment or so, there was silence between them. Further down the road, the rogue teenagers had succeeded in smashing the milk bottle into pieces, and were now kicking bits of it at each other.

Jack was first to speak. 'I never knew my mum. She died when I was born. My ol' man brought me up. 'E 'ated my guts, beat me black an' blue, the sod. I did a bunk when I was seven. Never saw ’im again. Good riddance.’

Beattie couldn’t understand why he was telling her all this. After all, she hardly knew him. And yet, there was something about him that fascinated her. It was to do with the way he talked without actually looking at her. He was a thinker. Beattie hadn’t met many people like that.

‘That’s when I learn ’ow ter nick. These geezers taught me, down the knackers’ yard.’ He flicked a glance at her. ‘That’s where they cut up the ’orse meat.’

He pulled one foot up, rested it on the coping stone, folded his arms, placed them on his knee, and rested his chin on them. ‘They used ter get me ter nick from the drunks when they come out the boozers. It was easy money. I didn’t get much of it, though. The geezers took most of it.’ He paused only long enough to wipe his nose on his fingers. ‘I come into me own later. Bigger fish. I didn’t go ’ungry. Not no more.’

‘Don’t yer feel guilty, robbin’ innocent people?’ asked Beattie.

‘Innocent?’ said Jack, looking out at the teenagers on the rampage along the road. ‘Who’s the innocent – me, or them wiv the cash?’

After a moment, Beattie got up. ‘I’d better be goin’. Fanks again, Jack.’

Jack grabbed hold of her arm, but he saw the surprise in her face, so he quickly released her. ‘Wot yer goin’ ter do when the kid arrives?’ he asked.

Beattie shrugged her shoulders. ‘Look after it, of course.’

‘Wot d’yer do for cash in the meantime?’

Beattie thought about this for a moment. 'I'll manage.'

'Well, if yer can't, yer know where to find me. Just ask Ma.'

He pulled his cap on straight again, put his hands in his pockets, and moved off.

Beattie watched him ambling down the road until he disappeared around the corner into the next street.

By this time, the rowdy teenagers were hurling as many milk bottles at each other as they could. In the distance, the burly figure of Big Ben was looming. Once again, the Bunk was on full alert.

Nagger Mills was turning out to be the kind of friend that everyone hopes to have, but rarely does. When Beattie left home, she was first to the rescue, taking Beattie back to share her room behind the cattle shed in the Caledonian Market; when Beattie moved into Ma Briggs' place in the Bunk, Nagger was first on the scene, bringing pots and pans to use on the gas ring in Beattie's room, an extra blanket and a feather pillow for her bed, a good supply of tea, sugar, a loaf of bread and a good lump of marge. She even treated her to a big pot of shrimps from Honest Harry's fresh fish stall up the market, and a pennyworth of Beattie's favourite peppermint-flavour bulls'-eyes from Gert Snell's sweet shop. The fact was, Nagger was really quite concerned about her old mate, and felt very protective towards her. She was anxious that Beattie hadn't decided to get rid of the baby, and she wondered how she was going to cope once it arrived.

Nagger could be quite a firecracker, though, like the time when she overheard Shiner Fitch taking the piss out of Beattie by telling his mates down the market as how she'd got herself 'a bun in the oven'. Lashing out at Shiner, Nagger told him, 'If yer arse was as big as yer mouf, we could auction you off wiv the rest of the bulls!'

On the first evening in November, Nagger took Beattie to the Palace Cinematograph Theatre on the corner of Seven Sisters Road and Devonshire Road, which most people knew as Pyke's, after its former owner Montague Pyke. The theatre was only a few years old, and was very popular with the residents of Holloway, despite the fact that, as the audience filed in, a member of the staff was there to hand out cough sweets to counteract the pungent smell of fag smoke that filled the auditorium during every performance. The programme that evening was a very popular one, for it featured several two-reeler films, starring firm favourites such as Little Titch, Pola Negri, Buster Keaton, Tod Slaughter, and Charlie Chaplin.

Beattie and Naggs were joined by some of Beattie's workmates from the candle factory, including Ivy West and Marj Barker, who were always good for a laugh. And laugh they all did, especially when the piano accompanist, Doris Bell, better known to the regulars as 'good ol' Doll', lost her place on her music sheet during a tense moment in Pola Negri's latest melodrama, and got everything out of sync with the film.

After the show, Naggs walked Beattie home to the Bunk, which gave her the chance to talk to Beattie about how she was going to cope once the baby was born. But there was one particular thing on her mind.

'Yer've gotta tell 'im, Beat,' she said, as they strolled arm in arm along Seven Sisters Road. 'Yer've gotta tell sailor boy about 'is kid.'

Beattie came to an abrupt halt. 'Now don't go fru all that again, Naggs,' she said abruptly. 'I've told yer, as far as I'm concerned, Ed Lacey don't even exist.'

'But 'e does, Beat,' insisted Naggs. 'Wot 'e's done is wrong, there's no two ways about that, and 'e's an absolute sod, but this kid is goin' ter be as much 'is as yours.'

Beattie tried to relieve the pressure on her bulging stomach by straightening her shoulders. 'What the eye don't see...' she said obstinately. 'I don't owe that man nuffin'.'

'That yer don't,' replied Naggs. 'But it's not right ter keep it from 'im. OK, so if yer do tell 'im, 'e could well decide ter take no notice and lay low. But if 'e wanted ter turn nasty – I mean, even more nasty – yer might end up in court.'

Until that moment, Beattie had only just realised that they had come to a halt on the corner of Hornsey Road, right opposite where the poor old Eaglet pub used to be. She stared hard at the shell of the building, and could still see herself and Edward Lacey standing at that bar. *Anchor's down, and here I stay.* His voice was echoing through her mind. *Edward. You can call me Ted.* A faint, wry smile came to Beattie's face.

'Look, Beat,' Naggs said, taking Beattie's arm again and moving on. 'Whatever yer fink of Edward bleedin' Lacey, it's not right ter take it out on the kid.'

Beattie was taken aback. 'The kid? Wot're yer talkin' about?'

'Yer could've got rid of it, Beat,' said Naggs, 'but yer chose not to. In which case, a kid needs a farver.'

Beattie was indignant. 'Who says so?'

'It's obvious, Beat,' said Naggs, doing her best to sound reasonable. 'Yer 'ave ter fink of all the problems of bringin' a kid up on yer own. A kid costs money. Where yer goin' ter get it if yer can't go ter work?'

'I'll manage,' replied Beattie, defiantly. 'Ma Briggs said she'd 'elp. There won't be no problems.'

'There's somefin' else too, Beat,' said Naggs, once again bringing them to a halt. ''Ave yer fawt about what people are goin' ter say – I mean, you, a single woman wiv a baby?'

'Who cares what they fink?' snapped Beattie. 'It's nuffin' ter do wiv no one but me.'

'But it is, Beat.' Naggs turned Beattie around to look at her. 'People can be cruel. They can make your life hell. It's not only your dad that feels the way 'e does. If the same fing 'appened ter me, my ol' man'd beat the bleedin' daylights out of me.'

For a moment, Beattie said nothing. Her mind was full of what options, if any, she really had. What Naggs was saying was right, it was only too plain to see that. Even in the Bunk word had got around that she was in the family way, without a husband, without a man. As her stomach swelled more and more, people she passed in the street were noticing her. Their looks were disapproving; she knew, she could tell. It was amazing how small-minded people could be, no matter where, or which side of the fence, they came from. On the opposite side of the road, there was a right royal knees-up going on in The Medina Arms pub. They were all having a good time all right, and Beattie wished she could be there with them. But even there, they would know. They would see that bulge of hers, and they would know. And then the questions would come. *'How long ter go now, dear?' 'Where's yer hubby then?' 'In the army, is 'e?'* And when they knew, when they found out that there was no husband, they would just be like all the rest. A woman with a kid and no husband? Must be a tart. Beattie felt two small feet kicking inside her stomach. That tiny creature was trying to tell her something. But what?

'I just don't want *you* ter be in the wrong, Beat,' said Naggs, her arm affectionately hugging Beattie around the waist. 'I couldn't care a monkey's fer sailor boy, but I do care fer you.'

'If I do tell 'im, what 'appens if 'e says 'e wants ter come back an' live wiv me?'

Naggs thought about this for a moment. 'D'yer want 'im ter come back?' she asked.

'Yer've got ter be jokin'!'

'Regardless of wot people fink?'

In the frail light of an early winter's evening, Naggs could see that the look on Beattie's face was more determined than ever.

'Regardless of wot people fink,' replied Beattie.

Naggs broke into a broad smile. 'Then tell 'im

ter get stuffed!'

Both of them roared with laughter.

Beattie crawled into bed and lay there, looking up at the grubby white ceiling which hadn't had a coat of paint since before the war. Although it was still only ten o'clock, or thereabouts, she felt drained. Two little feet inside her had shown her very little mercy during the day, and now she was resting on her back, that burgeoning life assured her that even if she was ready for sleep, *it* wasn't. Before getting undressed, she had turned off the gaslight on the wall without bothering to draw the blackout curtains. In any case, with rumours of an armistice at any time, many people had already discarded their blackout curtains, and as the residents of the Bunk cared little for decorum, at night it was now perfectly easy to peer into neighbours' front of house rooms as you passed by.

Even with no gaslight, the room was flooded with a bright, white glow, for the moon, although not full, was unhindered by any clouds. As Beattie lay there, her face bathed in the frosty rays of a cold November night, her mind was torn by indecision. Everything Naggs had told her was true; if nothing else, Edward Lacey was the father of the child she would bear. But when she dismissed him from her life, she did so in the knowledge that such a man was not fit enough to be a husband, let alone a father. Not that she would ever want to marry him or any other man, especially one from a world that was so different to everything she believed in.

And as she lay there, her mind slowly started to drift to other things. She wondered what was going on at home in Thornhill Road, and if what she had heard was true, that her father was unwell, and that Sarah had taken a job at Gamages. Since the early days of her pregnancy, she had thought a lot about her family, about her sister, Sarah, and all the years of lost opportunity – for both of them. She closed her eyes, and saw Sarah's face before her, smiling – that prim little smile – nodding her head graciously as if saying, 'It's wrong of you to do this, Beattie,' or 'It's wrong of you to do that.' A rare moment of guilt interrupted her thoughts. Who was to blame for their inability to get on? Was it Sarah, who was set in her ways and unable to compromise? Or was it Beattie herself, who could only see protest as a way to express herself. And then she thought of her mother, who tried so hard to retain the family in the traditional way. Poor, dear Mother. If there was any one person in the world who was likely to grieve over Beattie's absence, it would surely be her mother. Would she ever see them again? One day would they recognise that she herself was a mother?

Just when the two small feet inside decided to stop kicking in the walls of her stomach, there was an almighty thumping on her bedroom door.

'Beattie! Wake up! Wake up, Beattie!' It was Ma Briggs calling from the landing outside.

Beattie's heart was thumping hard at the shock, but she managed to sit up, lower her feet on to the cold lino floor, and get across to the door to open it.

'Beattie!'

Beattie's tired eyes could hardly focus on the old dear, who was out there with a lighted candle, and wearing a pleated nightcap and tattered pink nightgown. 'Wot is it, Ma?' she spluttered. 'Wot's up?'

Ma Briggs could hardly contain herself. 'It's over, Beattie! It's all over!'

'Over? Wot's over?'

Ma was talking faster than her lips would allow. 'The war, Beattie! The war! They're signing the armistice next week. Can't yer 'ear 'em in the street? Everyone's goin' mad!'

Beattie suddenly woke right up. Forgetting about the bulge in her stomach, she rushed across to the window, rubbed her eyes, and looked out. It was true. There were groups of people rushing up and down the street, some of them leaping up and down, others shouting and singing, and others doing an impromptu knees-up. Yes, it really was true. It was over. This long, bloody war was over at last. How much had it cost in human life? Beattie wondered. Would what happened from now on really be worth those years of bitterness, anger, and hate?

She turned with a start. Ma Briggs was still standing in the open bedroom doorway. She was sobbing hard, the candlelight picking out the tears rolling down her cheeks.

'It's all right, Ma,' Beattie said, throwing her arms around the old lady and hugging her. 'It's all over. Now we can start ter live again.'

When Ma Briggs had gone back down to her room, Beattie turned up the gaslight, collected a pencil and some notepaper, and returned to bed.

Then she set about writing a note to Edward Lacey. She had decided to tell him that during the next three months, he would become a father.

The armistice between the Allies and Germany came into force at eleven o'clock on the morning of 11 November 1918. Two days prior to that Kaiser Wilhelm II fled to the Netherlands, where he immediately went into hiding. There was great rejoicing throughout the United Kingdom, and it was the one event that was approved by the people of both Barnsbury – and 'the Bunk'.

On that morning, Beattie put on her working clothes as usual, had a cup of tea, cut herself a thick chunk of bread, plastered it with marge and a big spoonful of strawberry jam, and devoured it as quickly as she could. Although it was after nine in the morning, it didn't worry her, for she imagined that the candle factory would be joining in the celebrations just as much as everyone else. So, after wrapping herself up in a warm topcoat, and with a large woollen scarf over her head, she made her way downstairs.

As usual, Ma Briggs was waiting for her in the hall. It was a ritual that was beginning to irritate Beattie, for to her mind it smelled a bit of regularity. However, today the old lady had a reason for being there. 'Somefin' in the post for yer, dearie. Looks important. I 'ope it's a windfall!' She roared with hoarse laughter, and handed over the envelope.

Beattie took a good look at it, and realised at

once that it wasn't the reply she was waiting for from Edward Lacey. But in some perverted way, she was rather hoping that it wouldn't be. 'No windfall, Ma,' she said, despondently. 'More likely someone's after somefin'.'

Ma Briggs watched eagerly as Beattie ripped open the envelope and read the contents. She was surprised to see the lack of any kind of response on Beattie's face.

'Nuffin' important, Ma,' she said quite impassively. 'Do us a favour, will yer? Bung it in the bin for me?'

Ma Briggs took the letter and envelope from Beattie, then followed her to the door. 'We'll 'ave a little snifter tergevver ternight, dearie,' she called, as Beattie left the house. 'If yer feel like it, that is. We deserve a celebration.'

'Thanks, Ma!' called Beattie, as she made off down the street.

'See yer later!'

Ma stood in the open doorway, watching Beattie until she disappeared around the corner into neighbouring Fonthill Road. Then she went back into the house, closing the door behind her.

Still clutching Beattie's letter and envelope in her hand, Ma Briggs went into her front parlour and quickly searched for her wobbly, half-broken glasses. She found them on her breakfast tray, splattered with milk from her cup of tea. Quickly wiping them on her pinny, she cleared the tea tray to one side, and settled down at the table to read Beattie's letter, which was badly scrawled on plain notepaper, with no address.

9 November 1918

Dear Miss Beattie (I regret you did not add your surname),

Your letter addressed to my son, Edward, and dated 1 November, has been forwarded to me by the Royal Naval Training Depot at Dartford…

Ma Briggs wasn't very good at reading words, especially words that weren't written very clearly. But even with her modest skills, it took very little time for her to discover that the grand-sounding Lieutenant-Commander Lacey had written to tell Beattie that her sailor boy petty officer, father of her future child, was dead.

CHAPTER 7

Parliament was dissolved a fortnight after the signing of the armistice, and the Labour Party became the official Opposition to the new Coalition Government headed by David Lloyd George. But the aftermath of the war was a tide of upheaval, brought about by widespread unemployment, the inevitable outcome of rapid demobilisation. The brief economic boom turned out to be a false dawn, and within months the soup kitchens were busier than ever, with long queues waiting for the most modest state handouts. Public disorder became the curse of the new government. At the forefront of this was the newly formed Women's Movement, which strongly objected to women being asked to vacate their jobs in favour of returning ex-servicemen. Then, to add to the country's burdens, a deadly influenza epidemic wrought havoc on the population, with more than fifteen thousand deaths in the London area alone.

Geraldine Melford succumbed to the epidemic in the spring of 1919, at a time when the worst of the crisis was finally coming to an end. With such a shortage of drugs to tackle the virus, Sarah buried her pride and sought out every old wives' remedy she could find. This involved everything from soaking her mother in a hot bath spiced with malt vinegar, to a five-day course of warm black treacle mixed with dried, crushed dandelion seeds. The taste was, to say the least, quite disgusting, but Geraldine's temperature had remained high for so long that she wasn't even aware of the physical torture she was being subjected to. Luckily, the influenza took its own course, and Geraldine eventually recovered.

The greatest problem facing Sarah at this time, however, was the mental state of her father. After weeks pretending to go to his office at Gamages each day, Samuel Melford had finally lost his job. It had been a difficult time for Sarah, for, despite her denials that she was not related to the former General Manager, word had soon got round to the contrary. Fortunately, Gamages' personnel officer, the down-to-earth Mrs Hetherington, had become a staunch ally of Sarah's, having suspected all along who the girl actually was. But then rumours had circulated around the store that the real reason her father had been forced to leave his job was because of some financial irregularities that had only come to light during the end-of-year audit of the company accounts. Matters were made worse when, much to Mrs Hetherington's regret, Sarah herself had lost her job in the book department, in order to make way for a former male member of the staff who was returning from active service on the Western Front.

Only too aware that the family's finances were now under severe strain, Sarah searched the Situations Vacant columns of the newspapers. Since she'd displayed such determination to do paid work rather than have a stranger live in the house, all question of finding a lodger had been dropped. But despite her rapid response to any likely-looking job, by the time she had applied in writing, there were at least fifty or sixty applications before her, and, owing to her lack of any real experience, she was turned down on every occasion. In desperation, she started to search for less ambitious work, which meant tramping the streets each day, joining queues of the unemployed outside shops and offices where Situations Vacant cards had appeared in the windows.

Sarah's fortunes, however, changed quite suddenly, and in the most unexpected way. It happened during one of her endless visits to the employment exchange in Upper Street, which, since the end of the war, had been under siege by thousands of desperate unemployed people, many of whom were living from hand to mouth. Like all the other employment exchanges, the queues were dominated by males, most of them young and middle-aged ex-servicemen, willing to do any menial job they were offered. Of the few young women who were there, most were looking for domestic positions, such as scullery or bed maids. On this particular day, Sarah found herself standing in the queue behind a very rough and irate young girl, who was involved in a slanging match with a male assistant at the counter.

'What d'yer take me for?' yelled the girl, bringing the usual morning crowd of unemployed to a hushed silence. 'I ain't workin' fer no bloody coon, an' that's fer sure!'

The girl's objectionable manner prompted the

counter assistant, a restrained-looking middle-aged man with a neat grey quiff in his hair, and wearing a stiff white collar and tie, and rimless spectacles, to answer calmly, 'That's up to you, miss. Next, please!'

The girl was not taking that lying down. ''Ere you!' she screeched. 'Are you tellin' me that's the only job yer can offer me, workin' as a skivvy ter some black woman?'

'Next please!' called the assistant, ignoring the girl, and looking past her to Sarah, who was behind her in the queue.

The girl reluctantly stood aside, but was now intent on stirring up trouble with the rest of the crowd. ''Ere! 'Ave yer 'eard this then?' she yelled. 'All they can offer me is a job wiv a coon! Who won this bleedin' war then – us, or Kaiser Bill?'

In the present desperate climate of despair, her rabble-rousing did what the girl intended, provoking raised clenched fists, and yells of angry protests.

'It's time we stood up ter all this!' the girl continued. 'Stand up for our rights and demand decent jobs for a decent wage!'

This brought the crowd to a dangerous height of tension, with the prospect of a riot. But whilst everyone was busy giving support to the girl, two police constables appeared at the street entrance, and pushed their way through the crowd.

'Don't let 'em push us around, mates!' the girl yelled. 'A job fer every person in the country – man *an'* woman!'

This brought a mixed response, jeers from some of the men, cheers and applause from others, including the few women waiting in the queues.

During all the angry exchanges that had broken out behind her, Sarah, at the counter, remained quite still, too nervous to turn around to see what was going on.

The girl, her clenched fist now raised high to inflame the crowd even more, yelled, 'Demand yer rights!'

The crowd picked up her call, 'Demand our rights!'

At that point, the two police constables pounced on the rebellious young girl, each taking hold of an arm. Despite yells of protest from the crowd, she was led out of the exchange, closely followed by some of the more radical young unemployed men.

The counter assistant waited for the rumpus to die down, then returned to Sarah. 'Sorry about that,' he said, unmoved by what had been a potentially serious situation. 'Oh yes,' he said, adjusting his spectacles to look at Sarah's unemployment card, then he sighed. 'I'm sorry, Miss Melford. Nothing for you today, I'm afraid.'

Sarah looked crushed. 'Nothing at all?'

The assistant shook his head. 'It's not easy to find nice jobs for young ladies like you.'

Sarah was irritated. 'I'm not looking for a nice job,' she said. 'I'm looking for *any* job.'

The assistant gave her back her card. 'What can I say?' he replied apologetically.

Sarah was about to turn away, when she suddenly remembered what had sparked the girl's protest. 'What about the job you offered to the girl before me?'

The assistant looked up with a start. 'I don't think that would be suitable, miss,' he said, lowering his voice. 'Not for someone like you.'

'May I at least know what the job is?' Sarah asked politely.

The assistant studied Sarah's face briefly, then referred to a piece of paper on the counter at her side. 'It's a vacancy for a companion – to an elderly coloured lady. She's from Ceylon.'

'Ceylon,' Sarah said, almost subconsciously.

'It's in Asia,' said the assistant, in a rather superior way. 'Somewhere near Asia, I believe.'

'Just off the southern tip of India,' Sarah said, in an equally superior tone. 'It's an island.'

The assistant was not amused to be put down and he slid the piece of paper away from her.

'What does the work involve?' Sarah asked, refusing to be dismissed.

'It's manual work, Miss Melford,' he replied. 'The lady is housebound. She can't get around. Unfortunately she has no relatives in this country, so she needs someone to look after her during the day. It's a question of cleaning, and cooking – that sort of thing. If you don't mind my saying, I think someone of your breeding might find that – well, a little degrading, shall we say?'

Once again Sarah stopped him from pushing the piece of paper to one side. 'As a matter of fact, I wouldn't,' she replied, quietly insistent. 'I'm perfectly used to such tasks, and I'd be very grateful if you'd give me an introduction.'

The weary assistant sized Sarah up. After all he'd gone through that morning, he didn't quite know what to make of her. 'Can you cook?' he asked with an exasperated sigh.

'I can.'

'Scrub floors?'

'Yes.'

'Clean windows?'

'Yes.'

'Polish brasswork? Sew?'

'Most certainly.'

The assistant was now at the end of his tether. 'And would you be sympathetic and patient with an elderly lady who can't get around on her own, who spends most of her day sitting in an armchair by the fire?'

'I would hope so.'

'Would you feel the same about an elderly *coloured* lady?'

Sarah smiled. 'The island of Ceylon is a part of the British Empire,' she replied serenely. 'I would have thought her colour was quite immaterial.'

It was said that the difference between a street and a road was that a street had buildings on either side, and a road didn't.

Considering that most of the streets *and* roads in Holloway had houses or buildings of some sort on either side, it made nonsense of the definition. Arthur Road had houses on either side, built in the Edwardian period very solidly of bricks and stone on four floors, with just the suggestion of a small front garden to each. Arthur Road was one of those rather elegant back roads (or streets) which nestled quite comfortably behind the big, main Holloway and Tollington Roads, and if you were lucky enough actually to own a house there, as opposed to the less elegant Roden, Hertslet, and Mayton Streets just around the corner, you were considered to be not hard up for a bob or two.

Sarah took to Arthur Road the moment she turned the corner from the more modest Annette Road. The thing that struck her most about the long, wide terrace on either side of her was that not all the houses were identical, like so many other terraces around Holloway. Also, a few of them were semi-detached, with little alleyways in between, and the windows of some of the houses were quite large, either bow-shaped, or with high French windows and balconies on the first floor. She had no idea who the road had been named after, but whoever Arthur was, Sarah thought that he certainly had good taste.

The house she was looking for was about halfway down on the right-hand side, and she could see that it had once been beautiful, built on three floors, with a plain cement stucco border along the top at roof level, stretching all the way down on either side of the house to the small front garden below. Surprisingly, the street door had recently been painted, which must have been something of a coup during the long period of wartime shortages, but the elegant navy-blue colour was not enough to deflect the heavy, tarnished brass door knocker. At the employment exchange before she came, Sarah had had to sign for the front door key of the house, for the elderly lady resident was not really capable of responding to callers.

After first ringing the bell, and then letting herself in, Sarah closed the door quietly behind her, as she had been instructed to do, and stood for a moment or so in the hall to acclimatise herself. The first thing she noticed was a strong, unfamiliar smell, which seemed to pervade the whole place. For such a large house, the hall was quite narrow, more like a carpeted passage. There was a room on either side, and at the far end of the passage were the stairs, also carpeted, behind which was the room she had been told to make for. This she duly did, and knocked gently and called lightly, 'Hello!'

To her surprise, there was an immediate response. 'Come in!'

The moment Sarah entered the room, which turned out to be the kitchen, that unfamiliar smell hit her full in the face.

'Hello? Who are you?' Sitting at the kitchen table was a fairly elderly woman, with swept-back dark hair that had only recently started to turn grey. She was wearing what Sarah thought was a wonderfully exotically coloured, full-length dress of fine silk. Her narrow face carried no make-up, and her thin eyes radiated humour and intelligence. The voice was a cultured one, but tinged with a slight, fascinating Asian accent. In front of her was a bowl of some kind of creamy mixture, which she had been beating with a large wooden spoon, and much to Sarah's surprise, a cigarette was burning in an ashtray on the table alongside.

'Mrs Ranasinghe?'

'That's right,' came the reply. 'You must have

been sent by the agency.'

'The employment exchange,' replied Sarah. She held out her hand. 'My name is Sarah Melford,' she said, with a pleasant smile.

Mrs Ranasinghe stopped beating her creamy mixture. 'Sarah?' she said, more or less to herself. 'Yes. That's a good name.' She took Sarah's hand, and held on to it for a moment, as though trying to feel for the blood pumping through Sarah's veins. 'Twenty-two, twenty-three?'

Sarah was puzzled. 'I beg your pardon?'

'Your age.'

'Oh – yes, I'm twenty-four.'

Mrs Ranasinghe smiled and released Sarah's hand. 'So then, why don't you go and make us both a nice cup of tea? Kettle's on the stove. There's still some water left in it from my breakfast.'

Sarah couldn't get over how immediate and direct the old lady was, so much so that she found no difficulty in doing exactly what she was asked. Going straight to the gas cooker, which was tucked away in an alcove on the other side of the room, and on top of which a large saucepan of strong-smelling meat stew of some sort was bubbling away, she quickly checked that there was enough water in the kettle, found a box of Swan Vestas, and lit one of the gas rings.

'I can't tell you what a treat it is for someone to make me a cup of tea,' called the old lady. 'By the time I get out of bed in the morning, and wobble my way into this place, I'm so exhausted I feel like going straight back to bed again!'

Behind her, Sarah was having great success in

finding a teapot, milk and sugar, and cups and saucers. She also found a pile of dirty plates and crockery in the washing-up bowl.

'Come and tell me about yourself, young lady,' said Mrs Ranasinghe. 'I want to know why you want to look after a broken-down old mess like me.'

Sarah returned to the table, and sat down on the chair that Mrs Ranasinghe had struggled to pull out for her. 'I can't believe you're anything of the sort,' she said.

'How do you know?' asked the old lady. 'You don't know me.'

Sarah had no real answer, but nevertheless, she tried. 'You're so wonderfully clear and bright,' she said. 'More than I could ever be.'

The old lady roared with laughter. 'You must want the job badly!'

Sarah laughed with her. As she looked at Mrs Ranasinghe's pale brown skin, she wondered why that unpleasant young girl at the employment exchange had created so much fuss. The old lady's skin seemed only a tone or so darker than her own.

Mrs Ranasinghe picked up the remaining part of her cigarette that was burning in the ashtray. Then she took a small, delicate puff, and quickly exhaled very little smoke. 'A terrible habit,' she said, 'but I love it. I never used to do this back in my own country, you know,' she said, almost apologetically. 'More's the pity. It gives me so much pleasure.' She took another puff, exhaled in exactly the same delicate way, then stubbed out the butt in the ashtray. 'Can you believe, I left

Ceylon nearly ten years ago? Ten years! My husband died, and my family didn't like me. They said I was too "free-thinking"!' She roared with laughter again. 'So I decided to come to England. It's a good place to survive, England. And why not? After all, Ceylon *is* part of the British Empire!'

'What did they mean by "free thinking"?' asked Sarah.

'I apparently behave too young for a woman of my age. That's what they say, but what they really mean is that I am too independent. Ha! They should see me now.' She started to rub her kneecaps under the table; they were clearly giving her some pain. 'Riddled with every disease under the sun – if there ever was such a thing as sun in England. I have arthritis, bronchitis, a heart murmur, a spine disorder, and just about everything else. The doctors told me that if I didn't give up smoking, I'd kill myself. So what?' She stopped abruptly, and darted a quick look at Sarah. 'Do you think a woman should be independent, Sarah?' she enquired shrewdly.

Sarah thought for a moment before answering. 'As far as I'm aware, I've never been anything else.'

The old lady raised her eyebrows, then started a rapid cross-examination. 'Are you married?'

'No.'

'Never?'

'Never.'

'You live with your family?'

'My mother and father.'

'No brothers and sisters?'

Sarah thought for a moment before answering. 'None,' she replied.

The old lady sat back in her chair. Sarah clearly fascinated her. 'Don't you want to ask *me* some questions? About what work I would expect you to do?'

'I was told you needed looking after. They didn't mention that you were independent.'

'Does that worry you?'

Again, Sarah thought carefully before answering. 'If you wanted to employ me, I imagine my sole function would be to do only the things you want me to do. I presume that is why you have advertised this position.'

Now it was the old lady's turn to think carefully before continuing. 'I hate getting old. I don't like not knowing what is going to happen in the future.'

Sarah shrugged her shoulders. 'It can't be any worse than what's already happened.'

This time, there was a long pause. Sarah had no idea what the old lady was thinking. All she knew was that she was certainly a force to be reckoned with.

'I hope you can cook?' said Mrs Ranasinghe, quite suddenly.

'I do most of the cooking at home,' replied Sarah.

'I mean *real* cooking, not that terrible plain stuff you English eat.' The old lady started to beat her cream mixture in the bowl again. 'Egg hoppers, lamprais, fish curry, chilli sambol…'

Sarah was lost. 'I'm sorry?'

There was a broad but inquisitive grin on the

old lady's face. 'Don't worry, you'll learn,' she said, with a mischievous twinkle in her eye. Then she paused only long enough to point to the kettle, which was now steaming furiously on the gas stove. 'Now can I please have my tea? Surely you can tell that I am absolutely parched?'

Sarah did as she was told. She had learned already that her new employer did not like to be kept waiting.

It was a source of great sadness to Sarah that her mother and father no longer slept together. In the old days, they were, of course, inseparable, and Sarah had always cherished the thought that, each night, her parents were lying together in their huge double bed with the brass head rail, snuggled up together in each other's arms. But Samuel's illness had changed all that, for there was rarely a night went by when the poor man was able to get more than a couple of hours' sleep. And so he moved into the spare room on the same floor, leaving his wife to sob her way to sleep in the huge bed that now seemed to be without heart or soul.

There was, however, a more urgent worry for Sarah, concerning the deterioration in her father's mental state. Following Samuel's departure from his job at Gamages, Sarah had never tackled her father about the rumours circulating about the financial irregularities that had taken place during his final year as General Manager. As Samuel had never been visited by anyone from the police or the store itself, and as no charges had been levelled against him, she was willing to believe that the rumours were unfounded and spread by disgruntled members of his staff.

With so much time on his hands, Samuel now spent most of his days ambling along the towpath of the Islington Canal along Caledonian Road. When the weather was good, his favourite resting spot was an old cut-down treetrunk, which he perched on, enabling him to watch the coal barges on their way to the marshalling depots near King's Cross. But when it rained, he could usually be found crouched on the ground beneath the bridge over Caledonian Road, staring aimlessly down at his own reflection in the water for hours on end. At night, however, his behaviour was altogether more mysterious.

The grandfather clock in the sitting room had just struck eleven at night when, as regular as in his former commuting days travelling back and forth to Gamages, Samuel came quietly down the stairs, collected his jacket and homburg hat from the hall stand, and left the house. One night, though, he was not alone, for Sarah had been waiting for him, out of sight behind the kitchen door.

In the dark Thornhill Road outside, there was that kind of stillness that one only ever feels when the air is pure and the human race are in their beds. Spring had come and gone, and already the nights were showing the promise of a warm summer ahead. But Sarah was taking no chances, for even though her father was not wearing enough protection against the cool night air, she herself was well wrapped up in her favourite woollen topcoat with the rabbit fur collar.

Sarah only emerged from the shadow of the tree in the front garden when she was satisfied that her father was at a safe enough distance not to be aware of her presence. The moment she could see him heading off down Barnsbury Road, she stepped out, and carefully paced him. As she watched him shuffling off, head and shoulders stooped so low that it would have been impossible for him to see anything but the pavement at his feet, her heart was aching with the sight of this man, who only a few months earlier had been the perfect model of a husband and father, whose head was held high wherever he went. What had happened to bring him down to this level? Had it been shame or guilt at the realisation that he had cast his younger daughter out of his house without any recourse to balance or reason? What *was* going on in that tired mind, which had become so illogical, so detached from the realities of everyday life that nothing he said or did now made any sense whatsoever? Sarah felt a huge lump swelling in her throat, and she had to stifle her mouth with her hand to prevent the audible sound of the distress she felt.

Samuel and his daughter made slow but steady progress along Barnsbury Road, where the residents of the grand Georgian houses were long in bed, and where only the nightly gathering of stray dustbin cats were there to resent the human intrusion, their slinky eyes peering at them from the steps of every house basement along the road.

As Samuel approached the corner of Dewey

Road, the mystery of his nightly forays gradually became more worrying and sinister. Across the road, standing in the shadows of the White Conduit pub, was a shadowy figure who waved to Samuel as he approached. Sarah held back for a moment or so, but managed to conceal herself close enough to see her father cross the road and meet up with the man.

'You're late, sir.'

It was a voice Sarah recognised immediately: old Sid Perkins, the hot chestnut seller, whom she had passed on the corner of Richmond Avenue many a winter's evening.

'I'm sorry, Sid,' returned Samuel. 'It's not easy to get out without notice.'

'They've bin waitin' fer nearly 'alf an 'our, sir,' the old chestnut seller croaked in a tone that lacked his usual warm and friendly nature. 'Yer knows 'ow they 'ate ter be kept waitin'. It's a tricky business, wiv the law breavin' down their necks.'

On hearing this, Sarah's heart missed a beat. Her worst fears had been realised. Her father was mixed up in some kind of shady business. Oh God! What *had* he got himself involved in? She thought of everything, from a conspiracy to hold up a bank, to breaking into some wealthy person's house. Oh why hadn't she seen this coming? Why hadn't she got her father the care and medical attention he clearly needed?

Whilst she was agonising over all this, the old chestnut seller led her father into a yard at the side of the pub. Sarah waited a moment, then hurried across the road to follow them.

The pub itself had long since closed for the night and was in total darkness, but as the alleyway alongside came into view, Sarah could just make out a chink of light coming from what seemed to be some kind of large timber storage shed at the rear. She held back for as long as she could and watched whilst Sid Perkins tapped on the door of the shed, waited for someone to open it from inside, and then stood back to allow Samuel to enter ahead of him. The moment the door was closed and locked from inside, Sarah hurried along the alleyway, and tried to look in. Unfortunately, there was no hole big enough in the wood for her to see through. But as she moved slowly around the building, she eventually found a suitably safe spot to stop and put her ear to the outside wall. At first, all she could hear were men's voices. They seemed to be arguing angrily. Then she heard her father's voice, apologising profusely for keeping them all waiting. It seemed to take ages before the anger subsided. But then a different sound took over. It was a strange, brooding sound, which Sarah could not identify.

'Right!' called a heavily chesty-voiced man inside. 'This is yer last chance, Melford. Lose this one – and you're done!'

Sarah covered her mouth in horror. For as soon as the man spoke, there was a chorus of voices, ranting, shouting, and jeering.

But it was the other sounds that scared Sarah most of all. Sounds that she had unfortunately heard only too well – on more than one occasion.

CHAPTER 8

It was an irony that Young Ed had been given his father's name. But Edward Lacey's death had somehow infused Beattie with such a sense of guilt that her conscience pressed her into giving the boy some lasting connection with the father he would never know. Young Ed was also a bit like his dad, especially his eyes, which were bright, glowing, and the palest blue. But he had his mum's jawline, there was no doubt about that, for it was firm and determined, obstinate to the core. Ma Briggs said that on the whole, he was a good little baby, much better than her two had been, for not once had she heard him crying in the night, which was pretty good for a child who wasn't yet six months old. But Beattie had had a hard time during the delivery, mainly because the midwife had been impatient and wanted to get home to her supper, but also because the new arrival had come out at an awkward angle, and was a tight fit, causing his mum to scream the place down. Young Ed had kicked and bawled his way right out into the midwife's hands, but the moment he'd been cleaned up and Ma Briggs held him, the little monkey shut right up, and for the next half an hour or so, no one heard so much as a peep out of him.

Beattie's greatest problem now was, as usual, money, or rather the lack of it. The paltry wage she was earning at the candle factory was only enough to cover the very basic day-to-day essentials, and with a young baby in tow, it was now a struggle to survive. Fortunately, Ma Briggs had turned out to be the most wonderful landlady anyone could wish to have, not only did she charge Beattie the very minimum for her weekly lodgings, she also cared for Young Ed whilst Beattie went to work, from seven in the morning until six in the evening. This arrangement, however, did have its disadvantages, for Ma was a touch absent-minded, often forgetting what times she had fed the baby, as Beattie had requested. But she truly had a heart of gold, and there was no doubt that Beattie could not have coped without her help.

However, if ever there was a time when a daughter had need of her mum, this was it, and ever since the baby had arrived, Beattie had felt pangs of guilt that, apart from herself, her mother, the one other person in the world who had a right to be with the baby, knew nothing of him. And yet, every time she made up her mind to take the plunge and go back home to Thornhill Road to show off Young Ed to her family, she remembered what she had done to Sarah, and the hurt and pain she had caused her by robbing her of the child that should have been, by all rights, Sarah's own.

In recent months, a regular visitor to Beattie was Jack Ridley. At first she had been reluctant to become too involved with him, particularly knowing of his more nefarious activities. But as time went on, she found that she was attracted to him, despite his brash ways, he was the down-to-earth type of man she had always craved. However, kids were not part of Jack's plans, and he waited until the time was right when he would remind Beattie how much she owed him for the roof over her head. That time came one evening early in the summer, when young Ed was left in the care of Ma Briggs, whilst Beattie and Jack went for a drink at the Clarence pub, which was beneath the railway bridge in Seven Sisters Road.

'A job? What kind of job?'

Beattie's question brought a gleam to Jack's eyes. He leaned forward across the small corner table he had found for them, and gave her one of those intimate grins which made her fancy him like mad. 'One that yer get paid for,' he replied. As the Clarence was quite full that night, he had to raise his voice a little to be heard. 'Money that yer can do wiv right now.'

Beattie took one last drag on the half-finished fag she was smoking, then stubbed it out in the tin ashtray. Smoking was something that Jack had virtually forced on to her, and, as she really didn't care for the habit, she only did it when she was in his company. It also made her feel self-conscious, for like most other pubs in the area, the Clarence was a bastion of male companionship. 'If you're askin' me ter break the law,' she said, haughtily, 'yer can ferget it. I've got a kid ter bring up.'

'Precisely,' replied Jack. 'An' it costs money ter bring up kids. 'Speshully when they ain't got no farver.' He dragged his chair closer. 'The kind of job I've got in mind fer you, Beat,' he said, his mouth close to her ear, 'is just a bit of a lark really. It's somefin' you an' me could do tergevver.' Beattie attempted to interrupt him, but he talked over her. 'Before yer get all righteous wiv me, Beat, let me just ask yer somefin'. 'Ow much spondulix you got left in the kitty?'

Beattie, a sinking feeling in her stomach, tried to sit back in her chair, but Jack put his arm around her shoulders, and pulled her closer to him. As he talked, she could feel his warm breath in her ear. 'Kids cost money, Beat,' he said. 'There are easier ways of gettin' it wivout slavin' yer guts out ten or eleven hours in that bloody candle factory.'

'I make enuff, Jack,' Beattie managed to say. 'It's not much, but I can manage.'

'Manage now – oh yeah. But that's 'cos Ma looks after yer.' His lips were now practically touching the rim of her ear. 'But wot 'appens if Ma drops down dead termorrer?'

Shocked, Beattie swung round to glare at him.

'Oh, I'm not sayin' she will,' he said, with that tantalising grin on his face again, 'but yer never know. She ain't a youngster no more. She's 'ad a dicky 'eart fer years.'

'Don't talk like this, Jack,' Beattie pleaded. 'I don't like it.'

'What *you* don't like, Beat, is facin' up ter the facts er life.'

'These chairs taken, mate?'

Jack and Beattie looked up to find a navvy type standing there, two glasses of beer in his hands and a timid-looking girl at his side.

'Mind if we join yer?' the navvy asked.

'Piss off!' snapped Jack, giving the bloke a thunderous look.

The navvy was about to put down the two glasses of beer and take Jack on, but when Jack started to rise from his seat the girl pulled her mate away, leaving the two men to fight a scathing battle with their eyes.

Beattie was both horrified and excited by Jack's behaviour, but refused to show it. After a suitable moment of silence between them she downed the last of her shandy. 'I've 'ad enuff of this place,' she said.

A few minutes later, they were ambling at a leisurely pace down Campbell Road, Beattie with her arms crossed, and Jack, cap on the back of his head, fag in mouth, hands in trouser pockets. Neither of them spoke until they had almost reached Beattie's digs.

'This job,' Beattie said, trying to sound as casual as possible, 'is there any – danger?'

'Every job carries danger. Yer could set yerself on fire in the candle factory.'

For some perverse reason, this amused Beattie.

They came to a halt outside Ma Briggs' place. For a Saturday night, the Bunk was amazingly quiet, which made Beattie feel strangely ill at ease. 'Are you askin' me ter nick somefin'?' she asked.

Jack turned to face her. 'No,' he said. 'That's my department.'

Beattie was now intrigued. 'You scare me, Jack Ridley,' she said, watching the flicker of the street gaslight reflected in his eyes.

He drew a step closer to her. 'That's wot it's all about, in't it, Beat?'

After a brief pause, he put one arm around her neck, leaned closer to look at her lips, then, in one swift movement, he used the tip of his tongue very gently to caress her lips, before finally kissing her full on the mouth. This immediately aroused Beattie, and even though she had not set out to let this happen, there was clearly no way she could have prevented it.

It was only a short time later that Jack was seeing the inside of Beattie's room for the first time. He still had that smirking kind of grin on his face as he saw all the little things Beattie had done to brighten it up, to try to disguise the fact that it was really not much more than a dump. It was easy to see that Beattie was no housewife, for there were still dirty dishes in the china wash-basin, left over not only from breakfast, but quite probably from the night before as well. There were also plenty of baby's dirty nappies around, which had clearly been there for a day or so and accounted for the sour smell pervading the room. But Jack acknowledged the trouble she had taken in putting coloured pictures of animals on the walls above the baby's basket, which nestled neatly in the corner of the room near the bed.

'Turned out ter be quite the little mum, ain't yer?' Jack said, with more than a hint of sarcasm. Beattie was only too aware that, for him, the flea in the ointment was young Ed.

Beattie tried to turn down the gaslamp whilst she was getting undressed, but Jack would have none of it. He wanted to watch her, to see every part of her body as each garment was removed. She played up to him well, using every sensuous movement she could think of. It had been more than a year since this kind of opportunity had come her way. And Jack relished every minute of Beattie's act – the full breasts, flushed complexion, blue-green eyes that sparkled in the gaslight, the bobbed auburn hair, and the shapely, milky-white curves of her thighs. Once she had finished, Beattie pulled back the bedclothes, and climbed in.

Then it was her turn to watch, for Jack started to remove his clothes, slowly, methodically, taking off each item and placing it carefully on a chair as though it was worth a fortune. And all the time he was playing out this game he never once lost eye contact with Beattie, always watching her reaction, to see if she liked what she saw. When he had finished, Jack stood for a moment, hovering over her. Beattie's eyes searched every corner of his body – the broad shoulders, firm waist, and heavy-muscled arms with a tattoo of a woman dancing down one of them. Every part of him seemed to be so much more perfect than Young Ed's father; Jack Ridley was all man, she could see that now. And when he went across to turn down the gaslamps on the wall, she could see his fine, rounded buttocks moving together in perfect unison.

In his basket, Young Ed, thumb in mouth, was in a deep sleep, completely oblivious to his mum's goings-on.

Jack Ridley climbed in alongside Beattie, and for a moment or so, they lay on their backs, staring up into the darkened room. After the erotic lead-up, their silence was curious, only broken when Jack finally turned towards Beattie.

'Yer still 'aven't told me what this job is,' she said, resisting his advance.

'This is 'ardly the time now, is it?' asked Jack.

'Wot're yer askin' me ter do, Jack?' persisted Beattie.

Jack's shadowy outline leaned closer to her. 'It's a minor job. Ready cash –not much, but enough for us ter split fifty-fifty. You wouldn't 'ave ter do nuffin' 'cept keep a lookout. I'll do the rest.'

There was a pause before Beattie responded. 'Wot sort er place?'

'A shop. A small shop.'

'A shop?'

'It's got a good cash-till, plus quite a lot of – interestin' loot.'

'Wot d'yer mean – interestin''?'

In the dark she couldn't see the smirk on his face. 'Unusual.'

Beattie was getting irritated. 'Get ter the point, Jack!' she snapped. 'What kind of shop?'

Jack put his hand under the sheet and felt the warm flesh of her naked stomach. Then he started to raise himself on top of her.

'What kind of shop?'

Jack was now poised over her. 'A pawn shop.'

There was the briefest moment of delayed shock before Beattie gasped, 'Oh God – no!'

She tried to get up, but Jack had both her arms pinned down by the wrists. 'Relax, Beat! Relax!'

'No, Jack!' cried Beattie, struggling to sit up. 'Yer can't do it. Not Bob and Vera's place. Yer just can't!'

In his basket, Young Ed sounded as though he

was starting to wake.

'Why not, Beat?' growled Jack, who only had to use the minimum of strength to keep Beattie pinned to the bed. 'Yer need cash, don't yer? We boaf need cash. There's enuff in that till ter keep us going for a coupla weeks at least, maybe more. Then there's all that junk 'e's got stacked in those trays. Some of it could be worf a bob or two.' His face was now so close to hers that as he spoke he was practically spitting at her. 'There're some sparklers there, Beat.'

'No!'

'Some of it could be yours, yer stupid cow!' He was now having to fight with her as she tried to break loose. 'Don't yer want ter get that stuff back?'

'Bob Sluggins 'as bin good ter me!' gasped Beattie. ''E's 'elped me out of trouble time and time again.'

'An' wot about 'er – that ol' slag? Does she 'elp yer too?'

Beattie could now feel that Jack was fully aroused, which utterly confused her, because she was feeling exactly the same. 'Please, Jack,' she said in desperation, close to tears. 'I'll 'elp yer, I'll 'elp yer anywhere yer like. But not Bob. Not 'is place. Please don't do it, I beg yer…'

Jack gradually eased himself down on top of her, and she could feel the warmth of his naked body against her own. 'Now you listen to me,' he said. 'We're goin' ter do that pawn shop, boaf of us – you an' me tergevver. You owe me one, Beat.' His voice was almost a whisper. 'It's time ter settle up wiv me.'

He suddenly raised his body up again and, still pinning Beattie down to the bed, he entered her.

For three consecutive nights, Sarah followed her father to the old timber shed behind the White Conduit pub, where he rendezvoused with Sid Perkins. But on each occasion she had been unable to summon up the courage to confront them, and although she had so far been unable to find any way of seeing what was going on inside the shed, those terrible sounds that sent such a chill through her entire body were evidence enough. Each time she set out on her father's tail on the dot of eleven, the most awful thoughts went through her mind. Why had her father kept this dark secret for so long, and what *was* he doing in the company of such a gang of murderous thugs? And what did that man with the chesty voice mean when he shouted at her father, 'This is yer last chance, Melford! Lose this one – and you're done!' Whatever the consequences, Sarah decided once and for all that she had to know what was going on.

'You're just in time, sir,' called Sid, voice low, the moment Samuel Melford crossed the road to meet him. 'They've 'ad a bit of a 'itch ternight, so they won't be startin' fer anuvver few minutes or so.'

Without saying a word, Samuel hurriedly joined him, and after Sid had taken a careful look round to make sure that the coast was clear, they scurried off into the timber shed.

Sarah waited until the guard on duty had closed the door, then she emerged from the shadows on the other side of the street and quietly made her way towards the shed. When she put her head to the outside wall, she could again hear voices inside, but, as yet, not the horrifying sound that had distressed her so much during the previous three evenings. But tonight, Sarah had a plan. It would be daring and dangerous, but action had now become inevitable. Keeping well out of sight, she waited.

Her opportunity came no more than twenty minutes later. It was then that she heard those dreaded sounds again. It was time to move.

Coming out of the shadows, she made her way straight to the door of the shed. Then, pausing for a moment to summon up her courage, she took a deep breath, pulled back her shoulders and banged hard on the door.

Almost immediately, the door opened, and the guard peered out. But before he had time to register who was there, Sarah pulled at the door, and rushed straight in, where she was greeted by the most terrifying screeching sounds. 'Hey!' called the guard, as Sarah disappeared into the crowd of men gathered inside, but his voice was completely drowned by the shouting and jeering. 'Mr Rumbold!'

Sarah ignored the warning shouts, and pushed her way through the excited crowd, who were too involved in what was going on in the centre of the shed to notice that a woman had broken into their protected territory. Sarah's heart was pounding. But then she suddenly caught sight of the person she was desperately searching for. 'Father!' she yelled, over the roar of the crowd.

Samuel Melford turned with a start. He was standing right at the front of the crowd of onlookers, and when Sarah finally succeeded in pushing her way through to him, his face crunched up with distress, and he threw his arms around her.

'Oh, Father!' she said, her voice barely audible above the noise. But she was too overcome with horror to say anything more, for the spectacle before her was mounting to a climax, sending the spectators into a frenzy of excitement.

The chilling sounds Sarah had identified outside were now confirmed. Laid out before her was a circular cockpit, about twenty or so feet in diameter and scattered with sand, where two young cockerels were pitted against each other in a ferocious fight to the death. Sarah had arrived just at the point of kill, for the eye of one of the cockerels had been pecked out by its opponent, and its pure white feathers were splattered with blood. For Sarah it was a horrific sight, and her stomach retched with disgust and revulsion. It was not the first time she had witnessed the savage sport, for during her schooldays, she had twice come across teenagers pitting cocks against each other in a back street in the rougher part of 'the Cally', and the panicked screeching of those two poor doomed creatures was a sound that had lived with her ever since.

When the stronger cock had finally despatched its opponent, the crowd roared its approval, and the winners amongst them collected their cash.

'Oh, Father!' gasped Sarah, her arms holding him tight around his waist, her head buried in his shoulder. 'What are you doing here?' Then she looked up at him. 'How could you?'

Samuel was too confused to move. All he could do was to stare back at her, and ask, 'Sarah?'

'Yer shouldn't come 'ere, Miss Sarah!' said Sid Perkins, his eyes darting all round, looking out for trouble. 'Yer dad was on a winning ticket. It's the first time fer ages. 'E'll never pay off 'is debts if they know you're around.'

Sarah quickly pulled herself together, ignoring the men who were gathering round, glaring at her. 'You shouldn't have brought my father here, Sid,' she said sternly. 'You know how unwell he is.'

Sid was getting more and more nervous at the attention they were getting. ''E asked me, Miss Sarah. 'E begged me. Yer dad needs the lolly. This was the only way I fawt 'e'd have a chance of gettin' some.'

'Well, well now,' called an approaching voice. 'And what 'ave we 'ere?'

Sarah turned, to see a large, rotund, middle-aged man making his way through the crowds, who cleared a path for him.

'Yer didn't tell me yer was 'avin' a visitor ternight, Melford,' said the man, whose voice sounded so hoarse he must have suffered from asthma or bronchitis all his life. 'Yer know about the rules, Melford.' Menacingly, he leaned close to Sarah's bewildered father. 'Yer know, I really don't like people breakin' my rules.'

'If you have anything to say, sir,' said Sarah, defiantly, 'please address me, and not my father.'

The hoarse man turned his attention to her. 'Goodness grashush me,' he said, mockingly.

'Forgive me, miss. I was forgettin' we 'ad company – female company.' He took off his trilby and bowed. 'Allow me ter hintroduce myself. My name his–'

Sarah came back like a flash. 'I *know* who you are, Rumbold,' she snapped. 'Your reputation goes before you.'

Rumbold's face stiffened. 'Is that so?' he replied. 'I 'ad no idea I was so famous.' He turned with a false smile to Samuel. 'You didn't tell me yer 'ad such a lovely young gel, Melford. 'Ave yer told 'er that the female sex his not permitted in my establishment? 'Ave yer told 'er that when any of my customers lose at this game, I hexpect 'em ter pay out in full?' He leaned closer and stared straight into Samuel's weary, blank eyes. 'An' hif they don't–'

'I would advise you not to threaten my father,' growled Sarah, pushing herself between Rumbold and Samuel. 'The law does not take at all kindly to blackmail.'

Rumbold reacted to Sarah's rebuff with a mixture of rage and astonishment. 'Oh,' he said, 'so it's the law yer 'ave hin mind, his it?'

'It may well be,' returned Sarah. 'Unless, of course, you respond in a more businesslike manner.'

There were murmurs of astonishment from the gathered crowd.

'How much does my father owe you?'

Rumbold grinned. 'A small fortune, I'm afraid. Five quid.'

Sarah dipped into her coat pocket, took out her purse, and with all the startled crowd watching her, extracted a five-pound note and held it out to Rumbold. 'Five pounds!'

Rumbold hesitated for a moment, clearly taken aback. But he finally grabbed the note. 'Well, well now, gents,' he said, addressing the crowd. 'We appear ter 'ave a millionairess in our midst. We are indeed honoured.'

'Not a millionairess, Rumbold,' said Sarah, with firm clarity and defiance. 'Just one who takes care of one's hard-earned savings, and who does not spend them recklessly on out-and-out rogues!'

To Rumbold's humiliation and outrage, this provoked a roar of jeers and laughter from the crowd.

'You see, Rumbold,' continued Sarah, 'there are those in this life who do their best to live like decent, honest human beings. And there are others who feed off the misfortune of those who are incapable of defending themselves.' Now it was her turn to move a step closer to Rumbold. 'I would like to remind you of something, Rumbold,' she said, with complete abandon. 'You know as well as I do that cock-fighting – or whatever repugnant name you like to call these activities – is illegal.' She turned to the rest of the crowd. 'The government of this country abolished this odious business a long time ago. It would not go well if any of you people here tonight were caught betting and gambling on a fight to the death.'

At this point, Rumbold made a threatening gesture with his hand as if about to say something malicious to her. But Sarah was too quick for him.

'You may keep my five-pound note, Rumbold,' she said imperiously. 'But only on condition that I never set eyes on you or your "business activities" ever again.'

Rumbold again tried to speak.

'And if you think that I am intimidated by threats of physical violence,' she said, 'let me assure you that I do not scare easily.'

Apart from the cackling of some caged cockerels on the other side of the shed, there was complete silence.

For a brief moment, Sarah and Rumbold stared each other out. But Sarah was too overwhelmed by the stench of blood to stay any longer, so she took hold of her father's arm, and said, 'Come, Father. Let's go.' She started to lead Samuel through the crowd, who stood back to let her pass.

'Oh, miss? Miss Melford?'

Rumbold's voice calling to her brought Sarah to a halt. She turned, to find Rumbold coming slowly towards her. In his hands he was holding a beautiful white cockerel, with a full red mane, cackling and struggling to get away.

'Has a mark of respect,' he said, with a bow, 'I'd like ter make you a little hofferin'.'

With Sarah, her father, and everyone watching, he held out the struggling cockerel, and then with both hands wrung the poor creature's neck.

Sarah, needing all her courage to hide her fear at the implied threat, clearly intended to scare her, stared at Rumbold in utter contempt. Then, without another word, she led her father out of the shed.

CHAPTER 9

For no apparent reason, Bob Sluggins' pawn shop usually did very little business on a Tuesday afternoon. This was also the time when Bob's wife, Vera, made her weekly shopping visit 'up west' with one of her mates from Crawford's hardware store along the road. It was for these very reasons that Jack Ridley had chosen such a day to carry out his plan, which he had laid out in meticulous detail to a very unwilling Beattie.

'Sorry, mate,' said Bob, as Beattie plonked an old handbag on his counter. 'I've got enuff women's 'andbags in my back room ter last me a lifetime. Can't 'elp yer, I'm afraid.'

Beattie sighed. She was doing her best not to show how her nerves were tearing her stomach apart. 'Surely yer can give me somefin' for it, Bob?' she pleaded. 'That bag's genuine cow 'ide. My mum bought that for me on my eighteenf birfday.'

Bob was still shaking his head. 'Makes no difference, Beat, gel,' he said. 'If I took in anuvver one of these, my old woman'd give me bleedin' 'ell.'

Beattie sniffed indignantly, and replied, 'That's funny. I always fawt this was *your* shop.'

Bob flicked a quick look up at her. Beattie hadn't changed a bit; she still had her old sharp tongue. 'I'll give yer 'alf a crown for it. Not a farvin' more. OK?'

Beattie sighed, and smiled weakly. 'Thanks, Bob,' she said. 'You're a toff.'

'I wish I was,' he replied. 'I wouldn't be runnin' this place.' He picked up Beattie's handbag, but as he did so, there was the sound of a thump coming from the back of the shop somewhere. 'Wot was that?' he said, with a start, turning to go into his back parlour.

Beattie was shaking with nerves. 'I didn't 'ear nuffin',' she said quickly. Unfortunately, she knew exactly what it was.

'That thumpin' sound out back.' Bob, still puzzled, started to move off. 'Wot the 'eck was it?'

'Yer couldn't give me my ticket and the money, could yer, Bob?' Beattie was doing everything in her power to distract his attention. 'I've got ter get back ter the baby.'

'Baby?' he said, taken aback. 'You got a kid?'

Beattie was relieved that she had inadvertently found a subject that would distract him long enough to let Jack get in through a back window of the shop. 'Yes,' she said, finding it difficult to look at him. 'Nearly six munffs now. 'Is name's Ed Junior.'

'After 'is dad, yer mean?' Bob was hooked, and slowly came back to the counter.

''Is dad was killed in the war. 'E was an officer –in the navy.'

Bob was suitably shocked and sympathetic. 'Blimey, Beat,' he said. 'I din't know nuffin' about that. I'm sorry ter 'ear it.'

Beattie, trying to look courageous, lowered her head.

''Ow long was yer married then?' asked Bob,

who was already tying a tag on Beattie's handbag.

Beattie had to search for a quick reply, her eyes constantly flicking past Bob to see if she could see any sign of movement in the back parlour. 'Not long,' she said. 'I didn't even get the chance to tell him the baby was on the way.'

'Wot a bit er bad luck,' he said. Then after a brief moment's pause added, 'Tell yer wot, I'll give yer five bob fer the bag. OK?'

Although Beattie had been getting tensed up, she breathed a sigh of relief. 'Oh fanks, Bob,' she said, her eyes still darting back and forth to the back parlour door. 'That'll be a real 'elp.'

Bob turned away, put Beattie's handbag into a box with dozens of others behind the counter, then returned to his cash-till, which was hidden behind a thin timber partition set apart from the counter. Whilst this was going on, Beattie felt her heart beating faster and faster. Behind Bob's back, she could see movement through the curtained back parlour door, which confirmed to her that Jack Ridley had successfully found his way in. What happened from there on she could only guess, and dread. All she wanted now was to do as Jack had told her to, once she had given him enough time to get in – leave the shop as soon as possible.

'There we are, gel,' said Bob, genially, returning with the two half-crown bits he was forking out for Beattie's handbag. 'You just make sure you get yerself somefin' decent ter eat, and that youngster of yours too.'

'You're a real good'un, Bob,' said Beattie, taking the two coins from him, and putting them into her dress pocket. 'I won't ferget it.'

'An' don't you ferget ter bring young Ed in ter see me sometime,' said Bob, as Beattie was about to leave.

'Who?' she asked, momentarily confused.

'That's 'is name, ain't it?' asked Bob, a bit puzzled. 'Ed? Ed Junior?'

Beattie suddenly came to. 'Oh – yes. Yes, that's 'is name. I'll bring 'im in, that's fer sure.' She smiled, turned quickly, but as she made her way to the shop door her face brushed against the head of one of the many fox furs that were dangling down from a piece of rope across the shop ceiling. Taken by surprise, she gasped, but quickly recovered. Flustered, she called, 'Fanks again, Bob,' and as she reached the door: 'I can't fank yer enuff.' Before Bob had a chance to reply, she was gone.

In the street outside, Beattie felt quite sick, but she quickly took a deep breath, straightened up to regain her balance, and moved on. Her legs felt so heavy she wasn't sure how far they would take her, and as soon as she managed to turn the corner into Drayton Park, she stopped to compose herself. But she was just too agitated to relax, for the whole business of getting involved in Jack Ridley's plan was tearing her apart with guilt. All she could think about was how stupid she had been to let Jack talk her into it. It was one thing to help him to do a petty burglary at some rich person's house, but to do it to someone like Bob Sluggins was nothing less than a betrayal of everything she had ever believed in. Bob was a hard-working man who made only enough money to live on. Ever since she was a teenage girl, he had helped her by letting her pawn so much of her personal stuff that wouldn't have been worth a brass farthing anywhere else. As she stood there on the corner of two busy main roads, watching good, honest folk passing by on their way to their jobs or their homes, she kept asking herself time and time again how she could have allowed herself to be drawn into the world of someone like Jack Ridley. But the more she thought about him, the more she could see his face in front of her, and she knew only too well that it was not only sexual infatuation that was drawing her to him, but the sheer vibrant force of his personality.

Once she had cooled down, she felt brave enough to peer around the corner, and look down Holloway Road towards Bob's pawn shop. Fortunately, there was no sign of any disturbance, but she hoped that whatever Jack Riley was doing, he would not harm Bob in any way. Beattie could tell by the clock on top of the furniture store opposite that it was now over twenty minutes since she had entered Bob's shop, and so it was now rapidly approaching the time when she had arranged to meet up with Ridley, in the eel pie and mash café further along the road. But as she was about to move off, she was horrified to notice someone she recognised getting off a tram and making her way across the road to the pawn shop. It was the old slag herself, Bob's wife, Vera, whom Beattie had thought was 'up west' on her usual Tuesday afternoon shopping expedition. Beattie was now in a panic.

What would happen if the old slag walked into the shop and found Jack Ridley going through the place? Beattie was beside herself, and for a moment didn't know whether to run or to hang around and see what happened. Then suddenly she knew what she must do.

''Ello, Mrs Sluggins!'

Vera Sluggins, struggling to carry a large woven bag of shopping, turned with a start to see Beattie hurrying towards her. 'Who's that?' she growled, squinting in the sunlight. 'Can't see yer.'

'It's me, Mrs Sluggins. Beattie. Beattie Melford. Can I give yer a 'and wiv yer bag?'

Vera pulled away when Beattie tried to take the bag from her. 'I can manage on me own, fank yer very much,' she replied haughtily. 'Just move ter one side, please. I want ter get 'ome.'

Beattie was standing directly between her and the front door of the shop. 'I've just bin ter see Bob,' she said, deliberately barring the old slag's way. 'I've pawned my 'andbag. The one me mum gave me when I was eighteen.'

'I'm not interested in wot yer mum gave yer,' complained Vera, trying to move past. But she suddenly came to a halt. ''Ow much d'e give yer?'

'Five bob.'

The old slag nearly had a heart attack. 'Five bob! For a bleedin' 'andbag?'

Beattie's heart was racing again. Her eyes were darting back and forth to the front window of the pawn shop. 'It's a very good one, Mrs Sluggins, honest it is. Best cow 'ide.'

'I don't care if it's made of bleedin' tiger skin!' roared the old slag. 'I'll give 'im 'ell when I see 'im! Out of my way!'

Beattie was now beside herself. If Vera walked in while Jack was holding up her old man, it could be really dangerous. 'Bob did me a good turn, Mrs Sluggins,' she spluttered desperately. 'Yer see, I've got a baby boy. 'E's nearly six munffs old.'

The old slag stopped dead in her tracks. 'Oh yes?' she replied cynically. 'An' who's the farver?'

Beattie lowered her eyes mournfully. ''E was in the navy. Got killed on the last day of the war.'

Vera paused only briefly to take this in, then remarked without any emotion, 'Oh well, yer'll 'ave ter find 'im anuvver old man, won't yer?'

Beattie was too taken aback to answer her. All she could do was to stand out of her way, and let her pass. Fortunately, at that moment she caught a glimpse of Jack Ridley, who was waving to her from along Holloway Road, so breathing a huge sigh of relief, she hurried off to join him in the eel pie and mash café.

Ma Briggs could hear the row going on upstairs, and she just hoped that it wouldn't wake up young Ed, who seemed to sleep more than any baby she had ever known. So she just quietly closed her parlour door, and hoped it wouldn't last too long.

'You're mad, Jack,' yelled Beattie, at the top of her voice. 'Stark ravin' mad! I told yer not ter touch 'im! I told yer I'd 'ave no part in it if yer laid one finger on Bob. 'E's me mate. 'E's bin good ter me!'

'Don't you shout at me, yer stupid cow!'

warned Jack, who couldn't be bothered to raise his voice to Beattie. 'I told yer I'd do anythin' I 'ad ter do ter get that cash.'

'That didn't mean yer 'ad ter go an' tie 'im up and then knock 'im about. Wot 'appens if 'e's recognised yer?'

Jack was now getting really irritated with her. ''Ow many bleedin' times do I 'ave to tell yer, I tied somefink round 'is eyes. 'E never 'ad a chance ter see me.'

'An' wot about *'er?* Wot about Vera?'

This time Jack bared his teeth as he replied. 'Ditto!'

Beattie wasn't satisfied. Pacing up and down her room, she felt as though she was going out of her mind. 'Bob knows me, so does she. I was talkin' to 'er just before she went into the shop. If they put two an' two tergevver, they're bound ter know I was mixed up in it wiv yer.'

Jack, who was stretched out on the bed, suddenly sat bolt upright, and yelled back at her angrily, 'Fer Chrissake, why don't yer just shut yer mouff? It's all over, I tell yer! It's done! It's finished!'

'Yes – and for wot? Fifteen quid and a couple of lousy bracelets that ain't worf nuffin'!'

Jack suddenly sprang up from the bed, rushed at her, and grabbed hold of her wrist. 'If you'd given me the right info about the old slag,' he said, pointing his finger menacingly at her, 'fings might've bin diff'rent!'

Beattie was recoiling from him in pain. 'Vera always goes up west on Tuesdays. 'Ow should I know she was gettin' back early?'

''Cos you're the one that's s'pposed to've known all about their movements, not me!'

Beattie was now on the verge of hysteria. 'I should never've let meself get involved wiv someone like you. I must've bin out of my bleedin' mind!' As she spoke, she was practically spitting. 'Why? Why? Why?'

Jack grinned and pulled her close to him. ''Cos yer love me, Beat. An' there's nuffin' yer can do about it.'

Now completely unable to control herself, Beattie spat straight into his face.

Jack was so angry, he cuffed her across the face with the back of his hand. The severity of the blow sent her reeling across the room, knocking over the washstand and ending up sprawled out on the floor. Jack went across, and stood over her. Then, wiping Beattie's spittle from his face with two fingers, he growled, 'Don't you ever do a fing like that ter me again, d'yer 'ear?'

Beattie, lying flat on her face on the floor, refused to look up at him. 'Get out,' she said, quietly.

Jack grinned at her again, picked up his jacket from a chair, and threw it idly across his shoulders. Then he moved to the door, collected his cap from the hook there, and put it on the back of his head. Before leaving, he turned to take one last look down at Beattie. 'Don't worry, Beat,' he said flippantly. 'The first time's always the worst. Fings can only get better.'

Beattie listened to his footsteps as he went down the stairs. As he left the house, he called out to Ma Briggs, and Beattie heard the front door slam behind him. She lay where she was for several moments, her face pressed down on to the well-worn lino. Although she could feel blood trickling from her lip, and her right eye swelling up, she made no effort to get up. She felt no physical pain from the blow Jack had given her, but what she did feel was torment and anguish. Was this really the life she had chosen to live? Were these people, whom she had admired for so long, fulfilling her in the way that she had always dreamed they would do? What *was* so special about Jack Ridley? How and why could she have abandoned one life, only to be knocked down flat on her face in another? She, who had always fought for her independence and the right to mix with what she called 'the real people', was now yearning for a part of her life that she had lost. Oh how she craved for someone to pick her up, and care for her, to understand her, to hold her close and say, 'This is what you should do, Beattie. This is how your life should be.'

Tears were welling up in her eyes as she eased herself on to her knees and slowly stared round the room. Everything suddenly looked so tawdry, so cluttered, and so unnecessary. She felt dazed, and although her body was now aching and she could feel a graze on her knee, she managed to get to her feet. Then she lumbered across the room and picked up the washbasin and jug, which, because they were made of thick, chunky china, had miraculously survived the onslaught of her body being thrown against them. But the floor was soaking wet, for the jug had been half full of water, and she wondered what Ma Briggs was going to say if any of it had soaked through the ceiling of the tenant in the room below. But remorse and apologies would have to come later. Her first thought was whether her face looked as bad as it felt, so she made her way to the small handmirror, which was propped up on the window behind the washstand. Her eye was bruised, and beginning to close, and there was indeed a small trickle of blood from her mouth, which she tried to wipe away with the back of her hand. Tears were streaming down her cheeks, a sure sign that she was feeling sorry for herself. For some reason that she couldn't understand, she began to think about the one person who would know what to do, how to face up to the first real crisis in her life. It was her mum, her dear, caring, loving mum. And then she even thought about her dad, obstinate and ungiving, and how wise he had been to throw her out of the house. But the strongest image of all was of the person whose face was haunting, accusing, overwhelming her with shame and guilt. Her sister, Sarah.

Geraldine Melford had made up her mind. The estrangement with her younger daughter had gone on long enough, and despite her husband's objections, she was now determined to end it.

'You're going to see Beattie?' Sarah asked her, with incredulity. 'But you can't, I told you what that friend of hers up the Cattle Market said. Beattie lives with the baby in that awful Campbell Road. It's not safe for any woman to walk around a place like that.'

'I don't care where Beattie lives,' replied Geraldine, defiantly. 'My mind is made up. I shall go on Sunday afternoon, whilst your father is having his sleep. I shall take the omnibus in Caledonian Road. It goes all the way along Seven Sisters Road to Finsbury Park.'

Sarah had joined her mother in the garden for it was a hot summer's evening, and despite opening all the windows in the house, it was impossible to keep cool there. It was quite a large garden for a town house, and because Geraldine and Sarah both had green fingers, there was a fine display of early summer flowers, with the prospect of a good showing of roses in the following weeks.

'And what will you say when you see her?' asked Sarah, in a voice that could not conceal her disapproval.

Geraldine had to think about this for a moment. But she was able to contemplate well, for she was lying back in a striped canvas deckchair, cooling herself with a lace fan, one large ginger cat on her lap, and her eyes staring aimlessly up at the deep blue evening sky. 'I shall tell her – that I've missed her.' She swung a look across to Sarah. 'I have, Sarah. I've missed her terribly.'

Sarah, seated on a wrought-iron garden chair alongside, could not find it in herself to respond to her mother, so she merely lowered her eyes, and remained silent.

'I blame myself for what happened,' said Geraldine, shaking her head miserably. 'Whatever Beattie's done, she is still my daughter, and

I love her.' She was suddenly aware of Sarah's lack of response. 'I love you too, darling,' she said. 'I love both of you.'

Sarah finally looked up. 'Beattie doesn't want to know about family life, Mother. She's turned her back on us.'

'We turned our backs on her too,' replied Geraldine. 'That doesn't make it right. Beattie made a mistake, a huge mistake. But it was my duty to stand by her, and try to help her put things right. I failed her.'

'It was Father's decision,' Sarah reminded her.

'It was a wrong decision. I gave birth to Beattie. She's our own flesh and blood, and blood is thicker than water.' She turned away, and took a deep breath. 'How beautiful everything smells at this time of year,' she said. 'We're so lucky to have all this. Just think of that poor girl, being locked up in some terrible lodgings with a small baby and no fresh air.' She paused for a moment, then said, 'I long to see the baby, Sarah. Can you understand that?'

Sarah couldn't help but meet her mother's eyes.

Geraldine said, 'Do you realise I'm a grandmother? It's very hard to explain what that's like. It's like having a child of one's own all over again – like turning back the clock. But I don't even know whether it's a boy or a girl.'

Sarah waited a moment, then got up.

Geraldine did likewise, much to the disdain of the cat, who was immediately shoved off. 'Do you think you can ever forgive her, Sarah?'

Sarah was taken aback by this question. She wasn't really prepared for it. 'Forgive?' she replied, after a moment's thought. 'Oh, I can forgive. I just can't forget, that's all.'

Geraldine smiled gently, put her arm through Sarah's, and squeezed her affectionately.

'What about Father?' asked Sarah, after a pause. 'Have you thought about what he'll say if he knows you've been to see her?'

'Beattie is his daughter too,' she said almost guiltily. 'It's his duty to forgive. He'll never be at peace with himself until he does.'

Sarah tried to smile back at her mother. 'I'm going up to get ready for supper.' She kissed Geraldine on the cheek, and disappeared inside the house.

After Sarah had gone, Geraldine found herself being plagued by a large tabby, one of the more demanding of her cat quartet. 'Oh, Delilah!' she said, stooping down to pick her up. 'I'm sorry I didn't notice you. Yes, you are a beautiful girl.' Delilah broke into a loud purr the moment Geraldine started to stroke her. 'But, oh, Delilah,' she said, with a deep sigh, 'I hope for your sake you never become a mother. Children have such minds of their own. They think they know so much, but they actually know very little. Why can't they get on well with each other – hmm, d'you know? They both come from the same place, and yet … and yet, they hardly know each other. You know, Delilah, it takes a great deal of love to keep a family together.'

She was suddenly distracted by a ring on the front doorbell, so she quickly lowered Delilah to the ground and made her way back into the house.

'It's all right, Sarah, I'm here!' she called as she hurried down the hall. She gave her hair a last-moment pat to make sure that it was tidy, then opened the door. Her shock was immediate.

Standing on the doorstep was Beattie, holding young Ed in her arms. 'Hello, Mother,' she said, her voice barely audible. 'This is Ed. He's your grandson.'

For a brief moment, Geraldine seemed to be suspended in time, for all she could do was to stare hard at Beattie and the small baby she clutched in her arms. Then her face started to crumple up, and the shaky pitch of her breathing indicated that she was about to burst into tears. Her arms outstretched, she virtually threw herself at the two of them, embracing them, and hugging them vigorously. Laughing, crying, and smothering them both with kisses, all she could gasp over and over again was, 'Oh, my baby, my dear little baby!'

Beattie was completely overwhelmed. As she and her mother exchanged hugs and kisses, she felt as though her heart was about to break. It was a moment she would never have thought possible, even just a few days before. So she closed her eyes tight, and did her best to stop the tears from rolling down her cheeks. But when she opened them again, she found herself peering over her mother's shoulder, straining to see the silhouette of the figure who was standing at the top of the stairs, watching the extraordinary reunion.

It was Sarah.

CHAPTER 10

Samuel Melford looked at his grandson, and then at his younger daughter. Yes, they were alike, in some ways; Young Ed definitely had his mother's mouth, his full, pouting lips characteristic of her when she'd been his age. But Geraldine thought the baby had Samuel's eyes, dark and inquisitive, and she was certain that the moment she had him sitting on her lap at the kitchen table, he knew at once that she was his grandmother.

Much to Beattie's relief, her father had softened his opposition to her, and even allowed her to hug him. Young Ed had won over his grandfather completely, of course, first by making raspberry sounds at him, then by doing everything in his power to grab hold of the poor man's nose, which provoked gales of laughter from both Beattie and her mother. However, Beattie had been shocked to see how transformed her father was since the last time she had seen him, for his face was now white and drawn, and there was a vacant look in his eyes that she found strange and unsettling. There was no doubt how much her father had aged, and she felt nothing but guilt that this had probably been brought on by her own reckless behaviour.

Sarah's reaction to Beattie's sudden homecoming was, predictably, somewhat different to that of her parents. When she'd seen her young sister on the front doorstep, clutching a small baby in her arms, and witnessed the reunion with their mother, she'd retreated to her bedroom, and it was only the heartfelt pleas of Geraldine that finally persuaded her to join the family at supper in the kitchen. Beattie was only too aware that for Sarah to see Edward Lacey's child would be a painful experience, and she could hardly expect to be embraced by her sister after the way she had ruined her life. For her part, Sarah felt no pity for the predicament Beattie had got herself into, and when she listened to her sister's hard-luck tale of bringing up a child and trying to keep a job at the same time, she remained tight-lipped, her eyes lowered.

'Luckily, Ma Briggs is a treasure,' said Beattie, tucking into several slices of her mother's home-cooked ham. 'I don't know 'ow I'd cope if she din't look after Ed while I'm at the factory.'

Geraldine, cradling Young Ed on her lap whilst Beattie ate, looked concerned, and asked, 'But, dear, how can you manage to pay this Ma Briggs woman on the small wages you earn?'

Beattie's mouth was full, but she spluttered, 'Oh, I don't pay 'er nuffin', fank Gord. If I 'ad ter do that, we'd boaf end up in the work'ouse.'

Geraldine shuddered. The thought of her daughter and grandson confined to a workhouse filled her with horror. 'Your father and I would never let that happen to you, Beattie,' she said quite resolutely. 'You must make us a promise that if you ever need money you'll come to us.'

Beattie looked up with what she hoped was a startled expression. 'Don't be silly, Muvver,' she said, swallowing the next mouthful of ham. 'I'd never ask yer fer money. I've made me own bed and I can lie in it.'

Sarah listened to all this, but did not react. Her silence throughout the meal told Beattie all she needed to know.

'D'you know what I admire most in a person?' Samuel's sudden question caused everyone to turn and look at him. 'Stillness,' he said. 'Most people only have it when they die.'

For a moment, no one said anything. Beattie was thoroughly taken aback by her father's sudden, extraordinary comment; it seemed to have no bearing on the conversation. And when she turned to look at her mother for some kind of explanation, Geraldine could only shake her head sadly, and concentrate on stroking Young Ed's hair.

'I agree with you, Father,' said Sarah, covering Samuel's hand with her own. It was her first contribution to the conversation since the start of the meal. 'There's something beautiful about stillness. I wish I had it.'

Samuel nodded, but didn't really respond to Sarah, mainly because, these days, the moment he said anything, it usually slipped his mind.

'It's so good to have you home again, Beattie, my dear,' said Geraldine, quickly changing the mood. 'I've made up your room. It hasn't been touched since the day you left. Your father wanted us to take in a lodger, but–' she turned to look at Samuel – 'it wasn't really a very good idea, was it, dear?'

Samuel looked at her with a blank expression. He didn't really know what she was talking about.

'I can't stay, Muvver,' Beattie said awkwardly. 'I only come ter see yer, fer a visit. I've got an 'ome of me own ter go back to.'

Geraldine's whole expression changed to disappointment. 'But you've got a home – here,' she said. 'A home for you – and little Ed.'

Beattie shook her head slowly, guiltily.

'But why not?' asked Geraldine, holding on to young Ed as though she never wanted to let him go. 'I can look after him for you. He'll be safe with me, you know he will.'

'No, Muvver,' replied Beattie. 'It wouldn't be right. I 'ave ter do fings me own way. I only brought Ed up 'ere so's yer could see 'im. I wanted 'im ter see you.' Then she added poignantly, 'I did too.'

There was a moment's silence. Geraldine couldn't understand what was happening, why Beattie was so determined to continue her life of hardship. Then she looked down at Young Ed and felt so upset, tears came to her eyes.

'It's getting late, Mum,' Beattie said. 'I'd better be gettin' 'im 'ome.' She stretched out, and took the baby into her arms, saying, 'Got ter got ter work in the mornin', ain't we?'

Young Ed gurgled.

A short time later, Beattie bid her mother and father a tearful farewell, with the promise that from now on she would pay them regular visits. Just before she left, Geraldine discreetly slipped two one-pound notes into the pocket of Beattie's flimsy cotton dress. Sarah saw, but pretended she hadn't.

Outside the house, Beattie put Young Ed into a small, grubby pram. 'My landlady give it ter me,' she said. 'Apparently she used it fer both 'er own kids.'

Geraldine tried to smile, but it was an effort. 'Oh Beattie,' she said, anxiously, 'I can't bear the thought of you pushing the pram all that way. You'll be so exhausted by the time you get ho– by the time you get back to your lodgings.'

'There's no problem, Muvver, honest. It won't take long, no more than 'alf an hour. I'll be 'ome well before dark.'

The idea still tormented Geraldine, so she turned to Sarah, who was standing impassively behind them on the front doorstep. 'Sarah, dear, why don't you walk with Beattie for part of the way? It'll keep her company.'

Beattie had to smile at her mother's lack of judgement. But when she briefly flicked a glance at Sarah, she thought it wasn't such a bad idea after all. 'Feel like a stroll, Sarah?' she asked, half joking.

Sarah hesitated. Then, without saying a word, she went to the garden gate and opened it.

Geraldine waited on the doorstep, waving madly, until both her daughters and grandson were out of sight. Only then did she reluctantly turn back into the house and close the door.

Once Sarah and Beattie had cleared Richmond Avenue, their pace slowed to a stroll. They didn't actually say a word until they were well into Liverpool Road, and never once did Sarah so much as glance down at Young Ed, who was now fast asleep in his pram.

'Wot's 'appened ter Farver?' Beattie asked, quite out of the blue. ''As 'e 'ad some kind of breakdown?'

'Something like that,' replied Sarah, coolly. 'It was only to be expected.'

Beattie stiffened. 'Meanin', fanks ter me?'

'You're not the only problem in Father's life, Beattie,' said Sarah, pointedly. 'Just lately he's had rather a lot to cope with.' She turned to look at her. 'They have no money, you know. It's all gone. I've had to get a job.'

'I didn't come beggin', yer know,' Beattie replied, resenting the implication. 'An' I din't ask Muvver ter go an' put that money in me pocket.'

'I'm not suggesting that you did, Beattie,' Sarah said. 'But it's as well you know the situation.'

They walked on, Beattie pushing Young Ed in his pram, and Sarah at her side, arms crossed nonchalantly as she walked. The sun had already set, and the red-brick mansion blocks along Liverpool Road were gradually dimming in the summer twilight. But it was still warm, and although it would be dark within the next hour or so, there were plenty of people on the streets strolling aimlessly, and others sitting at their windows, watching the world go by.

On the corner of Offord Road, they paused a moment to let a horse and cart pass on its way to the coal merchant's in Brecknock Road. Whilst they were waiting, Beattie spoke, without turning to look at her sister. 'It ain't been easy, yer know,' she said, having to raise her voice to be heard over the sound of the horse's hoofs and the clatter of cartwheels. 'Fer me, I mean. These last few munffs.'

Sarah waited for the horse and cart to disappear before answering. 'What did you expect?' she asked, quite impassively.

Beattie looked at her. 'I shouldn't've done wot I did, Sarah,' she said. 'I was in the wrong, an' I admit it.'

'Then at least *something* has been achieved,' said Sarah, leading the way across the road.

When they got to the other side, Beattie brought the pram to a halt. 'I did yer a favour, yer know,' she said. 'If it 'adn't bin fer me, you'd 'ave bin lumbered wiv Edward Lacey fer the rest of your life. 'E wasn't worf it.'

'Is that why you had his child?' Sarah asked, cryptically.

Beattie lowered her eyes guiltily, and looked down into the pram. 'I know wot yer fink,' she said, doing her best to avoid Sarah's gaze. 'But it's not somefin' I wanted, or planned. I was careless, I know that. I 'ated wot I let that man do ter me. I didn't want 'is kid. I didn't want any part of 'im.' She sighed, then looked up again. 'But then, somefin' 'appened,' she said, aware that Sarah wasn't really looking at her. 'As soon as Ed was born, everyfin' seemed ter change. When I looked at 'im, 'e seemed so–' she looked down at Young Ed again, 'oh, I don't know – so small, so 'elpless. An' then I get ter finkin' – well, 'e din't ask ter be brought into this world, did 'e?' She paused again. 'Maybe it was because of wot 'appened to 'is farver. Maybe it's because I felt guilty, I just don't know. But once I saw 'im – I knew I 'ad ter do me best for 'im.' She looked up at Sarah again. ''E should've bin yours. Yer know that, don't yer?'

Sarah swung back and glared at her. 'I was never given the opportunity,' she replied, sharply.

'The opportunity was there, Sarah. The trouble is, yer never took it. Edward Lacey wanted me fer one fing only.'

'And you were perfectly happy to give it to him.'

Beattie hesitated, then walked on. But after just a few steps, she came to an abrupt halt again. ''Ow're we goin' ter put fings right then?' she asked. 'I mean – between you an' me?'

Sarah thought for a moment, then replied. 'We could start by taking one day at a time.'

Beattie did not reply straight away. 'Be seein' yer,' she said eventually.

'Beattie?'

Beattie stopped and looked back.

'Why did you do it?' Sarah asked coldly. 'Why did you take him from me?'

Beattie shrugged her shoulders. 'Yer 'ad somefin' I wanted,' she replied. Then she continued on her way.

Sarah stood watching her for a moment, then turned and walked back towards home.

Mrs Ranasinghe was very pleased with the way Sarah was looking after her. The house was cleaner than it had been for quite some time, and the Ceylonese meals that the old lady had been teaching Sarah to cook were improving every day, although, to her mind, Sarah was still not putting enough chilli in the chicken curry. 'Chilli is for us Ceylonese as mustard is for you English,' she insisted, 'except that chilli is far more civilised!'

Sarah's one problem, however, was keeping the old lady from becoming too bored with her life. In many ways, Mrs Ranasinghe was unique, for she never complained about the pain she was suffering, and quite often made fun of her condition, calling herself 'the old bag of bones'. She had even taken to smoking through a long cigarette holder. 'The doctor told me to keep away from cigarettes,' she joked, 'so that's what I'm doing!' It was an old joke, but Sarah laughed every time the old lady told it. Without realising it, Sarah was becoming very fond of her employer, and when they sat down to eat together in the kitchen, she listened in awe to the old lady's tales of life on her native island. Until now, Sarah had only read about a place where pineapples grew and coconuts could be picked off the trees, where beaches were almost as white as snow, and where native workers from India picked the tea leaf that eventually found its way into the teapots of every home in England. But now, thanks to this spellbinding old lady, all of these pages from books had come to true and vivid life, and listening to Mrs Ranasinghe, there were times when she felt as though she had been transported to the other side of the world.

But working as a companion for Mrs Ranasinghe was proving to be not only stimulating but also enlightening, for the old lady was turning out to be a mine of wisdom. This was never more evident than on one rainy afternoon in late September, when Sarah found herself being cross-questioned about her horoscope, which Mrs Ranasinghe had compiled, based on what she had learned about Sarah since she had come to work for her.

'I don't think there is any doubt in my mind,' said the old lady, with a sly twinkle in her eye, 'that romance for you, young lady, is just around the corner.'

Sarah tried to pretend that she was fascinated by this astounding piece of information, but she was more involved in trying to rinse the henna out of the old lady's hair, which she had just washed in the stone kitchen sink. 'I'm not really interested in romance,' she said. 'I think I'm getting too old for all that now.'

'Too old!' Mrs Ranasinghe pulled her head out of the sink so fast that streaks of black henna dye were running down her face. 'Too old at *your* age?' she spluttered, through her ill-fitting plate of false teeth. 'Ha! What is this thing that young people have about old age? Do you know what I said to my eldest daughter when she asked me why I couldn't grow old graciously? I told her I only wanted to grow old *un*graciously!'

Sarah laughed with her, then gently eased her head back into the sink.

Later, when the old lady was in bed ready for her afternoon sleep, Sarah tried to read her one chapter of Charles Dickens's *Old Curiosity Shop*. But Mrs Ranasinghe was in no mood to be read to, and wanted to talk.

'You must think it strange,' she said, reflectively, 'that a woman like me should want to leave her home and family, and all the things she loved most, to travel to the other side of the world where everything is so different – people, buildings, the weather, and religion. I came into this life as a Buddhist. I've remained so all my life. It gives me strength – oh not in the same way as in your churches, but in the way I've come to terms with myself. If it hadn't been for my faith, I think I would have thrown myself overboard from the boat on the way over to England.' Despite her efforts, her eyes were flickering for want of sleep, so she gradually slipped down beneath the sheets, rested her head on the pillow, and closed her eyes. But her mind was still wide awake. 'It's not easy for a family to accept that one of them is different to the rest,' she said, her voice firm and strong. 'After my husband died, I never did any of the things my daughters expected of me, me a good mother, and devoted widow. I learned to ride a bicycle! It was wonderful.' Her eyes suddenly sprang open. 'Do you know, I only ever fell off once!'

By the time Sarah had smiled at her, the old lady's eyes had closed again.

'I bought a dog. Her name was Chuti. She was a beautiful little creature, so small and fluffy. My girls detested her. They said dogs were dirty and carried disease. But I loved her. I went on the train on my own, right up to the hills, to Kandy. It was – exhilarating. Everything looked so lush and green. Just me – and Chuti. Oh, I did lots of things on my own, things that ordinary people would not expect of a respectable Ceylonese widow.' Her eyes sprang open again. 'But I value my independence, Sarah. Without it, I would die. That's why I can never go home. I suppose it must be some kind of disease, because when I decide to do something, I just can't stop myself.'

The old lady's eyes closed again, but this time she fell into an immediate sleep. Sarah waited until she heard her snoring soundly. Then she gently covered the old lady's shoulders with the eiderdown, and left the room.

Sarah went into the sitting room, and flopped down on to the sofa. All around her were mementoes of Mrs Ranasinghe's extraordinary life: cushion covers embroidered with elephants, brass ornaments in the shape of temples, and a wooden head of the Buddha, which meant so much to this strange old lady. But more significant to Sarah were the vast array of family photographs scattered around the place, on small polished tables, on the wall, and on the mantelpiece. There were group pictures, portraits of her daughters and her grandchildren, all either laughing or taking their pose terribly seriously. Nothing out of the ordinary about them really. And yet, Sarah found it odd that someone as fiercely independent as Mrs Ranasinghe should want to be reminded of the life she had so readily abandoned, the members of her family who frowned on one of their own who had chosen to become an outsider. But then, was it really so strange to be different? She leaned her head back on the sofa, and stared up at the white plaster stucco design around the ceiling. And as she lay there, she began to think about Beattie, who, just like Mrs Ranasinghe, had forsaken so much to take that dangerous, uncharted road to independence.

Beattie knew there was something wrong the moment she got back from work that evening. Now that autumn was in the air, the nights were already beginning to draw in, so by the time she got home, it was practically dark. Usually even as she put her key in the street door, she could hear Ma Briggs playing with Ed Junior in her front parlour. But tonight, she could hear nothing.

'Ma!' she called, knocking on the parlour door. 'It's me. I'm home.'

'Come in, dear!' came Ma Briggs' voice from inside. But as soon as Beattie entered the room, she could see no sign of Young Ed.

''Ad a good day, dear?' asked Ma, who seemed quite unruffled. 'Real autumn chill in the air now,' she said. 'Wot about a nice cuppa before yer go up?'

'Where is 'e, Ma?' Beattie asked quickly. 'Where's Ed?'

'Ed?' replied Ma, a bit taken aback. 'Why 'e's gone, dear. Like yer said.'

Beattie immediately panicked. 'Gone? Wot're yer talkin' about? Gone where?'

Ma was getting nervous. 'Jack took 'im. Over 'alf an hour ago.'

'Wot!'

Ma was now flustered. 'But – din't yer know? 'E told me yer asked 'im. 'E said yer asked 'im ter take little Ed fer a walk. Din't yer know? Yer must've–'

Beattie took hold of Ma's shoulders and shook her. 'Where, Ma?' she said over and over again. 'Where's 'e taken 'im?'

'I don't know, Beattie!' she cried, her face crumpling up with remorse and guilt. 'Honest ter Gord, I don't know. 'E just said–'

Before she could say anything more, Beattie had rushed from the room and out into the street.

The light outside was rapidly fading, and the street lamplighters were already lighting the gas mantles with their long poles.

In a wild frenzy Beattie looked all around her, from one end of the Bunk to the other. The street was deserted – no one to ask if they had seen a feller like Jack pushing a small baby in a pram. So, in desperation, she had to choose which way to go. She decided to try the Fonthill Road direction first, for that was where Jack usually made for when he used to leave her first thing in the morning.

'Jack!' she yelled, her voice echoing around the roofs and chimneypots as she went. 'Jack!'

So much was racing through her mind, for it had been some months since she had last seen Jack Ridley, the last time being when he had beaten her up for daring to criticise him. She was going crazy with fear. What was he up to? Was it possible that he was trying to kidnap little Ed as some kind of punishment because she had refused to have anything more to do with his ugly, unpalatable activities? Every time she thought about him, her flesh crept. Only by luck had she avoided being implicated in Jack's breakin at Bob Sluggins' pawn shop. It was bad enough to be questioned by the rozzers after the incident, but fortunately, no one had put two and two together, and that meant her and Jack Ridley.

'Jack!' She was now yelling hysterically. 'Jack Ridley, yer bleedin' sod! Where – are – yer…?'

Beattie's frantic yells had now brought people rushing to their windows and front doors, but no one wanted to get involved; no one came out to ask her what was wrong.

She finally reached the corner of Fonthill Road, but it was now so dark she could see very little. 'Jack…!' Her yells were now echoing along the entire length of the road. 'Don't … do … this … ter … me…!'

Standing alone on the corner of the darkened road, Beattie suddenly broke down into a fit of uncontrollable tears.

''Ere now, Beat,' said a voice, quietly, right behind her. 'Wot's all this then?'

Beattie swung round to find the dark shape of Jack Ridley, holding on to the handle of Young Ed's pram. 'Yer sod!' she squealed, immediately trying to push him out of the way. ''Ow could yer? 'Ow could yer?'

Jack placed himself in between Beattie and the pram, preventing her from getting to little Ed. 'Not so fast now, Beat,' he said. 'Don't want yer wakin' up the poor little bleeder. 'E's bin 'avin' a really good kip.'

Beattie suddenly lost control and went for him, thumping at his chest with her fists. 'I'll kill yer, kill yer!'

Jack deflected her blows, and held on to her

hands. 'Calm down now, yer silly cow,' he said quietly, and without fuss. 'No 'arm's come ter the kid. Go on – ask 'im,' he added, mocking her. Then he pulled her to him. 'I 'ad ter see yer, Beat,' he said, his face close to hers. 'Yer can't go on shuttin' me off – not all the time. This was the only way I could get to yer.'

Enraged, Beattie spat in his face.

Jack's immediate reaction was to cuff her, but he thought better of it and continued to restrain her. 'I love yer, Beat.'

Beattie was stopped dead in her tracks.

Jack moved close to her ear and whispered, 'I've never said that to anyone else in the 'ole wide world. Yer've got to believe me.'

Beattie took a moment to calm herself, then said, 'Is that wot love's all about, Jack? Beatin' up people?'

Jack squeezed her wrists until they hurt. 'I swear ter Gord, I'll never lay an 'and on yer again.'

'Not till the next job, eh, Jack?'

Jack refused to be riled. 'That's all over, Beat,' he said reassuringly. 'I don't need it no more. But I do need you.'

He now felt confident enough to release her wrists.

'You're a nutcase, Jack Ridley,' she said. 'Yer know that, don't yer?'

'I make mistakes, Beat,' he said. 'But I'm not mad.'

'Yer 'ate the kid. Yer've told me a dozen times.'

'I was jealous of 'im. I still am. But I don't 'ate 'im. 'Ere. See fer yerself.'

He stood aside and allowed Beattie to go to little Ed. She found him fast asleep in the pram, sucking away quite contentedly on his dummy. Relieved, she started to sob again.

Jack took her in his arms, and held on to her. 'I've never met anyone like yer before, Beat,' he said softly. 'I knew that the first moment I saw yer.' He leaned in closer so that as he spoke his lips were virtually caressing her ear. 'Let me tell yer somefin'. You an' me tergevver could conquer the world. Gimme anuvver chance, an' I'll prove it.'

CHAPTER 11

It had been two years since the war had ended, and yet, during that time, it seemed as though the world had learnt nothing. In America, the US Senate had rejected the Versailles Treaty, which, under the all-embracing name of the League of Nations, was at least an attempt by the Allies to restore some kind of peace and unity in Europe. There was turmoil in Russia after the White Army leader had been executed by the Bolsheviks. In Syria, the French occupied Damascus. The Poles were at war with the Russians. In Italy there was serious industrial strife. Nearer to home, Sinn Fein supporters and Unionists were rioting in the streets in Belfast; there were the usual scandals involving accusations of corruption amongst members of Prime Minister Lloyd George's administration, and as unemployment continued to soar, labour organisations threatened strike action if the British Government declared war on Russia. Yes, the world had gone mad, and if only Samuel Melford had been in his right mind, he would have had quite a few comments of his own to make on the matter. Unfortunately, however, those times had now passed.

Samuel's illness, which had gradually deterior-ated during the previous year, had been diagnosed by a hospital specialist as a form of premature senility. As each day passed, he seemed to know little of what was going on around him. Sometimes, when Geraldine and Sarah were talking together, he would simply watch them as though they were strangers, and the bewildered look on his face suggested that their conversation had no meaning whatsoever, and merely consisted of two human mouths with lips moving at enormous speed. There was now, of course, no prospect of Samuel returning to any kind of job, which made the upkeep of the family house in Thornhill Road difficult. To make matters worse, during recent months, Beattie had been paying regular weekly visits to her parents, which were apparently arranged so that the couple could keep in touch with their grandson. But Sarah knew her sister well enough to be deeply suspicious of her motives. Her worries became more acute when she noticed that various objects that had been in the family for years were disappearing from their usual places around the house. These included fairly valuable items, such as a small silver snuff box, a set of Royal Albert finger bowls, two double brass candlesticks, a small Wedgwood fine bone china country maid figure, and even an early Victorian hand-embroidered beaded table cover.

'Got rid of them?' Sarah asked her mother, with incredulity. 'You got rid of *all* those things? All those beautiful things that you and Father have been collecting ever since you were married? But why, Mother?'

Geraldine had been dreading this moment. She knew it would be only a matter of time before

Sarah noticed all the valuables that were missing, that she herself had been taking to Bob Sluggins' pawn shop in the Holloway Road. 'If you must know,' she replied, quite casually, whilst making heavy work of changing the sheets on her husband's bed, 'I was tired of them. In any case, we don't need all those silly things,' she said. 'They just clutter up the place and bring back memories.'

Sarah watched her mother with growing suspicion. There was a tense energy in Geraldine's behaviour, as though she was trying to make light of something that was in fact quite serious.

'Believe me,' Geraldine continued, as she pulled off the two soiled pillowcases and threw them on to the floor, 'when you've lived as long as your father and me, you learn that material things mean so very little.' She briefly flicked a glance over her shoulder at Sarah, without making eye contact with her. 'You'll know what I mean one day, when *you* get married and have a home of your own.'

These days, Geraldine was a changed person. Sarah had noticed it since they first became aware that Samuel's mind was drifting. As Sarah watched her mother each day, busying herself with unnecessary intensity over the most trifling housework, it distressed her to see the anguish in the poor woman's eyes. For Sarah, Geraldine had been the perfect mother, caring, loving, and always interested in anything her family was doing. But now, her whole life seemed to be obsessed by two things: the protection of her ailing husband, and a passionate need to spend as much time as she possibly could with her little grandson. It was strange to see this once beautiful, lively woman so ill at ease with herself and everyone around her. Even her former immaculate dress sense had been abandoned, and these days she seemed quite prepared to meet any visitors to the house wearing her long, dull pinafore dress. And her hair, once so well groomed, now frequently fell into straggly locks across her forehead. Of course, it was hardly surprising that she seemed to care so little for her appearance, for she no longer had a husband to look nice for, no husband to hold her in his arms in bed at night. Sarah was convinced that she had to find some way of preventing her mother from just giving up, and, most important of all, to stop Beattie taking advantage of her.

'Mother,' Sarah asked, as she helped her mother to make up her father's bed with clean sheets. 'What have you been doing with all the things you've got rid of?'

'What does it matter, dear?' Geraldine replied evasively. 'They've gone, and that's an end to it.'

'Have you sold them?'

'More or less.'

'What have you done with the money?'

This irritated Geraldine, and it showed in her voice. 'I really don't think that's any concern of yours, Sarah.'

Sarah stopped making the bed, and looked hard at her. 'Have you given it to Beattie?'

At this, Geraldine slammed down the sheet without tucking it in. 'I've given it to my grandson,' she snapped. '*My* own grandson, Sarah. Do you understand?'

Sarah felt chastened, but undeterred. 'You can't afford to spend your money like that, Mother,' she said. 'You and Father have little enough as it is.'

Geraldine angrily flicked away a lock of hair that had fallen over her eye. 'What sort of a person do you think I am if I can't even help my own flesh and blood?'

'But Mother, it isn't necessary for you to go and sell all your possessions like this. I know Beattie's not earning very much, but she certainly has enough to put a good meal inside her child's stomach.'

Geraldine came back at her immediately. 'When *you* were a child,' she snapped, 'you wanted for nothing – neither you nor your sister. You had food in your stomach – *good* food – clothes on your back, shoes on your feet, holidays down by the sea – all the things that a child needs in life. But this poor little mite has nothing, absolutely nothing.'

'With respect, Mother,' Beattie said, restrained, 'nobody asked Beattie to have an illegitimate child.'

Geraldine was taken aback. 'How dare you?' she gasped, glaring across the bed at Sarah. 'Has it ever occurred to you that little Ed is your own nephew?'

Exasperated, Sarah turned away.

'That child has a right to our support,' Geraldine said, coming around the bed to confront her. 'When you have one of your own, you'll feel differently. Remember this, Sarah. Once a child is in the womb, it becomes a living thing, and from that moment on we all have a part to play in its future – whatever the circumstances.' Sarah turned to go, but Geraldine quickly took hold of her arm. 'Sarah, I love you,' she said. 'I love you *and* Beattie. And I love my grandson. You've no idea how much that little boy means to me. Especially now.' She released Sarah's arm and sighed. 'There's a huge, empty gap in my life, Sarah,' she said. 'I can't tell you how much I need to fill it.'

Sarah looked at her mother, and felt the emptiness that had engulfed the poor woman's life. Yes, it was true. Now that Geraldine had virtually lost Samuel into this strange, twilight world, having little Ed around the place was helping her to fill that awful gap. In fact, for Geraldine, at this traumatic time in her life, her grandson probably meant as much, perhaps even more, than her own two daughters. 'It's all right, Mother,' she said, going to Geraldine and putting her arms around her. 'Everything's going to be quite all right. I'll do anything I can to make you happy.'

Geraldine's eyes were doleful. 'Then make it up with your sister,' she pleaded. 'Then your father and I will know we still have a family.'

Much to Beattie's irritation, Young Ed was beginning to look more like his father each day. Not that Beattie knew what Edward Lacey looked like at eighteen months old, but there was no doubt that his son had the same glowing, pale blue eyes, and even at this age the boy had the same mischievous look that Beattie remembered when she first met Lacey in the Eaglet back in 1917.

There was also no doubt that Young Ed was beginning to show signs of his own individual personality, such as a real appetite for picture books, which Ma Briggs bought for him every week when she picked up her ounce of pipe tobacco from the newsagent in Fonthill Road. Even when he was less than a year old, he was already identifying objects in the books, and always jumped up and down with excitement every time his mum or the old lady pointed out a cat or a rabbit or a cow. He also learned to pull himself up to his feet long before anyone had expected, despite his grandmother's warning that doing it so early could make the child bandy. But what was extraordinary was what a sensitive little boy Ed was developing into. When he was upset, it showed in his face. He never cried, but went immediately silent, lowering his eyes, and staring at his feet as though he was being punished. All this wasn't easy for Beattie, for she never wanted to have a baby, and although she was turning out to be a protective mum, a feeling nagged inside her that she didn't really love the child.

Life for Beattie was not easy, especially with Jack Ridley around the place. Despite her initial forebodings, during the spring of that year Beattie allowed Jack Ridley to move in with her. It had been an unwise decision, for despite Ridley's assurances that he was now a changed man and that he would be good for her, within a few weeks he had virtually taken over the household, losing his temper every time little Ed opened his mouth, and using his fist on Beattie whenever he wanted his own way. Ma Briggs knew what was going on, for on those all-too-frequent mornings when she noticed Beattie trying to cover up a black eye or a cut lip, she wondered whether she had been right to give her blessing to Ridley moving in, which she had only agreed to because she had known Jack since he was a youngster, and felt that it was a wonderful chance for little Ed to have the father he had so far been denied.

There were times when Beattie was in total despair, for her resistance had become so low that she had no idea how to cope with a situation in which she not only hated Ridley for being such a sadistic bully to both her and her child, but she felt troubled and confused as to why she should want to hang on to a man for whom she had an inextricably fatal attraction. What Beattie needed, and needed desperately, was someone to make up her mind for her, to tell her what to do, and shoulder the burden of bringing up Edward Lacey's child.

In Beattie's mind, that opportunity finally came one morning in September 1920, when she opened a letter addressed to her, with a Suffolk postmark. Both the envelope and the letter were written by someone with a rather shaky hand, and Beattie found such difficulty in making it out that she could only make sense of it by reading out loud.

The Old Manor House
Stickley
Nr Sudbury
Suffolk
21 September 1920

Dear Miss Melford,

I am writing to you on the advice of my solicitor, Mr Albert Cordell of Cordell and Winters, No 3A Gainsborough Street, in Sudbury.

You will recall that I last wrote to you acquainting you with the death of my son, Petty Officer Edward John Lacey, who was killed in an unfortunate naval accident on the final day of the war in November 1918.

For his own reasons, prior to his death my son failed to notify me of his relationship with you. Had it not been for your letter to him, that came into my possession on his death, I would not have known of your existence. You will therefore understand the pain I suffered when my solicitor's enquiries revealed that you had given birth to my son's child. I am sure you can understand the devastating shock this news caused me, and the knowledge that somewhere in this troubled world there was a small child, who, despite the circumstances of his conception, was my grandchild, the offspring of my only son.

You will, no doubt, have many questions to ask as to why I have taken this amount of time to make contact with you, and it is in this regard that I am now writing.

After reading this, Beattie found it hard to concentrate. Oh yes, she had plenty of questions all right, such as why her son's own grandfather had waited so long before even bothering to find out how she was coping with a fatherless child. But then, she had no illusions about what he really thought about her – that she was a little tart, who couldn't wait to get her hands on some spare cash. But when she read on, she wasn't quite so sure.

When I was first notified about Edward's death, I was utterly bereft. Although he and I often clashed about the way he conducted his private life, the thought that he had been struck down at such an early age filled me with remorse and guilt. But when I discovered that he had been responsible for your pregnancy, that guilt quickly turned to anger. I just wanted to close my mind and tell myself that it simply wasn't true. But it *was* true, and despite the loss of my son, nothing in the world could change what had happened. With that thought in mind, I finally decided that there was no way that I could go on ignoring the fact that I had a duty towards my only grandchild, his future, and his rightful inheritance.

Beattie's eyes lit up. She now couldn't read on fast enough.

I would therefore like to invite you to the Old Manor House, where we can discuss in detail what I have outlined in more general terms above. The village of Stickley is just two miles outside the small town of Sudbury, which can be reached by taking a train from Liverpool Street. On arrival at Sudbury, you will be met by a member of my household. In acknowledging receipt of this letter, please be good enough to advise a suitable date of travel. Enclosed please find two one-pound notes to cover cost of journey for self and child.

Yours faithfully,
J.L Lacey
Lt Comm R.N (Rtd)

Beattie put the letter down. Her hands were shaking; she could hardly contain herself. Despite the formal tone and the appalling presentation she was convinced that this was the break she had been waiting for. Now she would be able to bring Young Ed up in a civilised way instead of in the stifling atmosphere of her upstairs room. In her mind, she immediately started working out plans of how she and little Ed would move out of the Bunk into a flat of their own, or, if old Lacey offered her enough money, perhaps even into a small terraced house.

'We're movin' up in the world, Ed,' she called to the boy, who was stretched out on the floor using a black crayon to draw a big bushy moustache on a rabbit in one of his picture books. 'Wot d'yer fink about that then?'

Young Ed's response was to roar with excitable laughter. Beattie laughed with him, but for quite a different reason. She was thinking of how, with old Lacey's help, she would now have the chance to break with Jack Ridley once and for all. Or would she? As she sat down to write an immediate response to the letter, her mind was again plagued by indecision. Could she really go through with all this *without* telling Ridley? And if so, when he did eventually find out, what would he do to her then?

The Old Manor House wasn't nearly as grand as its name seemed to suggest. Beattie and Young Ed's first glimpse of it came as the pony and trap they had been collected in at Sudbury railway station turned off the small country lanes outside the village of Stickley, and headed along what could only be described as an overgrown path lined on either side by tall elm trees. The member of Lacey's household, who turned out to be the old gardener, and not at all pleased to be leaving his vegetable beds for a trip to the station, remained virtually silent all the way, so if Beattie had imagined she was going to be able to pump the man for any kind of information about his employer, she was vastly mistaken.

When the house finally came into view, Beattie's first impression was of an ancient building that had clearly once been quite beautiful, but which was now run down and sorely in need of repair. But as she and Young Ed were helped out of the trap, the splendour of the old red bricks, leaded windows, and fine sculptured stucco work around the exterior walls presented a picture of elegant grandeur, and reflected the type of people who must have lived there for generations.

The heavy oak front door was opened by an elderly housekeeper. 'The Commander is waitin' for you in the hall, miss,' she announced, in a country burr that Beattie recognised from her childhood when she and Sarah had spent a summer holiday with their Aunt Dixie, who lived in another part of Suffolk.

Beattie, with young Ed clutching her hand, entered the front hall, which had a stone floor, wood panelling, and a huge open fireplace. Little Ed's eyes were as large as saucers as he noticed the head and horns of a shot deer placed on the wall above the fireplace.

''Ook!' he cried, pointing to the amazing spectacle.

'Don't point, Ed!' scolded his mum. 'It's rude!'

The housekeeper showed them straight into the sitting room, which looked more like a room in a hunting-lodge, for there were more heads of culled animals jutting out from the walls, and a smell of decay mixed with rotting timber. 'Here we are, Commander!' she called.

'Ah!' said the man, who was standing with his back to the fireplace. 'Miss Melford?'

Beattie took Young Ed straight across to him. 'Please call me Beattie, Farver,' she said. 'After all, we're family.'

The Commander did not respond to this, but held out his hand for Beattie, who shook it. 'How do you do?' was all he said.

Beattie smiled and tried to identify some kind of resemblance between this man and his son, Edward, but, surprisingly, there was none. She was quite astonished that the retired naval officer didn't look at all old, in fact far younger than she had imagined, with dark blue vacant-looking eyes, short brown hair that showed not a trace of grey, and a moustache.

'This is yer grandson, Farver,' Beattie said, rather too well-rehearsed. She lifted up Young Ed to show the Commander. 'Say 'ello ter Granddad, Ed,' she cooed.

''Ello.' Despite his mum's warnings, Ed Junior looked a little nervous as he offered his hand to the strange man.

Beattie was a little puzzled that the Commander failed to take the child's hand.

'Can I hold him?' asked the Commander.

''Course.'

Beattie readily handed the boy over, despite the fact that the poor little thing was wary and ill-at-ease.

The Commander took the boy and, for a moment, held him at arm's length, as though looking him over.

But once again, Beattie was puzzled to see that the Commander was not actually looking directly at the boy's face.

'What colour eyes does he have?'

Beattie was completely taken aback by this question. Only when she watched him gently feeling around the boy's eyes with the tips of his fingers did she realise that he was blind. It took her completely by surprise. 'Er – blue,' she replied awkwardly. 'A kind of light blue.'

The Commander's face broke into a broad smile for the first time. 'Ah!' he said, to the boy. 'Then you truly *are* your father's son, aren't you,

Edward?' He put the boy down, and straightened up to face Beattie again. 'I'm sorry you weren't warned about my slight disability,' he said. 'I got it in an explosion on board my ship before the war. Stupid thing to happen. But you mustn't let it worry you. I can assure that I *can* see you – in a manner of speaking.'

Beattie was trying her best to cover up her awkwardness. 'I'm sorry,' she said. 'Edward never told me.'

The Commander gave her a wry smile. 'I don't expect he did,' he replied dryly.

The real purpose of the Commander's invitation to Beattie was not really addressed until all three had sat down to lunch at a long, highly polished table, where they were waited on by Mrs Routledge, the housekeeper, who served a meal of hot chicken broth, and cold beef and salad. Beattie knew that the only thing Young Ed would eat was a slice of bread and butter, for even back home his eating was generally confined to things like minced scrag end of mutton and mashed potatoes. But his eyes did light up when the main course was followed by treacle tart and custard, which he polished off very quickly. After the meal, Young Ed was allowed to leave the table, and with his mum and grandfather's permission, he was taken out into the garden by Mrs Routledge to look for frogs in the Old Manor House pond.

'As I wrote in my letter, Miss Melford,' said the Commander, once they were alone, 'or rather, as Mrs Routledge wrote for me, you must have been somewhat surprised to hear from me after such a long silence. And I wouldn't blame you for feeling angry at what I'm sure you must have felt was my complete indifference to the birth of my grandchild.'

Beattie tried her best not to show what she really felt about the way the old man had left her to struggle on, trying to bring up his son's child on her own for nearly two years. But until she heard how he intended to put things right, she was prepared to give him the benefit of the doubt. 'I don't see no point in bein' angry,' she said, without bitterness. 'It won't bring Ed's dad back ter life again.'

The Commander was intrigued by Beattie's candour, and it persuaded him to be more open with her. 'I'm not proud of the way I've behaved, Miss Melford,' he said, his eyes flicking aimlessly. 'You see, I've always believed that children should only be born within the framework of family life. It was a shock to know that my own son had–' He stopped abruptly, and turned his eyes in Beattie's direction. 'Did you love my son, Miss Melford?' he asked.

Beattie was taken aback by this question. And yet she understood why he asked it. After thinking about it for a moment, she replied, 'No, I didn't.'

The Commander looked impressed. 'If he had lived,' he asked, 'would you have married him?'

Again, Beattie hesitated before replying. 'Only for the sake of my child.'

The Commander sat back in his chair. He seemed well satisfied. 'Thank you, Miss Melford,' he said.

Beattie watched him carefully, and was struck by the way he sat so erect in his chair, shoulders squared, and with those lifeless dark blue eyes staring past her. 'When was the last time yer saw Edward?' she asked tentatively. But then quickly correcting herself, she added awkwardly, 'Wot I mean is – when was the last time yer was ter-gevver wiv 'im?'

'Oh, we hardly ever met,' he replied, suddenly brushing away what seemed to be imaginary food crumbs from the arm of his dark blue blazer. 'Edward only ever came when he wanted something. Usually money.' He hesitated, and Beattie could see that he was deep in thought. 'We didn't really get on well, you know. Chalk and cheese – that's what his mother always called us. She adored him, of course. Bit of a mother's boy, Edward.' He hesitated again before adding sadly, 'If I hadn't urged him to follow me into the navy, he'd be alive today.'

Beattie sensed his guilt, and for a brief moment, felt quite sorry for him.

'He once told me he'd never marry. Bit of a rogue, you know. I don't know what kind of a father he'd have made.'

'I'm sure 'e'd've bin marvellous,' said Beattie, reassuringly. She didn't believe a word she had said.

The Commander grunted. He didn't believe her either. 'So what are we going to do about this boy of his then?' he asked. 'Can't leave him to starve, can we?'

Although Beattie resented the implication that she was not somehow looking after his grandson, her heart started thumping at the prospect of some kind of financial offer of help. 'I'd never let Ed starve, Farver,' she said. 'Even if I 'ave ter go wivout meself, which I often do.'

The Commander ignored this, and carried straight on. 'Well, as the boy doesn't have a father, it's up to me to do what I can. He's part of my own flesh and blood, my own family. I'm the boy's grandfather. I won't let him down – nor his father.' He leaned forward in his chair, and directed his conversation straight towards where he could hear Beattie's movements. 'Tell you what I have in mind,' he said briskly. 'I've got quite a few nephews and nieces and godchildren littered around the world, so I can't go mad. And in any case, this house isn't worth as much as it used to be. Needs a lot doing to it.' He leaned back in his chair again. 'None the less, this boy is far closer to me than all the riffraff and hangers-on in my family, so I owe it to him to give him a good lift up in life. So I've instructed my solicitors to put him in my will.'

Beattie's heart was beating faster and faster.

'I want him to have a cut of the house, and five thousand pounds in cash. What d'you say about that, eh?'

Beattie clasped her hands so tightly together under the table that her knuckles went white. 'I – I fink that's – luvely of yer, Farver,' she replied falteringly.

Both turned their heads towards the large leaded bow window, as they heard Ed Junior laughing and screeching in the garden outside.

The Commander smiled, raised himself up

from his chair, and went to the window. 'I was tempted to leave him everything. But I believe a person should find his own way in life. If you make it too easy for them, they lose their energy and ambition.'

Beattie was biting her lip. To her mind, he was talking a load of old rubbish.

The Commander stood at the window, as though looking out into the garden, listening to the sound of Ed Junior giving poor Mrs Routledge quite a boisterous time. 'I want him to have something to fall back on,' he said contemplatively. Then he turned his attention back to Beattie. 'But it'll be his, you know. Whatever my grandchild gets from me goes to him, no one else. D'you understand what I'm saying, Miss Melford?'

Beattie felt her back stiffen. 'Nat'rally,' she replied, coldly but cautiously.

The Commander came back to the table, and leaned both his hands there. 'A child born out of wedlock,' he said, 'has a lot to bear for the rest of his life. He didn't ask to be brought into this world. And for all I know, it was not what his father wanted either.'

Indignant, Beattie sat bolt upright in her seat.

'Oh, I know how you feel, my dear,' said the Commander, fully aware of her outrage. 'But I would be deceiving myself if I thought I could trust you.'

Beattie slowly raised herself up from her chair. 'I fawt yer asked me 'ere to talk about yer grandson,' she snapped.

'Quite so, my dear,' he replied. 'But until I

know what kind of sacrifices you are prepared to make as the boy's mother, in the event of my death, none of the inheritance I have mentioned will be made available until my grandson reaches the age of twenty-one.'

CHAPTER 12

These were hard times for the Melford family. The winter had been bad enough, with leaks appearing all over the roof of Number 14 after a week-long downpour during November, which was followed by a big freeze-up in December. Geraldine, in particular, hated the cold, and as there was little money to buy coal for every fireplace in the house, she had to resort to wearing thick woollen underclothes, which was something she had shunned all her life. Samuel spent most of his days in his pyjamas and dressing gown, hunched up in front of the fire in his bedroom. But he seemed contented enough, especially when Sarah came back from work in the evenings and read him articles from the day's newspaper, which always seemed to stir something in his inner consciousness.

During the bad weather, Beattie's visits became less regular, but there was no doubt that whenever she called, little Ed's presence brought the house back to life. Despite her mother's pleas for her to 'make it up' with her sister, Sarah kept her distance, preferring to remain in her room while Beattie and her son entertained their parents downstairs. It was a painful experience for Sarah to hear the child romping around the place, laughing and yelling as he chased his grandmother's four outraged cats from one room to another. No matter how hard she tried, it was impossible for her to ignore that small, boisterous voice, the laughing eyes and podgy frame, a bundle of life and energy that should, in her mind, have belonged to her and her alone.

But Sarah's feelings towards her sister were to take a strange turn when, quite by chance, she and Beattie met each other in the Seven Sisters Road on the last full Saturday shopping day before Christmas.

'Didn't expect ter see you in my neck of the woods.'

Sarah always knew that it would only be a matter of time before she bumped into her sister whilst shopping for Mrs Ranasinghe, for these shops were only a stone's throw from Beattie's lodgings in the Bunk. But now it had actually happened, Sarah once again felt her whole body seizing up with tension. 'Hello, Beattie,' she said, without a glimmer of warmth.

'Ready fer Chris'mas, are yer?' Beattie asked, as she rested her large canvas shopping bag on the windowledge of Lipton's dried food shop. 'Got yer turkey yet?'

As Sarah had no intention of standing talking to Beattie for very long, she held on to her own small shopping bags. 'I'm afraid we can't afford a turkey this year, Beattie,' she replied, rather primly. 'We're having a chicken.'

'Roast chicken?' Beattie sighed wistfully. 'I reckon it's goin' ter be sausage an' onion rissoles for me an' Ed.'

Sarah was unmoved by what she considered to be Beattie's feeble attempt to gain sympathy. 'I seem to remember Mother telling you that you'd both be welcome to join us at home for a meal any time during Christmas.'

Beattie shook her head. 'I know,' she replied, pulling up her fake astrakhan coat collar as snowflakes began to flutter down out of a darkening sky. 'But it wouldn't work. Not wiv the usual crowd, the family an' that, all disapprovin'. 'Cept Aunt Dixie. She's always good fer a laugh.'

Sarah looked at her sister and thought what a fool she was. How could she even think about giving up so much for so little? How could she value independence more than the love and warmth of a good family, who were worth more than all her so-called working-class mates put together.

'I have to go, Beattie,' she said, starting to move off.

'I've just been ter see Bob Sluggins,' Beattie said suddenly and impetuously. 'Down the pawn shop.'

Sarah stopped.

Beattie took a step towards her. 'I saved up enough ter buy back Mum's silver snuff box. You know – that one Dad give 'er for 'er birfday a coupla years ago.'

Sarah looked at her, unsure how to react. For the first time in her life, she noticed that Beattie had a small mole at the base of her right cheek.

'I've bought back most of the uvver stuff she pawned,' Beattie said, her eyes showing the need she felt for Sarah's approval. 'I told 'er not ter do it, but she wouldn't listen. You know Mum. She always wants ter 'elp 'er kids.' She averted her gaze for a moment. Then: 'I've made up me mind, Sarah,' she said firmly. 'If I 'ave ter work twenty-four hours a day, seven days a week, I'm goin' ter get all those fings back for 'er. I'll give 'er the first lot back for a Christmas present. I know it's not the same, but at least it's somefink.'

Despite the heavy fall of snowflakes that were now settling on both women's heads and shoulders, Sarah felt a warm glow seeping through her entire body. As she looked at Beattie standing there in the ice-cold, she felt as though she hardly knew who this strange, vulnerable woman was. None the less, her face gradually loosened into a faint, appreciative smile. 'Thank you, Beattie,' she said, without the usual harshness in her voice. Then, after pausing briefly, she turned and moved off.

'Sarah!'

Again, Sarah stopped.

Beattie's eyes were glistening with the cold. 'Come back 'ome an' 'ave a cuppa tea wiv me.'

Sarah shook her head slowly. 'I don't think so, Beattie,' she replied with some difficulty.

Beattie clutched Sarah's arm. '*Please,* Sarah,' she pleaded. 'I'm only a stone's throw from 'ere. I'd like ter talk ter yer. I *need* ter talk ter someone. I'll go out of my mind if I don't. Just 'alf an hour's chinwag, that's all. We ain't done that in a long time.'

'We don't know *how* to talk to each other, Beattie,' said Sarah. 'We never have.'

Beattie drew closer. 'Maybe we 'aven't tried 'ard enuff,' she replied.

It was a long trudge along Seven Sisters Road,

for the snow was now falling thick and fast, and the earlier slight breeze had turned gusty, transforming the entire road into a dazzling carpet of white, where pavement, kerb and road were one. And even though it was a Saturday afternoon, in the middle of this great white blizzard a queue of men had formed outside the side entrance of a small copper works where, rumours had been circulating, there were job vacancies. It was a forlorn hope, for the yard gates remained stubbornly closed, leaving the men outside to freeze in the snowstorm, which seemed to have turned the long, thin queue into a white-capped caterpillar, whose only comfort came from a nearby street accordion player entertaining them with a shaky rendition of 'Good King Wenceslas'.

By the time Beattie and Sarah had turned into Campbell Road, the blizzard had started to abate. The Bunk wasn't at all as Sarah had imagined it to be, for before her was a winter wonderland, flanked on either side by houses that, in their massive coat of white, looked positively beautiful. There was no sign of the tawdriness for which the Bunk was so famous – no rubbish bins turned on their sides, no broken milk bottles littering the pavements. For this one lingering moment, Sarah could see no more than a street like any other, serene and tranquil in the snow-white mist that was gradually engulfing it.

Ma Briggs was certainly relieved to see Beattie when she came through the front door. 'I was beginnin' ter fink you'd end up as a bleedin' snowman, gel!' she bellowed, laughing out loud at her own rusty humour. But as soon as she saw another young woman hurrying in behind Beattie, she quickly tried to make herself look presentable, wiping her usual dewdrop from the tip of her nose with the back of her hand. 'Sorry, mate,' she said. 'Din't know yer 'ad company.'

'Ma,' said Beattie, putting down her shopping bag and taking off her snow-covered headscarf, 'this is me sister, Sarah. She's the brains in the family.' Then turning to Sarah, she said, 'I couldn't manage wivout Ma, 'ere. She's a real life-saver.'

Sarah held out her hand to Ma. 'Pleased to meet you,' she said formally.

In one hearty movement, Ma grabbed hold of Sarah's hands and shook them hard with both her own hands. 'Our Beat's sister!' she cried jubilantly. 'Well, there's a turn-up fer the books!' Then the old girl completely unnerved Sarah by suddenly leaning forward close and giving her a good looking-over. 'Diff'rent as peas ter pods,' she sniffed airily. 'Looks don't run in *your* family, do they, mate? Still, looks ain't everyfin' in this world. It's wot's inside that counts.'

Sarah had no time to respond, for Young Ed suddenly came rushing out of Ma's front parlour, shouting and yelling, 'Mum! Mum! Mum!' ignoring everyone, and charging straight past them and up the stairs.

'Be careful, Ed!' Beattie yelled. ''Old on ter the banisters!'

'I lit yer fire about 'alf-hour ago,' said Ma. 'Should be nice an' warm up there by now. Nice ter meet yer, young lady,' she bellowed to Sarah. 'Looks like your mum 'ad a good time wiv the milkman!' Roaring with laughter at her own cheeky joke, she disappeared into her room.

Beattie's room was, as Ma Briggs had promised, nice and warm when they got there, so the first thing Beattie did was to fill a large blackened kettle with a jug of water, taken from a bucket in the corner. Then she lit one of the two gas rings on the portable hob, and put the kettle on to boil.

Sarah was somewhat surprised by the room, for, although it was in bad need of decoration, at least everything was neat and tidy, the large double bed covered with a plain pink eiderdown, and the brass bed rail polished. There were clean floral-patterned curtains at the windows, an old chest of drawers with a snapshot picture of Beattie holding Young Ed in her arms when he was a baby, but, most surprising of all, no dirty dishes left in the china washbasin. Sarah thought it was all a far cry from the days when Beattie lived at home, with her bedroom constantly cluttered with clothes that had never been put away, and a bed that was never made until either their mother or Sarah herself had come in to do it. Sarah felt sad, however, to notice the open-sided cot that Young Ed was still forced to sleep in, for it was obvious that he was rapidly outgrowing it.

'Not exactly a palace, is it?' called Beattie, as she bustled around looking for two enamel mugs for the tea.

'You've made it very nice,' replied Sarah, tactfully. 'It's – comfortable.'

'Not big enuff fer free of us, though.'

Although Sarah was quite aware that Beattie and Young Ed shared their digs with a man, she did not react. She just looked across at the exuberant small boy, who was down on his hands and knees rolling a toy train engine across the cold lino floor. '*He* looks happy enough,' she said blandly.

Beattie pulled out a chair for Sarah to sit on, and they faced each other across the table. 'I share this place with my bloke,' Beattie said, stretching for a packet of Woodbines that were lying in an improvised tin-can ashtray on the other side of the table. 'Yer knew that, din't yer?'

Sarah sat up straight in her chair. 'It's none of my business, Beattie,' she replied, as she watched her light a cigarette. It was the first time she had seen Beattie smoking.

''E's got a temper like a ravin' loony,' said Beattie, resting her elbows on the table. 'Sometimes 'e knocks the livin' daylights out of me.'

Sarah stiffened and froze. 'Then why d'you stay with him?'

'Don't know really. Can't understand it.' Beattie took a deep puff of her fag, inhaled it down into her lungs, and exhaled less than half of it. 'I mean, it's not as though I love 'im,' she said, waving the smoke away with one hand. 'After wot 'appened wiv Ed Lacey, I vowed I'd never get 'ooked up wiv no more men. But then – along came Jack Ridley.' She flicked a quick glance at Sarah. 'Still, 'e's a good-looker, I'll say that fer 'im.'

'Is it enough?' asked Sarah, impassively.

Beattie thought about this for a moment. 'No.

It's not enuff. But when yer don't know wot life's all about, it 'elps.' She held the fag between her fingers, rolling it over and over and staring at it as though it were a living thing. 'I owe a lot ter Jack. 'E's bin good ter me. If it 'adn't been fer 'im, I wouldn't have this place.'

Sarah continued to stare at her. She was not convinced.

'I don't know where I'm goin', Sarah,' Beattie said, looking and feeling thoroughly downcast. 'I've got a kid I never wanted, and a man who's capable of killin' me.'

Sarah was shocked. 'Killing you?'

Beattie was still playing with her fag. 'Oh, I'm not sayin' 'e'd actually do it, but when 'e loses 'is temper I get really scared.' She finally took a puff of her fag. 'A few weeks ago, 'e give me a real fourpenny one – right 'ere.' She touched her right-hand cheek with the tips of her fingers. 'It puffed up like a football, all blue and bruised. That's why I 'aven't been to visit Mum an' Dad fer a while. I din't want ter upset them.'

Sarah leaned forward and looked straight at her. 'Beattie, why don't you just tell him to go?'

'I can't.'

'Why not?'

'I need 'im.'

Sarah stared at her in disbelief. '*Need* a man who tries to kill you?'

Although Beattie hadn't finished her fag, she stubbed it out in the ashtray. 'Sarah,' she said, putting the unfinished stub in her dress pocket, 'yer don't understand. When yer need somebody, it's not just fer sex, or money, or even friendship, it's becos, becos – they're there. And when they're not there any longer, no matter 'ow bad they've been, yer feel lost and rejected. I know, 'cos 'e once did leave me – only fer a few days, mind yer. We 'ad a row, about nuffin' at all really, but 'e flared up and just walked out on me. I nearly went out of me mind, sittin' 'ere night after night wiv no one ter listen to me, no one ter put up wiv all me grumbles. So I went ter this buildin' site where 'e was workin', and I burst into tears. 'E was so embarrassed, 'e came back 'ome wiv me. It's stupid, ain't it? Night after night I lay at the side of 'im in that bed, and I keep prayin' that 'e'll get out of my life and leave me alone, and then, when 'e does, I want 'im back. I mean, it's not as though I love 'im, 'cos I don't. 'E even asked me ter marry 'im, and I said not on yer nelly!' She looked across the table at her sister. Tears were beginning to swell in her eyes. 'Who'd be a woman, eh, Sarah?'

For a moment or so, there was silence between them – Sarah sitting bolt upright in her chair, and Beattie with hands clenched together on the table in front of her, her head bowed low. Then Sarah tentatively reached out to cover Beattie's hand with her own. It was something she had never been able to do before. 'Beattie,' she said quietly, tenderly.

But Beattie flinched, and quickly removed her hand nervously. 'I've forgotten the milk,' she said, getting up from her chair and hurrying to the door. 'When the kettle boils, could you fill the pot for me? The tea's already in. Won't be long.' With that, she was gone.

For a moment, Sarah was too numb to move. She just sat there, slumped in her chair, casting her mind back over all she had heard during the past few minutes. *'Who'd be a woman, eh, Sarah?'* kept ringing in her ears. Who indeed? she asked herself. It was all so depressing. How could her sister, her own young sister, have allowed her life to get into such a mess? After all, out of the two of them, Beattie was the one who had been the very essence of independence, outgoing, strong, and wilful, able to take on anything and anybody. What had happened to her? Why had Beattie allowed this brute of a man to dominate her life, a man she claimed she didn't even love? Sarah sat back in her chair, covered her face with her hands, and sighed. She found it extremely hard to come to terms with all that had befallen the Melford family over the past few years. Was there no end to their run of ill fortune? Oh God, she thought, if only they could turn back the clock and start all over again.

'Will yer play trains wiv me?'

Sarah removed her hands from her face with a start to find Young Ed standing right beside her, his face barely level with the top of the table. 'I – I...' She was so taken aback by the small boy's request that for a moment she didn't quite know how to respond.

'Please.' The small boy reached out, and tried to take hold of Sarah's hand.

Young Ed's pleas were irresistible, and Sarah knew that there was no way she could refuse. Taking hold of his tiny hand, she got up from her chair, and allowed him to lead her across the room to where his few pieces of train set were laid out on the floor. Both of them dropped to their knees, and within seconds, Sarah was joining him in making all the right train sounds, whistling, hooting, and being every inch the signalman. It was a very odd experience for Sarah, and she had to fight against her true instinct, which frequently reminded her who this small creature at her side really was. Every time she looked at the boy's face, she could see Edward Lacey, the same smile, the same pale blue eyes, even the way he tossed his head back when he laughed. Sarah couldn't explain the deep feeling of emotion that ran through her entire body. One part of her was so consumed with bitterness that she couldn't even bear to feel the boy's hand touching her own. But another part glowed with warmth and affection for him. It was as though their flesh was all from the same body. She suddenly felt an urge to take hold of the boy, and hug him. But she held back, afraid that she might be in danger of becoming fond of him. For a moment or so, she just watched the child, and gradually she saw her whole life flashing before her. Young Ed was what might have been, for her, and she for him. It was a daunting thought, and she agonised over it. She leaned forward, and gently stroked the boy's flaxen-coloured hair. It felt soft and fine in her fingers, and she caressed it affectionately. As she was doing so, she heard Beattie's footsteps coming back up the stairs, but when the door opened, another figure was standing there. It was Jack Ridley.

'Oh yeah?' he said, fixing his gaze on Sarah. 'An' who've we got 'ere then?'

Sarah glared at him only briefly. Then she turned away, as though he didn't even exist.

Christmas Day was a quiet affair for the Melfords. Because of the inclement weather, most of the usual family crowd decided not to turn out, and so, apart from Aunt Dixie, who would rather die than miss a whole day of food and drink, the party was a limited one. However, Geraldine's dream of bringing her two girls back together again under the same roof at last became a reality when, quite unexpectedly, Beattie turned up at the front door on Christmas morning. Jack Ridley, she said, had decided to go and spend Christmas Day with his brother in Stepney, although she wouldn't admit that the real reason was because Ridley couldn't bear to have the kid around his neck all day, and in any case, it would give him and his soak of a brother a chance to drink themselves into a coma for as long as they wanted.

Beattie and little Ed's presence transformed the atmosphere at the family home. Geraldine wept for joy as she watched her grandson playing with the decorations on the Christmas tree, and when they all sat down to open their presents, even Sarah was moved to see the smile on her mother's face. And when the boy climbed on to Samuel's lap, and started to sing 'Away in a Manger' to him, Aunt Dixie was so overcome with emotion that she had to retire to her bedroom for a while to pull herself together.

After Christmas lunch of roast chicken, Brussels sprouts, parsnips, cauliflower and roast potatoes, followed by Geraldine's traditional home-made Christmas pudding, everyone gathered round Geraldine's old upright piano whilst she played for a family singsong, which, apart from Christmas carols, included such favourites as 'Early One Morning' and 'Come into the Garden, Maud'. But the highlight of the evening's entertainment was, as usual, Sarah reading a chapter from Charles Dickens's *A Christmas Carol*, during which little Ed fell fast asleep in his grandmother's arms. At the conclusion of the chapter, at the moment when Ebenezer Scrooge became transformed into a figure of goodness to wish Tiny Tim a 'Merry Christmas', something quite extraordinary happened. Until that moment, Samuel Melford had sat in his armchair by the sitting room fire, his face blank, and his eyes transfixed on the glow from the burning embers. But quite suddenly, he sprang to his feet, and as if echoing what his daughter Sarah had just read out loud, he repeated the same greeting – 'Merry Christmas!' It was the first time for many weeks that he had responded to anything that had been going on around him, and it not only took everyone by surprise, but it was also the first real hope that perhaps a return to even a limited recovery was possible. Everyone sprang to their feet, and they all hugged him together.

Geraldine insisted that Beattie and little Ed stay the night, but as Aunt Dixie was using Beattie's old room, Beattie helped Sarah to make up the bed in the small spare room on the top floor. Little Ed slept through all the preparations, and hadn't even woken up enough to notice himself in a strange bed. Geraldine took Samuel up to his room, and then, reluctantly, she went to bed in her own room.

Aunt Dixie sat up talking to Beattie and Sarah for as long as she could, but when she realised that the bottle of sherry she had been drinking from all evening was getting perilously low, she decided to retire.

Now alone together, Beattie took off her shoes and curled herself up on the sofa, whilst Sarah sat in her father's armchair, and rested her feet on his red velvet footstool. Although the fire was beginning to fade, the room was steeped in a sweet, rich smell of burning elmwood. Sarah had already lowered the flames from the gaslamps on the walls, so that what light remained from the fire cast dancing shadows, which bounced up and down as if part of a magic lantern show.

'I've taken your advice, Sarah.' Beattie's voice was low, but still cut through the calm of the room.

Sarah looked up with a start.

'I'm goin' ter tell Jack Ridley ter push off. It's the best thing fer Ed an' me, an' it's the best fing fer 'im. I should've done it a long time ago, but I couldn't see straight till you 'elped me make up me mind.'

'You mustn't listen to what *I* say, Beattie,' replied Sarah. 'It's your life, yours and Ed's. Only you can make decisions that affect your future.'

'It's not my future I care about,' said Beattie, the dying glow from the fire reflected in her eyes.

'It's the kid's. I don't want 'im ter grow up watchin' me bein' bashed all over the place. An' if I ever saw Jack lay a finger on the boy, I don't know wot I'd do.'

For a moment they both stared into the fire without speaking. Eventually, Sarah asked, 'What happens if this man refuses to go?'

Beattie answered without turning to look at her. 'Then I'll pack me bags and take the kid somewhere else.'

'Where will you go?'

'There's always somewhere. Ridley don't pay me a penny fer 'is keep, so I'm not losin' out on nuffin'. Only trouble is, I'd miss Ma's 'elp. I don't know 'ow I'm goin' ter keep a job wivout 'er.'

'You could always come home.' A few weeks before, Sarah would rather have died than suggest such a thing. But she now knew how vital it was that her young sister should get away from this sadistic man, and she was prepared to do anything in her power to help her.

'No, Sarah,' replied Beattie, putting her feet on the floor, and leaning back on the sofa. 'I've got to work this out fer meself. All I know is, I've made up me mind,' she said firmly. 'I'm determined ter start the New Year by makin' sense of me life. Once I get rid of Jack Ridley, I never want ter see 'im again as long as I live.'

Sarah was relieved to hear her sister talking like this. Even if she didn't entirely believe her.

Geraldine lay in her bed in the dark, with her mind churning over all the things that had happened during the day. Most nights she couldn't sleep, and then she would lie awake reflecting on all the good times the family used to have, especially when Sarah and Beattie were children, and she and Samuel were able to enjoy all the love and comforts of married life together. But since Samuel's illness had first taken hold, she had spent so many nights in anguish and despair, fearing for her husband's state of mind, for her children, and for the future. Many a night she had cried herself to sleep, for there seemed to be no end to her problems, no future to look forward to. But tonight was different. She had seen her children get together under the same roof, sharing the delights of the family Christmas, her only grandchild laughing and romping around the house, and that restored her faith in what life was all about. For the first time in two years, she felt able to close her eyes, and fall asleep with a gentle smile on her face. It was all so perfect. If only Samuel was there to share the night with her, like he used to for so much of their married life – oh, how wonderful that would be. No more heartache, no more loneliness.

In her few moments of reflection, Geraldine had failed to notice the figure slipping quietly into her room. She couldn't see who it was sliding into her bed beneath the eiderdown, but she knew, and her heart started thumping with joy.

'I've come home.'

Samuel's voice was barely audible, but as Geraldine turned to greet her husband, they soon snuggled up together. It was just like old times.

As the New Year rolled in, the fortunes of the Melford family seemed to take a dramatic turn for the better. Not only were Sarah and Beattie making strenuous efforts to establish a relationship that they had both denied each other over the years, but Samuel's mind, although not as focused and logical as during his working life, was at least showing some signs of normality. However, although Beattie had always been Samuel's favourite, it was Sarah who gradually gave him the impetus to talk and take notice of life around him again.

One Sunday afternoon on the first weekend of the New Year, Sarah and her mother decided to try to reacquaint Samuel with the old towpath alongside the Islington Canal just beneath the Caledonian Bridge. For years this had been one of Samuel's most treasured spots, and when his illness became so severe that he was unable to go there alone, he sank into a state of abject despair. And so, with the blessing of his doctor, Samuel strolled with his wife and daughter to the bridge, and they made their way down the steps to the towpath, where, to their delight, a barge, towed by a magnificent long-haired black and white cart horse, was just coming into view. Samuel quickly took his place on his usual bench, and with Geraldine and Sarah at his side, he waited for the long, narrow, flat-bottomed boat to approach.

After the recent falls of snow, the towpath itself was still covered with a thin layer of slush that had turned to ice, and it was easy to see that the poor creature, who was attached to the forward section of the barge by a rope tied to its harness, had some difficulty in keeping its balance on the frozen grass.

'Wonderful! Wonderful!'

Samuel's excitement was a delight for Geraldine and Sarah to see, and as the barge drew closer and closer, they were thrilled by his enthusiasm, and his ability to recognise something that had meant so much to him in the past.

'This must be your New Year resolution, Father,' said Sarah, her arm around his shoulders. 'From now on, you must come to this favourite place of yours at least once a week.'

To Sarah's astonishment, he suddenly took hold of her hand and kissed it. Then he hugged his wife, who was seated beside him.

'Dear God,' said Geraldine, in soft, gentle prayer. 'Thank you for giving me back my Samuel. Thank you for giving me back my family.'

The old barge horse was now almost parallel with them, and for the first time, they could see that the cargo on the vessel was a pile of scrap iron, probably destined for a factory somewhere in the north of England. High above them, seagulls squawked, and, much to the disdain of the local sparrows, swooped low over the canal and skimmed the surface of the shimmering ice-cold water. By the time the horse and barge had reached the small party huddled together around the bench, the excitement proved too much for Samuel, and, to gales of laughter from his wife and daughter, he leaped up from the bench, and slowly followed the huge horse as it plodded its way along the path towards the bridge. Sarah and Geraldine also got up from the bench, and followed him.

'I mean what I said, Mother,' said Sarah, as they picked their way carefully along the icy path. 'We must bring him here as often as possible, get him used to things he did in the past. I'm convinced this is a new start for Father.'

Geraldine was clinging on to Sarah's arm as they walked. 'Oh, I do pray so, my dear. I do pray so.'

Samuel was now far ahead of them, following the barge horse as he gradually started to move along the towpath beneath the bridge. Then, delirious with the excitement of being back where he belonged, Samuel suddenly made a dash towards the old horse in what seemed to be an effort to pat it affectionately on the rump before it disappeared under the bridge. But in one swift movement, he tripped over the long towrope, and plunged head first into the icy waters of the canal.

Geraldine screamed out at the top of her voice, 'Samuel...!'

'Father...!'

Sarah couldn't believe what she had seen, for by the time she had reached the spot where her father had fallen in, he was struggling to keep afloat. She immediately fell to her knees, and despite the slippery conditions on the ice, she stretched out her hand in a desperate effort to grab hold of him. But her father, whose face was only just visible above the surface of the water, seemed quite bewildered, as though he couldn't understand what was happening to him, and although Sarah briefly managed to cling on to the shoulder of his overcoat, he quickly slipped away out of sight.

'No, Father! No…!'

'Sam – uel…!'

The cries of panic and despair soon brought a crowd of people hurrying down from the bridge above, and the skipper of the barge immediately brought his horse to a halt. But it was all too late. Samuel had been sucked down into the muddy, ice-cold waters of the canal.

PART 2

1930 – 1931

CHAPTER 13

Ed Melford was no cissy. Thanks to Jack Ridley, he could rough and tumble with the rest of them, despite the fact that his body seemed to be no more than flesh and bones, held together with short trousers that were cut down from an old pair of Ridley's, and braces that didn't have enough buttons to cling on to. The trouble was that Young Ed's passion was reading books – any books that he could lay his hands on, and newspapers too – and that, for an eleven-year-old from the wilder side of life meant that, to the gangs down the Bunk, he was his mum's darling, a number-one cissy. Ed, however, couldn't care less what any of the local 'spunks' felt about him, for what he lacked in brawn, he made up for with a brain that was constantly hungry for information. Mind you, it wasn't easy living with a mum who couldn't care less about what was going on in the world around her, and a stepfather who only ever read kids' comics such as the *Dandy*, and the *Beano*. Ed's interest was further roused by the fact that the country was going through one of the worst depressions of the century, with so many people out of work that, as a young, politically minded prodigy, he feared it would lead to riots in the streets.

Ever since she had taken the plunge and married Jack Ridley five years before, Beattie had spent most of her time either struggling, as the only wage-earner in the family, to keep her job at the candle factory, or fighting with her neighbours down the Bunk, who considered her a 'stuck-up little cow' who should push off back to her own type on the other side of Islington.

That wasn't, of course, Beattie's only problem, for during the past nine years the state of her relationship with Sarah had swung back and forth like a yo-yo. When Beattie had opened her heart to Sarah during that eventful Christmas at the family home in Thornhill Road, it seemed as though they would finally be able to create a close bond, and after their father died both had made strenuous efforts to become friends, if only for their mother's sake. But personal and financial pressures burdened the whole family and all changes seemed to be for the worse.

Since then, the diabolical economic recession had overwhelmed the country, and despite Sarah's efforts to keep up with the seemingly endless bills, it was becoming an impossible task to maintain such a large house. The crunch came the year before when, after a long illness, their mother died of pneumonia. Geraldine had never really got over the untimely death of her husband, and when she succumbed again to flu, then developed pneumonia, she had neither the energy nor the will to survive.

To everyone's dismay, neither Samuel Melford nor his wife had made a will. It was therefore left to Sarah to sort out the mess, and the first thing she did was to put the house up for sale. During this period, relations between Sarah and Beattie had once again become strained. It was clear that Beattie's marriage to Jack Ridley, which she had vowed was something she would never do, had completely undermined the new-found confidence Sarah had in her young sister.

'How can you marry a man who tries to kill you?' Sarah had asked, with incredulity. 'One minute he's everything you despise, and the next minute you're back in bed sleeping with him!'

Beattie had not taken Sarah's outburst lightly, especially when Sarah had accused Jack Ridley of frequently trying to 'touch' her whenever they had been left alone together.

'Yer'll never change, will yer, Sarah?' Beattie snapped back at her angrily. 'No wonder Edward bloody Lacey never laid 'ands on yer!'

After all the help and advice she had offered Beattie over recent years, this one remark had hurt Sarah most of all, and she vowed to herself that one day she would find a way to pay back her young sister for all the harm and pain she had caused her.

One day during the summer of 1930, Beattie discovered that she had yet another problem to cope with.

'Disappeared? The kid?' Ridley had only just got back home from another day job-hunting, and he was in no mood for any more bouts of Beattie's hysteria.

'I tell yer 'e should've bin 'ome from school nearly two hours ago!' snapped a near-panic-stricken Beattie, who had been waiting in desperation with Ma Briggs on the front doorstep of the house for Ridley's return. 'I went up the school, an' 'is teacher said 'e din't turn up all day.'

Exasperated, Ridley pulled off his flat cap, and scratched his head. 'So wot yer goin' on about then? Most kids 'is age do a bunk from school when they feel like it.'

Beattie came back at him like a flash. ''Ow would you know? You never 'ad a day's learnin' in yer life!'

Ridley wanted to cuff her, but with Ma there, he thought better of it. 'So wot d'yer want me ter do about it? Search the streets of bleedin' London?'

'See if yer can find Big Ben,' pleaded Beattie. ''E'll know wot ter do.'

'Big Ben!' Ridley almost choked. 'If yer fink I'm goin' ter ask fer a bleedin' bluebottle's 'elp, yer've got anuvver fink comin'. 'Aven't yer 'eard? Me an' the law don't mix.'

'Ed's only a kid, Jack,' protested Beattie. ''E's our son.'

'*Your* son,' retorted Ridley. 'Not mine.'

'Little monkey,' said Ma, whose eyes were anxiously scanning each end of the road. 'That's wot yer get fer too much book readin'. That boy's got too many fancy ideas in 'is 'ead.'

'This is no time ter keep goin' on about 'im!' spluttered Beattie, the palms of her hands pressed anxiously against her cheeks. 'Fer all we know 'e could be lying dead on some railway line. Remember that kid they found on the track at Canning Town the uvver week?'

Ma Briggs shook her head vigorously. 'Our Ed

ain't lyin' on no railway line,' she said confidently. ''E's got too much sense ter do fings like that.'

'If yer looked after yer bleedin' kids, yer wouldn't 'ave so much trouble wiv 'em!' The woman's voice shrieking from an upstairs window a couple of doors away caused everyone to swing round and look up.

'You talkin' ter me, cow face?' yelled Beattie, unceremoniously.

'You ain't got cloff ear'oles!' came the terse reply.

Beattie immediately rushed along to the front door gate of her rowdy neighbour, and, shaking her fist, yelled, 'You come down 'ere, mate, an' I'll show yer wot I've got!'

At that moment, an empty milk bottle came crashing down from another upstairs window in the same house, landing in pieces on the pavement just behind where Beattie was standing. This was followed by another woman's voice yelling, 'Go back 'ome an' look after yer kids, loud mouff!' This was followed by a man's voice yelling out to all of them, 'Keep yer voices down! Wot d'yer fink this is, a bleedin' circus?' Within seconds, people's heads were peering out of their windows, shouting, yelling, waving, most of their abuse directed at Beattie, who was taking them all on. Pretty soon, bits of rubbish were being hurled at her by some of the Bunk's teenage gangs, which prompted Ma Briggs to take up the cudgel. 'If any of this stuff catches me,' she bellowed, 'I'll 'ave yer guts fer garters!' Beattie and Ridley had to duck as pieces of roof tiles came hurtling towards them.

'All right then,' boomed a deep-throated voice from nearby. 'Let's 'ave yer!'

Beattie turned with a start to find Big Ben, the burly PC Ben Fodder, hurrying straight across the road towards them.

'It's about time you turned up,' Beattie yelled. 'They're all bleedin' mad round 'ere!'

Big Ben's massive frame towered above her, and he carried so much weight that one or two of his tunic buttons were positively tugging at their holes. But his was a kind face, completely round and podgy. 'So what's goin' on, Mrs Ridley?' he asked, aware that at the precise moment of his appearance, Jack Ridley had discreetly disappeared back inside the house.

'My boy, Ed – 'e 'asn't come 'ome from school,' replied Beattie, feverishly. 'Yer've got ter find 'im!'

'Take it easy now, missus,' said Big Ben. 'Let's get some facts down first. Wot time was 'e supposed ter be back?'

'Over two hours ago,' chimed in Ma Briggs. ''E's usually back dead on five past four every day.'

Big Ben passed only a brief, dismissive glance at Ma. He'd known her for years. ''As 'e gone off wiv 'is pals, or somefin'?' he suggested. 'Maybe they've gone off ter play football up Finsbury Park.'

'Yer don't understand,' said Beattie, urgently. ''E didn't turn up at school all day.'

Big Ben took a beat, and straightened up. 'Ah!' he exclaimed. 'Playin' 'ookey, is 'e?' He took out his notebook and pencil from a top pocket in his uniform. ''Asn't anyone round 'ere seen 'im all day then?'

'This lot?' snapped Beattie, scathingly. 'Just look at 'em – scum of the earth!' But when she turned round to glare back at her tormentors, the entire street was deserted, not a soul now at any of the windows.

To Beattie's irritation, Big Ben was busily scribbling in his notebook. 'I'll get this down to the station down 'Ornsey Road right away,' he said. 'If your lad's playin' truant again, our boys in blue'll find 'im.'

Beattie and Ma Briggs exchanged a puzzled look. 'What d'yer mean playing truant *again?*' Beattie asked. 'Are you sayin' 'e's done this before?'

Big Ben looked up from his notebook. 'Who – young Ed?' he answered with a wry smile. ''Course 'e 'as. Well, that's wot they told me down the school. I give the boy a good talkin'-to after the last time. I told 'im next time 'e did a bunk, I'd be on ter 'im faster than a dose of salts.' Then, aware of Beattie's pained expression, he added, 'Now don't you go worryin' yerself, Mrs Ridley. I'll find your boy if I 'ave ter scour every street in Islin'ton.'

Sarah got home late from work that day. Usually she left Mrs Ranasinghe round about four in the afternoon, but just lately the old Ceylonese lady had been in talkative mood, which was a sure sign that she was desperate for company, so by the time Sarah got on the bus in Tollington Road, it was already past six in the evening.

The bus journey home took less than ten minutes, and Sarah always used the opportunity to relax and look out of the downstairs window. The Caledonian Road looked particularly busy today for Cattle Market day always brought a stream of visitors from outside the borough, which meant that the shops were full. Sarah wondered how, in a time of such poverty and depression, people managed to find the money to buy anything. None the less, every time she came on this journey, a faint, wistful smile came to her face, particularly when she passed the tobacconist's shop on the corner of Offord Road, where she could still visualise her dear late mother going to buy her husband one of his favourite brands of cigar. But the recession had taken a toll on so many small shops and businesses. Sarah's favourite chandler shop, where she could buy anything from candles to split peas, had been one of the first victims, closely followed by Peg's Wool Shop, Ernie White's China, overflowing with jugs and washbasins and commodes decorated with grass and poppies, the Cally Live Snake Market, and Mr Murphy's Funeral Parlour, where both Samuel and Geraldine Melford had been laid out in open coffins prior to their burial in the Islington Cemetery. As she looked out on to what was once a thriving shopping area, Sarah felt nothing but disdain for the endless stream of politicians who, over the years, had reduced the country to such a parlous state. The current offenders, Ramsay MacDonald and his Labour Government, had a lot to answer for.

Once she had got off the bus, Sarah stopped briefly to buy six pennyworth of sweet broken biscuits from Mrs Miller's, the baker on the corner of Richmond Avenue. Then she made her way home, passing St Andrew's Church on the way, where she could hear the sound of choir practice taking place in preparation for the Harvest Festival service in a few weeks' time.

'Sarah!'

Sarah turned, to find her long-time friend Winnie Carter waving to her from across the road. Holding her hand was her four-year-old daughter, Melanie. Sarah waved back.

'I was beginning to think I'd never see you again,' Winnie called, as she led her little girl across the road to talk to Sarah. 'I thought you must have sold the house at last. You haven't, have you?'

Sarah shook her head. 'No such luck,' she sighed. 'I don't think I ever will.' She leaned down and smiled sweetly at Winnie's little girl. 'Hello, Melanie,' she said. 'And how are *you* today?'

'Say hello to Auntie Sarah,' urged Winnie. But the small child turned away and hid behind her mother's back. 'Don't be so silly, Mellie,' Winnie chided. 'You know Auntie Sarah. She's our friend.'

Sarah decided not to pressurise the child, who was prone to tears. But she was pleased to see Winnie again, if only for a few fleeting moments. Since her mother had died, Sarah seemed to have drifted apart from so many of her friends, mainly because the worry of trying to keep on the family house was weighing down on her.

'It seems so absurd that you haven't been able to find a buyer,' said Winnie. Marriage to Bank Manager Frederick Allsop clearly suited her well, for she had filled out immensely since the days when she and Sarah used to spend so much time together. 'How long is it now since you first put it on the market?'

Sarah shrugged her shoulders. 'I can't remember, Winnie,' she replied. 'It feels like years.'

'It's a crying shame,' asserted Winnie. 'It's such a beautiful house. If it wasn't for the fact that there's so little money around these days, I'm sure it would have been snapped up a long time ago.' She put her hand affectionately on Sarah's arm. 'You've had such rotten luck, Sarah.'

Sarah smiled at her. Dear Winnie, she thought. She must try to see her more often. 'Other people have more to put up with, Winnie,' she said. 'At least I have a roof over my head.'

'Well, as I've told you before, and I'll tell you again–' Sarah could tell that Winnie was in one of her practical moods, for the shoulders of her small, ample frame were now pulled back firmly – 'if ever you need any help, you know where to come. Thank God, Frederick is still earning a good salary, and we can always loan you something till you get on your feet.'

Winnie's words really cheered Sarah, so she leaned forward and kissed her gently on the cheek. 'Thank you, Winnie,' she said warmly. 'You really are such a good friend.'

'And you're a good friend to me too,' insisted

Winnie. 'You always have been, and always will – even after we've gone.'

Sarah looked at her with a start. 'Gone?' she asked.

'I haven't seen you to tell you, Sarah,' she said. 'Frederick's been told he has to take over a new branch. He can't say no, not the way jobs are at the moment. It's down in Kingston, in Surrey.'

Sarah put her hand to her mouth in dismay. 'In Surrey. Does that mean you'll be moving down there – to live?'

Winnie nodded. 'The house comes with the job. But it's not really all that far,' she said reassuringly. 'You must come down and see us – spend a Sunday with us all. It'll be like old times.'

Sarah smiled back bravely. 'Thank you, Winnie,' she said. 'I'd like that.' But as she took her leave of her friend, she found it difficult to disguise her dismay.

Clutching her modest bag of broken biscuits, Sarah made her way back home. She hardly noticed which street she was walking along, for her mind was too weighed down with the news she had just heard. It wasn't just the fact that Winnie was leaving the neighbourhood that hurt, but the pain she felt for the aimless direction of her own life. Now that she had passed thirty years of age, Sarah had begun to think of herself as an 'old maid'. Even if she had wanted to find a man and get married like Winnie, she saw no prospect of ever doing so. Between them, Beattie and Edward Lacey had thoroughly demoralised her, made her feel sexless and unattractive. But the main problem was that she wasn't yet self-sufficient enough emotionally to live a life without close friends like Winnie.

As she turned into Thornhill Road, she paused briefly to look up at the house that had been at the heart of the Melford family for so many years, and for one fleeting moment she wondered whether mere bricks and mortar were worth all the heartache she had had to endure since the death of her parents. The iron gates at the front garden entrance had still not been replaced since they'd been removed by the Borough Council to provide scrap for the war effort in 1915, and this somehow immediately presented an image of a house that had had its day, and was now only waiting for the winter of its life. But as she made her way up to the front door, Sarah refused to let her despair affect the deep sense of love she felt, and would always feel, for this very special place.

Inside, Sarah again had to face an intrinsically depressing atmosphere. With so much of the furniture sold to pay the bills, it was no longer the home it used to be. The rooms were barren and soulless, the walls were desperate for a coat of paint, there was a smell of emptiness and decay about the place, and as she moved from one room to another, her feet echoed on stone floors that no longer had any carpets. But despite her feelings of desolation, Sarah refused to feel sorry for herself. Life couldn't be like that, she thought. After all, the good Lord had only given every one of us a certain amount of time to live, so life had to be practical and uplifting. Striding across the hall that had once reverberated to the sounds of two small sisters rushing up and down the stairs, to her father arriving home at the front door after a busy day in his office at Gamages, and to the sweet, pervasive smells of her mother's home-cooking, Sarah made her way straight into the kitchen.

After placing the bag of broken biscuits on the kitchen table, she put the kettle on to make herself a cup of tea. As she took off her small summer hat and placed it on a chair, she was suddenly alarmed to hear a movement coming from the pantry. She wasn't quite sure what the sound was, for it was only slight, which led her to believe that a mouse had moved in. Warily, she approached the pantry, and in one swift, brave act, pulled open the door.

'Oh my God!' she gasped.

Curled up beneath the lower pantry shelf, doing his best to make himself as tiny as possible, was Beattie's boy, Young Ed.

'Ed!' Sarah cried. 'What on earth are you doing here?'

Reluctantly, the boy crawled out, and allowed his aunt to help him to his feet. 'I came ter see yer,' he said awkwardly.

'Well, couldn't you just come to the front and knock on the door? How did you get in without a key?'

'Yer left the window open. Over there.' He pointed to a tiny window high up on the wall near the door, which was open, but hardly big enough for a cat to crawl through, let alone a growing eleven-year-old boy.

Sarah shook her head in disbelief. 'Does your mother know you're here?'

The boy shook his head.

'You should have asked her first.'

Ed shrugged his shoulders.

It had been almost a year since Sarah had last seen her nephew, and she was dismayed at how thin he was, hardly enough flesh on his bones to make a meat stew, as her mother used to say. 'Are you hungry?' she asked.

He nodded vigorously.

Sarah led him across to the table. 'Come and sit here and have some biscuits. I'll make you a dripping sandwich.'

Ed did as he was told, and immediately started tucking in.

Sarah made him a sandwich of beef dripping. It was only a matter of minutes before he started gorging himself on what was, for him, a feast, the first meal he had had all day. Whilst she watched him eating, Sarah poured him a glass of ginger beer, and when he downed it without coming up for breath, she quickly poured him another. It was a curious experience for her to see the boy sitting at her own kitchen table, and it took all her self-control to discard all thoughts about the role his father had played in her life. She waited until he had practically demolished both the biscuits and the dripping sandwich before she started to question him.

'Why did you come here, Ed?' she asked.

Before answering, the boy wiped his mouth on the back of his hand. 'I told yer. I wanted ter see yer.'

Sarah removed her hat from the second chair, then sat opposite him at the table. 'You've never tried to see me before, Ed,' she said. 'What do you want with me?'

The boy burped, then pulled himself up, and sat cross-legged on the chair. Sarah noticed how dirty he looked, but decided against forcing him to have a wash until he had had a chance to talk.

''Ave yer got any books?' the boy asked.

Sarah was puzzled. 'Books?'

'*Any* books,' continued the boy. 'I can read, yer know. I'm not so good at writin', but I can read anyfin' yer like.'

Sarah could hardly believe what she was hearing. 'You mean, you've come all the way up here to ask me for a book?'

Ed nodded.

Sarah scratched her head. 'Don't they give you books to read at school?'

The boy snapped back immediately, 'I don't like school, an' the books they give yer are stupid.'

'Stupid?'

'They're fer kids.'

Sarah found herself smiling. For some strange reason, she felt good. 'So – what kind of books do you *like* to read?'

Again the boy answered immediately. 'About foreign countries. About politics.'

Sarah was not sure if she was hearing right. Although she remembered how advanced at talking the boy had been at a very early age, it seemed incredible to her that at the age of eleven, he could possibly have an interest in such an absurdly grown-up topic as politics. 'Why haven't you asked your mother to get you some books like that?'

'Mum never talks ter me,' Ed replied, seemingly more interested in playing with his foot than concentrating on what his aunt was saying to him. 'All *she* ever says is that working-class people are the scum of the earth.'

Sarah's eyes opened wide in disbelief. Could it really be possible that, after all these years, Beattie was turning against the very type that had meant so much to her?

'She's stupid, my mum,' continued the boy. 'She don't know nuffin' about the rich an' the poor.'

'And do *you* know?' asked Sarah.

'Poor people 'ave ter work fer their livin',' the boy replied, instantly. 'Rich people don't. They 'ave uvver people ter do the work for them.'

Sarah certainly found it illuminating to hear this from such a young mind. But in a strange kind of way, despite the simplicity of the boy's thinking, there was a sort of logic there somewhere. As she watched him sketching out imaginary figures on the tablecloth with his fingernail, she couldn't help imagining what the boy's father – his real father – would have thought about him. 'You know, Ed,' she said, trying to make eye contact with him, 'as you grow older, you'll discover that it takes all sorts to make a world. The poor need the rich, as much as the rich need the poor. In a sane world, there shouldn't be any poor. But what's really important is that we all talk to each other. Your grandfather used to say that if people ever stopped talking to each other, the world would come to an end.'

'Did you ever talk to *your* dad?' asked Ed.

The boy's question was so reasonable, but so direct, then it took Sarah by surprise. 'Yes,' she recalled. 'Your grandfather and I often used to talk together.'

'What about?'

'All kinds of things. We used to discuss what we read in the newspapers.'

'The only newspapers *I* read are the ones they let me 'ave down the chip shop.'

Sarah reached across the table, and was about to touch his hand. But then she thought better of it. 'It won't always be like that, Ed,' she said reassuringly. 'Some day you'll be able to afford a newspaper of your own.'

'Can I 'ave a book then?'

Sarah sighed. 'I'll see what I can find.' She got up from the table, but before she made for the door, said, 'If you want, you can come and see me again. When you come home from school.'

Ed replied, without looking up, 'I don't go ter school.'

'What do you mean?'

'I told yer. I don't like goin' ter school. The teachers don't know nuffin'. They're all stupid. Mum finks I go ter school, but I don't. I stay away lots of days.'

Sarah was horrified. 'Ed!' she snapped. 'Are you telling me you play truant?'

He merely shrugged his shoulders.

She rushed back to him, and made him sit up in his chair. 'Now listen to me. If you keep away from school, then you can keep away from me. Do you understand?'

He shrugged again.

'School may not be perfect, Ed,' she continued, 'but it's the best hope you have of learning all the things you want to know about. Now I'm going into the next room to see if I can find something for you amongst Grandfather's collection of books. If I let you have one, you must promise me that from now on, you won't miss one single day of school. And even more important, you won't lie to your mother. Is that clear?'

Again, the boy shrugged his shoulders.

Sarah shook her head in despair. Then she left him while she went off to look for a book in one of the large packing cases in the sitting room. She eventually came across a mammoth-looking thing called *The Class War – Struggle for Survival*, and was convinced that if that wasn't enough to put an eleven-year-old off politics for the rest of his life, nothing was. Hardly able to carry the monstrosity, she returned to the kitchen.

When she got there, Beattie's boy was curled up on the floor. He was fast asleep.

CHAPTER 14

At the beginning of September, Sarah had an unexpected offer for the family house in Thornhill Road that she couldn't refuse. It was a pretty paltry offer, almost half the real pre-war market value, but as she was desperate to pay off the mountain of bills outstanding on even the basic maintenance of the house, she had no alternative but to accept. It was a hard decision for her to take, especially as the buyer, a repellent character with the flowery name of Sebastian Plomley, was a property speculator, who clearly had no intention of using the place as a residence for himself, but was acquiring it purely as some kind of business investment. His spoiled young wife, Dora, was little better, for on first sight of the house her only comment was that it smelled like the place hadn't been lived in for years. Dealing with people like this had confirmed a feeling that had been growing steadily in Sarah's mind for some years, that people who had money generally lived their lives wanting more money. It had also not escaped her notice that, with the exception of Aunt Dixie, since the death of Sarah's parents, none of their families had offered any financial help, nor even consolation for the predicament Sarah had found herself in. Fair-weather friends, she told herself. There was no doubt that she was gradually becoming disillusioned by the so-called middle-class values she had been brought up with.

It was fortunate that, following her initial meeting with the unpalatable Mr Plomley and his spouse, Sarah had no need to deal directly with them. However, on the day that contracts on the sale were finally exchanged, Sarah had a quite different, though not entirely unexpected problem to deal with.

'No money left over? Who're *you* kiddin'?'

It was clear from the start that Beattie attached no little importance to the day's events, for she had turned up at the house with not only young Ed in tow, but also Jack Ridley. It was an incongruous sight, for all three were togged up in their Sunday best, and Sarah was astonished to see Ridley wearing a tie, an accoutrement she had always firmly believed he did not possess.

'I'm afraid it's true, Beattie,' said Sarah, as she led the bizarre trio into a sitting room now stripped bare of everything but for two wooden stools, and a pouffe. 'If you remember, I warned you a long time ago that the expenses for maintaining this house far outweighed what I was able to afford out of my own modest income. However, it is just possible that once the legal costs of selling the place have been settled, there may be a little something left over for the two of us to divide between us.'

Beattie's eyes narrowed suspiciously. 'A little somefin'?' she pressed. ''Ow much?'

For a brief moment, Sarah stared directly into her sister's eyes. She found it hard to believe that those were the same eyes that had once pleaded with her for forgiveness. 'I don't know where I'm going,' Beattie had sobbed. 'Who'd be a woman, eh, Sarah?' It seemed a lifetime away. What she saw before her now was a self-confident, calculating little creature who had worked it out in her mind that she might be missing out on something. Or was it her? With someone like Jack Ridley at her side, Beattie was stripped of all sense of decency, and was quite capable of anything.

'A few pounds,' replied Sarah.

Beattie's eyes darted back at her. 'A few pounds? Does that mean 'undreds?'

'It means no more than a *few* pounds, Beattie.'

Beattie exchanged a quick, angry look with Ridley, then immediately turned back to Sarah. 'It's not possible,' she growled. 'Wot about all the furniture yer sold, an' all the rest of the stuff? That must've brought in a penny or two.'

'I sent you a list of everything I've sold. Every penny was put towards Father's debts.'

'You're not tellin' me that there wasn't enuff there ter cover the bills?' insisted Beattie.

Exasperated, Sarah went to the mantelpiece, picked up an old filing box, plunged her hand in, and pulled out a wad of bills. She thrust them at Beattie. 'Here!' she snapped. 'Take a look for yourself.'

Beattie, taken aback, had no alternative but to take the bills.

'You will find there a monthly account of all outstanding bills to date. Once payment of three thousand, two hundred pounds has been received for the sale of this house, the account will be in credit to the sum of approximately six hundred and twenty-four pounds.'

Beattie's face immediately lit up. 'There you are then! There *is* somefin' left over.'

'That, of course,' said Sarah, cutting straight through her sister's fatuous remark, 'is before the main outstanding debt has been accounted for.'

Beattie looked puzzled. 'Wot yer talkin' about?' she asked, half suspiciously but also warily.

Sarah, who had been waiting for this moment with Beattie for a very long time, decided to make the most of it. 'Two years before he died,' she said, turning her back on Beattie, and strolling to the window with arms firmly crossed, 'Father took out a mortgage to cover the debt he had incurred through gambling.'

Beattie was now really shocked. 'Father – gambled?' she gasped.

Sarah, at the window, turned round to face her. Her figure was now little more than a silhouette. 'Everything – from horse racing to cock fighting. At the time of his death, he owed more than one thousand, seven hundred pounds.'

Beattie suddenly dropped the wad of bills to the floor. Young Ed rushed forward, and on hands and knees, scrabbled round to pick them up.

As she slowly strolled back to join her sister, Sarah could smell the smoke from Ridley's fag. Ever since they'd entered the room, she had been constantly aware of his presence, for although he kept silent throughout, she knew that he was taking in every word she said. 'Soon after Father died,' she continued, 'I went to see Mr Levinson,

Father's bank manager. He told me that the debts were now the responsibility of our father's estate, and that his heirs would be expected to honour them. After careful persuasion, Mr Levinson agreed to let me take out a ten-year loan. I've been paying it back ever since.' She turned round to look at Beattie, who was now in such a state of shock that she had had to sit down on one of the stools. Satisfied that she had taken the wind out of Beattie's sails, Sarah concluded, 'At the current time, the outstanding balance stands at three hundred and ninety-two pounds, seven shillings, and seven pence.'

Young Ed finally succeeded in picking up the last of the bills, which he offered to his mother, who pushed them away. So instead he gave them back to his aunt, who put them straight away into the filing box.

'Why din't yer tell me about all this before?' asked Beattie, who looked shattered.

'You never asked me,' replied Sarah, acidly. 'In fact, as I recall, the only single thing you have ever asked me since our parents' death was in reference to what funds might legally be available to you – as your birthright, of course.'

'I fink that's bein' a bit 'ard on yer sister, Sarah,' said Ridley, as he strolled across to join them. 'I mean, she was only enquirin' about wot she's entitled to.'

'Really, Mr Ridley?' Sarah replied. Ever since she had first set eyes on the man, she had stubbornly resisted calling him by his first name. 'In that case, I'm sure your wife will be willing to share the responsibility of paying off the remainder of our father's debts. That would amount to the sum of one hundred and ninety-six pounds, three shillings, and ninepence halfpenny. Under the circumstances, I'll be willing to forego the rest of Father's debts that I myself have paid off over the past few years.'

Ridley had a wry smile on his face. ''Ow generous of yer.'

'Thank you,' Sarah replied, with her own wry smile.

For one very brief moment the two of them stared hard at each other. Both had wills and determination of their own, and though Ridley was a manipulator and Sarah a pragmatist, there was definitely a spark of mutual recognition.

'I fink we should go 'ome,' said Beattie, getting up wearily from her stool. 'No point in 'angin' round 'ere.' She looked round the cold, unwelcoming room, and for the first time, it suddenly dawned on her that she would never again see the place in which she had spent the formative years of her life.

''Ang on a minute, Beat,' said Ridley, who was still sizing up Sarah. 'Yer 'aven't asked yer sister wot 'appens to 'er now she 'as ter move out of 'ere.'

Beattie shrugged her shoulders, and made for the door.

'Oh, you mustn't concern yourself about me, Mr Ridley,' replied Sarah, with false politeness. 'I've found myself some suitable accommodation – elsewhere. But thank you for your concern. It's much appreciated.'

Ridley now had a broad grin on his face. He

liked, even admired Sarah's boldness. No one had ever played this kind of defiant game with him before, and it intrigued him. 'Well, if we can 'elp yer out any time,' he said, 'yer know where we live. Give us a shout.'

Sarah's expression was fixed as she watched Ridley put on his cap and follow Beattie to the door.

He turned to give a lingering look at Sarah. 'Be seein' yer then.'

Sarah watched him go without replying. All the time she had been in his presence, she had felt quite sick.

'Yer didn't sell Granddad's books, did yer?'

Until that moment, Sarah had forgotten about Young Ed, who had spent most of the time sitting cross-legged on the bare floorboards in the corner of the room, mesmerised by a small brown cockroach, which had somehow toppled over on to its back, its tiny legs kicking helplessly in the air.

'No, Ed,' replied Sarah, going to him. 'I haven't sold any of Grandfather's books. I've kept plenty of them back for you.'

'Why did Granddad lose all 'is money?' asked the boy, quite innocently, whilst keeping his attention firmly fixed on the cockroach.

Sarah sighed. 'He made mistakes, Ed,' she replied, squatting down alongside him. 'It's something we are all capable of doing from time to time, but some people don't know how to put things right.'

'Was 'e a bad man?'

Sarah shook her head. 'No,' she replied. 'Your

grandmother and grandfather were two of the kindest, most wonderful people who ever lived. When you were little, they loved you dearly.'

'I wish I was dead, too,' said the boy. 'I could meet Granddad, an' we could talk about all sorts of fings – about 'is books an' fings.'

A cold shiver ran up and down Sarah's spine. For one brief moment, her young nephew's chilling remark had distressed and amazed her. But the more she thought about it, the more she realised what truth it had. Yes, young Ed and his granddad would have had a fine old time together talking about books – any books. In fact, Sarah reckoned that Samuel Melford would have found quite a lot in common with his grandson.

Beattie didn't sleep that night. She lay awake for hours thinking about her father's gambling, and the pile of debts he had incurred. Try as she may, she couldn't rid herself of the guilt she felt for letting Sarah take on the burden of paying back those debts, and for daring to imagine that she, Beattie, should be entitled to any kind of inheritance. Jack Ridley, of course, was no help. These days, their relationship hardly existed. They rarely slept together, and even when they did, it was usually when Ridley came home drunk and collapsed on to the bed. Night after night, Beattie asked herself why she had ever married such a man, for she knew for a fact that he was sleeping around with every whore in Islington, and he treated Young Ed as though he was nothing more than a bit of horse dung. She had never worked out why he had married her either. At least, not until today. *'Yer stupid cow!'* he had ranted the moment they had left Thornhill Road after Sarah had dashed their hopes of a windfall. 'Can't yer see, she's pulled a fast one on yer? She's made a bucket out of that house and you've let 'er get away wiv it!' Beattie turned restlessly from one side to the other. Yes, she was a stupid cow all right, for not realising before what Ridley was after when he practically frog-marched her to a five-shilling wedding up the registry office. If it wasn't for Young Ed, she would be glad that there was no money from the sale of the old family home. But when she sat up in bed, and looked across at the boy, and saw him snuggled up on his pathetic second-hand mattress on the floor in the corner, she felt consumed with guilt and frustration that she had ever allowed herself to be dragged down by such a two-faced go-getter as Ridley. The only thing she did not regret was the time when she had secretly got rid of the baby he had forced inside her. 'Good riddance ter bad rubbish!' was all she felt now.

Her throat was parched with anxiety, so she got out of bed, found her enamel tea mug, and quietly got herself a drink of water from the bucket beneath the washstand. For a few minutes, she went to the window and just stood there, sipping her water, and staring down aimlessly into the barren street outside. The gaslamp just outside the house was still not working properly, for the mantle had a large hole in it which caused the light to flicker, and sent dancing shadows all along the fronts of the houses on one side of the street. The flickering light danced across Beattie's face too, and it showed exactly how she was feeling. How she hated that street. The Bunk was certainly the right name for it, not only for the filthy smell-hole of a place that it was, but also for the people who lived there. God, what a lesson she had learned! How could she ever have thought that all working-class people were the same, that they were the 'salt of the earth' and could do no wrong? They were just as bombastic, opinion-ated, and self-centred as any of that lot in Barnsbury. The only difference was that in the Bunk they'd tell you what they thought of you to your face; in select Barnsbury, they'd merely whisper it behind closed doors. As she stood there, turning things over in her mind, Beattie made a decision to do something to improve her lot in life. Somewhere, somehow, things *had* to change.

The following morning, Beattie turned up at Sedgwick's, the candle factory where she worked, to find her old mate Nagger Mills waiting for her.

'I'm gettin' married, Beat!' Nagger said, shaking with excitement. 'Taffy asked me last night. It's taken 'im bleedin' long enuff. We've been walking out fer nearly six years!'

Both women roared with laughter, as Beattie hugged her. These days they only got the chance to get together when Beattie was able to take a bus up 'the Cally', where Nagger still worked the tea urn for the farmers in the cattle pen. Although Beattie was quite jealous of how her old mate managed to look younger than her twenty-eight years, every time she was with her she felt as though she hadn't a care in the world. 'It's wonderful, Naggs,' said Beattie. 'Just fink of it, an honest woman at last!'

'Yer can say that again,' retorted Nagger, lowering her voice. 'I'll only just make it in time.'

Beattie gasped. 'You're jokin'?'

Nagger sighed deeply. 'I wish I was,' she said miserably. 'I only found out a coupla days ago. Fank Gord Taff din't fink twice about askin' me ter marry 'im.'

'An' so I should fink!' returned Beattie. ''E gave yer the bun, so 'e can pay for it!'

Again they laughed.

'Anyway,' continued Nagger, hurriedly, 'we're 'avin' a booze-up ter celebrate down the Albion ternight. D'yer fink yer could make it?'

Beattie pulled a face. 'I don't know, Naggs. Young Ed's got an 'abit of slippin' out as soon as me back's turned.'

Nagger's normally sunny smile turned a bit sour. 'Wot about that bloke of yours?' she asked scornfully. 'Can't *'e* keep an eye on the kid?'

Beattie was tight-lipped. Remembering how Ridley had practically knocked the daylights out of Ed on the evening he came home after calling on his Aunt Sarah when he should have been at school, she had no stomach to say what she really felt about Ridley – not even to her best mate. 'I'll find a way, Naggs,' was all she would say.

Ironically, the Albion pub was just a stone's throw from Number 14 Thornhill Road, which gave Beattie mixed feelings about accepting Nagger's invitation. But she told herself that her old mate's booze-up was far more important than what she felt about being so near to the old family home, so she turned up at about eight in the evening.

The Albion itself was one of the more pleasant pubs in the Barnsbury area; when it was first built in the nineteenth century, it was a fashionable tea garden, where the wives of rich businessmen passed their afternoons in hot gossip about their husbands' mistresses, and their own 'amours'. It was a very different establishment to the White Conduit pub just down the road, where Samuel Melford had spent so many of his latter years, drinking in the private bar, and in the cock-fighting shed in the back yard.

By the time Beattie arrived, Nagger's booze-up was in full swing in the public bar. As she expected, it was a pretty rowdy affair, for most of the menfolk present were already well oiled.

'So you're makin' an honest woman of 'er at last, are yer, Taff?' Beattie asked Nagger's intended.

'If yer ask me, I think it's the other way round,' replied the Welsh boy, who was a few years younger than Nagger, smaller, and decidedly plump. 'Got me under 'er thumb, and that's for sure,' he said, his accent thicker than a tin of treacle. 'Mind you, I'm a willin' party. At least I'll get my breakfast in bed every mornin'.'

This produced a roar of approval from all of the men, and jeers from the women. 'Some 'opes!'

roared Nagger.

In a matter of minutes, Beattie had a glass of bitter thrust into her hand. She didn't usually drink alcohol, but the way she was feeling these days, she was prepared to try anything. After all, this was a special occasion, and she was determined to enjoy herself. It felt so good to meet up again with so many of her old mates from the Cattle Market, and for a few fleeting moments, it helped her to forget the disenchantment she felt for her neighbours up the Bunk.

''Allo, stranger.'

If it hadn't been that she felt his hand on her shoulder from behind, Beattie wouldn't have heard who was talking to her. But it didn't take her long to recognise Shiner, one of her gang from her days knocking around the streets up 'the Cally'. 'Blimey!' she said, half a pint of bitter in her hand, and a fag in her mouth. 'Where'd they dig you up from, Shiner?'

'I've been around, mate,' he replied, with his usual gleam in his eye. 'Yer just 'aven't looked 'ard enuff fer me.'

Cheeky as he was, Beattie couldn't help liking him, though he was always taking liberties. She always knew how to handle Shiner, and he always knew how far he could go with her; it was a kind of mutual respect. And as she looked at his well-defined features, his dark eyes, and flat boxer's nose, it didn't escape her notice how much he had changed since she first knew him. Not only had he grown his hair so that it flopped over one eye, but he was dressed well in a black long-sleeved shirt, dark trousers, and a black trilby hat which was pushed to the back of his head. It was hard for her to believe that he was pushing thirty.

'Come up in the world, ain't yer, Shine?' Beattie asked.

'When yer put yer mind ter somefin', yer can't lose,' he replied.

Beattie was impressed. 'So wot *'ave* yer been puttin' yer mind to?' she asked.

'Aw – you know – this an' that.' Shiner's appearance may have changed, but he was just as evasive as ever. 'Let's just say that me work involves – 'ow shall I say – lookin' after the public interest.'

Beattie didn't have to ask any more. He was clearly up to something that was *not* in the public interest.

'An' wot about you?' Shiner lit himself a fag, but he was watching Beattie all the time.

'Wot about me?' Beattie replied chirpily.

'No man in yer life yet?'

Beattie's reply was haughty. 'As a matter of fact, I'm married.'

Shiner grinned. 'Married? Wos that?'

'Sounds as though you 'aven't 'eard of such a fing.'

'Marriage?' retorted Shiner. 'Greatly overrated, Beat,' he assured her.

At that moment, the Guv'nor of the pub, George Beckwith, offered everyone in the bar a free drink to celebrate Nagger and Taff's forthcoming wedding. Shiner immediately collected two bitters – a half for Beattie, and a pint for himself. They had only just started to down them when the place suddenly erupted into a singsong, with Fred Gardner stomping out a string of current pub favourites on the old joanna, such as 'Daisy, Daisy', and 'Nellie Dean'. Most of Nagger's pals had a whale of a time, yelling their heads off and swaying back and forth to the music, and by the time they got to 'Knees up Muvver Brown', the place vibrated so much that the Guv'nor was beginning to think that his 'drinks on the house' was not such a good idea after all.

Shiner partnered Beattie in the knees-up, and she found herself enjoying herself for the first time since before she had Young Ed.

'Yer know somefin', Beat?' yelled Shiner, above the roar of the party. 'I still fancy yer!'

Beattie tried half-heartedly to push him away. 'I told yer, I've got an 'usband.'

'So wot?' called Shiner. 'I'm not fussy.'

Beattie wanted to show her disapproval, but she just had to laugh. 'If your brain was as big as yer mouff,' she yelled, 'you'd make a fortune!'

'That's not very friendly,' replied Shiner.

''Ow friendly should I get?' asked Beattie.

Shiner didn't wait to be asked again. He just grabbed hold of her, and kissed her full on the lips.

Beattie struggled to pull away, but just when she had managed to do so, he kissed her again. This time, she did not try to resist.

Nagger, who was hard in the middle of the knees-up, gave an approving smile, seeing what her old mate and Shiner were up to.

Beattie and Shiner didn't wait until throw-out

time. After saying their farewells and wishing Nagger and Taff their best for the future, they left the Albion and went back to Shiner's place in Leslie Street, just off 'the Cally'. They weren't bad digs, and Beattie was quite impressed to find that there was actually a lavatory on the landing halfway up the stairs. She hadn't anticipated having a fling with anyone that night, let alone Shiner, but now that she was there, she felt really good. At least somebody had shown that they wanted her, and that was something that hadn't happened to her in a long time.

As Ma Briggs was looking after Young Ed that evening, Beattie could only stay with Shiner for a couple of hours. During that time she hardly thought once about Jack Ridley. She was also relieved when, just before she left, Shiner became a little more forthcoming about the nature of his work. It appeared he had just got himself a job as a recruitment officer for some kind of new political group.

The name of the bloke who was trying to get it up and running, he said, was some geezer called Mosley.

Towards the end of August, Sarah put the shutters up at the windows of her beloved house in Thornhill Road for the last time. It wasn't easy for her to say goodbye to so many years of memories, and as she turned the key in the lock of the street door, her hands tingled and her whole body felt empty and lost. No matter how hard she tried, she would never be able to think of the house as anything but a friend, whom she was deserting in its time of need. But she refused to look back, for if she did, she knew that the tears would come, and this was something she had promised herself she would not do. In her mind it would be a betrayal of her mother and father.

A taxi was waiting for her in the road outside, for she had already decided that when she left her home for the last time, she wanted to go quietly and quickly. She had no wish to imagine what the new owner would be doing to the place, but she hoped they would be kind.

The Melford house in Thornhill Road deserved nothing less.

CHAPTER 15

Mrs Ranasinghe brushed her thick black hair in front of the mirror. The henna dye, which helped to disguise her grey streaks, was holding up well, and the special oil she used kept her hair soft and moist. Despite her age and disabilities, she was determined not to lose her dignity, and so every morning she was up early to do her ablutions before Sarah arrived to start her day's work. Unfortunately, the old lady's arthritis was now so debilitating that most days she had to have help to get dressed, but she still made quite sure that she changed into a different sari each day. Today was to be rather special, so she chose the pale blue silk one, trimmed with gold, which, after a great deal of effort, she managed to swathe around her body with immense elegance. However, her feet remained stubbornly bare, which was a habit she had brought with her from Ceylon many years before, and which she had resolutely continued ever since. She also resisted any kind of make-up, calling it simply 'a western fad, which will never last'. The truth was that her face was strong and dramatic without any kind of embellishment.

That morning, Sarah arrived a little earlier than usual. Now that she had moved into a ground-floor flat just a few doors away, there was no worry about her having to wait for hours in a bus queue. In many ways, the old lady felt quite guilty that when Sarah was forced to leave her family home, she didn't offer to let her have a room in her own house. After all, there was plenty of room in the place, for the house was laid out on three floors, and the only occupant was herself. But Mrs Ranasinghe had always been very set in her ways, and as much as she had come to love and admire her young companion, she wanted no one to share the house with her. It wasn't something she was proud of. In fact, when she thought of how many homeless people there were around these days, she felt positively guilty. None the less, she was her own person, and she felt she had to follow her own instincts and fears.

'Mrs Ranasinghe! You look beautiful!'

The moment Sarah walked into her bedsitting room, the old lady shimmered with pride. 'It's nothing,' she said, failing miserably to sound modest. 'In Ceylon we wear things like this every day of the week.'

'Yes, I know,' replied Sarah, crouching down in front of the wheelchair to admire what the old lady was wearing. 'But this is so special, so colourful. What's the material?' she asked, delicately touching the gold rim of the sari between her fingers.

The old lady stiffened. 'Pure silk, of course!' she replied, haughtily, her accent still thick even after so many years in England. 'It's woven in a very exclusive shop I know in Kandy, in the hill country.'

Sarah continued to admire the sari, and the fact that the old lady had managed to wrap it around on her own. 'It really is beautiful,' she said. 'I'm quite envious.'

'English girls should wear English clothes,' said the old lady, imperiously. 'A sari is for we natives from the East.'

Sarah wanted to chuckle, but thought better of it. In any case, she thought, the idea of her wearing a sari would be quite bizarre.

'I think it's about time I made you a cup of tea,' she said, getting up from her crouching position.

The old lady straightened herself up in her chair. 'I'll wait until we get next door,' she said.

'Next door?'

The old lady leaned forward, and looked rather stern. 'It's over a week now since you moved into your flat,' she said. 'You still haven't invited me in.'

Sarah was taken by surprise. 'Goodness,' she said. 'I had no idea. Don't tell me you got dressed up just to pay me a visit?'

'Partly,' replied Mrs Ranasinghe. 'Partly not. As a matter of fact, I have one or two rather important things I want to discuss with you.'

A little later, Sarah was pushing the old lady in her wheelchair along the street outside. It was a fine summer's morning, and as they went, there were calls from the neighbours, such as ''Ello, ducks! You're lookin' rosy!' and 'You're lookin' marvellous, gel! Keep up the good work!' Mrs Ranasinghe waved back imperiously, like Queen Mary. She was very grateful that the people of Arthur Road appreciated her.

When they reached the rusty gate outside Sarah's new ground-floor flat, Sarah went ahead and opened the street door. Whilst she was doing so, Mrs Ranasinghe suddenly became hysterical when a ginger tomcat rushed past her feet. Sarah hurried back and quickly wheeled the old lady into the house. If there was one thing that was sure to give Mrs Ranasinghe nightmares, it was the sight of a cat. 'They should round them all up and drown them,' she had told Sarah on more than one occasion.

Sarah's bedsitter overlooked the street at the front, with the kitchen at the rear overlooking a small back garden. 'I'm going to try and plant a few roses,' she said, as she stood beside Mrs Ranasinghe, who was craning her head to look out at the garden through the kitchen window. 'But since I don't own the place, I don't really want to spend too much.'

The old lady agreed.

As the front room and the kitchen were all joined together as one, Sarah was able to make the tea whilst still talking to her employer. Mrs Ranasinghe liked the room, because it was very similar in shape and size to her own. But by her expression, she showed very clearly that she disapproved of the modern wallpaper design, which Sarah had inherited from the previous tenant, and which was a complete contrast to the old lady's plain white walls. However, she did approve of the few personal belongings Sarah had managed to bring with her from Thornhill Road, particularly the small round polished table, which was covered with a clean pastel lemon tablecloth, a couple of red velvet-covered dining chairs, and Sarah's own single brass-rail bedstead. The old lady's hawklike eyes soon picked out the framed family photographs on the mantelpiece above the small tiled-surround fireplace.

'Was *that* your mother?' she asked, rather jealously, pointing to a small oval-framed sepia photograph.

'Yes it was,' answered Sarah.

'Let me see.'

Sarah brought the photograph across to her.

The old lady studied it. 'Yes,' she said, looking back and forth from the photograph to Sarah. 'I can see the resemblance – the same rigid expression, same nose, that pale complexion. Yes – *very* English.'

Sarah stiffened. 'What's wrong with that?' she asked indignantly.

'Don't be stupid, girl!' retorted the old lady, pushing the photograph back at her. 'That was meant to be a compliment.'

'Oh, I see,' Sarah said humbly. 'Thank you.' Although she had been working for Mrs Ranasinghe now for over eleven years, she still often wondered what went on beneath that beautiful swath of dyed black hair.

'Was she a good mother?' asked the old lady.

'I've told you so many times,' replied Sarah. 'She was the best mother any daughter could ever have.'

The old lady grunted, and wheeled herself to the kitchen part of the room at the back. 'I'm a terrible mother,' she said. 'Always have been.'

'I'm sure that's not true,' said Sarah, preparing two cups and saucers for tea.

'Oh yes it is,' insisted the old lady. 'What would you say if your mother had walked out on you and the family, and ended up on the other side of the world?' She didn't wait for Sarah to answer. 'It was wrong. I was too busy thinking of myself. I had a responsibility to my two daughters, and I deserted them.' She began to light up one of her Capstan cigarettes in her long, thin holder.

'I think you're being too hard on yourself,' Sarah said.

Mrs Ranasinghe took a puff of her cigarette, and, as usual, coughed as she exhaled. 'No,' she said, shaking her head. 'I was wrong to leave them. My poor Michael, my dear husband. He must be turning in his grave.' She stared forlornly at her lap. Then she suddenly looked up. 'Did you know he died exactly twenty years ago today?'

'Today?' Sarah asked. 'Really?'

The old lady nodded. 'Now you know why I'm all togged up like this,' she said, her expression proud but not sad. 'It's a celebration of a life that was rich and wonderful.'

Sarah went to her, and gave her a hug.

'And now for the bad news,' Mrs Ranasinghe said. 'That letter you brought in from the postman yesterday, it was from my daughter, Marla. She's on her way over to see me.'

Sarah's face lit up. 'Mrs Ranasinghe!' she exclaimed. 'That's wonderful!'

'I doubt it,' returned the old lady. 'But since I wrote to her and asked her to come, I have to put up with it.'

'You asked her?'

The old lady put the cigarette holder into her

mouth, turned her chair, and wheeled it back into the bedsitting room. Sarah followed her. 'I'd been thinking about asking her for a long time, ever since that doctor came to see me about my varicose veins. He said it was about time I started to think of putting my house in order.'

Sarah was puzzled. 'I don't understand,' she said. 'What does he mean?'

'He means that I'm not getting any younger, and I should be prepared if anything – should happen to me.'

Sarah was outraged. 'What nonsense! That doctor! How dare he say such a thing? He doesn't know what he's talking about!'

Mrs Ranasinghe smiled wryly. 'Perhaps,' she said, with that twinkle in her eye that told Sarah she was enjoying herself. 'But there are certain things I want done when I'm gone, and I want to make quite sure Marla does them.' With the cigarette holder clenched firmly between her teeth, she took a sly look at Sarah. 'And that's where you come in.'

'Yes?'

'I intend to tell Marla that if – when – something happens to me, I want to make quite sure that you are taken care of.'

Sarah turned away. 'I don't want to hear you talk like this,' she said dismissively. 'You have many years ahead of you–'

The old lady's determined voice carried loud and clear across the room. 'I intend to make quite sure that you are taken care of. And that's final!'

Sarah refused to listen. She went straight to the

hob, removed the kettle which was boiling there, and briskly poured hot water into her mother's teapot. She couldn't bear to hear the old lady talking like this. Time enough to discuss such things when they happened, but not now, not when the old lady was still alive and fully alert. Just like her own mother, she said to herself, always planning and plotting things, so wretchedly practical. But then it occurred to her why she was feeling so upset. In the eleven years she had been working for this extraordinary old lady, she had actually grown fond of her. It seemed impossible to feel such warmth for someone whose background was so different in every way from her own, a woman from the other side of the world, who wore strange clothes, dyed her hair, and smoked cigarettes through a long holder. And yet, here she was, feeling in some strange, inexplicable way as close to this peculiar old woman as if she were her own mother.

'All this is quite unnecessary, Mrs Ranasinghe,' she said quite forcefully. 'I really am quite capable of taking care of myself.'

'That is the precise reason why I want to help you,' sniffed the old lady, on the verge of becoming tetchy. 'Oh, don't worry, I have no intention of telling you how. You'll have to wait for that until you hear from my solicitor, and *that,* by the will and grace of Lord Buddha, won't be until after my ashes have blown away in the wind.'

The soup queue outside the People's Mission Hall in Upper Street was longer than it had ever been. For most, it meant a wait of almost an hour just to get a bowl of chicken broth and a lump of bread, and by the time the poor wretches at the end of the queue had reached the front, more times than not, supplies had run out, which often resulted in riots and fist-fighting. With unemployment now at an all-time record, people in the street were beginning to wonder whether it had been worth winning the war, for ever since 1918, the country seemed to have entered one recession after another. In the soup queues up and down the country, neither the Conservative Government of Stanley Baldwin, nor the succeeding Labour Government of Ramsay MacDonald offered any real help to those who were starving; they firmly believed that politics were for the rich and middle classes, not for the poor.

After waiting in the sweltering heat of a late September afternoon, Jack Ridley collected his pathetic lump of bread and mug of lukewarm chicken broth, and took it as far away from the queue as possible. He eventually settled down on some church steps, just around the corner in Almeida Street. He ate the meal, or whatever it was, as though he hadn't eaten for days, which, considering he hadn't been home for nearly a week, was more than likely. Then he took the empty chipped mug and pumped himself some water from the well just alongside a trough used by local cart horses. Although he was supposed to return the mug to the Mission Hall, once he had drunk down the water, he merely tossed it into the trough and left it floating there, until it finally filled with water laced with dead insects, and disappeared beneath the surface.

'You look like a bloke who could do wiv a decent meal.'

Ridley didn't have to look to see who was talking to him. It was 'Ritz' Cooligan, one of the Dillon boys, a gang of former criminals who knocked around the Bunk. Ritz, who got his name after being sent down for eighteen months for a breaking and entering job at the Ritz Hotel in Piccadilly, was, at the age of twenty-four, already a hardened criminal, whose main aim in life was to make sure he never reformed.

'I never eat wiv strange men,' replied Ridley, dourly. He took the remains of a dog-end from behind his ear, shoved it into his mouth, and stretched out his hand to Ritz.

Ritz automatically handed him a book of matches. 'That's a pity, mate,' he said. ''Cos I know 'ow yer can afford a slap-up meal of yer choice.'

Ridley lit his dog-end, blew out the match, and tossed it on to the pavement. 'Oh yeah?' he replied, with just a passing glance.

Ritz moved closer and, making quite sure no one was watching them, said, 'Sedgwick's. They've got a lock-up round the back.'

'Sedgwick's?' said Ridley, sceptically. 'It's a candle factory.'

Ritz grinned. 'A bit more than that, mate,' he said, 'from wot *I* 'ear.' He leaned closer. 'Sounds ter me like they keep more than candles in their lock-up – at least fifty crates of 'igh-quality booze *I* was told – Johnnie Walker's whisky.'

Ridley's eyes lit up. ''Ow much?'

'It's worf a bob or two.'

''Ow much in it fer *me,* yer knuckle 'ead?'

'Depends wot we can get under the counter,' replied Ritz, keeping a close watch all around as he talked. 'We'll cut it five ways.'

'Who else is in on it?'

'The usual. Me an' the boys. Wot d'yer say?'

Ridley thought for a moment. 'Depends.'

'On wot?'

''Ow yer intend ter get in.'

'Piece of cake,' replied Ritz, confidently. 'Mind you, we could use a bit of inside 'elp.'

'Meanin''?'

Ritz took a deep breath before he answered. 'Your missus works there, don't she?'

Ridley stiffened. 'No way!'

'All she needs to do is make sure the door's left open after work hours.'

Ridley pulled the dog-end out of his mouth, and threw it down hard on to the pavement. 'I said – no way!' he snapped, grinding the dog-end angrily into the ground with his boot.

'OK, OK! Keep yer 'air on!' pleaded Ritz, backing away a step or two, the palms of his hands held up as if to protect himself. 'I was just tryin' ter fink of a way ter make fings a bit easy for us.'

'Then forget about Beat,' Ridley growled angrily. 'She ain't fer sale.'

Ritz shrugged his shoulders apologetically, then waited a moment until he was quite sure Ridley wasn't going to hit him.

As they stood there, two small kids came

running up to them, as though they were racing to see who could get there first. One was a boy, the other a girl, and both were dressed in tattered clothes, and looking more filthy than the pavement itself.

'Got a fag, mister?' asked the boy, cheekily.

'One each,' added the girl.

'Bugger off!' roared Ridley, raising the back of his hand as though he was about to lash out at them.

The two kids turned on their heels and ran for their lives, calling 'Stupid sod!' and 'Fat arse!' as they went. At the corner of the road, they even had enough gall to stop and make as many obscene gestures at Ridley as they could think of.

Ridley watched them go, but his anger quickly turned to apathy and frustration. Is this really where we've come to? he asked himself. This lousy, rotten world is turnin' us all into a bunch of bloody loonies! For Chrissake, how are we expected to survive without food in our stomachs and money in our pockets? 'Right!' he said, suddenly turning back to Ritz. 'I'm in. But no Beattie. Is that clear?'

Once again, Ritz held up his hands. 'Anyfin' yer say, Jack,' he sniffed. 'Anyfin' yer say.' Then he added, 'In any case, I agree wiv yer. It wouldn't be right ter bring Beat in on somefin' like this – oh no. I reckon she's got quite enuff ter keep her occupied as it is.'

Mick Wilson, the street lamplighter, had only just left the Bunk. He was late tonight, for he had had quite a lot of trouble with at least two or three of the gaslamps along the road, which were not working because someone had smashed the glass plates around the mantles. Mick didn't want to hang around in the dark for long; he knew the Bunk only too well, and if he didn't get out soon, he might not get out at all.

The moment Mick had scurried off into Seven Sisters Road, the Bunk fell into an eerie silence. The whole place looked as though it had died, and any moment now, great apparitions would spiral up from the sewers below, float across the rooftops, and gradually slither down the chimneypots. And yet there *was* life, if only the dancing shadows cast by that same faltering gas mantle right opposite the house where Beattie, Ed, and Ma Briggs lived.

Amongst the shadows that night was one that actually moved without the help of that faltering gas mantle. It was a tall, elongated human image, that emerged from behind a front garden wall, where it had been hiding since twilight. Only now, as the thick darkness of night took over, did the image dare to move into the false white glare of that flickering gaslamp.

Jack Ridley's face was taut and grim. As he slowly crossed the road, his eyes remained firmly fixed on the upstairs window where Beattie and Young Ed were, or should be, fast asleep. The room, on the second floor, was in darkness.

Ridley quietly let himself into the house using his own front door key. He closed the door behind him as softly as he had entered. As always, the only sounds he could hear were the distant snores of Ma Briggs, who slept in a back room on the ground floor. He knew only too well that even if the roof fell in, the old girl would probably sleep through it, so he had no worries about disturbing her.

Helped by a distorted filter of light beaming through the two frosted glass panels on the front door, Ridley slowly and silently found his way to the foot of the stairs and made his way up. As always, different smells competed with each other, from the remains of the gas from the extinguished wall lamp, to the pork trotters that had been boiling earlier in the kitchen, and finally to the pungent smell of the DDT disinfectant, which was helping to combat the nightly invasion of cockroaches.

It was only when he got to the first-floor landing that he heard a sound. He knew it wasn't old Rogers, Ma Briggs' new lodger on that floor, for he usually worked a night shift at the PO sorting office at Stroud Green. No, the sound he could hear, nothing more than a murmur at this stage, was coming from the upper floor.

Anyone who has ever tried to climb quietly up creaking stairs must know how impossible Ridley found it to make any progress without being discovered. None the less, he was gradually succeeding, and as he approached the final landing, the murmurs he heard earlier could be identified as two voices. Inch by inch, he crept his way towards the door of Beattie's room, then stopped, put his ear against the door, and listened. Beattie? Ed? He gently tried the door knob. The door was locked.

Without a moment's hesitation, he suddenly

threw all his weight against the door, and burst into the room. From inside came a shriek and a gasp.

For a moment, standing in the dark in the open doorway, Ridley's silhouette appeared as a terrifying, menacing unidentified shape. But then he lit a match and cast a narrow ray of light on to the bed where two figures were sitting up, huddled in shock together.

It was Beattie and Shiner.

'Oh my God – Jack!'

In the dark, Ridley rushed across the room, and lunged straight at Shiner. Grabbing him by the throat, he yelled, 'I'll give yer exactly one minute ter get out of this room!'

Ridley's reputation had gone before him for years, and Shiner knew that he was in no position to argue with such a roughneck bruiser as this. Saying nothing, the moment Ridley released him, he leaped out of bed, made for his clothes, which were piled up on a kitchen chair, and rushed to the door. Although Ridley couldn't see him, he knew that the bloke was stark naked.

The moment Shiner had left the room and rushed down the stairs, Beattie got up and tried to go after him. 'Shine!' she yelled. 'Don't go...!'

Ridley barged straight in front of her, and slammed the door back on to its broken lock.

'Who gave you the right?' shrieked Beattie. 'Who gave yer the bleedin' right ter come bargin' in 'ere...?'

Ridley smashed the back of his hand straight across her face. The blow sent her reeling to the floor.

As he reached down to feel for her, it was obvious that she too was naked.

Growling, sobbing, fighting for her breath, Beattie tried to slide away from him. But he caught hold of her hand, and dragged her back to him. 'Where's the boy?' he demanded.

'Yer can't touch 'im!' she yelled hysterically. ''E's wiv Ma! Yer can't touch 'im!'

Ridley dragged her up, turned her around, and pulled her arm up behind her. 'I'm goin' ter say this once, and once only,' he said quietly but menacingly.

Beattie tried to scream, but he clamped the palm of his hand over her mouth.

'Wot's goin' on?' yelled a voice from the bottom of the stairs. It was Ma Briggs, who was clearly not as heavy a sleeper as Ridley had imagined.

'Once, and once only,' Ridley repeated to Beattie, whom he now held in a vicelike grip. 'If I ever catch you wiv anuvver man, I'll kill the bleedin' pair of yer. Do I make myself clear, Mrs Ridley? Do I?'

CHAPTER 16

Eunice Dobson had two things in common with her friend, Sarah. She was in her mid-thirties, and she was still unmarried. In some ways this was a blessing in disguise for both women, for when they got together they were able to pour out their hearts to each other about their inability to find the right kind of person to settle down with. Eunice was the younger of the two by six days, a fact of which she never stopped reminding her friend. But in other ways, the two of them were chalk and cheese. For a start, Eunice had come from a middle-working-class family from St Paul's Road up at Highbury, as opposed to Sarah, who was *pure* middle class. Eunice was also tall and lanky so that she towered over Sarah even without her shoes on, and she wore more make-up each day than Sarah would wear in a month of Sundays. But what they did share was the same sense of humour, which sometimes caused raised eyebrows, especially when they went out shopping together, or to an amateur variety show in the Emmanuel Church Hall in Hornsey Road. When Eunice laughed out loud, heads turned, and Sarah spent most of her time trying to keep her quiet.

There was no doubt that ever since they'd met at a church dance a few years before, they had formed a close bond. In fact it had been Eunice who had drawn Sarah out of her shell, warning her that unless she forgot about the past and concentrated on the future, she would end up on her own, bitter and twisted for the rest of her life. Consequently, despite her previous determination never to walk out with a man again, Sarah had in fact managed to have 'flings' with three or four different chaps, most of whom, to her surprise, she quite liked. One of them, a young man called Blake Courtenay, worked as a marine underwriter at Lloyd's, in the City and, despite the severe economic recession in the country, he clearly earned enough to offer her a secure lifestyle. But there was one factor against Blake – he was too young for her, in fact several years younger than Sarah, and after her experience with Edward Lacey, she was not prepared to get mixed up with someone simply because of their good looks. Whatever happened, however, she remained as determined as ever not to give herself physically to anyone unless she was quite certain that it was for love.

At the beginning of October, Eunice concocted a plan for Sarah to meet Freddie Hamwell, a barber from Upper Street, who was a friend of her elder brother, Ernie. Freddie, who had become a widower after just two years of married life, was in his forties, and considered by nearly all who knew him to be a thoroughly lovely man. For Eunice, however, it was a tricky business bringing Sarah and Freddie together, for Sarah was getting wise to her friend's endless attempts at matchmaking. On one occasion, she had arranged an 'accidental' meeting between Sarah and the manager of a local piano workshop, but when they discovered that the man was a confirmed bachelor, who preferred the company of his young male friends, Eunice burst into so many gales of raucous laughter that she and Sarah had been forced into a hasty retreat. However, an opportunity did finally arise, when Eunice attempted an evening on which her brother and Freddie Hamwell would, coincidentally, go to the cinema together at the same time as Sarah and herself.

The queue outside the Blue Hall cinema in Upper Street stretched almost to the Islington Angel. After the rip-roaring success of Al Jolson's first feature-length talking picture, *The Jazz Singer,* everyone wanted to *hear* what was going on up there on the screen as well as to see, and the follow-up musical drama, *The Singing Fool,* again with the inimitable Jolson, was clearly going to be as big a sensation as its predecessor.

Despite the fact that Sarah had no idea what had been planned for her, she looked wonderful. Gone were the days when she dressed practically for a night out; these days, she wore dresses that were shapely, tight-fitting, cut just above the knee, and colourful. What's more she now made all her clothes herself on an old Singer sewing machine Mrs Ranasinghe had given her, and they were stitched to perfection.

'Let yourself go!' was Eunice's motto, and Sarah took her advice, for she had now put the past behind her, and had started to live her life for herself and not just for others.

'Goodness!' cried Eunice, as she and Sarah

arrived outside the cinema to find the long queue. As usual, it was a very badly acted reaction, for she knew very well that her brother, Ernie, and Freddie Hamwell were already queuing, and were very near the front. 'There's my brother!' she called unconvincingly. 'He'll get us in.'

As they quickly made their way to where the two men were standing in the queue, Sarah wasn't, at this point, quite sure whether it was a bit of luck, or yet another of Eunice's well-planned plots.

'Ernie!' squeaked Eunice, in that unmistakable high-pitched voice. 'How good of you to keep our places for us.'

The comment was clearly intended for the people queuing up behind rather than for Ernie, and they knew it. 'Get ter the back, mate!' growled one angry man, 'No pushin' in!' grunted one of two elderly women who had come straight from the fish stall in Chapel Market, and smelled to high heaven.

'You'll pardon me,' said Eunice, haughtily, putting her arm through Sarah's, 'but my friend here is just getting over a very *nasty* illness, and my brother and his friend very kindly offered to queue up for us until we got here.' She turned to her bewildered brother. 'Isn't that right, dear?'

Ernie dutifully nodded his head. He'd gone through all this kind of thing with his sister before.

Sarah didn't know where to look. All she knew was that from this moment on, she had to act as though she was near death's door.

As far as Eunice was concerned, no more explanations to the rest of the queue was necessary. So she immediately turned to her brother's friend. 'Hello, Freddie!' she squealed, all wide-eyed innocence. 'What a lovely surprise to see you here.'

Freddie Hamwell was a pleasant, if not particularly handsome man. He sported a small dark brown moustache beneath a small nose, and because he was a bit short-sighted, it was difficult to see the colour of his eyes behind his thick, metal-framed spectacles.

'Nice ter see yer again, Eunice,' he said, raising his trilby politely.

Eunice hardly allowed him to finish. 'This is my friend, Sarah,' she said gushingly, whilst practically pushing Sarah straight into his arms. 'Sarah. This is Freddie Hamwell.'

The barber raised his hat again, and offered his hand. 'Pleased ter meet yer, miss.'

Sarah smiled back, and shook hands. 'Hello, Mr Hamwell,' she said dutifully. Now perfectly aware that all this was yet another of Eunice's plots, she tried not to meet the barber's eyes for too long. But in the fraction of a second that she did, she thought that he looked quite ordinary – very ordinary in fact. He had beautiful manners, though, and she was impressed to see that he treated going to the pictures as an occasion, for he was dressed in a three-piece brown suit, with a gold watch and chain in his waistcoat pocket, and brown shoes that were well polished.

Eunice's manipulation of the queue worked wonders, and the shilling front-row seats in the circle they managed to get were certainly the best in the cinema. Ernie was furious when Eunice quietly insisted that he pay for them. Eunice immediately made sure that Sarah and Freddie sat next to each other, whilst poor Ernie was made to sit next to his sister, which meant being apart from his own best mate.

The Blue Hall, which some insisted was the first cinema in the country, had a beautiful Victorian auditorium, with a cream and gold décor. Tonight it was thick with cigarette smoke, for the audience from the previous two performances had hardly had time to clear before the place was filled again. Ernie smoked, but although Freddie usually smoked a pipe, this evening he merely kept it unlit in his mouth. To Eunice's dismay, all during the commercial slides, not a word passed between Sarah and the barber. But hope came at the final moment, when just as the lights were going down, Freddie asked Sarah, ''Ave yer seen a talkin' picture before, Miss Sarah?'

'Yes, I have,' replied Sarah, brightly. 'Eunice and I came to see *The Jazz Singer.*'

The barber drew breath, like a cat hissing. 'T'rrific, wasn't it?' he said. 'D'yer know, I saw it five times. Cried like a bloomin' baby, I did.'

Sarah smiled back bravely. 'Yes. It was quite sad, wasn't it?'

Eunice listened to this fascinating conversation, convinced that she had finally found the perfect match for her best friend. As the auditorium was finally plunged into darkness, she crossed her fingers tight and hoped for the best.

The Singing Fool turned out to be just as much

of a tear-jerker as its predecessor, and by the time Al Jolson came on to sing 'Sonny Boy' in that famous full-throated, powerful voice, there wasn't a dry eye in the house. Inevitably, the barber dabbed his eyes too, at the same time holding out a bag of sweets to Sarah. 'Bull's-eye?' he croaked. Sarah declined graciously, and did her best not to laugh. Eunice was unable to take one either. She was far too busy sobbing her heart out.

In the Angel pub after the picture show, Eunice tried to consolidate what she considered to be a good evening's matchmaking. 'Freddie's got a lovely barber shop just up the road,' she said eagerly. 'You must show it to her some time, Freddie.'

'Any time,' replied the barber directly to Sarah. 'It'll 'ave ter be outside workin' hours, though,' he added. 'I don't allow ladies in durin' the day, except when they bring in their youngsters.'

'Oh?' Sarah said, with raised eyebrows. 'And why's that?'

'A barber shop is a gentleman's sanctuary,' replied Freddie, rather stiffly. 'Ladies 'ave their own establishments fer 'airdressin'.'

Sarah's reaction was quite uppity. 'With respect, Mr Hamwell, that's absolute tosh.'

Eunice was quick to step in. 'Oh, I don't know, Sarah,' she said quickly. 'Men have all sorts of things in a barber shop that women shouldn't know about.'

'Really?' she asked mischievously. 'What kind of things?'

'Oh, don't be silly, Sarah,' Eunice replied,

trying hard to keep her voice low. '*You* know.'

Ernie, who was already on his second pint of bitter, was nodding his head furiously. 'A woman's place is in the home, I always say,' was his contribution. 'I mean, just look at that suffragette woman, the one that threw herself under the King's horse.'

Sarah swung around with a start. 'What about her?' she asked, tersely.

'Bleedin' loony, that one,' insisted Ernie.

'Because she fought for something she believed in?'

Ernie was beginning to get riled. ''Cos she was a woman. Women've got no right to a say in how the country's run. That's a man's job.'

'Do you think a man has a right to a say in how his child is brought up?' asked Sarah, who was clearly in a combative mood.

'You'll fergive my sayin', Miss Sarah,' interrupted the barber, almost apologetically, 'but surely that's an entirely diff'rent question.'

'Is it?' retorted Sarah, swinging her attention back to him. 'But if a woman has a child who happens to be a boy, part of her is inside that boy when it grows up. What I'm saying is that a boy is influenced as much by his mother as by his father.'

Eunice was getting really worried now. This was not how she had imagined her matchmaking efforts would turn out. 'I don't vote meself,' she said, quickly trying to change the subject. 'I couldn't care less who runs the country.'

'Well, you should care, Eunice,' said Sarah, scoldingly. 'How could we bring down a corrupt government if we didn't exercise our right to vote?'

'That sounds a bit left wing, if you ask me,' sniffed Ernie, downing the last of his second pint of bitter.

'It has nothing to do with left or right wing, Ernie,' Sarah snapped. 'What we're talking about here is equality.'

The barber puffed on his pipe and said, 'Well, I still won't allow women ter come inter my shop – equality or no equality.'

For a brief moment, Sarah remained silent, then she smiled at the barber and said, 'That, Mr Hamwell, is your loss.'

Eunice slumped back in her chair. Once again, her matchmaking efforts had failed – miserably.

Beattie poured herself a large glass of Johnnie Walker whisky. For most of her life, she had carefully avoided alcohol because she just didn't like the taste, but these days, it was different. She could see no future for herself, so she could see no harm in taking an occasional glass of the hard stuff to dull the hopelessness. She still didn't like the taste, but the more she drank, the more she grew used to it – it helped her to forget things, to forget what a mess her life was in. It also helped her to cope with Jack Ridley, whose vicious threat still rang in her mind. She had no doubt, no doubt at all, that he *would* kill her if he found her with another man. Many a time in the last few weeks she had told herself that if it hadn't been for Young Ed, she would have done the job for him. Thank God for Sedgwick's, she reckoned, and their under-the-counter discount whisky trade. Easy to nick, even for an amateur like her.

'You goin' ter go on boozin' all night?' asked Ed, as he watched his mother pour her second glass of whisky.

'If I do,' she replied, already beginning to slur her words, 'I shan't ask *your* permission – mate!'

Ed was squatting on his mattress on the floor, trying to read one of the books he had borrowed from his Aunt Sarah. But with his mother sipping booze and slamming around the place like a caged animal all the time, it wasn't easy. In fact, she had been hard to handle ever since the night Ridley had come home late and beat her up. She still had an unhealed cut above the eye, which clearly depressed her every time she had a wash and looked at herself in the mirror. At his young age, Ed had gone through many rough nights with Ridley living in the same room, but on that occasion, when Ridley had found his mum with Shiner, it had been like a nightmare.

'It's not fair, yer know,' he said, getting up from his mattress and going across to his mother. 'I'm not old enuff ter 'ave an old woman who's pissed every night.'

Beattie looked up from the table, where she was trying without success to wind some wool on her hands. 'Don't use language like that on me,' she said firmly, but slurring. 'I don't like it.'

Ed stood beside her at the table. 'Why won't yer tell me wot it's all about?' he asked. 'Maybe I could 'elp.'

Beattie gave a dismissive laugh. Her face was blotched, and puffed. 'Kids can't 'elp no one,' she replied. 'They only take. They never give.'

'If it's money you're worried about, I could get a newsround job. That shop in Fonthill Road's lookin' fer someone.'

'Ferget it.'

'They pay two or free bob a week. I'd give it all ter you.'

Beattie slammed down her tangled wool on the table. 'I said ferget it! Don't worry – you won't starve!'

The boy looked quite hurt. 'That's not wot I meant,' he said. He drew closer, but this time stood behind her looking at the back of her head. He could see several grey hairs there, which seemed wrong in a woman who was still only in her early thirties. For those few precious moments, he felt sorry for her. Suddenly he felt angry, really angry. His mother's life, and ultimately his own as well, was being torn apart by a man who couldn't care one twopenny-ha'penny for anything or anyone. 'Why don't yer just kick 'im out?' he asked.

Beattie slowly turned to look at him. It wasn't easy to focus. 'Wot're yer talkin' about?'

'Jack. We don't need 'im. Yer should kick 'im out.'

Beattie got up quickly from her chair, knocking it over as she did so. Without warning, she slapped the boy across the face. 'Don't you say fings like that ter me,' she barked, wavering back and forth shakily on her feet. 'Don't you *ever* say fings like that ter me, d'er 'ear? Jack Ridley's your farver, an' 'e deserves respect. I don't want to ever 'ear you talkin' about 'im like that again!'

When his mother's hand struck him, Ed hardly flinched. His response was to look back at her with a mixture of cold anger and pity. Then he turned, moved away from her, and flopped down on his stomach on the mattress. He could hear the bedsprings as his mother climbed on to her bed. He tried to imagine what she was thinking, whether she regretted what she had just done. He tried to persuade himself that he didn't care – didn't care about his mother, and didn't care whether she lived or died. But that was hardly true, for the pillow on which he was resting his face was wet with tears.

CHAPTER 17

Sarah was none too pleased when her front doorbell rang at seven in the morning. Now that the long winter nights were setting in, she found it hard to get up at the best of times. Also, it was still dark outside and as her flat was freezing cold, the moment she got out of bed she quickly had to put on her warm fleece-lined dressing gown, which her mother had given her as a Christmas present soon after the war. She was halfway to the front door when the bell sounded impatiently again, and as she opened the door and peered outside, she was astonished to see a small, frozen figure on the doorstep.

'Ed!' she gasped, pulling the door wide open to let her young nephew in. 'What on earth are you doing here so early in the morning?'

The boy, trying to warm his hands under his arms, marched straight in. 'Got ter see yer,' he said, his teeth chattering with the cold. 'It's urgent.'

Sarah feared the worst. Putting her arm around his shoulders, she led him into her sitting room. 'Is it your mother?' she asked. 'Is she ill?'

The boy blew into his hands to warm them. 'I just want ter talk to yer,' he said.

Sarah quickly retrieved a box of matches from the mantelpiece, and lit the gas fire. 'Come and warm yourself,' she said, bringing the boy forward so that he could crouch on the rug in front of the fireplace. 'Would you like a nice hot cup of tea?'

'Don't drink tea,' replied Ed, warming his hands.

'I know what I'll make you,' she said busily. 'How about a cup of cocoa? That'll soon get rid of the cold. Just let me go and get the milk.'

Ed shrugged his shoulders.

Sarah disappeared for a moment, to collect the morning delivery of milk from her doorstep. When she returned, she made straight for the kitchen at the far end of the room, where she poured some milk into a saucepan. 'You poor thing,' she said, as she lit the gas. 'You must be frozen, walking all the way here in this weather.'

The boy, now huddled up in front of the fire, didn't reply.

'What's happened, Ed?' she asked, whilst mixing cocoa in two cups.

Ed stared into the fire as he replied. 'Mum's on the booze,' he said.

Sarah stopped what she was doing, and joined him. 'She doesn't drink alcohol,' she said. 'At least, she never used to.'

'Well, she does now,' he replied impassively, his eyes still focused on the fire.

It was pure luck that Beattie managed to wake up in time to go to work. Most mornings she got up around seven, had a wash, and a piece of bread and marge and a mug of tea for breakfast, then, after getting dressed, took a leisurely stroll to Sedgwick's candle factory, which was no more than five or six minutes' walk away. But just lately, things were different. These days, after a heavy night's drinking, she failed to wake up until there was only just enough time to get her clothes on and rush to work.

This morning, when she eased herself out of bed, it was no surprise for her to realise that she was still wearing her day clothes. She couldn't remember much about what had happened the evening before. All she knew was that it felt like someone had thumped her over the head with a sledgehammer. 'Go downstairs an' get the milk, Ed,' she called, rubbing her eyes and without actually looking to see if the boy was still lying in. When she eventually did manage to focus, the first thing she noticed was that the boy was not on his mattress. Her immediate reaction was to go to the door, open it, and call out, 'Ed! You down there?' There was no reply, so she called again. 'Ed? Can yer 'ear me?'

The reply from the bottom of the stairs came from Mrs Briggs. ''E's gorn out, Beat!' she bellowed. 'Went first fing.'

'Where'd 'e go?' yelled Beattie.

''Aven't the faintest,' called Ma. ''E does wot 'e likes, that boy. In an' out like a dose of salts.'

Beattie heard Ma go back into her parlour and slam the door behind her. She closed her own door, and made her way to the washstand. It was only when she began to revive herself by dousing her face in cold water that it all came back to her.

The evening before, she had had yet another interminable bust-up with Ed. She remembered how, when he criticised her for her boozing, she went for him and accused him of being just as worthless as his real father. Oh God, what a shouting match! She looked at herself in the mirror above the washstand, water running down her cheeks, and couldn't recognise herself. Is this what I've become? she asked herself. How could she bring up a child, and let him see her like this? In that one moment of reflection, she decided that something had to be done. When the boy came home, she would tell him that from now on, things were going to change, that she would never touch booze again as long as she lived, and that she would start being a real mother to him. A new leaf, that's what it was going to be. At least she was lucky to have a job in times like this. At least there was *some* money coming in.

A few minutes later, she was on her way to work. Somehow, the day looked brighter than she had expected, even though there was no sun, and the sky was full of the usual dark grey clouds. Yes, as far as Beattie was concerned, this was going to be a new beginning: no more rows with Ed, no more Jack Ridley, no more booze. Last night had been the turning point. From now on, she had the chance to start all over again.

When she arrived at Sedgwick's to clock in, she found the foreman, Charlie Pearson, waiting to talk with her. Five minutes later, she was out on the street again. She had been given the sack for continuous bad time-keeping.

Sarah and Ed were sipping hot cocoa together, he squatting on the rug in front of the gas fire, and she sitting in the armchair at his side. In profile, she could see the shape of his young face, the slightly jutting jaw, pallid complexion, and ears that were more protruding than his father's. Sarah found it difficult to take in that this was Beattie's boy. A few years ago, she wanted to know nothing about the child that had ruined her future, but it was a strange act of fate that had brought the two of them together. The youngster had, for whatever reason, discovered in his aunt someone he could talk to, someone who could help him to sort out his problem. And in him, she recognised an enquiring mind, a thirst for knowledge, which, in her opinion, was at least a ray of hope for a boy with his limited education and traumatic upbringing.

'Try to remember, Ed,' she said, as they both stared into the red glow of the gas fire. 'When was the first time you noticed she was drinking?'

Ed had his hands wrapped around the cup of cocoa to keep warm. 'Soon after *'e* found 'er wiv this bloke.'

Sarah lowered her eyes.

The boy suddenly turned to her. 'Ridley. 'E come 'ome in the middle of the night. I was downstairs wiv Ma, but I 'eard 'im bashin' the daylights out of 'er. If I'd've bin up there, I'd've killed 'im!'

Sarah felt herself tense inside. She could now envisage the whole situation. 'You said a few minutes ago that you hardly ever see your – you hardly ever see Jack Ridley?'

Ed looked back into the fire. 'Never see 'im, not from one week to anuvver. Then 'e suddenly walks in an' expects everyone to go runnin' after 'im.'

Sarah drained the last of her cocoa, got up, and put it on the small coffee table nearby. 'Does he have a job, Ed?' she asked.

'Who – Ridley? Ha! Don't make me larf!' The boy had a rim of cocoa around his mouth. 'The only job *'e* ever does is breakin' an' enterin'.'

Sarah paused a moment, then turned back to him. 'Then how does your mother manage about money?'

'She don't,' he said bluntly, wiping his mouth on the back of his hand. 'We're broke.'

Sarah took the empty cup from him. 'Then how does she manage to buy alcohol?'

Again, the boy grinned. 'Nicks it, don't she?' he said. 'From up where she works. They don't only sell candles, I can tell yer.'

Sarah put the cup on the table, went to the window, and pulled back the heavy wooden shutters. It was now light outside, and when she pulled back the lace curtain she could see the pavement on the other side of the road glistening with early morning frost. 'I don't really know what to say to you, Ed,' she said with a sigh.

'Come an' see 'er,' the boy replied immediately.

Sarah did a double take. 'What do you mean?'

'If yer talked to 'er, she might stop drinkin'. She might try an' pull 'erself tergevver. She'd listen ter you.'

Sarah shook her head. 'I doubt that, Ed,' she replied. 'Your mother and I haven't really talked properly to each other in a very long time.'

'Yer could try.'

Those pale blue eyes of his were so appealing, and yet so vulnerable, and it didn't seem natural to Sarah that a boy of his age should have dark rings beneath those eyes. 'I wish I could help you, Ed,' she said, 'but it wouldn't be right. You see, your mother and I don't see eye to eye with each other, and if I interfered, I might end up doing more harm than good.'

'If anyone could 'elp Mum, it's *you.*'

'What makes you think that?' Sarah asked, surprised.

''Cos you 'elp me,' Ed answered immediately. 'Yer talk ter me about books an' fings.'

'That's not help in the way you mean it, Ed,' Sarah replied. 'When we talk about a book, I'm merely sharing with you what I've got out of it myself. In that way, we can both learn an awful lot.'

'I learn much more from books than goin' ter school,' said the boy, now sitting cross-legged on the rug in front of her. 'I don't mean about addin' up, an' fings like that. I mean about 'ow people do fings, and why. When I read about the people who run the country, I get really angry.'

Quite unexpectedly, this brought a smile to Sarah's face. 'Reading is not only about people who run the country, Ed,' she said, slightly teasing. 'It's about letting someone transport you to a world you may never know. It's about getting away from the harsh reality of life.'

'That's wot I mean,' said the boy. 'If you could talk ter Mum like that, if you could make 'er believe it, fings'd get better.'

Sarah looked hard at him. She couldn't believe

that she was only talking to an eleven-year-old boy. But having a conversation like this with Ed was one thing, having the same thing with his mother was quite another.

Jack Ridley met up with Ritz Coogan and the Dillon boys in the Highbury Tavern, a seedy pub halfway between Finsbury Park and Highbury Grove. Nobody in their right mind set foot in the place after six in the evening, for the Tavern had a reputation for being the watering hole for some of the most hardened criminals in the neighbourhood. 'Snare' Riley, the pug-nosed Irish landlord, encouraged this type of clientele, for whenever they did a job, he usually got a cut for providing the right kind of cover. The cover tonight for the Dillon boys was Snare's back parlour.

'The week before Christmas. It'll be perfect timin', 'cos the place'll be jam full of booze for the 'oliday.' Charlie Dillon was not only the eldest of the three brothers, he was also the brains behind most of their jobs. There wasn't much of a resemblance between him and his two brothers, Phil and Joe, except that he dressed as though he was a City stockbroker, whilst the younger men stuck to flat caps and dungarees.

'Do we know yet wot kind of booze they're floggin'?' asked Ritz, whose Weights fag had almost burned down to his lips. 'Last time I 'eard, they said it was mainly Johnnie Walker.'

Charlie sat back in his chair, with a pint of Truman's brown ale in his hand. 'Far as I know, most of it is,' he replied. 'But by Chris'mas, there'll probably be plenty of uvver stuff.'

'Yeah,' said his younger brother, Joe. 'The number-one problem is, 'ow do we get it out?'

Charlie turned to the middle brother, Phil.

'Leave that ter me,' said Phil. 'I've got a Morris van. Once we've got into the place, I can back it through the rear yard.'

'Be a bit noisy, won't it?' warned Ritz.

'It'll be the middle of the night,' said Charlie. 'There's only one bloke on watch. We'll take care of 'im.'

Ritz looked a bit uneasy.

'So where do I come in?' asked Ridley.

'Good question, Jack,' replied the sharply dressed Charlie.

'We need some muscle,' said Joe. 'The way it's lookin', we're goin' ter 'ave ter move about an 'undred crates.'

'An 'undred!' gasped Ridley. ''Ow long's it goin' ter take us ter do that?'

The three brothers exchanged a knowing look. 'It can't take longer than fifteen minutes, Jack,' said Charlie.

'Maximum,' said Phil.

Ridley thought about this for a moment, and drew on his fag. This was the first time he'd worked with the Dillon boys, and he wasn't at all sure. Charlie Dillon had already done two years for a pretty heavy-handed break-in at Samuel's, the jeweller's shop in Holloway Road, in which an assistant was badly injured. Petty larceny was one thing, a violent break-in was something quite different. 'Wot about the law?'

'The fuzz?' asked Joe. 'They couldn't care less

what goes on around the Bunk. If they know wot's good fer them, they'll keep their noses clean.'

'Wot about Big Ben?' Ritz reminded them. ''Is nose can sniff out somefin' goin' on a mile away. I wouldn't want ter come up against *that* fifteen stone of fat in the dark,' he moaned, nervously gulping down the remains of his whisky.

'Don't underestimate Ben Fodder,' said Ridley, with a rare show of unease. 'That flatfoot's bin my shadow fer years. 'E's just waitin' fer a chance to send me down.'

Charlie smiled gently at Ridley. He didn't like him, he'd never liked him, but he was right for this job, because he was desperate for money. And anyone who was desperate for money would be willing to take chances. 'Yer know somefin', Jack?' he said, putting his arm round Ridley's shoulder, and giving him an insincere hug. 'Yer worry too much. There's a lot in this fer you, fer all of us. All you've got ter do is ter trust us. Savvy?'

Ridley stubbed out his fag in an ashtray, and looked up at his new boss. Oh yes, he savvied all right. But he certainly didn't trust him.

Beattie left the labour exchange in Seven Sisters Road, and slowly made her way back home. It had been an agonising morning. First, the shock of getting the sack from that short-arsed little squirt at Sedgwick's, Charlie Pearson, and then hours of queuing up at the labour exchange to see if there was a job – any job – she could do that would keep her and Ed going until something better came along. There had been nothing for her.

Try as she may, she could not erase the deep feeling of bitterness she felt, not only for Charlie Pearson, but for just about every living person in the world. Only a few hours before, it seemed as though she was going to get a new lease of life, but suddenly, everything had collapsed around her. She was beside herself. Where would she get the money to pay Ma Briggs for her digs? Where was the money coming from to buy enough food just to keep her and Ed going for the next few days? It was an impossible situation, and, for the time being at least, she hadn't the faintest idea how she was going to cope.

'Yer've got a visitor,' announced Ma Briggs, the moment Beattie came through the front door. 'It's yer sister, Sarah.'

Beattie did a double take. 'Sarah – 'ere?'

'Young Ed brought 'er 'ome wiv 'im,' said the old girl, as Beattie left her and hurried up the stairs. 'I told 'im ter make 'er a cuppa tea!'

When she got to the top-floor landing, Beattie found the door to her room open. Inside, Sarah was at the kitchen table, sipping the cup of tea Ed had made. 'Wot you doin' 'ere?' Beattie said unceremoniously.

Sarah stood up immediately to greet her. 'Hello, Beattie,' she said awkwardly.

'I asked Aunt Sarah ter come and see yer,' said Ed, also getting up. 'She said I ought ter ask you first, but I said yer wouldn't mind.'

'Did yer?' Beattie snapped, practically slamming the door behind her. 'Well next time – *ask.*'

The boy looked crushed, and Sarah went to put her arm around his shoulders. 'I'm sorry, Beattie,' she said. 'I told him it wouldn't be right–'

'Sit down and finish yer tea,' Beattie said, taking off her coat and hat, and hanging them behind the door.

Sarah exchanged an anxious glance with Ed, who begged her to sit down at the table again.

'So,' said Beattie, coming across. 'Wot's this all about?'

Sarah hesitated before answering, 'I wanted to see you, Beattie. It's been some time. I wanted to see – how you're getting on.'

'Why this sudden interest?'

'Mum!' protested Ed.

'I didn't ask *you!*' said Beattie, turning on him.

Already Sarah realised that it had been a mistake to come, though she'd wanted to help Beattie because the boy had asked her to. 'Ed tells me you've been having a bad time just lately.'

Beattie glared at the boy. 'Did 'e now?' Then, turning to Sarah, she quipped, 'Everyone's 'avin' a bad time. Ain't you 'eard?' She pulled back the chair that Ed had vacated for her, and sat down facing Sarah across the table. 'I lost me job terday.'

Ed gasped. 'Mum!'

'I'm sorry, Beattie,' Sarah said, dismayed.

'I asked fer it,' said Beattie, eyes focused on the table. 'I've bin goin' in late every mornin' fer weeks.' She looked up. 'Yer learn lessons the 'ard way.'

Sarah asked her, 'How will you manage?'

'Manage?' replied Beattie. She shrugged her shoulders. 'Why?'

'I'd like to help.'

Beattie narrowed her eyes suspiciously. ''Elp? Why should you 'elp *me?*'

'I don't know,' replied Sarah, nonchalantly. 'Perhaps it's because you're my sister.'

Beattie smiled wryly at her. 'And *'ow* would you intend to 'elp me, Sarah?' she asked.

Sarah thought for a moment. 'I could let you have some money. Not very much. But it might tide you over until things improve.'

Beattie tossed her head back and laughed. 'Improve!' she spluttered. 'That's a good one, that is!'

Ed couldn't bear to hear the way his mum was talking. 'Look, Mum,' he said. 'I asked Aunt Sarah ter come an' see yer 'cos she can fink straight. She can tell us some way we can get out of 'ere.'

'Get out of 'ere? Wot d'yer mean, get out of 'ere? This is our 'ome. This is where we live. Just fink yerself bleedin' lucky yer've got a roof over yer 'ead, and food in yer stomach...' The words stuck in her throat, for at that moment she broke down.

Sarah immediately got up from her seat, and signalled to Ed to leave them alone. 'Beattie,' she said, tentatively putting her arms around Beattie's shoulders.

Beattie immediately stood up, went to the window, turned her back, and wiped her tears away with her hands.

Ed made as though he wanted to stay, but again Sarah signalled to him to leave the room, which he finally did.

Sarah waited a moment, then went across to Beattie. But this time she didn't attempt to touch her. 'Beattie,' she said quietly and without emotion. 'Let's for just a few minutes try to forget who we are, or where we came from. Let's try to pretend that we're two strangers who know absolutely nothing about each other.' She moved closer, so that she was now standing alongside Beattie, both of them looking out of the window into the street below. 'If we know nothing about each other, then we can be totally objective. What I mean is, we have no past to look back on, no memories of bad times together. It means that we can do things for each other without the past hanging around our necks.' She paused a moment before continuing, 'You know, Mother used to say that if you and I could only find time to stand still occasionally, and find out what each other actually looks like, we'd get on so much better.'

She slowly turned to look at her sister. Beattie also turned. Both stared hard at each other, Beattie with tears still glistening in her eyes, and Sarah trying desperately hard to elicit some kind of feeling from her.

It lasted only a brief moment, for Beattie suddenly broke away and went to sit on the edge of the bed. 'Why *did* yer come 'ere, Sarah?' she asked, taking out a small handkerchief from her dress pocket, and dabbing her eyes with it. 'Was it to 'elp me, or was it ter prove that you was right, and I was wrong?'

Realising that she was wasting her time, Sarah went back to pick up her gloves, then made for the door, but she stopped when Beattie called to her.

'Ed belongs ter me, Sarah – ter me, an' 'is farver. I'll never let yer take 'im away from me – never. I may not be the perfect muvver, but as long as I've got blood in me veins, I'll go on doin' me best for 'im.'

Sarah waited no longer. As she left, Beattie called out to her. 'Keep away from 'im, Sarah! Keep away from boaf of us!'

CHAPTER 18

Freddie Hamwell wiped the remnants of shaving foam from old Arthur's cheeks, and finished off the haircut and shave by puffing some talcum powder on to his customer's neck. This immediately caused the old boy to sneeze, and he was relieved when Freddie removed the towel from around his shoulders, so that he could lever himself up from the heavy leather-covered barber's chair. Freddie prided himself that he gave one of the smoothest shaves in Islington, mainly because he used the same cutthroat razor and strap that his late father had used during his long career as a gents' barber. Once the old boy was on his feet, Freddie used a small clothes brush to remove the surplus grey hairs from his tattered jacket. 'That'll be a tanner, please, Arfur,' he called. He had practically to shout into the old boy's left ear because he was as deaf as a post.

'A tanner!' protested Arthur, with a thunderous look. 'Don't nuffin' get cheaper round this place? 'Ighway bleedin' robbery, that's wot it is!'

Freddie grinned. He was used to the old boy's protest, for he made it every time he came in, which was usually once a month.

Arthur dug deep into his trouser pocket, came up with a handful of change, sorted through it as though it was all he had in the world, and handed over the sixpenny coin. ''Ighway bleedin' robbery!' he repeated grudgingly.

''Urry up, Granddad!' called a small boy from one of the seats lined up along the wall behind. 'I'm gettin' fed up 'angin' round 'ere.'

Arthur turned with a start, and growled back at the boy. 'Oy! Who d'yer fink *you're* talkin' to, 'Arry? You just keep yer tongue between yer teef, or I'll get yer dad on yer!'

Freddie laughed, as he put the old boy's tanner into his till. 'Next customer, if you please!' he called.

Harry, Arthur's eight-year-old grandson, got up from his seat, tugged at his braces, and went across to the big chair his granddad had just vacated. He was so small that Freddie had to lift him up into it.

'Wot'll it be terday, then, young man? Short back an' sides?'

The old boy answered for him. ''Is mum's asked fer the puddin' basin,' he rasped. 'Straight line all round.'

'Puddin' basin it is!' replied Freddie, tucking a towel into the boy's shirt neck.

Young Harry groaned and resigned himself to his fate.

Using comb and scissors, Freddie battled to untangle the snotty-nosed kid's blond locks. When he was satisfied that he had made progress, he collected a small porcelain pudding basin from a cupboard beneath the sink, and plonked it on to the child's head.

'Owch!' protested Harry. 'That 'urt!'

'Not 'alf so much as if I wallop yer!' called his granddad, flat cap on his head, and now settling back to read a copy of the *Daily Mirror* whilst he waited.

It was when Freddie got to the point where he was able to use his cutthroat razor on the line of hair beneath the pudding basin that he suddenly heard someone tapping on the shop window. He couldn't believe his eyes when he recognised Sarah peering in and waving. He immediately rushed out to meet her.

'Miss Sarah!' he exclaimed, beaming.

'Hello, Mr Hamwell,' she returned, with a courteous but awkward smile. 'I hope I'm not disturbing you.'

'Not at all!' he replied instantly. 'Please, come in!'

'Oh no,' replied Sarah, holding up her hands in polite refusal. 'I wouldn't want to embarrass your customers.'

'You could never do that, Miss Sarah. Please come in ... no, I insist!'

Reluctantly, Sarah allowed him to lead her into the shop.

'Blimey!' protested Arthur. 'A woman! Wot's the world comin' to?'

'It's all right, Arfur,' Freddie quickly explained. 'Miss Sarah's a friend of mine.'

'Oy!' called a small voice from the barber's chair. ''Ow much longer do I 'ave ter sit wiv this fing on me 'ead?'

'Comin'! Comin', 'Arry!' Freddie was now dithering between Sarah and his outraged young customer. 'Take a seat, Miss Sarah. I'll be wiv yer in just a tick.'

Sarah did as she was told, and sat in a chair at

the side of Arthur.

The old boy glared at her, grunted, and moved on to the next chair along.

Whilst she waited, Sarah was like a child in a toy shop. Everything around was so new to her, so different from Martha's Ladies' Hairdressers in Caledonian Road, which she had visited regularly for so many years. There were two huge barber's chairs that swivelled around to enable Freddie to reach every hair of his customers' heads, an assortment of shaving brushes, sticks, and lethal-looking razors, and colourful displays that ran down the sides of the mirrors, advertising everything from Wright's Coal Tar Soap and Player's Navy Cut cigarettes, to Doctor William's Rejuvenating Hair Lotion. She also noticed a small certain small wall cabinet, which had an intriguing notice pinned on the door, marked 'FOR GENTLEMEN'. She imagined that this was what Eunice meant when she'd said, 'Men have all sorts of things in a barber shop that women shouldn't know about.'

Much to young Harry's relief, it took Freddie no more than a few minutes to finish off the kid's pudding-basin trim.

'There you are, young man,' announced the barber. 'You wait till yer gelfriend sees yer now!'

Harry treated Freddie's joke with complete contempt, waited for the towel to be removed from his shoulders, then jumped down from the chair.

''Ow much?' sniffed the kid's grandfather, rising from his seat, again dipping into his pocket for some coins. 'Five nicker fer kids, I s'ppose.'

Freddie laughed and wiped his hands on the towel. ''Ave this one on the 'ouse, Arfur,' he replied.

The old boy glared at him. 'Oh no yer don't!' he growled indignantly. 'I don't need no 'andouts just 'cos yer lady friend's wiv yer.' He sorted out a couple of penny coins, and practically pushed them into Freddie's hand. 'Twopence!' he cried. 'An' that includes yer tip!' He turned, and made for the door. 'Come on you!' he called to his grandson.

Freddie quickly went ahead of him, and opened the shop door.

Arthur gave Sarah a scathing look as he passed. 'Next fing yer know, they'll be 'avin' lady barbers!'

He marched out of the shop, closely followed by the kid with his brand-new pudding-basin haircut, who acknowledged no one as he went.

Freddie closed the door behind him. 'I'm sorry about that,' he said, turning back to Sarah. 'Old Arfur's a bit of a ranter when 'e wants ter be.'

'I'm the one who should apologise,' said Sarah, rising from her chair. 'It's just that I happened to be in Upper Street, and I remembered Eunice had said that your shop was in St Alban's Place–'

'Oh no,' said Freddie, quickly. 'No need ter apologise ter me. I'm really glad yer popped in.'

Sarah felt a bit embarrassed. 'What I mean is, I came to apologise for my behaviour the other evening – when we were in the public house with Eunice and Ernie.'

Freddie was puzzled.

'It was very rude of me to criticise you for not

encouraging the opposite sex into your shop. Everyone has the right to make their own rules and regulations. I was extremely foolish.'

'Miss Sarah,' returned Freddie, who was clearly taken aback, 'there was nothing rude about your behaviour. Quite the reverse, in fact. I was the one who should've known better – I'm getting too set in me ways. I s'ppose I 'ave me dad ter blame fer that. 'E was very strict about keepin' ladies out of men's establishments.'

Sarah smiled gratefully at him. She wasn't going to let on that she had made the journey from the Nag's Head to Upper Street not by chance, but because she had a natural instinct to know about something that was denied her. But now that she was here, she was pleasantly surprised, not only by the shop, but by the barber himself. He somehow seemed different from when she had last seen him, not nearly so ordinary. In fact, whilst she had been watching him work on young Harry's pudding-basin trim, she had noticed what a fine head of hair he had himself. Whilst she had been talking to him in the pub, he had never once taken off his hat, so she was unable to see that his hair was dark brown with a neat quiff at the front, and a parting that was clear and straight enough to have been drawn. His moustache was also much thinner than she remembered, which made him, in her eyes, much more attractive. Attractive? As she had watched him at work, she pondered on this. Yes, she had to admit that, in a strange way, he *did* have quite a pleasant face, not nearly as ordinary as she had at first imagined.

'So, can I tempt you, Miss Sarah?'

The barber's voice brought her out of her momentary trance with a start. 'I – I beg your pardon?' she said nervously.

'I asked yer if yer'd care fer a cuppa tea,' said Freddie, apparently repeating the question she had not heard. 'It won't take a jiff ter boil the kettle.'

Saturday morning down the Bunk was a time when most of the young kids and teenage gangs would just hang around on the street, trying to work out what mischief they could get up to next. Weekends, however, were not popular with the people who lived in the neighbourhood, for it usually meant that fights broke out between rival gangs, or someone had fun throwing a milk bottle through a neighbour's window, or, for some really enjoyable entertainment, a stray cat or dog was tied to a railing whilst brave youngsters taunted it.

On this particular Sunday morning, Young Ed was with one of the only mates he had anything in common with, a boy called Mick Cantor. The two of them spent most of their time aimlessly kicking an old corned beef tin up and down the kerb, much to the anger of a young unmarried woman in Number 27, who'd been trying to get her new baby off to sleep all morning. Ed's only reaction was to put two fingers up at the woman and yell obscenities back at her, and as he was something of a hero in his mate's eyes, Mick did likewise. What they hadn't noticed, however, was the approach of Constable Big Ben Fodder, who had Ed by the scruff of his neck before the boy had time to turn.

'Right then!' proclaimed the burly fuzz. 'I fink we've 'ad quite enuff of that, fank you, young man!'

'Get orff! Leave me alone!' yelled Ed, who, despite kicking and punching, hadn't a chance in hell of breaking loose from the firm grip around his neck. 'Mick!' he called. 'Get 'im orff!'

Mick, however, had other plans. He had already run for his life down the street, and disappeared into Seven Sisters Road.

''Old on now, old son, 'old on!' said Big Ben, as he finally brought Young Ed under control. 'This is no way ter be'ave in front of yer visitor.'

Ed pulled himself away, and glared. 'You get away from me!' he growled. 'You got no right–' He stopped dead. He had not noticed that someone was standing with the constable.

'Hello, Edward,' said the tall, well-dressed stranger. 'That *is* your name, isn't it?'

'No, it ain't!' snarled the boy. 'It's Ed!'

The stranger resisted the temptation to move closer to the boy, just in case he ended up with a black eye. 'But you *do* have another name?' he said. 'A family name?'

Rubbing his neck after Big Ben's heavy-handed grip, the boy snapped back, 'Wot's it to yer, mate?'

'No lip now!' warned the constable. 'Answer the gent's question.'

The boy hesitated, then answered cockily, 'Melford. You can call me *Mister* Melford!'

The stranger exchanged a bemused smile with Big Ben. 'And where would I find your mother,

Mister Melford?' he asked.

'She's at work.'

Big Ben butted in. 'She don't work at Sedgwick's no more.'

The boy sniffed dismissively at him. 'Know everyfin', don't yer? Well, she's got a different job now. A much better one.'

'And where is that, Edward?' asked the stranger.

The boy's bottom lip stiffened obstinately. 'Mind yer own!' he growled. 'I ain't tellin' *you* nuffin'!'

Beattie hated sweeping up the tunnel. She had done it five times during the past week, and every time she did it she felt sick from the smell of urine. But at least she had a job, even if it was only working part time as a temporary cleaner with London Transport. The tunnel in question was part of the entrance to Finsbury Park underground station, and was a popular haunt for drunks, who used it as a short cut from Seven Sisters Road to Wells Terrace, at the rear of the station. During the week or so that she had been there, she had seen two rats scampering along the stone floor, several cockroaches crawling over some discarded apple cores, and a long line of black ants marching in regiment down the white-tiled walls. It was a pathetic way to earn a few bob a week, she kept telling herself, but something was better than nothing at all.

Being a Saturday morning, the tube was busy with passengers going into the West End for the day to spend what little money the recession had left them for Christmas shopping, whilst others turned up for a half-day of work in offices, cafés, and shops in nearby Seven Sisters and Blackstock Roads. In other words, if there had been anyone she knew who was amongst the passing crowd of passengers, she wouldn't have noticed them. But she saw Ed the moment he came running down the tunnel from the Wells Terrace entrance.

'Mum!' he called several times, as Beattie strained to see his silhouette flanked by so many others against the daylight streaming in from the far end of the dimly lit tunnel.

'Ed?' she called, her voice echoing and bouncing off the walls. 'Wot yer doin'?'

The boy finally reached her. He was out of breath. 'This bloke wants ter talk to yer,' he said, very agitated.

'Hello, Mrs Melford,' the stranger said, as he approached. But when he offered to shake hands with Beattie, she pulled back.

'Wos this all about?' she rasped. 'Who're you?'

'My name is Johnson,' said the lanky stranger, who towered above her. 'I'm from a law firm who represent the late Lieutenant-Commander Lacey.'

Beattie wiped her face with the back of her hand. She looked bewildered. 'Who?' she croaked. But then she suddenly remembered. *'Him!'*

'Is there someone a little more private – where we can talk?' asked Mr Johnson.

'This is as private as I ever get,' Beattie replied wryly. 'Did you say "late"?' she asked. ''As

Edward's old man snuffed it then?'

Johnson's expression became funereal. 'Yes,' he replied. 'I'm afraid he has. Just over a month ago.'

'Good riddance!' was Beattie's response. She never had any time for the old ratbag, and she showed it.

All three were now caught up in the crowd who had just come streaming up the stairs from a newly arrived train.

Johnson waited for them to clear before talking again. 'I'm sorry you feel that way, Mrs Melford,' he said, 'because your son is a beneficiary of the late Lieutenant-Commander's will.'

'Oh yes, I know all that. A few bob when 'e gets ter twenty-one – right? An' stop callin' me Mrs Melford. Melford was me maiden name. Take it or leave it, me name's Ridley now.'

This was unexpected news for the law man. 'Oh, I see. You mean, you married again?'

Beattie gave a dismissive laugh. 'I was never married in the first place.'

As they stood there, one of the regular tube tramps came up to them. On his threadbare army tunic he wore a row of war medals. 'Anyone got a fag?' he asked with a chesty wheeze.

'Bugger off!' snapped Beattie.

Mr Johnson dug deep into his inside jacket pocket, took out a packet of cigarettes, pulled one out, and gave it to the man. The man took the fag, shoved it in his mouth without attempting to light it and, with an appreciative salute, scurried off. 'Do I take it then,' continued the law man to Beattie, 'that your financial situation is somewhat improved since you last saw the

Lieutenant-Commander?'

Beattie roared out loud, her voice echoing along the tunnel. 'Oh yes, mate! Looks like it, don't it?'

Johnson was becoming increasingly ill at ease. 'Well, my instructions from the Lieutenant-Commander's executors are that you be notified of one of the codicils made by him just prior to his death.'

Now it was Beattie's turn to look baffled. 'Come again?'

The law man continued. 'As you know, some years ago our client notified you of his intention to bequeath a certain amount of money to your son, but not, as you rightly indicated, until he had attained the age of twenty-one.'

Beattie grunted.

'However,' continued Mr Johnson, who was eager to relieve himself of his duties as promptly as possible, 'our client decided that, if the period of time between him passing and the twenty-first birthday of your son should be in excess of five years, an interim sum should be paid to you for the continuation of his education and general welfare.'

Beattie was still not quite sure what the law man was going on about, but her eyes widened when she saw him unclip the leather briefcase he was carrying, and take out a long, buff-coloured envelope.

'You will find here a letter of intent, Mrs – er – Ridley,' said Johnson, very formally, handing her the envelope.

Before taking it, Beattie leaned her broom

against the wall and wiped her hands on her coat. 'Wos it all about then?' she asked tentatively.

With the conclusion of his business close at hand, Johnson was already doing up the buttons of his overcoat. 'It gives you formal notice,' he said, 'that a cheque in the sum of one hundred pounds will be forwarded to you by post within seven calendar days of this meeting.'

Beattie's heart was thumping hard. Clasping the envelope to her chest, for once in her life, she was at a loss for words.

'Do you have any questions, Mrs – Ridley?' asked the law man.

Beattie was too stunned to answer. She merely shook her head.

'If by any chance you do not receive this bequest during the time stated,' Johnson added, 'please contact me at the address on my business card.' He gave her the card, which he had already taken from his briefcase. 'I am there most days of the week, Monday to Friday.' He clipped up his briefcase again, and offered his hand to Beattie.

This time, Beattie shook hands with him eagerly.

'I'll bid you good morning,' said the redoubtable Mr Johnson. And turning to Ed with a wry smile, he said, 'And to you too, Edw– young man.' With that, he made his way back out of the tunnel.

'Is it true, Mum?' Ed asked. 'Are we really gettin' an 'undred quid?'

Beattie was still speechless. All she could do was to lean against the tunnel wall, look at the boy, and marvel at the way fate had decided to give them another chance in life, especially whilst they were stuck right here – in the middle of a urine-stinking tunnel.

It had been several days since Sarah had seen Freddie Hamwell. During her visit to his shop, she firmly believed that it would be the last time she would ever set foot in the place, but try as she may she couldn't get him out of her mind. Yes, she had heard several times from Eunice what a pleasant and kind man he was, and she certainly didn't doubt that. What she hadn't appreciated, however, was what an interesting person he was, for during that hour following young Harry's pudding-basin haircut, when, unusually, not another customer came into the barber's shop, she and Freddie had talked over a whole range of subjects from the negligence of the present Labour Government, to the heated subject of raising the school-leaving age to fifteen.

Gradually their talk turned to more personal matters, and Sarah was sad to hear how Freddie had lost his wife to a rare blood disease after only two years of married life. He also had much more of a sense of humour than she had at first imagined, especially when he poked fun at himself by referring to his shop as 'Sweeney Todd's of Upper Street'. By the time they parted, she found she had promised to go out with him.

It was therefore a pleasant surprise when she arrived home one day from shopping to find a note from Mrs Ranasinghe pushed through her letterbox, informing her that a young man had called to see her, and that he would be returning that evening around eight.

With only a couple of hours to spare before Freddie was due to arrive, Sarah bustled around, tidying her small flat so much that, in her estimation, it was fit enough even for the King and Queen to visit. By a quarter to eight, she had changed into a long-sleeved navy-blue crushed-velvet dress, with a solitary small rhinestone in the shape of a cat pinned just below her left shoulder. She also brushed her hair back behind her ears, so that it was gathered together behind the head, and tied with a navy-blue ribbon to match her dress. As always, she wore only a minimum of make-up – a touch of pale red lipstick, a mere suggestion of face powder, and a very faint trace of eyeliner. She completed her outfit with a pair of half-heeled navy-blue suede shoes, which she'd bought herself for her birthday that year. By two minutes to eight, she was ready to entertain her caller.

The front street bell, however, did not ring until almost half-past. By that time, all her good thoughts about the barber were beginning to fade. But when she opened the street door, who was standing there but Jack Ridley.

''Ello, Sarah,' he said, even touching his cap. 'Long time no see.'

'What are you doing here, Mr Ridley?' she asked tersely.

'Din't your old gel tell yer I was comin'?' he asked quite innocently. 'She wrote a note for yer, got me ter put it fru yer letterbox.'

'What do you want, please?' was Sarah's curt response.

'Wanna chat wiv yer.'

'What about?'

'Ain't yer goin' to invite me in? I'm yer bruvver-in-law, remember?'

Sarah stared right through him for a moment, then reluctantly stood back to let him in. 'In there,' she said, closing the front door, and indicating the sitting room to him.

Ridley took his cap off, went in and looked around. 'Hm,' he commented with an approving nod. 'Not bad. Not bad at all.' He turned to look at her. 'Got *your* 'ead screwed on the right way, an' that's fer sure.'

'What do you want, Mr Ridley?' Sarah asked uncompromisingly.

'The first fing I'd like,' he said, 'is fer you ter stop callin' me Mister Ridley. I 'ave got an 'andle to my door, yer know.'

Sarah's refusal to respond was indication enough to Ridley that she had no intention of warming to him.

'I come ter speak to yer about Beat,' he said. 'She's bin goin' fru a rough time, did yer know?'

Sarah crossed her arms. 'My sister and I are not in contact,' she replied implacably.

Ridley sighed as though he were sorry. 'Yeah, I know,' he said. 'That's a real shame. 'Cos she's always goin' on about you.'

'Oh really?' replied Sarah, impassively.

'Oh yes. She reckons you ain't bin fair to 'er over the years. She reckons you've – misunderstood 'er.'

Sarah's arms were still crossed as she turned her back on him, and wandered off towards the fireplace. When she turned round to face him again, she was startled to see that he had sat down and made himself comfortable in her armchair.

'Mind if I smoke?' he asked mischievously.

'Get to the point, Mr Ridley,' Sarah replied, becoming irritated. 'I don't have the time to talk with you.'

Ridley took the fag from behind his ear and lit it, then looked around for an ashtray in which to deposit his matchstick. 'Yer know wot I fink?' he said. 'I fink it's about time you two got tergevver and sorted fings out. Your trouble is you're boaf so much like each uvver. Yer need yer 'eads bangin' tergevver.'

Sarah found an ashtray and put it in front of him. 'It's very touching that you appear to be so interested in the welfare of my sister and myself, but I can assure you that our differences are deep-rooted.'

Ridley took a puff of his fag and leaned back in the armchair. 'Yeah. I know wot yer mean,' he said. 'You've got so much more class than 'er.' He brought his head up suddenly. 'She's a whore, your sister. Did yer know?'

Sarah froze. 'I beg your pardon?' she said icily.

'I come back one night and she was in bed wiv this bloke. Broke me 'art, I can tell yer. I mean, if yer can't trust yer own wife, then who can yer trust?'

Sarah's response was instant. 'I suppose it depends on how good a husband you are yourself.'

Ridley smiled back at her knowingly, took a

puff of his fag, and got up. 'Well, when it comes down to it, I reckon life is fer livin'. Wot say you, Sarah?'

She just glared at him.

Ridley started to pace the room, giving the impression that he was interested in the place. 'You've got good taste, Sarah, anyone can see that. Worf a bob or two, some of this, eh?'

Sarah was watching his every movement, and when he came to stand in front of her, she refused to budge.

'I admire you, Sarah,' he said, looking directly into her eyes. 'I always 'ave. Yer know that, don't yer?'

'I think it's time you went,' she replied.

He stepped closer.

Sarah looked at him, and for one fleeting moment she could see why Beattie had been so devastated by him. His was quite simply a rugged, handsome face, a real man's face, that any woman would surely find hard to resist.

'Wot I like about you,' he continued, staring deep into her eyes, voice low, 'is yer've always been yer own person. Not like Beat. She's like a kid. No sense, no feelin'...' He leaned forward, and made as though he was about to kiss her.

'Is that why you beat her up, Mr Ridley?' Sarah asked, as cold as ice.

Ridley hesitated, and moving his attention from her lips to her eyes, replied with a grunt and a smile. 'See wot I mean?' he said.

Sarah turned, and moved away from him. 'A whore doesn't need to have sense or feeling, Mr Ridley,' she said. 'A whore is just there for her body. But I'm sure I'm not telling you something you don't already know.'

Ridley casually followed her across to where she had her back to the shuttered window. 'It's not only your body I want ter know, Sarah,' he said, close to her again. 'It's *this.*' He pointed to his own forehead.

If she hadn't known by this time what Ridley had come for, she certainly knew now. She allowed him to look deep into her eyes, and could smell the aroma from the cheap soap he had used, could see the bristles on his face and chin that, given the chance, could scratch her flesh. Desire swept through her, and for one moment she felt that this could be her chance to get her own back for all the heartache and misery Beattie had caused her. As Ridley pressed closer and closer towards her, she thought of Edward Lacey, and all that he had ever wanted from her, but never got. She thought of love, hate, fear – and treachery. The time had come, and now that she had got this far, she would not lose her chance.

Ridley was now close enough to kiss her, and he closed his eyes for the final assault.

Suddenly Sarah stepped out of his way and struck him a thunderous slap across the face. 'Get out!' she growled. 'Get out – now!'

After the force of the blow, which caught him completely off guard, Ridley took a moment to recover himself. Then he looked at her. His face was grim and full of menace.

Although Sarah was convinced that he would now do to her what he had done to Beattie, she stood her ground and refused to be intimidated.

'If you ever try to do that to me again, *Mister* Ridley,' she warned, 'I won't be responsible for the consequences.'

Ridley's expression slowly changed, and menace gradually dissolved into a broad grin. Without another word, he collected his cap, silently made for the door, and left.

As soon as Sarah heard him in the passage outside, she called out, 'My sister is not a whore. And don't you forget it!'

There was a moment's silence. Then she heard the street door open and close, then the iron gate outside.

Sarah stood in the middle of the room. She could still smell Ridley's cigarette burning in the ashtray. She went across and stubbed it out. Her whole body was shaking.

CHAPTER 19

Beattie saw her opportunity, and she was now determined to take it. The cheque for a hundred pounds that she had received from the estate of Edward Lacey's father meant that she could not only pay Ma back the five pounds she owed her for rent, but she had the chance to move out of the Bunk for ever. With Christmas now only a week away, this was going to be an occasion that she would never forget.

Once she had discovered the way to cash the cheque at a bank, Beattie set two pounds aside for Christmas presents for both Ed and Ma. For Ed she found a second-hand book about life amongst the peasants in Spain, plus a new pair of shoes, which he had never had in his life. For Ma she bought a pink cotton petticoat from a stall in Chapel Market, which she knew would give the old girl immense pleasure and bring a tear or two to her eyes. Then she put thirty shillings away to buy a chicken, some vegetables, a small Christmas pudding (from another stall in the market), and a pound of liquorice allsorts to round off what was clearly going to be a slap-up Christmas dinner.

But despite all the elation, there was still the little matter of Jack Ridley to face up to, for once he found out that she was in the money, he would be down on her like a ton of hot bricks. But –

how to keep it from him?

The solution came when Beattie heard of a place that was going in Mitford Road, which was just off Hornsey Road, a district that was several cuts above the Bunk. When she and Ed went to look it over, they found that it consisted of three rooms on the ground floor of a terraced house that hadn't been occupied since the death, two years before, of the elderly couple who had lived there. It even had an inside lavatory, and, at the rear, a small back yard with just enough room for a few potted flowers. Despite the fact that the property was clearly in need of a coat of paint and some plasterwork, Ed thought it would be like a dream come true if they could live in such luxury.

'Oh Mum, please let's live 'ere,' he pleaded. 'I promise yer won't 'ave no more trouble from me ever again!' Beattie needed no persuading, but knew only too well that everything would depend on how much she would have to pay for rent. To her astonishment, however, she discovered that the place, which was being handled by the Borough Council, was, owing to the recession, going for a snip at thirty shillings a week.

'You're goin' – ter move?'

Beattie hadn't intended to tell Ma about the place in Mitford Road until after Christmas. But, having lived so close to the old girl for so many years, and having relied on her kindness, she wanted to prepare her before the actual move.

'We're not goin' till the New Year, Ma,' said Beattie, only too aware of the anguish she would be causing the poor old soul. 'An' me an' Ed wouldn't even fink about doin' it unless we was sure that yer could come and see us whenever yer want.'

Ma was in her kitchen making Ed a bread pudding when she was told the news, and was too upset to reply. But she was determined to put a brave face on it. 'We all 'ave ter do wot's fer the best,' she replied. 'Yer've boaf got yer lives ahead of yer. Yer can't go round finkin' of old gels like me.' Beattie put her arm around her, but Ma was not giving way to sentiment. There was plenty of time for tears after they'd gone. Practical as ever, she asked, 'So wot yer goin' ter do about Jack, then?'

This brought Beattie down to earth. 'I don't want 'im ter know, Ma,' she said, with a look that told Ma what she already knew.

Ma, her hands covered with soaked stale bread, looked up at her. 'If an' when I see 'im, 'e won't 'ear nuffin' from me,' she said reassuringly. 'I'll tell 'im yer just upped one night and did a moonlight flit.'

Beattie sighed with relief. 'Fanks, Ma,' she said.

'Don't fank me too soon,' she warned, grim-faced. 'You know Jack. If 'e finks 'e's missin' out on somefin', as sure as God made little apples – 'e'll find yer!'

Jack Ridley and Ritz Coogan met up in the Ton O' Feathers pub in Stepney High Street. It wasn't one of their favourite 'houses', but, as it was well away from their normal neck of the woods, they were less conspicuous.

'It's all set fer ternight,' croaked Ritz, who was

sounding more chesty than ever after smoking too many of his rolled-up fags. 'Phil's got the van. If we play our cards right, we can pile the 'ole lot in the back.'

Both men were propped up with their pints on the end of the counter in the saloon bar, their backs turned to the other customers.

Ridley was shaking his head. 'I still say it's pushin' it ter get an 'undred crates of booze in the back of a van in fifteen minutes. If the fuzz get wind, we're done.'

As if to reassure him, Ritz put his hand on Ridley's arm. 'Look, Jack,' he said, voice low. 'This job's a cinch. We've got five pairs of 'ands ter pull it.'

'Yeah,' quipped Ridley, 'an' free knuckle 'eads ter make a piss-up.'

Ritz stiffened, and immediately looked over his shoulder, just in case any of the Dillon boys were around. 'Wot's up, Jack?' he asked. 'Don't yer trust Charlie?'

'Trust Charlie?' he said with a dismissive snort. 'Now yer *are* jokin'!' His face tensed. 'I wouldn't trust any of that lot ter take my missus on a day out ter Soufend.'

Somehow, this amused Ritz. 'Well if yer put it that way, Jack,' he croaked, with a grin, 'yer could 'ardly blame 'em, could yer?'

'Wot d'yer mean by that?'

Ritz shrugged his shoulders. 'Well, she's a good-looker, ain't she, your old woman?'

Ridley answered with a steely look in his eyes. 'I wouldn't know, Ritz,' he said. 'You obviously know more than I do.'

Ritz could have bitten his tongue. He'd known Ridley long enough to be wary of any comments about his private life. 'I din't mean nuffin', Jack,' he said defensively. 'It's just that I was finkin' 'ow useful she could've bin if we'd 'ad 'er in on this job. I mean, 'er workin' fer Sedgwick's on the inside an' all that.'

'Well, she ain't,' said Ridley, stubbing out his fag. 'So ferget 'er.'

'You're right, Jack, absolutely right,' said Ritz, eager to change the subject. 'Anyway, now she ain't there any more, it don't make no diff'rence.'

'Wot d'yer mean, she ain't there?'

Ritz looked surprised. 'Your missus,' he said. 'She's left Sedgwick's. Got the push fer bein' late, or so I 'eard. Got a job up Finsbury Park tube station. I fawt yer knew.'

Ridley thought about this for a moment, then drained his glass. 'I'm not interested,' he said acidly. 'Wot my missus gets up to is 'er own business. I've got far more important fings on me mind.'

Sarah had never been to a music hall before. When she and Beattie were young, they were only taken to places like museums or art galleries, which is what all middle-class children were expected to do. But what they were not encouraged to do was to visit places of entertainment that were, by and large, the preserve of the working classes. With this in mind, Freddie Hamwell decided to extend Sarah's education by taking her to Collins Music Hall on Islington Green, which was probably one of the most famous music halls in the country, maybe even the world.

It made no difference that during the week prior to Christmas, variety had given way to a thrilling melodrama entitled *Maria Marten or The Murder in the Red Barn,* for in one way, this was as much an entertainment as singers, jugglers, or even male impersonators. Starring Tod Slaughter, a great dramatic artist of his day, the story of a wicked squire who is haunted by the ghost of his pregnant mistress was ripely played, and brought chilling gasps from every audience.

Freddie sat through almost the entire performance with his eyes covered, but from the moment the curtain went up, Sarah was unconvinced by the whole thing, deciding that she had witnessed far more horror in real life than on the stage that night. What did enthral her, however, was the sheer magic of the theatre's ambience, rich in colour and atmosphere. She had never experienced anything quite like it, and tried to imagine what it would be like to be present during *Dick Whittington,* the pantomime that was due to take over from the ghostly Maria Marten on Boxing Day.

Sarah was surprised how much she had taken to the 'demon barber of Upper Street', which was Freddie's own light-hearted nickname for himself. Although she had met him just a few weeks before, she felt she had known him all her life. Apart from his gentle manner, she was utterly won over by his courtesy. There was hardly ever a time when he allowed her to cross a road without first making quite sure that the way was clear, and on more than one occasion, he had taken out his handkerchief in a public place to wipe a chair that Sarah was about to sit down on. She was also very impressed at the way he treated his young teenage assistant, Tinker, always taking the trouble to show the lads the tricks of the trade, and giving him the opportunity to wash the hair of selected customers. But Sarah's great revelation about herself was the fact that she was now virtually walking out with someone who was so very positively from the working class.

After all the thrills of Miss Marten and her Red Barn, Freddie took the plunge and asked Sarah whether, as it was a reasonably mild night, she might like to walk back home to Arthur Road rather than take the tram. He was overjoyed when she replied that there was nothing she would like better.

It was indeed a mild evening, and hard to believe that in a couple of weeks' time they would be entering another New Year.

As they made their way along the widest stretch of Upper Street, Freddie found himself taking all sorts of risks. 'Sarah,' he said daringly, 'I 'ave a confession ter make.'

Sarah laughed. 'Don't be silly, Freddie,' she teased. 'I'm not a Roman Catholic priest. You don't have to confess things to me.'

'Oh, but I do,' insisted Freddie, deadly serious. 'I want to.'

Sarah was suddenly quite worried. Confession? What? Was this meek and mild man now going to reveal all sorts of skeletons in his cupboard? Did he have a mistress who was just waiting to blackmail him, or perhaps he had an illegitimate child languishing in an orphanage somewhere. Her curiosity was now well and truly aroused. 'Then tell me, Freddie.'

The moment he had her attention, Freddie regretted it. But after a moment's deep thought, he finally plucked up enough courage to say, 'I once killed a man.'

Sarah brought them to a halt and turned to look directly at him. 'You – killed someone?'

Freddie nodded. This confession was clearly going to be painful. 'It happened during the war. When I was in the army.'

Sarah sighed with relief. 'In the army?' she said. 'You mean you killed one of the enemy?'

Freddie shook his head sadly. He was consumed with guilt and anguish. 'Me own best mate.'

Sarah clasped her hand to her mouth. Her initial relief was short-lived. 'You killed – one of your fellow soldiers?' she asked timidly.

'Executed 'im,' replied Freddie. ''E was up on a court martial for tryin' ter make a run fer it. They found 'im guilty, an' we 'ad ter shoot 'im.'

Sarah felt total despair for him. 'Oh, Freddie,' she said, clutching his arm. 'How terrible.'

''Course, it may not have bin my bullet,' he continued, 'but one of 'em was. 'E 'ad ter be blindfolded. Fank God 'e never saw me. But 'e knew I was there. Oh yes.'

For a moment, there was silence between them, until quite spontaneously, they started slowly to move on.

'I never forgave the army fer wot they did,' said

Freddie. 'Derek wasn't even eighteen. When 'e took the King's shillin', 'e lied about 'is age. But they still tied 'im to a post an' got us ter shoot 'im down. It was murder, Sarah, nuffin' short of cold-blooded murder. An' I was part of it.'

'It was a vile war, Freddie,' Sarah said comfortingly. 'One day, they'll realise what they've done. All we can hope is that it never happens again, neither the war nor the killings.'

Once they'd passed Highbury Corner, Sarah took the initiative and put her arm through his. Until that moment, they had merely walked side by side, like mere acquaintances, but as they slowly strolled together down the good old reliable Holloway Road, they behaved like two people who had known each other all their lives. The more Sarah thought about Freddie's heartfelt 'confession', the more she realised how close they were becoming, and in so short a time. It seemed as though, during their few outings together, Sarah had heard practically the whole of Freddie's life history. She'd been told about his early days as the son of a local barber, and a mother who doted on him because he was the only child she was capable of bearing. She heard about all sorts of people – aunts, uncles, gran and granddad, cousins (especially cousin Lil, who'd had an affair with a man more than twice her age), friends, neighbours, and customers. She loved the way he described them all, and the obvious affection he felt for his family. How sad then that she was unable to respond with tales of her own happy family life. Listening to the way Freddie talked only convinced her more and more of the gulf that seemed to exist between the classes.

When they finally turned into Arthur Road, most houses seemed to be plunged into darkness, for it was now very close to midnight, and the unusually mild evening was already showing signs of giving way to a frost. As they passed, Sarah pointed out to Freddie the house where she worked for Mrs Ranasinghe, and even now, it seemed impossible not to notice the exotic smell of hot spiced curry that was still seeping out through the front street door.

When they stopped outside the gate of where Sarah lived, she asked Freddie whether he would like to come in and have a drink or a cup of tea. The moment she had suggested it, she could hardly believe how forward she had been. *She* of all people, asking a *man* into her flat late at night! No matter how innocent the offer, it showed how far she had come since those unnatural days with Edward Lacey. Fortunately or not, Freddie declined the invitation, either because he was nervous of being accused of taking advantage of someone he had become very attached to, or because he was just plain prudish. Either way, he thanked her for her company, and in what Sarah thought to be a wonderfully old-fashioned gesture, he took hold of her hand, and gently kissed it. But the moment he looked up at her again, she leaned forward, put her hands on his shoulders, and gave him a firm, but proper kiss. Once again, her own rash act took even her by surprise. When she pulled away, she said, 'Forgive me, Freddie.'

Freddie hesitated not a moment longer. Pulling her back to him again, he gave her a firm, lingering kiss.

When it finally came to an end, they continued to embrace, Sarah with her head resting on his shoulder, the taste of his pipe tobacco still fresh on her lips.

'My dearest Sarah,' he whispered, his soft breath warming her ear. 'I want you to know that this is the most wonderful night of my life.'

Sarah, eyes closed, heard his delightful old-fashioned words, and smiled to herself brighter than she had done for such a long time. 'Would you believe it, Freddie,' she replied, holding him tight, 'it is for me too?'

Sedgwick's candle factory had been established in Fonthill Road for a good many years. Nobody seemed to know for exactly how long, but it was certainly there before the start of the Great War, during which time it did a brisk business, thanks to the endless cut in power supplies for gas lighting. The founder of the firm, a man by the name of Bertram Sedgwick, was said by those who worked for him in those early days to have been a good and fair boss, but when, after his death, the firm passed into the hands of a local wide boy named Ricky Mercer, wages were no better than slave labour, and the business, quite literally, fell apart. Consequently, Mercer began to deal in other forms of activity, such as the illegal sale of discount booze. Most of the people employed there knew something of this bizarre trade, or how it worked, for most of the merchandise was kept locked up in a warehouse at the back of the premises, and supervised only by a carefully selected band of thugs. However, the business of making candles continued, and, because the endless recession was hitting hard, the law turned a blind eye.

Nob Koshak was on watch that night. The boss trusted him, because he got double time not just for night work but for keeping his mouth shut. Koshak, formerly a Jewish *émigré* from Bohemia, spent most of his nights playing cards in the back room of the warehouse. He rarely ventured out, for his room had the luxury of a wood-burning grate, which kept the place beautifully warm and cosy. Koshak had never been known to sleep on the job, which was why he was so highly thought of by the boss, but he did have a tendency to help himself to the odd bottle of Johnnie Walker from the pile of crates stacked high in the warehouse, and it was not unknown for him to go off duty first thing in the morning weaving from side to side as he walked.

By the time Jack Ridley and Ritz Coogan arrived outside Sedgwick's rear entrance, Joe Dillon had already used a pair of strong wire cutters to force a hole through the protective mesh fence. The whole area was virtually in darkness, the only light coming from a distant public gaslamp in nearby Wells Terrace. Joe, the youngest of the three Dillons, had dressed for the occasion, everything black – sweater, jacket, trousers, and cap – which made his face look absurdly conspicuous whenever the moon decided to make a brief appearance.

'Charlie's already inside,' he whispered. 'By now 'e's done the watcher.'

Ritz swallowed nervously. The one thing he wasn't looking for on this job was rough and tumble.

'Wot about the van?' asked Ridley. ''E was s'pposed ter be 'ere before us.'

'Keep yer 'air on,' replied Joe. 'Phil's parked it in the cul-de-sac at the back. There's no point in bringin' it across till we get the stuff out.' He suddenly ducked out of sight. 'Wotch it!' he cracked. 'Someone comin'!'

Ridley and Ritz dropped to their knees and took refuge in the shadows. A dark figure came out through the rear door of the warehouse. Not until it approached the fence did they see that it was Charlie Dillon.

'Right!' he called, voice low. 'We're clear. Joe, tell Phil ter bring the van.' He suddenly caught sight of Ridley and Ritz. 'You two,' he snapped. 'Let's get goin'!'

Inside the warehouse, Ritz was relieved to see that, apart from being blindfolded, gagged, and hands and feet tied together, no real physical harm had come to Koshak.

Using his own flashlight, Ridley took a good look at the stacks of crates, each containing bottles of good-quality Johnnie Walker whisky. It was only when he lifted one of the crates that he realised how heavy it was. 'Fifteen minutes fer this lot?' he called, his voice so low it was straining to be heard. 'You're bleedin' loony!'

Ridley's comment irritated Charlie. 'You're bein' paid for yer muscles, Ridley,' he snapped, 'not yer brains!'

Ridley gritted his teeth; he wanted to smash Charlie's face in but he thought better of it, and went to meet the van as soon as he heard it pulling up at the rear door.

Within moments, the place was a hive of activity, with the beams from flashlights criss-crossing the dark roof and walls of the warehouse, and lighting the way for the frenzied convoy of crates being rushed into the Morris van at the rear door. Every so often, Charlie would shout in muted voice, 'Move it!' and it took every bit of brute force the five men could muster to do just that.

At the end of ten minutes, only half the crates were in the van, but the pace was visibly slowing. Ritz was fit to drop, and even the younger Dillon boys were feeling the strain.

But just as Charlie was trying to make the all-important decision whether to carry on moving as much of the stuff as possible, or to cut their losses and take what they had already, the whole place suddenly echoed to the sound of a voice booming from the yard outside: 'Stay where yer are! The 'ole lot of yer! You're under arrest!'

Everyone froze.

'It's Ben!' gasped Ridley.

'Christ!' croaked Ritz.

'Don't move!' ordered Charlie. 'There's too many of us. 'E can't take us all!'

Ritz was first to break. He made straight for the watcher's room at the rear of the factory, closely followed by Ridley.

Charlie and his brothers were less fearful. The

first thing they did was to arm themselves with anything they could lay their hands on. Joe ripped off a lump of wood from one of the crates, Phil found a long metal spanner in a tool box, but Charlie's vicious-looking crowbar was the most lethal weapon of all.

As all three made a dash out to the van, the sound of Big Ben's shrill police whistle pierced the night air.

'Stay where yer are!' Ben repeated. 'No one moves!' But by the time he had reached the van, the Dillon boys were already inside, with the doors locked.

The van moved off at speed, with Ben chasing after them. But the constable's heavy frame prevented him from keeping up with them, and his only recourse was to blow his whistle again and again.

Back inside the warehouse, Ridley and Ritz had succeeded in climbing through the window into the factory, where they were able to find a way out into Fonthill Road. Ritz was in a state of terror and confusion.

'Bloody fuzz!' he yelled.

'I told yer!' Ridley panted, as the two of them made off as fast as they could down the road. 'I told yer Ben'd be on to us!'

As they spoke, the Morris van came roaring out from the rear of the building, and with brakes screeching, skidded round the corner into Fonthill Road. Following laboriously on foot was Big Ben, still furiously blowing his police whistle.

The van picked up speed, and rapidly approached the corner of the Bunk. But Phil suddenly turned the steering wheel too sharply, and before anyone could do anything, the van skidded again, shook from side to side, and toppled over.

Whilst the three Dillon boys were scrambling out, Big Ben came puffing round the corner in hot pursuit. The worst hurt was Joe, who had blood streaming down the side of his face from a cut on his forehead, though Charlie and his younger brother, Phil, seemed to have escaped unreasonably unhurt. But when his two brothers started to make a dash for it, Charlie, flaming with anger, called them back. 'Stay where yer are!' he ordered.

'No, Charlie!' pleaded Joe. ''E's right be'ind us!'

'We've gotta get out of 'ere!' insisted Phil.

'I said – stay where you are!'

Charlie's voice boomed along the road, where faces were now beginning to peer behind the curtains of windows on both sides.

With the sound of Big Ben's boots rushing towards them, Charlie stood his ground. 'We can't let 'im get away wiv this!' growled the eldest, and most dangerous of the Dillon boys. ''E knows who we are. They'll root us out, an' they'll frow the book at us.'

'Charlie!' pleaded Joe.

'Let's go!' begged Phil.

Charlie refused to move. He glared angrily as the heavyweight flatfoot came charging along the road.

Within moments, Ben, truncheon drawn, and panting heavily, was upon them. But for a moment, he kept a wary distance. 'Done it this time, ain't yer, boys?' he called. 'Looks like you're not goin' ter enjoy yer Christmas this year, mates!'

Much to the disbelief of his brothers, Charlie strolled up quite fearlessly to the constable. 'Yer know somefin', Ben?' he said calmly. 'You're becomin' a bloody nuisance.'

'Really, Charlie?' replied Ben, with a satisfied grin. 'Well, I must say, I'm glad ter 'ear that.' He came forward slowly. 'Now please do me the honour of lyin' down flat on yer stomachs – all of yer!'

For a moment, nobody moved.

Charlie stared at him, a faint wry smile on his face. Then, almost in slow motion, he started to fall to his knees. But just at the point when it seemed as though he was fully complying with Ben's command, he suddenly sprang back up, and, producing the crowbar from behind his neck, crashed it down on the constable's head.

Ben yelled out, and tried to protect himself with his hands, but it was too late. The blow struck him on the side of the head so hard that, despite any protection he might have had from his helmet, he crunched up and dropped heavily to the ground.

Simultaneously, Joe and Phil started to make a run for it, but once again, Charlie yelled at them. 'No! Get back 'ere!'

'Fer Chrissake, Charlie!' cried Joe.

'Let's get out of 'ere!' called Phil.

'No!' growled Charlie. 'If we leave 'im now, we're done for! We've got ter finish 'im off!'

Joe and Phil exchanged a look of disbelief. Even in their fast and furious world of petty street crime, they had never anticipated anything like this.

Charlie's eyes were scanning the kerb. He found what he was looking for. 'Get 'old of 'is feet,' he barked. The two brothers hesitated. 'Now!'

With blood streaming from a vicious cut at the side of his forehead, Big Ben was groaning, and only half-conscious. Reluctantly, Joe and Phil took one foot each.

'Get 'im over 'ere!' commanded Charlie with urgency.

The two boys did as they were told, and with great effort managed to drag the badly injured police constable to the edge of the kerb. With horror and incredulity, they watched whilst their elder brother struggled to pull off the metal grate of the water drain. Once he had accomplished this, he turned to the others, and rasped, 'Get 'is 'ead down there!'

The two brothers looked thunderstruck.

'D'yer wanna be topped?' he snarled.

The brothers were in anguish.

'Then get 'im down there!'

Charlie bent down, pulled off Big Ben's helmet, and with his reluctant brothers pushing from behind, gradually eased the head of the massive human frame down into the drain. It was a difficult job, and Ben's shoulders had to be forced and wedged into the restricted space. But then, with Charlie urging them on, between them they all finally managed to upend Ben's huge body, and submerge his head beneath the water line halfway down the drain.

From a distance came a shrill cacophony of police whistles.

'Let's get the 'ell out of 'ere!' yelled Charlie.

The Dillon brothers made off as fast as they could, leaving Big Ben's body upended in the drain.

From the corner at the end of the road, Jack Ridley looked on in abject horror. Then he turned, and fled for his life.

CHAPTER 20

The brutal murder of Police Constable 'Big Ben' Fodder sent shock waves throughout the entire community. Even by the low standards of the residents of Campbell Road, it confirmed the Bunk as a bastion of wild criminal activity, and the Metropolitan Police were castigated by both the local and national press for their inability to control the situation. And, as if to enhance their reputation as one of the most dangerous areas in London in which to live, the residents of the Bunk built their own wall of silence around the grim events that had taken place in their very midst on that dark, cold night, only one week prior to Christmas. Despite exhaustive police investigations, it appeared that no one in the entire street witnessed anything other than some kind of fight amongst a gang of youths, the kind of thing they had grown used to over the years. But when anyone was asked if they could identify any of the youths present, their replies were identical, that it was a dark night, and that they knew what could happen to them if they poked their noses into things that didn't concern them. Even Sedgwick's watcher had been of no help. Bound, gagged, and blindfolded, he could recognise no one, and even if he could, Rick Mercer, his boss, was, for obvious reasons, determined to keep the events of what happened that night as low key as possible.

Sarah read about the Bunk murder in the newspaper the following day. Although she was not altogether surprised at anything that went on in such a place, her immediate thoughts were of Beattie. Despite the fact that she had no time for the way her young sister was living her life, her natural instinct was concern, and she wondered how much longer Beattie would be able to bring up Young Ed in such an unsavoury environment.

When Beattie heard the news, she felt quite sick. Both she and Ed had heard the rumpus going on in the street the previous night, but it was too far along the road for them to see what exactly was going on. But there was no doubt that the savage murder of the burly flatfoot had left even her in a state of shock. It seemed such a cruel, mindless act that anyone could hate a person so much that they would resort to something so horrific.

'Wicked sods, that's wot they are!' growled Ma Briggs, tears in her eyes, and voice cracking with anger. ''Ow could anyone do such a fing? I mean, I never cared much fer the man, the way 'e strutted up an' down the place like 'e owned it, but fer Gord's sake, 'e was a 'uman bein'! Just fink wot sort of a Christmas 'is poor missus an' kids are in for next week.'

Beattie and Ma were standing in the open front doorway, watching all the activity going on in the road outside, the place quite literally crawling with flatfoots. 'Wot're we goin' ter say ter the flatties when they come round askin' questions?' asked Beattie, anxiously.

'Well, I can't tell 'em nuffin',' replied the old girl. 'I slept fru it all, din't 'ear a fing. Sometimes it pays ter be deaf. I tell yer this much though.' She wiped her eyes, and then her nose, on her pinny. 'I 'ate this bleedin' road. I 'ate everyfin' about it. I only wish ter Christ I could get out of the place, an' never set eyes on it again.'

'Then why don't yer, Ma?' Beattie said impetuously.

'Wot d'yer mean?'

'Come an' live wiv me an' Ed. There's a spare room upstairs. We could offer the Council five bob a week extra for it, an' you could come an' go as yer please.'

Ma was slowly shaking her head.

'Why not?' asked Beattie. 'You're like a second mum ter me. An' ter Ed too.'

The old girl's face crumpled up. 'It wouldn't be right. You're a married woman. Now that Ed's gettin' older, you're entitled to a life of yer own. And anyway, yer've got quite enough problems ter cope wiv.'

'Such as?' asked Beattie.

'Wot about Jack boy?'

Beattie's expression changed immediately. Yes, she thought, suddenly tense and anxious, what about Jack Ridley? What would *he* say once he knew that his loving wife and her son had disappeared out of sight, and taken Ma Briggs with them? But there was more on her mind than that. Where, she wondered, was Ridley during the time Big Ben was being shoved down the drain just along the road? Even as the thought occurred to her, two men were approaching her and Ma, one in plain clothes, the other in police uniform.

'Pardon me, madam,' said the uniformed flatfoot. 'We're looking for a Mrs Ridley.'

On Christmas Eve, Beattie finished her cleaning job early, and she and Ed joined the crowd of carol singers who had gathered round a huge Christmas tree just outside the entrance to Finsbury Park. It had now become bitterly cold, and although there was as yet no sign of a white Christmas, during the past twenty-four hours the temperature had fallen dramatically, and the danger now was of ice patches forming on all the side roads. None the less, the seasonal atmosphere was in full swing, and as everyone rushed about to do their last few hours of shopping, it was hard to resist the temptation to join the throng of carol singers who were filling the twilight air with the uplifting sounds of 'Good King Wenceslas' and 'Silent Night'.

The sound of voices joined together in harmony and Christmas cheer helped Beattie in some part to cope with the feeling of total despair that had overtaken her since the murder of Big Ben just a few days before. And, young though he was, Ed was sensitive enough to know how his mum was feeling, and uncharacteristically, whilst they stood there, joining in the communal singing together, he had put a comforting arm around her waist. Much to his surprise, Beattie responded by putting her arm around the boy's shoulders. However, the brief moment of lost care came to an abrupt halt when Beattie suddenly felt someone's chin resting on her own shoulder, and a familiar voice close to her ear saying her name. 'Beattie.'

Beattie, immediately panicked by Jack Ridley's voice, tried to turn.

'Don't move!' he demanded. 'Carry on singin'!'

Beattie did as she was told, but Ed refused to co-operate. 'Leave us alone!' the boy snapped.

Ridley, clearly tensed up, dug his knuckle into the boy's back.

Beattie pulled Ed back towards her.

'I need ter talk to yer,' came the voice from behind. 'I'll see yer in the park in five minutes, on the bridge. I'll go first.' He paused a moment, then added, 'Leave 'im 'ere!' To show who he meant, he again dug his knuckle into Ed's back.

A few minutes later, Beattie made her way through the park entrance, and headed off towards the railway bridge close to the football pitch. The light was now fading, and Beattie was afraid the park would soon be closing. But she pressed on regardless, and pulled her long woollen scarf around her head and shoulders to protect her from the first signs of a biting cold drizzle. When she got to the metal steps leading up on to the bridge, she felt her heart thumping, for as she climbed the steps, Ridley came into view. He was waiting for her, his cap pulled down close over his eyes, the collar of his jacket pulled up in a pathetic attempt to keep his neck warm, and his hands tucked beneath his arms. As usual, there was a lighted dog-end in his mouth, and the smoke from it curled through the metal railings of the bridge.

The moment she reached him, she was astonished to see how pale and drawn he looked. 'Wot 'ave yer done, Jack?' she asked directly.

Ridley pulled his shoulders back, and stared straight at her. It seemed as though he was about to square up to her. But quite suddenly, his whole appearance changed, for his face crumpled up, and he burst into tears. 'I didn't do it!' he spluttered, pulling the dog-end from his lips and tossing it over the bridge on to the line below. 'I didn't bleedin' do it!'

Beattie couldn't believe what she was seeing. Never in all her time with Jack Ridley had she seen him go to pieces like this, blubbering like a baby. Although her instinct was to rush forward and throw her arms around him, she knew why this was happening, and, for the moment at least, there was no way she could respond.

'The law,' she said, grim-faced, 'they've bin round askin' questions. They've bin askin' everyone. They asked me – and Ed.'

Ridley, who had been covering his eyes with one hand, slowly looked up at her.

'We told 'em we 'adn't seen yer,' Beattie continued. 'We told 'em yer ain't part of our family any more.'

'I didn't do it, Beat,' said Ridley, wiping his eyes with the back of his hand. 'I saw 'em do it, I saw wot they did to 'im. But I 'ad no part in it. I swear ter God I din't!'

What a pathetic sight, Beattie thought to herself. What happened to the big, tough bully who would sooner use his fists on a woman or a kid than find a decent way to survive this hell of a life? 'There's a rumour goin' round the Bunk it was you an' the Dillon boys.'

Ridley shook his head strenuously.

'Oh, don't worry,' Beattie assured him, 'nobody's goin' ter split on yer. Unless, of course, there's somefin in it for 'em.'

As she spoke, a railway train approached at full speed making its way north, leaving a trail of thick black smoke behind to engulf the bridge above. When it had cleared, Ridley drew closer, glanced all around, then lowered his voice. 'Listen ter me, Beat,' he said, with almost a look of begging in his eyes. 'I was in at the job at Sedgwick's, but I split the moment I 'eard Ben comin'. The boys – they did the rest. I was round the corner at the time, at the end of the Bunk. There was nuffin' I could do.'

'Really, Jack?' replied Beattie, staring coldly at him. 'Yer mean yer couldn't've stopped the cold-blooded murder of a man whose 'ead was pushed down a drain just because 'e was doin' 'is job?'

Ridley took hold of her arms. 'You don't know the Dillon boys, Beat,' he said earnestly. 'If I'd've put one foot out of place, they'd've topped me too.'

Beattie was quite impervious to his plea. 'D'yer know 'ow many kids Ben has?' she said. 'Five. The eldest is seventeen, the youngest is two. They took 'is missus off ter the 'ospital when she 'eard. Merry Christmas – eh?'

Ridley again shook his head in anguish. ''Elp me, Beat,' he pleaded. 'Please 'elp me.'

'Wot d'yer expect *me* ter do?' she asked acidly.

'I've got ter get away. I need some cash.'

Beattie turned, and started to move away.

Ridley went after her, and held her back. '*Please,* Beat!' he begged. 'If I turn meself in, they'll top me.'

'If yer didn't 'ave anyfin' ter do wiv it, then why should they top yer?'

Ridley stared hard at her. ''Cos they 'aven't an 'ope in 'ell of findin' the Dillon boys. The Dillons've got their contacts; they can vamoose wivout any trouble at all. This is a flatfoot killin', Beat. The fuzz are goin' ter want ter get someone, even if it ain't the right man.'

Beattie thought about this for a moment, and she saw that what Ridley was saying made sense. A police killing was one of the worst crimes anyone could commit. Ben's pals in the fuzz would never rest until they took their revenge on anyone who was even remotely involved. 'Where are yer making for?' she asked reluctantly.

'I don't know,' he replied. 'Somewhere – anywhere. But I've got ter find some way of gettin' out of the country. Maybe go ter Ireland or somefin'. But I need some cash. I ain't got a farvin' in the world.'

''Ow much?'

Ridley shrugged his shoulders.

Beattie sighed and moved a short way from him. Through the narrow metal grille of the bridge, she could just see the tiny figure of Young Ed, who was waiting for her on the deserted football pitch down below. And then she thought about all the plans she and the boy had made about moving into their new home, their hopes, their aspirations. How could she betray the boy by giving up the best part of a hundred pounds to a man who had abused both her and the son that she had brought into this world? Ed deserved the right to a new start in life, she was telling herself. He was a kid with a good brain, who deserved to be given a good education, a good home to live in, and a chance to show what he could do. But then she thought about what would happen if Jack Ridley were to turn himself in. Like it or not, he was still legally her husband, even though he had never treated her like a wife, in or out of bed. And how would it be if her son went through life branded with the stigma of having a stepfather who was hanged for murder? The dilemma was tearing her apart. After a moment, however, she turned back to Ridley. 'All right, Jack,' she said firmly. 'I'll give yer wot I've got.'

Ridley breathed a sigh of relief.

'But on condition,' added Beattie, 'that neivver me nor Ed ever 'ave ter set eyes on yer again. 'Cos if we do, I swear ter God – I'll turn yer in.'

Being a Buddhist, Mrs Ranasinghe didn't recognise Christmas as the most important festive season of the year. However, she always celebrated it, even if devilled chicken, vegetable curry and rice, and seeni sambol were her preferred Ceylonese favourites to roast turkey and Christmas pudding. This being a special year, because her married daughter Marla was visiting her in England for the first time, her small annual dinner party was held on Boxing Day. Although Sarah was in the strict sense an employee, the old lady now considered her to be more of a friend, so after helping Marla in the kitchen, Sarah took her place at the dining-table alongside her 'gentleman friend, the barber', who had also been invited. The only other guest was Mrs Elsa de Silva, an old friend of Mrs Ranasinghe, who had left her husband in Colombo over twenty years before, and had lived in London ever since.

Despite the old lady's constant carping about how old-fashioned her daughter was, the moment Marla had arrived, Sarah took a liking to her. Unlike her mother, Marla was quite a tubby little woman, who, oddly enough, preferred to wear western-style clothes to the traditional Ceylonese sari. But she had a great sense of humour, and knew exactly how to keep both her mother and Mrs de Silva in check.

Sarah loved the way the two old ladies had built their relationship on one-upmanship. Several times during the evening she had listened to them reminiscing about their childhood days in Kandy, and she frequently had to suppress a giggle when the two of them nearly came to blows over their different versions of events.

There was also a tricky moment when Mrs de Silva asked everyone, 'Tell me, does anyone know why the English insist on calling today Boxing Day?'

To everyone's surprise, Freddie immediately came up with more or less the right answer. 'Actually, Mrs de Silva,' he said, with gentle courtesy, 'my gran once told me that in the old days, employers usually gave their Christmas boxes to their employees on the day after

Christmas Day. I s'ppose that's where the name came from. Of course, it's all changed now.'

Mrs Ranasinghe looked very smug. 'You're quite right, Mr Hamwell,' she said. Then, turning to her old friend, added, 'After all the years you've been in England, Elsa, I'm surprised you didn't know that.'

Mrs de Silva grunted, and turned to look the other way.

'Actually,' said Marla, interrupting like a mediator, 'I heard that Boxing Day had something to do with taking a collection in church for the poor.'

'You're probably right, Marla,' said Sarah. 'We could do with some of that today. After all these years, the country is still plagued with poverty.'

'Well, you only have Ramsay MacDonald and this damned Labour Government to blame for that!' Mrs de Silva sniffed.

Mrs Ranasinge sat bolt upright in her wheelchair. 'Come now, Elsa,' she said touchily. 'What makes you think Baldwin and the Conservatives would do any better?'

'The Conservatives are a better class of person,' returned Mrs de Silva. 'They know how to handle business.'

'Poppycock!' spluttered Mrs Ranasinghe, indignantly. 'Anyway, it's very rude of you to discuss political matters when you're not entitled to the vote!'

Marla exchanged a resigned sigh with Sarah.

'It's not only in England where there's trouble with business and the economy,' said Freddie, quickly diffusing the situation. 'Just look at other countries – unemployment, rows and fights, people on the dole everywhere. I'm afraid it's goin' ter get worse before it gets better.'

'I think it's time I did the washing-up,' said Sarah, quickly rising from the table.

'I'll come and help you,' said Marla, also rising, and collecting the dishes as she went.

As they made for the kitchen, both Sarah and Marla took one last wicked look back at Freddie, who was clearly quite concerned at being left alone with the two old warhorses.

'Actually, I've been wanting to talk to you, Sarah,' said Marla, drying the dishes as Sarah washed them. 'Mother got her appointment to see the specialist the other day. Did she tell you?'

Sarah shook her head. 'Anything concerning her health she usually keeps from me,' she replied with a smile. 'It's nothing serious, though, is it?'

'I hope not,' said Marla. 'But I've been a bit worried about these pains she's been getting in her chest.'

Sarah turned with a start. 'Pains in her chest?' she asked anxiously. 'She didn't tell me about that.'

'I don't think it's anything to worry about,' said Marla. 'As you know, she likes her food a lot, so it may be indigestion. But I think it's best to be on the safe side. Anyway, we shall find out definitely in the New Year.' She started to pile the dry dishes on the kitchen table. 'But one thing I must say,' she said, 'is how wonderful you've been to my mother. I don't know how she would have coped without you all these years.'

'Oh, it has nothing to do with me,' replied

Sarah. 'Your mother is a very determined lady. She knows what she wants, and she knows how to get it – regardless of anything I do.'

They both laughed gently at this.

'Mother thinks highly of you, you know,' said Marla, whose firm and cut-glass accent sounded as though it came straight out of an English public school. 'I think she'll miss you a great deal when she has to go back home.'

'You mean, that's a possibility?' Sarah asked tentatively.

'I think it's inevitable sooner or later,' replied Marla. 'If anything should happen to her, it would be better for her, and for us, if she was home amongst her own family. Despite what she may have told you, we all love her very much.'

Sarah smiled, but she couldn't help feeling a little sad inside. They were interrupted by a ring on the doorbell.

'Who on earth is that at this time of night?' asked Marla. 'I thought the carol singing was all over now.'

'It's probably one of the neighbours coming in to cadge a drink from your mother,' Sarah said lightly. 'Don't worry, I'll take care of it.'

'No,' said Marla, making for the door. 'One look at me, and they'll run for their lives!'

Sarah laughed. She carried on washing up, concerned by what she had heard about her employer. Although she had tried to dismiss the thought from her mind, over the past few weeks the old lady had indeed been less lively than in the past, and even more disturbing was the way she had stopped talking about the plans she was making for the house, something she had done since the first day Sarah had come to work for her.

'You have a visitor,' announced Marla, as she returned.

Sarah was astonished to see who Marla had brought in with her. 'Ed!' she cried, drying her hands on the wiping-up cloth, and going to him. 'What are you doing here?'

The boy hung his head low, and didn't reply. He looked not only cold, but thoroughly miserable.

Sarah exchanged a concerned look with Marla. 'I'm sorry, Marla,' she explained. 'This is my nephew, Ed. Say hello, Ed.'

Ed could only manage a quiet grunt.

Marla held up her hand to Sarah. 'I'll leave you two together,' she said with an understanding smile as she made for the door. 'Take your time.'

After she had gone, Sarah took the boy's flat cap off, and led him to the table. 'What is it, Ed?' she asked, sitting him down. 'What's happened?'

The boy looked up slowly at her. His eyes were raw from crying. 'It's Jack Ridley,' he said. ''E's stopped us from movin'.'

'Ridley? Stopped you?' said Sarah. 'But I thought you told me it was all arranged. You were supposed to be moving to Mitford Road some time in–'

'I tell yer, 'e's stopped it. We ain't goin' – not now, not ever!'

'But why?'

The boy looked slowly up at her. His eyes were now once again swelling with tears. 'She's given

’im the money, the money we got from Granddad. She’s given ’im the money. ’E’s a killer, an’ I ’ate ’im! An’ she’s given ’im the money!’

CHAPTER 21

The year of 1931 was already turning out to be even more of a mess for the country politically than the dark years of the General Strike. In February, Oswald Mosley resigned from the Labour Party in protest at the parlous state of the economy. This was followed by his forming his own radical 'New Party', which fomented as much trouble as it possibly could on the streets, particularly the poorer districts of London. With unemployment now more than three million, the long-term unemployed were enraged when they were asked to submit to a means test before receiving any further relief from public funds, and their grievances, on top of everything else they had endured over the years, threatened to turn into another full-scale showdown with the government.

The situation abroad was little better. In Spain there was the real prospect of a civil war when the government of General Berenguer was forced to resign and King Alfonso XIII had to flee the country. In Germany too, the years of crisis since the end of the war were taking their toll on the population. With unemployment there also at record levels, there were signs that a thuggish type of political uprising was becoming a very real threat.

For Beattie and Ed the year had started better

than they had anticipated. The great life-saver was, of course, being able to move into the new property in Mitford Road after all. The bonus was Ma Briggs, who had been persuaded to give up living in the grime and hate of the Bunk, and who had immediately taken it upon herself to make sure that the new premises were scrubbed out thoroughly with DDT from top to bottom, so that by the time she had finished there wasn't a cockroach in sight. She had also helped Beattie and Ed to put up wallpaper, which was a new experience for all of them. But both women were surprised to see what a dab hand Ed was at painting the woodwork. His joy at moving into such a place, with his own bedroom, an inside lavatory, and a yard out back, had clearly given him a new lease of life.

For Beattie also, moving away from the Bunk and all its implications was a gift from heaven, or rather from Jack Ridley. She had never stopped thanking God for the day that Ridley had waited for Ed outside his school, and handed back the eighty pounds Beattie had given him to help him get out of the country. Although Ridley's apparent change of mind didn't make him any better a person, at least it showed that he had some degree of conscience.

Beattie's main preoccupation now was to put the events of the week before Christmas behind her. She hoped that, three months since the callous murder of Big Ben Fodder, the residents of the Bunk might have come to their senses and at least made an effort to restore some kind of decency to their tarnished community.

Beattie's priority now was Ed. The moment she left the Bunk, she was determined that with the prospect of the school-leaving age now being raised to fifteen, the boy was to be given all the support he needed to catch up on his lost education – no more truancy, no more kicking tin cans around the street. She had been given full-time work as a cleaner at Finsbury Park tube station, and she was able to give Ed a small weekly allowance with which to buy the books he craved.

She rarely thought about Sarah, whom she hadn't seen since the morning she flew into a rage at her for what she suspected was an attempt by her sister to turn the boy against her. But she held no malice against Sarah, and in some ways even regretted the fact that they were no longer in contact. With her new attitude of mind, Beattie decided that, when the time was ripe, she would make the effort to improve the atmosphere between them. Unfortunately, even the best intentions go awry.

On one fine spring morning in March, Beattie found herself sitting just a seat away from Sarah on a number 38 tram, heading up Holloway Road and Upper Street towards the Angel, Islington. At first, their contact was no more than a double take, but after they had established full eye contact, Beattie had no alternative but to move into the seat next to her sister. 'Long time, no see,' said Beattie, which was her usual greeting when she was taken by surprise.

'Hello, Beattie,' replied Sarah, stiffly, moving up as much as she could to give Beattie more room.

The lower deck of the tram was jammed, and every so often the standing passengers swayed to and fro as they struggled to hold on to the overhead straps.

'So where yer off to then?' asked Beattie, who was surprised to see her sister with a new hair-style, and looking far younger and more radiant than she'd hoped.

'I'm going to see a friend of mine,' replied Sarah, who thought that Beattie was looking tidier, and wearing more suitable clothes than she could ever remember. 'He's a barber. He has a shop near the Angel.'

'Oh yes,' replied Beattie, who wasn't too interested. 'That's nice.'

'So how've you been?'

Beattie perked up immediately. 'Oh,' she said, 'fings couldn't be better. When Lacey's farver died, 'e left us – I mean, 'e left Ed – a nice little nest egg. 'E probably told yer about it.'

'If he did, I don't remember,' replied Sarah, carefully. 'I don't see Ed very much these days,' she said tactfully.

Beattie was in a quandary. The moment she saw Sarah, she wanted to put things right, she wanted to tell her that they should bury the hatchet and try to become friends again. But then, before she could do anything about it, she found herself wanting to make an impression, to make Sarah jealous that things were actually going well for her. 'Me an' Ed 'ave moved into a nice little place up Mitford Road,' she said proudly.

'That's wonderful, Beattie,' replied Sarah,

genuinely pleased. 'I'm so happy for you both.'

'Oh yes,' Beattie continued, trying hard not to show that she was boasting, even though she obviously was. 'We've got a room each, an' a kitchen/diner. We've got our own lav – toilet – an' a lovely little garden at the back. Yer must come an' visit us some time.' Even as she said it, she wished she hadn't.

'That's very kind of you, Beattie,' said Sarah. 'Some time.'

The tram rattled its way along the Holloway Road, and when it reached Highbury Corner, it was a relief for both sisters to see so many people getting off. But once the last of them had cleared the platform, a queue of new passengers filed on board.

'So what's happened to your husband?' asked Sarah, as casually as she could manage. 'Has he moved in with you?'

Beattie hesitated only briefly. 'Oh no,' she replied cagily. 'Jack's gone abroad. He's got a job.'

'Oh really? That's nice.' Sarah didn't sound at all convincing.

'Me an' Jack are not really tergevver now,' said Beattie, who kept fidgeting and tidying her dress uneasily as she talked. 'These fings 'appen, though.'

'Of course.'

'But 'e's bin good about our new place,' she added, again trying to impress Sarah. 'Oh yes. In fact we 'ave 'im ter fank fer us gettin' most of the cash. It's just that 'e ain't cut out ter be a family man, that's all.'

Sarah smiled, without giving anything away. 'I'm so pleased to hear that things are going so well for you, Beattie,' she said. 'Especially after the terrible time you must have gone through at Christmas.' She paused only long enough to think what she was going to say. 'I hear the police are looking for some local men who were involved.'

Beattie was quick off the mark once more. 'Oh, those bruvvers, yer mean?' Her reaction was again accompanied by fidgeting. 'If it's the lot I remember, they deserve everyfin' they get. They used ter play dice an' fings down our road. Poor old Ben was always after 'em. They gave 'im an 'ell of a lot of lip.' Then she added as an afterthought, 'Jack was always tellin' 'em ter leave the poor man alone.'

Sarah nodded, her smile fixed. 'That was brave of him,' she replied. Her remark carried more meaning than Beattie would ever know. 'But then, he was always a man of many surprises, wasn't he?'

Tinker Murdoch swept the barber shop floor. It had been quite a busy morning, for Freddie had done eight haircuts without a break. The hair left over on the floor was a wonderful kaleidoscope of colours, curls, and just plain straight. There were three different shades of brown, two greys, a couple of blondes, and even a bright ginger. Young Tinker had a broad grin on his face as he swept it all up into a pile, because every selection of discarded hair reminded him of the head that it had come from. And what a collection it was!

One or two of them were casual customers, but the regulars, such as Mr Mooney from the flower shop in Upper Street, and Mr Pyle, the commissionaire from the Blue Hall cinema, had the most wonderful habits, which were a gift to a mimic such as Freddie's young apprentice. For instance, Mr Mooney often quite unconsciously picked his nose, which always ended up in his sneezing his head off, and Mr Pyle's face never failed to stop twitching with anticipation when he knew that he was the next customer to be attended to. There was also a young chap who came in every fortnight, whose girlfriend always waited outside, peering in the window and waving at him, which somehow made the chap feel quite good, as though everyone was envious of his undoubted attraction to the female sex. Whenever she came into the shop during the lunch hour, Sarah loved Tinker's impersonations; she was always telling him that he should be on the stage.

Sarah arrived at the shop at exactly one o'clock, but as the last customer before lunch had already left, Tinker had put up the 'CLOSED FOR LUNCH' sign on the inside of the shop door. The moment he saw Sarah, Freddie went to meet her. Tinker covered his eyes when they embraced and kissed, saying he was far too young to witness such goings-on. He never, of course, referred to his own girlfriend, who was waiting for him in the caff just down the road, but before he went off to join her, he did manage to get in one quick impersonation of one of the morning's customers, who spent the whole time whilst

Freddie was cutting his thinning hair admiring himself in the mirror facing him. As usual, Sarah absolutely loved Tinker's turn and was in fits of laughter.

Once Tinker had left, Sarah noticed that there was something different about Freddie. 'You're looking awfully smug today, Mr Hamwell,' she chided.

'I'm glad yer noticed, miss,' he quipped, before suddenly disappearing into his back room, to re-emerge almost immediately clutching a huge bunch of daffodils. 'Compliments of the management!' he announced grandly. 'Mr Mooney in the flower shop chose 'em 'imself.'

Sarah was taken aback as Freddie passed them to her. 'But – why, Freddie?' she asked.

'Do I 'ave ter 'ave a reason?' he asked.

'Well, no, no of course not,' she replied. 'But–'

'They're a celebration,' he said.

'Celebration?'

'It's the anniversary of our first meetin', when yer came up 'ere ter see me. Five munffs this week.'

Sarah laughed. 'Thank you, Freddie,' she said, giving him a gentle kiss. 'But you've got it all wrong. The first time we met was in the queue outside the Blue Hall, with Eunice and Ernie.'

'Yeah, but that was diff'rent,' said Freddie. 'When yer first saw me, yer 'ated the sight of me.'

Sarah's expression changed immediately to concern. 'Oh, Freddie, that's not true. I could never hate anyone like you. You're one of the sweetest people I've ever known in my entire life.'

Freddie beamed. 'Then your old lady was right.'

Sarah was puzzled, as he put his arm around her waist and led her to the row of customers' chairs along one side of the shop. 'Old lady?' she asked. 'Who are you talking about?'

Freddie eased her down on to one of the chairs, and then sat alongside her. 'Your boss. Mrs Rana-thing.' He was thoroughly enjoying the game he was playing. 'She told me, long ago, if I din't ask yer ter marry me, I'd be the biggest chump in the 'ole world.'

Sarah's mouth dropped. 'Freddie!' she gasped.

'Wot about it, Sarah?' he asked, with a begging, longing look in his eyes. 'I want ter marry you, an' I want us ter live tergevver fer the rest of our lives.'

Sarah was half-laughing, half-crying. 'Freddie, I don't know what to say.'

'Just say yes,' he replied quickly. 'If yer like…' He suddenly dropped to his knees in front of her, and in a mock attempt at the old-fashioned proposal ritual, took hold of both her hands and looked up at her… 'I can do it the proper way.'

Sarah was laughing. 'Don't be so silly,' she said.

'Well, will yer – or won't yer?'

Sarah was at a loss for words. If someone had told her a few years ago that she would be sitting in a men's barber shop, with a funny little working-class man proposing to her, she would have laughed in their face. But Freddie Hamwell was different. What he lacked in sophistication, he made up for in warmth, care, and understanding. And what he didn't understand, he made it a point to find out. There was nothing dark or mysterious about Freddie, and though he had his weak points, like sulking when someone contradicted him, or refusing to let other people do things for him, he was basically honest and open, a man of intense compassion. But could she marry him? Was he the one she would want to share the rest of her life with? Could she be sure? Could she be absolutely sure? Whatever her doubts, her mind was made up. 'If you really want me, Freddie,' she said, staring into his eyes, 'I'd be very proud to be your wife.'

The wide beam on Freddie's face told it all. He immediately got to his feet, eased Sarah up from the chair, threw his arms around her and hugged her. Over his shoulder, he could see an eager face peering through the shop window. He gave the thumbs-up sign.

Tinker's cheeky face lit up. Then he pulled off his cap, and threw it straight up into the air.

'Married?' barked Mrs Ranasinghe, who had reacted to Sarah's news as though it had come as a complete surprise. 'Who to?'

'You know perfectly well who to!' chided Sarah. 'In fact, you put him up to it, you know you did.'

The old lady had a mischievous twinkle in her eye. 'Oh, if you're talking about that barber fellow, then it's all right.' Having made her approval obvious, she held out her hands to Sarah, took them, and pulled her down so far that she could give her a kiss on the cheek. 'I shall miss you, young lady,' she said with hidden significance.

'Miss me?' Sarah returned immediately. 'Well, don't think you're getting rid of me as quickly as that. Freddie and I won't be able to get married until next spring at the earliest. We've got so many things to do, and plans to make.' She was so breathless with excitement, she was practically tumbling over her words. 'We're going to live in Freddie's room above the shop – just for a while, until we find somewhere bigger and more permanent. Freddie's got all sorts of ideas where he wants us to go. I'm leaving it all up to him.'

Marla then came over to her. 'It's wonderful, Sarah,' she said, hugging her. 'I'm so happy for you. We both are, aren't we, Mother?'

The old lady sniffed. 'I suppose so,' she said, clearly determined not to show how thrilled she was. 'At least you won't have to pay to have your hair done any more!'

Sarah and Marla laughed. But despite the old lady's apparent happiness, Sarah could sense that both Mrs Ranasinghe and her daughter were trying to put on brave faces. It was this thought, and the odd exchange of looks that passed between Marla and her mother that gradually changed Sarah's expression to one of concern.

'Is anything wrong?' she asked, addressing her question to both of them.

Marla hesitated, then looked at the old lady. 'I think, Mother,' she said awkwardly, 'you have something you want to say to Sarah.'

Sarah switched her look from Marla to her mother.

Mrs Ranasinghe was looking very pale and drawn. Sarah hadn't really noticed before now that the old lady was developing lines to the sides of her mouth and beneath her eyes, on what had been until recently a beautiful, clear pale brown face. 'It seems my family want me to go back home,' she said. 'My other home, that is.'

Sarah felt her stomach tense. 'Oh, I see,' were the only words she could find.

The old lady settled herself back in her wheelchair. 'I fear they want to keep an eye on me, just in case something should happen when they're not around.' There was just a suggestion of that wry smile on her face that Sarah had come to know and love so well. 'It's all poppycock, of course. I intend to live for at least another twenty years – if not more!'

'Indeed you will, dear lady,' said Sarah, brightly. She could feel Marla's eyes searching for hers. They clearly had a different story to tell. 'So – when are you planning to leave?' she asked stoically.

Marla answered. 'If we get things cleared up here in time, there's a boat from Tilbury on the twenty-ninth of next month.'

Sarah felt a sense of despair. 'Goodness. That's less than a month. We'll have quite a lot to do before then.'

Marla was looking at her. There was a pained expression on her face. She wanted to say something, to explain, to make it all sound as though there really wasn't anything to worry about. But the words just wouldn't come. 'Why don't I leave you two to have a chat?' she said tactfully. 'You've got a lot to talk through.' She smiled gratefully at Sarah, and then left the room.

The old lady wheeled herself to the window. It

was a glorious day outside, and the spring sunshine was streaming through the lace curtains, casting weblike patterns across her face. 'I can't remember the number of times I've sat at this window on my own, staring out at the same old things, same people, big dogs, little dogs, awful cats, the milkman, the baker, the postman. And yet, one way or another, they're all different. You know, I often wonder what your God or mine was thinking about when He made the human race.' She turned briefly to throw a look at Sarah. 'I mean, we really are a peculiar lot, aren't we?'

Sarah came across to her and placed her hands gently on the old lady's shoulders. 'Not all of us,' she said. 'People like you are quite special.'

The old lady chuckled. 'Oh yes, I know,' she said, with a wave of her hand. 'I bet you say that to all your old ladies.'

Sarah laughed with her. Then, for a moment or so, they both remained silent, their faces streaked with patterns of light.

It was finally Mrs Ranasinghe who broke the silence. 'I want you to promise me something,' she said. 'I want you to promise that you'll keep in touch with Marla. She likes you, respects you. I hope one day you and your husband will come to visit her out in Ceylon. I won't be there to greet you, but I'll certainly be there in spirit.'

Sarah increased the loving pressure of her hands on the old lady's shoulders. She knew what she was trying to tell her, but she was making quite sure that she would not betray the unspoken understanding they had between them.

'You would like it out there,' continued the old lady, eyes still fixed firmly on the street outside. 'We're a very close-knit community, always conniving against each other. But it's all part of the game, you see. We're actually quite nice, quite harmless.' She reached up for one of Sarah's hands, and then covered it. 'You'll have a lot of new things to experience in life, Sarah, so many exciting, wonderful things. One day, you will wake up and find that everything is suddenly in focus. You will finally know where you are, where you are going.' Again she paused briefly to look up at Sarah. 'That's how it happened to me,' she continued. 'The time came when I knew that I had a family, a family who needed me, and who I needed myself. One day, it'll be like that with you and your sister. Not that blood is thicker than water, but that you will both realise that you have a need to be part of each other again. One day, your Beattie will also wake up and wonder what has happened to her sister, Sarah. And when that day comes, that need will bring you closer together than you have ever been before.'

She spun the wheelchair around to face Sarah. 'When you walked through that door for the first time, with the awful smell of Yorkshire pudding and Brussels sprouts all over you, I was absolutely convinced that, by bringing you into my home, I was making the biggest mistake of my life.' She paused, and swallowed hard. 'I want you to know, young lady, that I couldn't have been more wrong.'

Sarah's eyes swelled with tears. She leaned

down, and hugged the old lady as hard as she could.

There was never a dull moment at Liverpool Street Station. During the war its platform had been invaded by British troops on their way to and from their training camps in the East of England en route to the battlefront in France, and during peacetime, it had been destined to become the heartbeat of office workers who were forced to commute every morning and every evening in a relentless circle of drudgery. It was also the hub of cross-Channel activity, for, together with Victoria and Waterloo Stations, it handled many of the ferry services to the European continent. This grandly built station was also used for the boat train service to Tilbury, where ocean liners took passengers to far-distant destinations such as Australia, the Far East, and South East Asia.

The boat train service for the Orient Line *Orion* ocean liner was scheduled to leave at eleven o'clock, and it was rare for it to depart late. With that fact in mind, Mrs Ranasinghe, Marla, and Sarah arrived at least half an hour early for the service, for it was obviously going to take quite a time for the old lady's wheelchair to negotiate both platform and railway carriage steps. Mrs Ranasinghe's huge trunks, together with Marla's four suitcases, and vast collection of goods that had been bought in London to take back to Ceylon, had already been sent on in advance by road to the docks at Tilbury, which made the prospect of the rail journey far less cumbersome.

As soon as she arrived at the platform, Sarah was astonished to see such a vast mixture of brown and white faces. In all the years she had been working for Mrs Ranasinghe, it had never really occurred to her that there might be other people like her boss and Mrs de Silva living in this country. She was also fascinated to see the exotic colours of the ladies' saris, and the formal white tropical suits of the male passengers, which all seemed a little incongruous in the winds and drizzle of London in April. This, coupled with the rising hum of excited chatter, and tearful farewells, presented a picture that could have come straight out of a painting in an art gallery, so alive, and so full of emotion.

'If they call this first class, I dread to think what the poor devils in third class are suffering!' Mrs Ranasinghe was not amused by what she considered to be a less than inferior railway carriage, for there were grease marks on the windows, and particles of black coal dust on the off-white head rests. It was, however, at Marla's insistence that her mother was to travel first class back to Colombo, for, as had become only too clear to Sarah since she was first informed about the reasons for her employer's hasty return home, the least she was entitled to for this one last journey was a little luxury.

Sarah took out her own handkerchief, and tried to rub off the grease from the carriage window, but the more she tried, the worse it got. After a while, she gave up. At least the irritation of having it there would keep the old lady's mind occupied for the duration of the journey to Tilbury.

Once she was satisfied that Mrs Ranasinghe was comfortable, Sarah prepared herself for the moment that she had been dreading. 'I must say, I envy you,' she said bravely. 'How wonderful to cruise along the Mediterranean, and then through the Suez Canal. Six weeks at sea is such a splendid prospect.'

'It is if you don't get seasick!' complained the old lady.

'You don't, do you?'

'Not Mother,' said Marla, who looked so anxious, it was as though she was already about to plough through the choppy seas of the Indian Ocean. 'I'm the one who suffers. On the way out, I spent nearly the entire journey lying in my bunk in the cabin. I just wanted to be left to die!'

Sarah laughed sympathetically.

'Write to me!' the old lady suddenly demanded.

Sarah smiled, and covered the old lady's hand with her own. 'Of course.' Until this moment, she had tried to avoid making direct eye contact with Mrs Ranasinghe. She had tried to forget that Marla had told her about the doctor's fears that her mother's heart condition would probably kill her within a year. She tried to forget that this was going to be the last time that she would ever see this remarkable woman. 'I think you should write to me too, though,' she said.

'You know I hate writing,' replied the old lady, her Ceylonese accent already more pronounced after hearing her fellow passengers jabbering away in Sinhala. 'But I won't forget you.'

Their eyes finally met. There was recognition

there, a complete understanding of what both were feeling.

'And if there are any more wars,' said the old lady, trying to conceal her feelings, 'you and your husband are to get on the first boat and come out to us!'

'There won't be any more wars,' replied Sarah, with a smile. 'After what happened last time, the world has to come to its senses.' Her eyes momentarily flicked up to a railway travel advertisement on the wall just above the old lady's head. It read: 'FRANCE, LAND OF PEACE AND BEAUTY'.

The first shrill guard whistle filled the air. There was an immediate hustle amongst the crowds milling around the railway carriages, and the slamming of doors all along the platform.

Sarah felt quite chilled. She knew that if she spoke one more word to Mrs Ranasinghe, she would make a fool of herself. So she turned first to Marla, and they embraced. Then, finally, she returned to the old lady, bent down to her, and quickly hugged her. 'I'll never forget you,' she said. Then she rushed off the train.

As she reached the platform outside, the final whistle echoed. The excited chatter amongst the well-wishers subsided instantly. Even before the train's departure, loved ones were standing at the carriage windows, waving frantically, and trying desperately to touch the hands of those they were leaving behind, perhaps for the last time.

Gradually, the train started to move, and with it moved the platform crowds, all trying to keep up with it as it went.

Sarah walked with them. All she could do now was to place her hand on the carriage window, where Mrs Ranasinghe was doing her best to take one last look at her. And then, just as the tips of Sarah's fingers were pressing hard against the glass, the old lady leaned as close as she could manage, and, placing her lips against the window, kissed Sarah's fingers through the glass.

Within moments, the train had twisted its way along the platform, its thick dark smoke curling up into the glass and metal roof of the station as it went, until it finally disappeared out of sight.

Suddenly, there was silence. Excitement had turned to emptiness, laughter to tears.

Sarah watched the train until she could neither see nor hear it any more. Then she turned, and started to make her way slowly back along the platform towards the gates. She passed through them, and found herself on the vast station concourse. She was too numb, too disoriented to know where she was going, and it took her several minutes to work out which exit would lead her to her bus stop.

Eventually, she found her way to the main station entrance, and then to the street outside. For Sarah, bidding farewell to Mrs Ranasinghe was like a chapter of her life coming to an end. And yet, in another sense, it was only just beginning.

As she ran for her bus, which was just leaving the stop, she failed to notice a news vendor's placard board nearby, which had been poorly scrawled with the words: 'GERMANY: THE NEW REVOLUTION'.

PART 3

1940 – 1941

CHAPTER 22

Ma Briggs was convinced that her time had come. Three times in the past week, the house in Mitford Road had been shaken from top to bottom, and on one occasion, when she and Beattie had got back from the Anderson shelter in the back yard, she found that part of the ceiling in her room had collapsed on to her freshly ironed clothes. The language she had used then was not exactly that which was becoming of a lady, but then, as Ma had never considered herself to be one, it didn't really seem to matter. None the less, it was obvious from the name she frequently called Herr Hitler, Goering, and that rat-voiced Lord Haw-Haw that she considered they had the misfortune to be fatherless.

The country was now at war with Germany for the second time this century, and there was hardly a family in the land that had not been affected by it. After nearly ten years of rebuilding her life, Beattie was now having to cope with a new kind of hardship, such as the rationing of everything from food to clothes. Just over a year before, when war had been declared, it seemed as though life was carrying on more or less the same as it had done for years. But in September 1940, the so-called phoney war came to a dramatic end, when the German Luftwaffe began their massive daily onslaught on the civilian population of London and the Home Counties. Since then, Beattie had divided her time between her job as a clippie on the buses, and getting herself and Ma safely down the air-raid shelter.

Despite the war, Beattie seemed to have found a new purpose in life. With the turmoil and horrors of the Bunk long behind her, she had settled down to a much more coherent routine, which gave her the will and the energy to survive even the most difficult situations. In many ways, she had returned to her roots, embracing many of the middle-class values that, as a young woman, she had spurned with such disdain. This was especially reflected in her home. It wasn't exactly a palace, but with the regular wage she had been earning since she had got her job on the buses, and the modest wage Ed had earned working in the Islington Central Library after leaving Holloway Grammar School, the house in Mitford Road had been transformed into a comfortable, lower-middle-class home. With Ma's help, Beattie had learned how to wash clothes properly in an aluminium bath, and to mangle, and then iron. She had even learnt how to sew on buttons, and darn Ed's socks when they sprouted holes in the heels. Domestication, which had once been anathema to her, had now transformed the young rebel into an organised woman, who was progressing towards middle-age with a new-found confidence.

These days, Beattie was also more responsible about her own personal appearance. When she was not in her bus conductress uniform, she always managed to look good in smart, belted dresses, or a stylish blouse and skirt that she had bought in either Selby's department store in Holloway Road, or the North London Drapery Store in Seven Sisters Road. She even took trouble with her hair, which she spent time in the mornings combing up into a bunch of curls on the top of her head, a style currently so fashionable in Betty Grable musical films. And if ever she went out for the evening with any of her clippie mates, she sometimes donned a small pillbox hat, which she wore at a cheeky angle, with hair piled up all around it.

Another extraordinary change in Beattie was that, despite the fact that her job brought her into contact with working-class people, the cockney slang she had affected for so long in her younger days had gradually given way to a more gentle North London way of talking.

'Jairmany calling! Jairmany calling!'

The phoney upper-class English voice of William Joyce, better known as 'Lord Haw-Haw', the Nazis' chief English-language propagandist broadcaster, echoed out of Ma Briggs' wireless set, crackling with static and false information. His nightly commentaries on how Britain was losing the war infuriated anyone who was foolish enough to tune in to him. ''Ere 'e comes agin, the snotty-nosed git.' Ma was in good form, for Lord Haw-Haw was the one she most loved to hate. 'Goin' ter tell us that we're done for, are yer?' she barked at the wireless set.

'Poor little Englanders,' sneered the assumed cut-class voice, 'time is running out for you all, I fear.'

'There yer are!' protested Ma, angrily. 'Wot'd I tell yer?'

'Soon,' continued Ma's sworn enemy, 'the powerful boots of the Führer's troops will be leaving their glorious mark all over the faded white cliffs of Dover...'

'Some 'opes!' yelled Ma, shaking her fist at the wireless. 'Just wait till we get our rope round your neck, mate. We'll separate yer from yer bleedin' breff!'

'Ma!' called Beattie, who was half-laughing whilst ironing at the kitchen table. 'Why d'you always listen to that stupid man? You *know* he only does it to work us all up.'

''Cos I like ter work out in me mind wot an 'orrible bleedin' fissog 'e's got, an' 'ow I'd like ter get my 'ands round 'is froat an' wring the bleedin' daylights out of 'im!' Ma had her hands stretched out towards the wireless set as though she was about to strangle the creature sheltering inside it.

Beattie was getting used to Ma's nightly ritual. One minute the old girl was laughing her head off at Tommy Handley in *ITMA,* and the next, she was lambasting Winston Churchill and the entire government for not sending out a raid party to capture her pet hate in the wireless set.

Even so, in time of war Ma was an inspiration, a real morale booster. Now a sprightly eighty-two-year-old, she had more energy and drive than many people half her age, so much so that she still insisted on washing her own hair in the kitchen sink every week, and putting in the same curlers she'd kept in her old mum's 'vanity box' for what seemed like a hundred years. And, despite the wartime rations, she had managed to fill out to nearly twice the size she'd been when she'd run her boarding house back in the Bunk.

'Of course,' continued Ma, relentlessly, 'yer know this git used ter be in the Fascist Party, wiv ol' Mosley?'

Beattie didn't reply. Ma told her the same information every night she listened to Lord Haw-Haw, so there was really very little she could say. But every time Ma mentioned it, Beattie thought of Shiner, whom Jack Ridley had once threatened to kill if he ever tried to sleep with his wife again. Like the dangerous Fascist agitator himself, he had been detained in prison for the duration of the war.

'I tell yer this much though,' Ma whined, still glaring with venom at the wireless set, 'the way 'e reads that stuff, yer can tell that 'e ain't got a bleedin' brain in 'is–'

'Ma – quiet!' Beattie suddenly shut her up.

'Wos up?'

'Listen!' said Beattie, going to the wireless. 'I want to hear what he's saying.' To Ma's astonishment, she turned up the volume.

The plummy voice of the Nazi collaborator now filled the room. '…and after the invasion of Egypt by the brave forces of our victorious Italian ally, Marshal Benito Mussolini, the totally demoralised men of your English 8th Army are now being chased through the Western Desert, in one of the greatest humiliations in British military history.'

'Lyin' sod!' yelled Ma.

Beattie turned off the set abruptly.

Ma was no fool. She knew at once why Beattie had reacted in such a way. Struggling to her feet, she went straight to her, and put her arms around her. 'Don't listen to 'im, Beat,' she said comfortingly. 'No 'arm'll come to our Ed. 'E's far too clever.'

Beattie smiled weakly. 'Of course, Ma,' she said. 'I know.'

At that moment, they were distracted by the distant wail of the air-raid siren.

'Oh blimey!' groaned Ma. ''Ere we go again!'

'You go ahead,' said Beattie, quickly shunting the old girl towards the back yard door. 'I'll join you down the shelter as soon as I've put the ironing away.'

Ma left, grunting and groaning. 'Take no notice!' she called, as she went. ''E's a lyin' sod!'

After the old girl had gone, Beattie closed the door, and drew the blackout curtain across. For a moment or so, she stood in the pitch-dark, listening to the distant anti-aircraft gunfire. But her mind was occupied with something far more important than the start of yet another night's aerial bombardment. She was thinking of Ed, and how the worst moment of the war had been when he had volunteered for military service. Every time she thought about it, she ached inside. God knows, it had been hard enough to accept that her only son had been taken from her, but to know that his life would be in constant danger was just too much to take.

Her mind drifted back to the day when the boy tried to find a way of getting to Spain to fight against the Falangists in the Civil War, despite the fact that he was no more than seventeen years of age at the time. Then, when he was barely twenty-one, going straight into the army, to be sent within weeks to fight in France with the British Expeditionary Forces, only to return shell-shocked and traumatised from the horrifying retreat at Dunkirk. And if that wasn't enough, active duty again 'somewhere in North Africa'. It didn't make sense, rhyme, or reason. Oh yes, Ed had guts all right, but he was still her son, and he was only made of flesh and bones. Damn Lord Haw-Haw, she thought.

The droning of enemy aircraft grew closer and closer, and the house shook beneath the barrage of ack-ack fire that greeted them. Damn Lord Haw-Haw, Beattie fumed again. Damn him and all those who made him possible.

She opened the door, and went down to join Ma in the shelter.

Sarah swept the glass on the pavement from Freddie's barber shop window, and piled it into the kerb, to await, along with all the other bomb damage debris, the Borough Council collection. It had been another night of intense bombing by Jerry, in which poor old Essex Road nearby had copped a high-explosive bomb on a sweet shop, which had caused considerable damage throughout the neighbourhood right up to the Angel.

'Well, we've been lucky so far,' said Freddie, who was already fixing a 'BUSINESS AS USUAL' sign on his front door, now boarded up with strong timber planks. 'It was bound ter be our lot sooner or later.'

Sarah had just finished the clearing up when it started to rain. 'It's those poor devils in Maynards I'm thinking about,' she said, coming back inside with Freddie. 'They say it was a direct hit, nothing left of the sweet shop. I don't see how anybody could survive that.'

'Yer mustn't upset yerself, dear,' said Freddie, closing the shop door behind him. 'I'm afraid it's goin' ter get worse before it gets better. This could well be Jerry softenin' us up before 'e pays us a visit.'

Sarah was alarmed. 'Oh God, Freddie,' she said. 'D'you really think there *will* be an invasion?'

Freddie immediately wished he hadn't said that, so he put his arms around her. 'No, of course I don't, yer silly fing,' he said, holding her to him. 'If Jerry ever tries ter set foot on Blighty, we an' the gang'll be waitin' for 'im.'

Sarah pulled back, and looked at him. After eight years of married life, she had grown terribly protective of him. 'I don't want to hear you talk like that, Freddie,' she said, deadly serious. 'You're fifty-four years of age now. Fighting should be done by young men.'

'Wot young men?' asked Freddie.

Sarah thought about this. It was true. Most young men, just on the threshold of life itself, had been called up, taken away, and plunged into a useless exercise to prop up the retreating French troops whose positions had collapsed before the advancing German military machine. Young men like Tinker, Freddie's former apprentice, barely twenty-five years of age, killed in action in France after stepping on a landmine. It was cruel, so very cruel. 'Please don't take chances, Freddie,' she said with pleading eyes. 'I couldn't bear anything to happen to you.'

Freddie kissed her lightly. 'The 'Ome Guard don't take chances, Sarah,' he said with a comforting smile. 'We're just around in *case* of trouble.'

Until the start of the Second World War, life had been good for Mr and Mrs Freddie Hamwell. They were married in the spring of 1932 at St Mary's Church in Upper Street, with Sarah looking beautiful in a modest three-quarter-length wedding dress of white organza set off at her neck by a fluted lace collar, and a thin, half-length cotton veil topped by a small cluster of spring flowers – all made by herself. Both families were there, but Freddie's side far exceeded Sarah's, except that Aunt Dixie made up for all those who weren't there, by drinking as much gin as she could lay her hands on at the wedding reception afterwards at the Freemasons Hall in Clerkenwell Road. Against her instinct, Sarah did invite Beattie to the wedding, but was much relieved when she declined, 'owing to a prior commitment'. However, Young Ed did turn up, and created a big impression amongst the two families by talking with great intelligence about such things as the danger of Oswald Mosley and his New Party, and the suppression of the peasants in Spain. Despite his opinions, the reception was a huge success.

Since then, there had been two major disappointments in Sarah and Freddie's marriage.

The first was that, despite Freddie's early promises, they had still not moved from his cramped two rooms and a kitchen above the shop, which made life very difficult whenever Sarah wanted to invite family or friends over for tea. But the greatest sadness had been for Sarah to discover from a gynaecologist that she was unable to have children. For a time, this gave her a terrible complex, for she felt guilty, blaming herself for betraying Freddie, and denying him one last chance of becoming a father. But when Freddie told her, 'Having you as me wife is the most precious thing I have,' she realised what a special man he really was, and why she loved him more than anything or anybody else in the whole wide world.

Within an hour or so, Sarah and Freddie between them had cleaned up the shop, so that by their normal opening time of half-past eight, business could resume – despite Jerry's determination that it should do otherwise. And sure enough, at exactly half-past eight, the first customer arrived. It was old Arthur Ballard, who some years before had regularly brought his young grandson into the shop for a pudding-basin haircut. But the boy was now a teenager, and, according to Arthur, would soon be getting a free haircut, courtesy of the army barber. Now pushing ninety, the old boy had the most wonderful shock of white hair.

'Reckon it's about time 'e give yer double time fer this job,' quipped the old boy, taking his seat in the barber's chair. 'Mind you, I still don't 'old wiv wives workin' fer their 'usbands.'

Sarah smiled, and put a clean towel around his neck. 'I'm not working *for* him, Arthur,' she said. 'I'm working *with* him.'

'That's right, Arfur,' said Freddie, combing back the old boy's hair. 'There ain't no lads around these days. They're eivver called up, or makin' some fast cash in better-paid jobs.'

'This bleedin' war!' growled the old boy, as Freddie trimmed his hair. 'It's breakin' up families all over the place. Yer can't tell if the kids're alive or dead!'

Sarah shuddered as she thought of Ed, and wondered if she would ever see him, or Beattie, again.

'Business as usual! That's wot I like ter see!' The bright and cheery voice calling from the shop door was Frank, the postman. In his outstretched hand he was clutching just one letter. 'Lucky ter get somefin' terday, mate!' he called. 'They got the sortin' office last night. 'Ole lot went up in smoke.'

Freddie reluctantly took the letter from him. 'If it's a bill, yer can stick it!'

Frank laughed. 'Don't expect me ter pay it!' he joked as he left.

Freddie looked at the letter. 'Fer you, dear,' he said. 'Don't worry, it don't look like a bill.'

Sarah took the plain white envelope from him. The address was written by hand, but all in capital letters. She tried to read the postmark, but it was none too clear. When she slit open the envelope with one finger, she looked straight to the end of the hand-written letter to see who had sent it.

Fortunately, it wasn't a bill. It was from Beattie.

Beattie had only been a clippie on the trolleybus for a couple of months. Before that, she had been operating on the number 14 route, which was a good old-fashioned double-decker petrol bus that crossed London all the way from Hornsey Rise in the north, to Putney in the west. But although the trolleys were clearly the transport of the future, Beattie didn't care for them, mainly because they worked off overhead power lines, and whenever the two connecting poles came off, and started to flap around in midair, it was her job to slide out the long, cumbersome pole from underneath the bus and get the overhead connection working again. But at least it was a smooth ride, and one advantage the trolleys had over the petrol buses was that they were wider and easier to move around in.

On the morning after the Essex Road sweet shop bomb, Beattie was on duty on the 609 route to Moorgate. There were, as always, plenty of passengers, and Beattie found herself going up and down the stairs continually. On the upper deck, she could hardly see through the thick haze of cigarette smoke, and as no passenger ever seemed to want to open a window, the atmosphere was stifling. None the less, her ticket machine was kept busy, punching out tickets at a penny, twopence, and threepence. Very few passengers were travelling the entire journey, and some of those who did tried to insist that they had only got on at the previous bus stop.

As the bus reached Highbury Corner, Beattie

tried to peer through the protective gauze-covered windows, where it was obvious there was quite a lot of activity after the bomb blast the previous night. Shopkeepers were sweeping up broken glass from their windows, and others were busily boarding up the devastated shop fronts. All along Upper Street, fire engines were racing past heading off to the worst-affected areas where water mains and electric power lines had come down. It was a scene of utter chaos everywhere, and one that was becoming more and more familiar as the aerial onslaught continued.

'Wanna a pair of nylons, mate?' one of the younger male passengers asked Beattie as she punched him out a twopenny ticket. 'Goin' cheap. You've got the legs ter fill 'em!'

Beattie gave him his ticket, and wanted to tell him where to stuff his black-market nylons. But she thought better of it, took the bloke's coins, gave him the ticket, and with a stern, disapproving look, moved on.

Her next customer was an elderly lady, who had a large mongrel dog wedged in between her. 'One adult and one dog to City Road, please, dear,' she said.

Beattie took one of the coins from the palm of the old lady's hand. 'Let's forget about the dog, shall we?' she replied, with a grin. 'He's not a seat-paying passenger!' She put the coin in her satchel, took a penny ticket from her machine, punched it, and handed it over.

The old lady winked at her, and mouthed a silent 'Thank you.'

'I'm not a seat-payin' passenger eivver,' said the man sitting at the window, just in front of the old lady. 'Can I go free too?'

Beattie was just about to give him one of the pat answers she always kept in reserve for passengers who were too fresh, but when she looked at the man, she did a double take. Not only had she recognised the voice, but, despite the fact that he had lost his moustache, and had grey hair sprouting over both ears, there was no doubting who he was. 'Christ!' she said.

It was Jack Ridley.

29A Mitford Road
N7
26 Oct 1940

Dear Sarah

I know this will seem strange to you, my writing to you after so long, but just lately I've been thinking a lot about you.

Freddie Hamwell listened with rapt attention as Sarah read aloud the contents of the letter she had just received from her sister.

This war has brought home to me so many things that I've never really thought about before. I often think about the times when we were kids together, how you were always the one who knew how to play games or put things together, and how furious I was when I couldn't do anything myself. I also remember how many times we argued, how many times I sulked if I didn't get my own way. When you think about it, and I'm sure you have lots of times, I've been quite a failure as a sister. I'm not much good at being a mother either, but, in spite of everything, I *have* tried.

What I'm getting at is, I'd really like to see you again. I know you're married now, and Ed told me what a lovely man your Freddie is, but I would like to see you. You could, if you wanted, come here to tea, or even for a meal if you like. But I know you probably wouldn't like that. So, if you can bring yourself to forgive your sister for all the stupid things I've done in my time, maybe we could meet up on 'neutral territory' or something. I promise you, I'd sleep better at night if we could.

I miss you, Sarah. Sounds ridiculous, doesn't it, especially after all these years of distance between us. But I *do* miss you. There's a gap I can't fill, and I don't know why.

Please write. I would appreciate it. And please give my best to your Freddie. I'd love to meet him some time.

Love
Your sister, Beattie

Sarah put down the letter. She found it hard to take in what she had just read. 'Why?' she asked.

Freddie removed his spectacles, and ran his fingers through his greying hair. 'She misses yer.'

Sarah slowly shook her head. 'It's not possible. Every time we've met, she's been aggressive and unpleasant. She's never liked me.'

'She's older now,' said Freddie. 'So are you.'

'You mean, older and wiser?' asked Sarah.

'Yer never know.' Freddie, with his arm around Sarah's shoulders, was sitting next to her on the customers' row of chairs. 'Sounds like she needs you,' he said.

'It would be the first time.'

Freddie squeezed her shoulders. 'There's always a first time for everyfin',' he said. 'Who knows? P'raps you need her too?'

CHAPTER 23

'I'm a changed man, Beat.'

Despite the fact that his physical appearance had mellowed, Jack Ridley's words seemed as hollow as ever. The good looks were still there all right, but now that he was in his mid-forties, his rugged build had surrendered to a paunch, which suggested a period of good living. And if some of the aggression he had as a young man had been knocked out of him, he had certainly not lost the quick tongue, nor the flashing dark eyes, that had so captivated Beattie in her young days.

'They say travel broadens yer mind,' Ridley continued. 'Well, I've certainly 'ad me share of that. Been all over Ireland, from norf ter souf. It's a wonder I 'aven't turned into a bleedin' leprechaun!'

Ridley's humour failed to impress Beattie. She just sized him up over a mug of tea in the London Transport caff at the Moorgate turnaround.

'Got a lot ter tell yer, though, Beat,' Ridley said, rolling his own fag. 'Got meself a bob or two in Dublin. The war don't mean much ter the Paddys. No bombs over there.' He licked the ends of the fag paper, then stuck it between his lips. 'I managed ter set up me own business,' he said enthusiastically. 'You know – plasterin', brickie, that sort of fing. Mind you, I 'ad ter lay low fer a while. The fuzz never give up after wot 'appened ter old Ben.'

Beattie was doing her best to find some compassion for this man, but as she watched him lighting his fag, all bright and full of himself, she couldn't help casting her mind back to the last time she had seen him, his face crumpled up and crying like a baby, pleading to her to help him get away.

''Course, yer must've 'eard wot 'appened ter the Dillon boys – ter Phil and Joe?' He didn't wait for an answer, but carried right on talking. 'Caught their lot in a nicked car crash, up in Liverpool or some such place, or so I 'eard. At least they won't 'ave ter swing fer wot they did.'

Beattie watched him take a deep, uneasy draw on his fag.

'Not so wiv Charlie, though,' he continued. 'Ritz told me 'e got out ter Australia just before the war started. 'E's probably leadin' a 'ighly respectable life as a sheep farmer or somefin', wiv a wife an' six kids!' He flicked a quick glance up at Beattie, who had hardly spoken since they'd sat down at the table. 'Yer look good, Beat – not a day older. Must be almost ten years. Time flies.'

Beattie finally broke her silence. 'What d'you want from me, Jack?' she asked.

Jack hesitated before answering. 'I want yer back, Beat.'

Beattie sighed, and sat back in her chair.

'I'm not all bad, yer know,' said Ridley. 'Oh, I know I've got me faults–'

'Faults!' Beattie spluttered, in disbelief. 'You treat me like an animal, you beat up me – and my son – you get yourself involved with a gang of murderous thugs, then you run off and leave me to take the can back for ten years. And you tell me you have *faults?*'

Aware that the other bus crews in the canteen were watching them, Ridley stretched across the table and covered her hand with his own. 'I know I've made mistakes, Beat,' he said, voice low. 'But deep down inside, I've always 'ad a soft spot for yer.'

Beattie snatched her hand away. 'Don't talk to me like that, Jack!' she growled. 'I'm not a child. I'm not one of your pick-ups from the pubs down Stepney High Street.' She leaned across the table and faced him eye to eye. 'I've moved on, Jack. I'm not only older, but I've also come to my senses. You walked out of my life ten years ago, and that's an end to it!'

Ridley's expression hardened. He was far too vain to have expected this kind of response. 'So wot d'yer want ter do about our marriage then, Beat?' he asked, his face set firm. 'In case yer've fergotten, you're still me wife.'

Beattie couldn't believe that she was having this conversation with him. It had been sex, not love, that had brought them together, but as she looked at him now, with his square, obstinate jawline and dramatic but shifty eyes, she found him to be just about the most unappealing creature she had ever known. 'I want a divorce, Jack,' she said firmly.

For a moment, Ridley was stung. But then, as he sat back in his chair and took another drag of his fag, his face broke into that old, familiar grin.

'Do yer now?' he replied. 'An' wot if I say no?'

'You won't, Jack,' she replied. Then, after a perfectly timed pause, added, 'Because I know too much.'

Having sized her up in silence, Ridley finally leaned forward, stubbed his fag out in the tin top ashtray, and said, 'Yor'll 'ave ter find me first.'

But as he started to rise from the table, Beattie said: 'There is one thing I have to thank you for, Jack. If you hadn't returned that money, Ed and I would never have been able to get away from the Bunk. I shall be grateful to you for that for the rest of my life.'

Ridley looked at her as if she was mad. 'Wot're yer talkin' about?'

'That eighty pounds I gave you – after Big Ben's murder, the money you needed to get away. Ed told me what you'd done, how you'd given it to him, and told him to return it to me. I think it was very noble of you to go it alone.'

Ridley hesitated, then burst out laughing. 'Me – *noble?*' He laughed even more. 'Let me tell yer somefin', darlin',' he said. 'I don't know an' I don't care wot your son told yer. *I'm* tellin' yer that that money came in 'andy. An' I would never've given it back if yer come crawlin' on 'ands an' knees!'

With that he was gone.

Ma Briggs was none too pleased about her bloomers. Two pairs she'd lost when that last bomb fell. As it was, she only possessed four pairs in the entire world, and to lose two of her warmest flannelette ones, which Beattie had bought her for her birthday, was too much to bear. How would she ever be able to get a boy-friend now? she wondered, chuckling to herself.

Ma never stopped thanking the good Lord for giving her Beattie. Whatever good deeds the old girl had done for her had been more than repaid since they moved into Mitford Road, and since she hadn't seen any member of her so-called family for years, Beattie and Ed were the nearest she had to a daughter and a grandson. Even so, she worried continually about Beattie. It seemed to Ma that a young woman had no right to be all alone in this world. She needed a man about the place to spoil her and look after her.

Ha! she thought. A man – look after her, look after anyone. No hope! They're only out for themselves, for what they can get, not for what they're prepared to give – you only have to look at Jack Ridley for that, and her own late husband too. Bleedin' stupid old sod, killin' 'imself with booze before he was even fifty. It's not easy being a widow for over thirty years. But that Beattie, she's different. She should find herself a nice man, not over good-looking, but just a nice down-to-earth hard worker, who can give her all she wants in life – and a bit more beside.

Ma was suddenly jolted out of her daily after-noon snooze in the armchair in front of the gas fire in her bedroom. Someone was banging on the front door, but with her rheumatism, it was going to take her some time to get there.

'All right! All right!' she yelled as she carefully lowered herself heavily down each of the seem-ingly endless stairs that she counted every time she went up and down them. The heavy thumping on the street door continued, which only made Ma more and more tetchy. 'Wot's up wiv yer?' she yelled. 'Who d'yer fink I am – an Olympic bleedin' runner?' When she finally reached the door and opened it, she was surprised to see a teenage telegram boy waiting there on the doorstep.

'Afternoon, dear old lady!' the boy said brightly, holding up an orange-coloured telegram envelope. 'One telegram for a Mrs Ridley.'

Ma snatched the envelope from him. 'None of your bleedin' cheek,' she said, about to close the door.

'Wot – no tip?' asked the boy mischievously.

'Yes!' snapped Ma, irritably. 'Tip of my boot!'

She slammed the door in the boy's face, unaware that he had put two fingers up at her after she had done so.

Once the door was closed behind her, Ma's confidence disappeared immediately. A telegram! Oh Gord in Heaven, she thought. No one gets a telegram these days unless someone died – or been killed in action. With shaking hands, she made her way into the kitchen. She couldn't see what was written on the front of the envelope, for she hadn't got her glasses on, so she quickly found them, took the envelope over to the table where the light was better, and read out what it said. IMPERIAL TELEGRAM. MRS B RIDLEY.

Torn by worry and fear, Ma pondered on what to do next. Should she open the telegram herself right away, or wait until Beattie came home that evening? But then, she asked herself, if it was bad news about Ed, wouldn't it be better if she herself broke it gently to Beattie? For several minutes, she stood there, trying to decide what to do. She finally decided on the solution. Going to the gas hob, she put on a kettle of water to boil. When the steam started to appear at the spout, she held the sealed side of the telegram envelope over the steam and gradually prised it open. With fear and trepidation, she carefully unravelled the telegram and read it:

HOORAY! STOP. I'M COMING HOME ON LEAVE. STOP. LOTS OF LOVE. STOP. ED. STOP.

Ma, overjoyed, felt her heart miss a beat. Then she quickly put the telegram back into the envelope, and sealed it down.

Sarah looked wonderful in her sari. Freddie told her so the moment she came out of the bedroom and gave him a fashion show all to himself. Although Sarah had been left the sari by Mrs Ranasinghe, after the old lady's death eight years before, she had kept it locked up in her bottom drawer. She had always considered it to be far too precious actually to wear, and in any case, she still had such fond memories of her former employer wearing it on the anniversary of her husband's passing. She also never forgot the wonderful letter Mrs Ranasinghe's daughter Marla had written to her at the time, in which she mentioned her mother's last wishes, which consisted of one thousand pounds in cash, together with the sari 'which my dear girl liked so much, and who will wear it with dignity and charm'. It was a poignant departure, and one that Sarah would never forget. The thousand pounds had immediately been put into a savings account, ready for the day when she and Freddie were able to afford to move into their first real home, and the pale blue sari with the gold trim was wrapped up in tissue paper, and stored safely. But today was a special occasion, Freddie's birthday, and Sarah felt that this was the time when that wonderful old Ceylonese lady would want her to wear her very special bequest.

That evening, Sarah cooked a birthday meal for Freddie unlike anything he had had before. In keeping with her appearance, and as a tribute to the memory of Mrs Ranasinghe, she cooked a full Ceylonese meal of rice and curry, dried vegetables, and fruit chutney. Freddie was a bit suspicious of it all at first, but once he'd got the taste, he was a convert. 'Best birfday I've ever had,' he said, 'even if there weren't no Yorkshire pud!'

A little later, Sarah gave him his birthday present: a pair of gold-plated cufflinks, each in the shape of a pair of scissors. But there was a shock in store for Sarah when Freddie told her that he had a present for her too.

'I've put a down payment on a house,' he announced, quite suddenly.

Sarah was totally taken aback. 'Freddie!' she exclaimed. 'Wot? Where?'

'For the time bein', yer'll just 'ave ter be

patient,' he said, clearly enjoying the game he was playing.

'But Freddie,' said Sarah, who was initially excited, but was now nagged by doubt, 'why didn't you talk it over with me first? After all, if we're both going to live there, we should choose it together.'

Freddie looked hurt. Suddenly, the 'gift' he had planned so carefully seemed to have gone sour. 'I couldn't really tell yer, dear,' he said sheepishly. 'I wanted it ter be a surprise. Yer see, it's very special.'

'Even more reason why you should have discussed it with me.'

Freddie looked worried, as Sarah collected the dishes and took them to the sink. He could tell that she was upset with him. Going across to her, and putting his arm around her waist, he said meekly, 'Don't be angry with me, dear. I did it 'cos I love yer.'

Sarah wanted to say that everything was quite all right, but there was something inside her that wanted to sulk, to show her disapproval. In nearly nine years of marriage, this was the first time she had ever shown any real irritation with him. She also showed irritation with herself as well, for she knew she was being inflexible and selfish. But after a moment or so, she was willing to try. 'Can you at least tell me where it is?' she asked.

Freddie was concerned. 'If I did that,' he said mournfully, 'it wouldn't be a surprise any more, would it?'

Sarah put the last of the dishes to soak in the

sink, then wiped her hands on the drying-up cloth. Then she turned to face him. 'Don't let us ever keep secrets from each other, Freddie,' she pleaded. 'Because secrets between married people can only lead to – problems.'

'Do you have any secrets, Sarah?'

Freddie's extraordinary question came like a bolt out of the blue. 'What do you mean?' she asked.

'Oh, I don't know,' he replied. 'I suppose everyone 'as a dark secret in their life at one time or anuvver. All I mean is that if yer did, yer would tell me, wouldn't you?'

'Of course,' she replied with some surprise. 'I would never keep anything from you.'

'Nuffin'?' he asked. 'Nuffin' at all?'

Sarah was now quite unnerved by the way he was putting her on the defensive. 'Freddie,' she said, uneasily, 'I don't know what you're getting at.'

Freddie put his arms around her waist, and pulled her close, her head resting on his shoulder. 'I was just wonderin',' he said, 'who that man was who come in lookin' for yer terday.'

Beattie got home from her day shift on the Moorgate route at about seven in the evening. She was dog-tired, and the first thing she did was to go straight into her bedroom and kick off her shoes. Then she pulled off her uniform beret, and threw it on to the armchair by the fireplace, followed by her uniform jacket, which she hung on a hook behind the door. Absolutely dead on her feet after running up and down bus stairs all day long, she quite literally flung herself on to the bed, and lay spread-eagled there.

After a moment, there was a tiny tap on the door. 'Come in, Ma!' she called, wearily.

'Sorry, Beat,' said the old girl. 'I 'eard yer come in, and wondered if yer'd like a nice cup of tea.'

Beattie sighed hard, sat up, and rubbed her eyes. 'You're a dear, Ma,' she replied. 'But I think I'd like just like to have a wash before we have to get down the shelter again.'

Ma looked anxious. 'Come on, dear,' she said, trying to coax Beattie, 'it won't take long. I've got it all ready. It's on the table.'

Beattie felt quite sick inside. She didn't want to hurt Ma's feelings, because she knew the trouble she always took to look after her. 'Just five minutes then.'

Ma beamed, and left her to it.

A few minutes later, Beattie came down the stairs, but she was curious to know why Ma seemed to be waiting for her in the passage. 'Anything wrong, Ma?' she asked.

'Wrong?' asked Ma. ''Course not!' she replied. 'Tea's on the table. I'll leave yer to it.'

Beattie watched the old girl disappear into the kitchen, then wrapping her winceyette dressing gown around her, she went into the front room. Her face was a picture, as she immediately saw someone standing by the fireplace, his back turned towards her. He was quite a tall, skinny young man, with a short back and sides haircut that made his ears protrude far more than they would if his hair had been longer. But when he smiled at her, there were no guesses as to who this young man in army uniform was.

'Oh Christ – Ed!'

'Hello, Mum!' he said, beaming.

With that, she ran straight into his arms.

Even in his wildest imagination, Ed had never guessed that he would be spending his first night home on leave in an Anderson air-raid shelter in the back yard. Not that he wasn't used to life in a dugout, but that was on the front line, where soldiers were expected to keep their heads low, and try to protect themselves against enemy shells and sniper bullets. This was different. This was a hole in the ground for civilians, with a cold, unfriendly, sloping roof made out of corrugated iron, which, if you were tall like Ed, dared you to stand up and not bang your head. And the noise of ack-ack gunfire was just like the chaos at the front, relentless, night and day, day and night. He found it hard to believe that his own mother was having to survive this kind of life; in many ways, he found it far more frightening down in this particular English hole than in any old mud-filled dugout in France.

'I had my heart in my mouth when I heard Lord Haw-Haw boasting about the destruction of the British forces in Egypt.' Beattie was half-dozing in an old wicker armchair with Ed at her side, an affectionate arm around her shoulders. 'After your last letter, I was convinced they'd sent you out to the desert. I had no idea you were in Greece.'

'We were part of an advance party,' said Ed, trying to be heard above the racket going on outside. 'Everyone knows Jerry and the dagos are going to invade sooner or later. We were there to help the Greeks set up their defences.'

'It's all so frightening,' said Beattie.

'Not really,' Ed assured her. 'Yer can't just let the Fascists take over the world. There has to be a time when you say, "That's it, mate. That's as far as you go!"'

In the lower bunk behind, Ma was snoring so loud, it sounded as though she was trying to compete with the constant drone of enemy aircraft overhead.

Beattie leaned her head against Ed, and she felt the surge of warm blood rushing through his body. This was the child she never wanted, and yet she felt sick every time she knew he was in danger. 'What I can't get over,' she said, 'is why they brought you home? I mean, if it's as bad as you say it is out there, surely they need all the men they can get?'

'Good point, Mum,' he replied with a knowing grin. 'But I wasn't really much good to them with my wound.'

Beattie sat bolt upright. 'Wound?' she gasped. 'You mean, you've been injured?'

Ed laughed, and gently kissed her on the forehead. Now that he had outgrown that snotty-nosed kid in the Bunk, he was much closer to his mother than he had ever been during those days. 'Nothing to worry about, Mum,' he said reassuringly. 'Someone dropped a shell on my foot, broke two bones. I had to spend two weeks in the field hospital. They said I wouldn't be much use if I suddenly had to make a break for it.'

Beattie almost looked relieved. 'Does that mean you won't have to go back?' she asked hopefully.

Ed smiled. 'I wouldn't bank on it,' he replied gingerly.

For the next few moments, they just sat there deep in thought, thinking about the past, the present, and what the future was likely to hold for not only them, but for the whole of the human race.

'I saw Ridley,' Beattie said quite suddenly.

'Oh?' Although Ed was shocked, he tried not to show it. 'So they haven't caught up with him?'

'I doubt they ever will,' replied Beattie. 'He's too clever by half. But if they do...'

'If they do,' said Ed, carrying on where she'd left off, 'God help him.' He pulled himself up, took a cigarette out of a packet in his uniform trousers pocket, and lit it. 'Has he changed much?' he asked.

'Ridley will never change,' replied Beattie. 'He wouldn't know what to do if he did.' She paused for a moment, then said, 'He wanted me to get back with him again.'

Ed laughed, and practically choked on his cigarette. 'That's a joke!' he spluttered.

'No, he meant it,' said Beattie. 'The thought of it practically gave me a nightmare.'

'I'm not surprised.'

For a brief moment, the barrage of ack-ack fire seemed to cut out, to be replaced by an ominous silence, but for the deafening chorus of Ma's snores.

Then, quite out of the blue, Beattie asked, 'D'you remember all those years ago, just before

Ridley skipped the country, how you told me that he'd given you back the money I'd given to him? D'you remember that time, Ed?'

Ed drew on his fag. 'I remember,' he replied quietly.

'Well, a funny thing happened,' she said. 'He told me he never gave you any money at all. And yet, when you came back that day, you had that eighty pounds. Where did it come from, Ed?'

Ed leaned back in his vastly uncomfortable wooden upright chair. With his cigarette in his mouth, his eyes were transfixed on the sloping ceiling of the shelter, where condensation was running down slowly then gathering speed down the walls. He was now a one-pip lieutenant in the Royal Fusiliers, and his training as a commissioned officer had prepared him for just a situation such as this – decision, tact, and truth in the face of all adversity. 'Does it really matter now, Mum?' he asked. 'It was a long time ago.'

Beattie turned to look at him. 'It matters to me, Ed.'

Without holding the fag between his fingers, Ed blew out smoke from it. 'It came from Aunt Sarah.'

'Sarah?' Beattie said in absolute astonishment. 'My sister?'

'*My* aunt,' replied Ed. 'I went to see her. When there was a chance that we'd lose this house, I asked her to help. No, I begged her.'

'Oh God, Ed!' she gasped. 'You didn't?'

'She took the money out of her savings, then told me what I should tell you. She wanted you to think that Jack had paid it back. She never wanted you to know the money came from her.'

'Ed, how could you have done such a thing?'

After a brief moment's thought, Ed turned to look at her. 'I did it because I wanted to, because I *had* to. Aunt Sarah needed to do it, Mum. Because *she* needs you, as much as *you* need her. Sooner or later you're both going to realise that.'

The barrage of ack-ack gunfire opened up again. By then, both Ed and his mother were looking hard at each other.

It was almost daybreak. They'd been talking all night.

CHAPTER 24

If the first few days of November were not exactly an Indian summer, they were certainly milder than usual for the time of year. But what with the combination of the early blackout, the dreary long nights, and regular nightly air raids that began at dusk and continued until dawn, the weather was no real help to the morale of the thousands of people who had to spend their nights in an air-raid shelter. But there was certainly no doubt that since the unexpected success in September of the RAF's campaign to combat the German Luftwaffe, there had been a decisive turnaround in the nature and scale of the London Blitz, as it was now called. For a start, so many enemy aircraft had been shot down or destroyed in midair that the German pilots now found it far too dangerous to carry out bombing missions over London and the Home Counties during daylight hours. Subsequently, the strategy changed to massive air strikes against civilian targets under cover of dark, which inevitably caused widespread damage. But there was one element of night-time raids that even the superior power of the Luftwaffe could not cope with.

Sarah hated fog. It scared and disoriented her. Once, when she was a child, she had got lost in the fog in the garden of the old family home in

Thornhill Road, and she'd screamed so loud that her mother had had to come out to rescue her. To Sarah, fog was sinister and threatening, and whenever it came down, she tried to make sure that she was safely at home. This evening was a real pea-souper, and she had been caught out in it, as it had come down quite suddenly as she made her way home from collecting the bagwash in Upper Street. She immediately began to panic, for the blanket of thick, choking fog seemed to engulf her, forcing her to lose all sense of direction. Although she could hear voices in the distance, all traffic seemed to have come to a standstill, and she couldn't make out whether she was still on the main road, or hadn't inadvertently turned a corner into a side street. She cursed herself for not having brought her torch, even though it would have been no use in such conditions, as the beam would only have produced a blinding glare. So her only solution was to ease her way towards the shop fronts, and quite literally feel her way to the corner of St Alban's Place, where she would find it easier to locate the barber shop. Her task was made more difficult for as it had already passed blackout time, there were no lights in the shop windows. Fortunately, she did bump into a young couple, who were having as many problems as herself in finding their way about, but their only response when she asked if they knew where they were was, 'Sorry, missus. 'Aven't the foggiest!' She cursed them too, as their silly giggles disappeared into the murky grey blanket behind her.

Her spirits were raised, however, when her hand suddenly identified the rolled timber shutters over the shop window of her neighbour, Mr Timmins, the tobacconist. All she had to do now was to feel her way past the walls of the other few houses along the quiet side street. She was just a few doors away from the barber shop when she heard a movement directly in front of her. She stopped dead, and called, 'Is someone there? Freddie? Is that you?'

There was no response. In the claustrophobic box she was enclosed in, her voice sounded dull and blank, and she was almost overpowered by the smell of coal fires, pumping out thick black dust from chimneys all over London. Again, she heard something, or rather sensed it.

'Please,' she begged, nervously, 'if there *is* someone there, say something.'

'Sarah.' She was answered by a man's voice, little more than a loud whisper.

Sarah took a step backwards. She was frightened. 'Wh-who are you?' she asked anxiously.

The eerie outline of a man slowly materialised, but as the fog was now dense, there was no way he could be identified. 'Don't worry,' he said. 'I'm not going to 'urt yer.' He moved closer. 'It's yer bruvver-in-law, Sarah, yer long-lost bruvver-in-law.'

It took Sarah a moment to take it in, and then it dawned on her that it was Jack Ridley's voice. 'You!' she gasped, no longer nervous, but angry. 'What the devil d'you think you're doing?'

'I come ter see yer, Sarah,' he said, trying to sound as though he was hurt. 'I'm sorry I din't choose the right time.'

'There's never a right time to see you, Ridley!' she snapped. 'How dare you call on my husband and tell him we're close old friends?'

'Ah!' replied Ridley, a grin in his voice. 'So 'e told yer, did 'e? 'Ow d'yer know it was me?'

'Oh, I knew!' replied Sarah, scathingly.

'Even after all these years?'

'Oh yes,' she said. 'Even after all these years. The moment he described you, I didn't have to think twice.'

'I'm flattered.'

Sarah thought about making a run for it, but she was so disoriented she just didn't have the nerve. 'What do you want, Ridley?' she asked.

'I could do wiv some 'elp, Sarah,' he said, his outline distorted by the drifting fog. 'I need some – respectability, shall I say?'

'What the devil are you talking about?'

Voices were heard in the distance, distraught passers-by on Chapel Street, trying to work out which way they were heading.

Ridley waited a moment until they had gone, then withdrew his shadowy outline back into the fog. 'I want a wife, an 'ome, a family,' his voice coming from nowhere. 'I want *my* wife, my 'ome, and *my* family.' He had now moved into a position somewhere at her side. 'In uvver words, I want ter get back wiv your sister again.'

'Why?'

Ridley was stung by her question. ''Cos I love 'er, of course.'

'Don't talk nonsense, Ridley,' she said. 'What have you ever done to love my sister?'

'I married 'er, din't I?' he snapped. 'In't that enuff?'

Sarah paused. 'No, *Mister* Ridley,' she replied. 'That is not enough.'

There was an unnerving pause from Ridley whilst he gathered his thoughts. During the years he had been lying low in Ireland, in his mind he had often rehearsed this moment with Sarah, gaining her support to help reinstate him. Despite what he had told Beattie, for the past ten years his life hiding away in Ireland had been a hell on earth. From one day to the next, he never knew whether someone would turn up at his room in the middle of the night and take him back to England, to gaol, and the real possibility of a walk to the gallows. 'Sarah,' he said, finally, 'I don't want ter run any more.'

'You should have thought about that before you killed that poor man.'

'I din't 'ave nuffin' ter do wiv wot 'appened ter Ben!' he insisted firmly, though in a low voice. 'I 'ad no part in it!'

'Then go to the police and tell them so.'

'It's all in the past, I tell yer,' Ridley pleaded, his voice cracking with frustration. 'Nobody cares wot 'appened nearly ten years ago!'

'His wife and five children do,' replied Sarah.

She started to move on, but Ridley suddenly appeared from behind, clutched her arms, and held her. 'Look. All I want is a chance ter get a job and settle down. Talk ter Beat for me. She'd listen ter you. Tell 'er that I'm not the man I used ter be. Tell 'er I'll do anfyin' I can ter make 'er 'appy.'

Sarah hesitated, then said, 'Go away, Ridley.

Leave us alone – all of us.'

She started to move again, but Ridley suddenly increased his hold on her arms. 'Tell me somefin', Mrs barber shop lady,' he said, his voice more like his old self. 'Wot d'yer fink your lovin' 'usband'd say if 'e knew about – you an' me?'

Sarah swung round. 'I beg your pardon?' she snapped indignantly.

'If I wanted to, I reckon I could tell 'im a fing or two – wouldn't you say? I mean, 'e'd 'ave ter draw 'is own conclusions about whevver it's the truth or not. But it ain't easy, is it? There's never no smoke wivout fire, is there?'

Ma Briggs had lost her false teeth. She distinctly remembered taking them out before she went to bed in the air-raid shelter the previous night, so there was absolutely no doubt in her mind that that's where they were. But Ed took a different view. He was just as sure that before Ma went down to the shelter the previous night, she hadn't had her teeth in. Whatever the truth, both his mum and himself had searched the house from top to bottom without success, but the elusive pearly whites were still missing.

'Don't worry, Ma,' said Ed, 'I'll buy you a new pair.' Then added teasingly, 'We'll leave your old pair to scare the mice away!'

Ma was not amused. She was very sensitive about talking to people without her teeth in, so from now on when she did so, she would have to cover her mouth discreetly with her hand.

Ed's teasing did not, however, lessen the great affection she had for the boy. Practically the moment he walked through the door, she had thrust one of her home-made bread puddings, his all-time favourite, into his hands. Over the years, their relationship had developed into a deeply loving one, and in spite of the fact that he still called her Ma, he really thought of her as his grandma. When Ed was a small boy, they would sit alone together and discuss his mum, and all the problems they had to face up to, especially Jack Ridley. ''E's not all bad,' Ma would often say, 'but 'e can be a real pain in the arse.' Now Ed was all grown up, if ever there was anything he needed to know about his mum, it was always Ma he turned to. But on his second day home on leave there was something he particularly wanted to ask her.

'Boyfriends? Yer mum? Ha! That's a larff, that is!' Ma was taking full advantage of having Ed all to herself whilst Beattie was doing her day shift on the buses. 'Well,' she said, correcting herself, 'that's not altergevver true. There is this bloke in 'Ornsey Road she's quite keen on – 'e's a schoolteacher or somefin'. But every time she finks 'e's gettin' serious, she backs orf. If yer ask me, she's worried about once bitten, twice shy, if yer know what I mean.'

Ed did know what the old girl meant. His mum's experience of men had been none too happy, and she had now fallen into a style of life that seemed to suit her best of all. Or did it? He was now adult enough to know that, for whatever reason, people need people, and his mum was too young and too good-looking a woman to be wasted on a solitary existence. 'But doesn't she ever go out anywhere?' he asked. 'I mean, to have an evening out with anyone?'

Ma stopped peeling the spuds, and shook her head. 'Only wiv her old mate, Nagger Mills. But Nagger's got an 'usband an' family of 'er own ter look after. She don't 'ave much time for gallivantin'.' She plopped a spud into a saucepan of water in front of her. 'Mind you,' she said, wistfully, 'it's a pity yer mum don't keep in touch wiv 'er sister, Sarah. I mean, look at 'er. She's 'appy as a sandboy that one, good 'usband, good 'ome. I often wonder why they don't just bury the 'atchet and get tergevver. I know yer mum'd like to. Gord knows, she's always goin' on ter me about it.'

Ed was astonished. 'Mum says she'd like to get back together with Aunt Sarah?'

'Oh yes,' replied Ma. 'She's always goin' on ter me about 'ow badly she treated 'er sister Sarah, and 'ow, if only fer the sake of yer gran and granddad, she'd like ter put fings right.'

Ed was fascinated to hear all this. Only a couple of nights before, when he'd told his mum about the eighty pounds Aunt Sarah had taken from her savings, his mum had more or less indicated that she didn't really care if she ever saw her sister again.

'Does Mum still never try to make contact with Aunt Sarah?' he asked.

'Just once,' replied the old lady. 'She wrote to 'er, coupla weeks ago. She asked if they could meet up, an' talk fings over. I mean, when yer fink 'ow proud yer mum is, that took quite a bit of doin'.'

'Well, what did Aunt Sarah say?' asked Ed.

'Not a word.'

Ed was puzzled. 'You mean, she didn't reply?'

The old girl shook her head. The ordeal of talking without her precious pearly whites had been too much for her.

Freddie Hamwell finished getting into his Home Guard uniform. All he needed now was his khaki topcoat, his gasbag, and his rifle. Sarah didn't like him doing night duty, for it meant that as she had herself volunteered for civil defence work in the Women's Voluntary Service, they had been forced to spend many nights apart. At the moment, this was even more worrying, for ever since his birthday supper, when he'd casually asked Sarah who the man was that had been into the shop enquiring after her, he had remained stubbornly uncommunicative.

'Why are you sulking, Freddie?' asked Sarah, with concern, handing him his gasbag.

'Don't know wot yer mean,' he replied awkwardly and coldly.

'You know very well what I mean. You've hardly spoken to me since your birthday. Why can't we talk about it?'

'Nuffin' ter talk about,' he said, putting his gasbag over his shoulder.

Sarah was rapidly losing her patience. She knew what was nagging at him, and she was determined to have it out with him. 'Freddie Hamwell, I won't have you treating me like this. I'm your wife and you're my husband. If something is wrong, we should bring it out into the open.'

'I've got ter go, Sarah,' he said, edging his way towards the bedroom door. 'I don't want to be late on duty.'

She took hold of his arm, and yanked him back. 'Don't be so silly, Freddie,' she said, scolding him. 'I know very well that you're not on duty until seven o'clock, and it's not even six. What's this all about?'

'Please, Sarah,' he said, trying to pull away. 'Let me go.'

'D'you think I'm having an affair with another man?' she asked, point-blank.

'Couldn't tell yer,' he replied, indifferently.

'Oh really, Freddie,' she said, straightening his khaki tie. 'After nearly nine years, I honestly thought you knew me better than that. I'm a married woman. It's ridiculous to think that I go around having secret liaisons.'

'Why not?' replied Freddie, sulkily. 'You're an attractive woman.'

'Sit down, Freddie,' Sarah said calmly.

'I've got to go.'

'For God's sake!' she snapped. 'Sit down and let's discuss this like rational human beings.'

Freddie hesitated then, like a naughty schoolchild, he went back to their bed and perched himself on the edge.

'I know what this is all about,' she said, going to him. 'I know you think that the man who came into the shop looking for me was – well, what you think he was.' She perched on the bed beside him. 'You've got it all wrong, Freddie. I want to tell you about it. I *have* to tell you about it.' She took his hand and gently cupped it in her own.

'The man you saw was my sister's husband.'

Freddie swung a look at her. 'Jack Ridley?'

'Yes.'

'But you told me they didn't live together, that he'd run off to Ireland or some such place.'

'All that's true,' she said. 'But what I've never told you is *why* he ran off.'

Freddie looked at her in bewilderment as he listened to her harrowing account of the murder of Big Ben Fodder in the Bunk, of Ridley's involvement with the Dillon boys, and the way he had beaten up Beattie ever since the day they married. She also told him about her relationship with Edward Lacey, how he had jilted her, and why. It wasn't easy for her to open her heart to him, for her involvement with Lacey had left a permanent scar on her pride and dignity. But she knew that she owed it to him to tell the truth, especially since he not only knew Young Ed, but he liked him a great deal. In the period before the boy joined the army, every time the two of them met, Ed often talked enthusiastically to Freddie about books, and all the things he had learned from them. Although Freddie himself hadn't been very well educated, he was a wonderful listener, and this gave the boy the most tremendous encouragement.

When Sarah had finished pouring her heart out to him, Freddie took off his gasbag, laid it on the bed behind him, and put his arm around her waist. 'Why din't yer tell me all this before, yer silly gel?'

Sarah leaned her head on his shoulder, and sighed. 'I didn't want to lose you,' she said.

'Yer won't lose me that easy, Mrs 'Amwell,' he said, hugging her.

But a sudden thought occurred to her. 'Freddie,' she asked anxiously. 'What are we going to do about Ridley? He frightens me.' She sat up straight and faced him. 'Years ago – he tried to take advantage of me. And last night...'

Freddie lowered his eyes.

Sarah continued with difficulty. 'Last night, he was waiting for me outside, in the fog. He tried to get me to persuade Beattie to have him back. He said if I didn't, he'd tell you that his advances towards me all those years ago – had not been rejected.'

Freddie still couldn't look at her. 'An' were they, Sarah?' he asked, grim-faced.

Sarah put her hand underneath his chin and gently raised it. She was now looking straight into his eyes. 'What do you think, Freddie?' she asked.

Freddie took her hand and held it.

After a pause, Sarah continued, 'In some ways it's not his fault. Ridley is a victim of his own upbringing. He's like so many of his kind who've cut themselves off from their families. Beattie once told me his was a lost childhood, a childhood without hope, without any form of direction. Unfortunately for everyone else, however,' she said with an anxious sigh, 'Ridley *is* dangerous. He could do Beattie a lot of harm. He could do us all a lot of harm.'

As she spoke, the shrill call of the air-raid siren pierced the air outside.

CHAPTER 25

London was now in the grip of an intense campaign by the German Luftwaffe to bomb the daylights out of it. But it was night after night that they came, one great aerial armada after another, engines droning like a dragon's roar, and hundreds of high-explosive bombs raining down on the homes, businesses, and places of worship of the rich and poor alike. But if the intention of Herr Goering was to bomb the spirit out of the civilian population, it clearly wasn't working.

'Show me the way ter go home!' Wave after wave of people's voices belted out the words of a popular morale-raising song, and the magnificent sound they made echoed out loud across the River Thames at the Victoria Embankment, right in the heart of London Town. Further up river, the flickering glow of massive fires surrounded the mighty dome of St Paul's Cathedral, turning the waters of the river into an inferno. There was frantic activity everywhere, with mere handfuls of exhausted firemen desperately trying to tackle major incidents with the most limited resources, and women from the civil defence units and auxiliary emergency services there to give all the support they could, from medical aid to life-saving cups o' char. On the other side of the river, there was competition from a Salvation Army band, who were determined to obliterate the whining sound of high explosives and Molotov cocktail incendiary bombs, with the strains of 'Yes, Jesus Loves Me!' in words, song, drums, and tambourines.

Sarah and her old friend Eunice Dobson were on WVS mobile canteen duty just near the Embankment entrance to the Kingsway tram tunnel. After a hard night pouring endless cups of tea for the exhausted teams tackling the persistent fires around Charing Cross and Northumberland Avenue, it was now approaching daybreak. But, weary though they were, the two women joined in the rousing song, Eunice's squeaky voice piping above the rest.

Despite the fact that she was now a married woman with three kids of her own, Eunice always defied regulations by leaving the top buttons of her uniform tunic open, which left very little to the imagination of the firemen. 'Poor sods!' she squeaked to Sarah, usually after yet another admirer had given her a lustful grin, 'they've got ter 'ave a little somefin' ter look forward to, 'aven't they?'

Amongst the usual nightly crowd of firemen and rescue workers, there was always a fair number of special reserve police constables, and members of the armed forces. Many a night the two women had been told by soldiers just back from the front somewhere that they felt safer where they'd come from than taking their chances on the streets of London. There was always someone to chat to, someone to comfort, or someone to tell that they were perfectly safe and that no harm would come to them. But whilst Sarah was in the middle of trying to serve a small animated group of servicemen, who had all descended on her in a mad rush, she suddenly picked out a face that took her totally by surprise.

'Oh my God!' she cried. 'Ed!'

Her young nephew beamed. 'Hello, Aunt Sarah!' he called from the seething crowd, his hands trying to reach out to her. 'How are you?'

Sarah couldn't hear what he was trying to say, and in any case she dare not stop pouring cuppas for the crowd that was besieging her and Eunice. 'See you after the all clear!' she mouthed.

'Can't hear you!'

'She said, she'll see yer after the all clear!' answered one of the firemen, standing at the front of the queue. 'Wot's up wiv yer, mate?' he quipped, amidst weary laughter from the others. 'Got cloff ears or somefin'?'

It was half an hour later that the all clear siren wailed out across the river. By then, the rescue workers were moving on to reinforce their embattled colleagues in the City of London, where scores of fires were still raging out of control. With the night's events now at an end, Eunice told Sarah that she would wash and clear up the cups to enable Sarah to go off for a chat with her nephew.

It was strangely quiet along the Embankment at six o'clock in the morning, for, after the frenzied activities of the night, most of the clearing-up operations seemed to be confined to the areas that had had direct high-explosive hits. As they strolled down Northumberland Avenue,

Sarah and Ed had to step carefully over the last of the dozens of hose pipes, which had snaked all the way back to Trafalgar Square.

As they strolled, Ed told his aunt about all that had happened to him since they had last met, careful not to alarm her too much about the dangerous missions he had been involved in. At the Embankment, they crossed the road, and made for Cleopatra's Needle. Here, Sarah and Ed perched on the riverbank wall and looked out at the mighty London river, now just beginning to shed its thin layer of early morning November mist. To their left, they looked out on to the City skyline, with numerous pockets of thick dark smoke still curling up into the murky grey clouds from the night's savage firebomb onslaught. And to the right stood the great clocktower of Big Ben, impervious to all the provocation, standing proud and contemptuous to the overhead intruders, a true inspiration to the 'Mother of all Parliaments', which had itself been damaged in an air raid during the autumn.

'I never thought I'd live to see this day,' said Sarah, taking off her tin helmet and shaking out her hair. 'Bombs on so much of this lovely city – it's a crime.'

'Not only London,' said Ed. 'Just think what they did to poor old Coventry the other night. Practically destroyed the whole city. God knows how many were killed.'

'They can destroy our cities,' said Sarah, 'but they'll never destroy the people's spirit.'

Ed lit a cigarette, and for a moment or so they both just sat there, unwinding from the night's traumatic events, staring out along the river, undaunted in the early morning light.

'I thank God you're safe,' said Sarah. 'I've often told Freddie how concerned I am for you.'

'I've been concerned for you too, Aunt Sarah,' replied the boy.

Sarah gave him an affectionate look. 'Thank you, Ed,' she replied gratefully.

There was again a moment of silence, of deep thought between them. Their eyes glistened in the weak winter sunlight. A gentle breeze carried the smoke from Ed's cigarette down river.

'I was looking at a photograph I keep of you the other day,' he said, quite out of the blue.

'Really?'

'It was of you and Mum when you were small kids together. She said it was taken when Gran and Granddad took you on holiday to the Isle of Wight.'

'Oh yes,' she said with a faint smile. 'It was a glorious fortnight. I think I only quarrelled once with your mother.'

They both chuckled. Their eyes, however, remained turned towards the river, which was now swelling in the oncoming tide.

'I'm very flattered that you keep a photograph of me, Ed,' said Sarah. 'It's a sweet thought.'

'It's not the only photo I keep,' he continued. 'I've got a whole lot of them in my wallet. Every time I think I might not get back from a pretty dicey mission or something, I always take them out first and have a look. It never fails. I'm still here.'

Sarah felt quite sick inside. She knew that if she

turned to look at him she would cry, so she merely felt for his hand and gave it a loving squeeze.

'You know, Aunt Sarah,' he said reflectively, 'you've given me so much in my life. I don't know how I'd have done what I have if it hadn't been for you.'

Sarah was embarrassed. 'That's not true, Ed,' she said. 'What you've achieved, you've done all on your own.'

'Oh no,' he insisted. 'I remember those days back in the Bunk. It was like being locked up in a prison. When I came to see you, I could talk to you about all the things inside me that were trying to get out. I learned so much from Granddad's books that you gave me.'

'He would have liked that,' replied Sarah.

'I learned about people, the way they talk, the way they think, the way they can make you happy or inflict pain. I learned about the gulf between the rich and the poor, and about inequality. It was thanks to you that I started to think things out for myself, to use my own mind, to have opinions and make decisions. It was the reason I wanted to go to Spain, to help the weak in their struggle against the powerful. It was the reason I joined up at the start of the war. I can't bear the Fascists. I can't bear injustice.' He tossed his cigarette into the river and turned to her. 'As much as I love Mum,' he said, 'she couldn't give me what you've given me.'

Before Sarah could answer, he gently put his fingers over her lips. 'If you could do all that for me,' he said, 'why couldn't you do it for her?'

Sarah lowered her eyes. 'You're a young man, Ed,' she said. Then she raised her eyes again. 'One day you'll know a lot more about your mother and me.'

'I know more than you think,' he said. 'I know that she loves you. And she needs you now more than ever before.'

Ritz Coogan hadn't changed a bit. In ten years, he still looked as dumpy as ever, and there was hardly a line on his chubby little face. His only concession to advancing years, however, was his hair, which had once been dark and wavy, but which was now pure white, due no doubt to the fright he got when he heard how the Dillon boys had dealt with Big Ben. Since those days, he had spent most of his time in Belgium, making as much money as he could doing casual labour. He never remained in one place long enough for anyone to get to know him properly, which was just as well, for Scotland Yard, back in the home country, had never closed their investigation into the murder of one of their own.

Over the years, there had been very little contact between Ritz and Jack Ridley. Their paths only crossed occasionally once Ritz had found the place in Ireland that Jack had mentioned as being the perfect backwater to hide out in. Since then, although they kept their distance, they agreed to stay in touch, just in case of unwelcome developments.

These days, the two men kept away from the pubs, not only because they would be the first place they would be recognised, but because some of the old clientele would only be too glad to shop them. And so, when Ridley decided that he had something he needed to talk over with his former criminal sidekick, he chose as a meeting place the back row of the stalls in the Marlborough cinema in Holloway Road.

The good old 'bug-hutch' was fairly empty that afternoon, with no more than a handful of regular elderly patrons there to watch Gary Cooper and Ray Milland in *Beau Geste,* a stirring tale of courage and cowardice in the French Foreign Legion. The cinema was a perfect place to meet, for the lighting was very poor, with the only real light coming from the picture screen itself.

'Got a little job for yer, Ritz,' said Ridley, careful to keep his voice down. 'No risk involved. Just a little visit to my lovin' wife.'

After the last job he was involved in with Ridley and the Dillon boys, Ritz was a bit cagey. 'I dunno, Jack,' he replied, whilst digging into a tub of synthetic ice cream. 'I've 'ung up my gloves these days. As far as I know, the fuzz still don't know fer sure that I was involved wiv the Dillon boys. I don't wanna take no chances.'

Even in the old days, Ritz had always irritated Ridley. But he knew that, on this occasion, he needed him to help him do a job that had – immense possibilities. 'I told yer, Ritz, there's no risk involved,' he said. 'An' if yer keep yer cool, there's a grand in it for yer.'

Ritz's eyes widened. 'A grand!'

'No 'olds barred,' continued Ridley. 'Let me tell yer.' He leaned his head sideways, drawing close to Ritz. 'Yer see, my wife is sittin' on a real little nest egg – or at least 'er boy is.'

'Ed, yer mean?'

'The very same.' He quickly sat up straight again, when the beam from an usherette's torch flashed across the seats further down the aisle. He waited whilst she showed two old ladies to their seats, turned off her torch, and disappeared again through the back exit. 'It would appear,' he continued, leaning his head back to meet Ritz's, 'that my young stepson is on the verge of inheriting – shall we say – a considerable sum of money. In uvver words, 'e's sittin' on a bleedin' fortune!'

Ritz, thunderstruck, bent down, as though picking something up from the floor. ''Ow come?'

Ridley joined him, so that they were now both out of sight below the seats. ''Is ol' man's farver – rich as a row of bean poles – died years ago, but 'e left the kid everyfin'–'

'What!'

'On one condition,' continued Ridley. 'The kid can't get 'is 'ands on it till he reaches the ripe ol' age of twenty-one.'

'An' when's that?'

'Next Friday week.'

Ritz's teeth nearly fell out from his dropped jaw. 'Christ!'

'Precisely.'

'But 'ow d'yer know all this?'

Again, Ridley was irritated by Ritz's naïve question. 'Let's just say I know a geezer who knows a geezer – who *knows*.'

Ridley raised himself up in his seat again. Ritz did likewise.

On the screen, a pitched battle was taking place between the heroic Legionnaires and the marauding Arabs. As if the gab Ridley was giving him was not riveting enough, the sound of frenetic gunshots was unnerving the daylights out of Ritz.

'But wot's this got ter do wiv yer wife?' he said, trying to be logical. 'If the cash 'as bin left to the kid, wot's in it fer 'er?'

'Fer Chrissake, Ritz,' Ridley snapped. 'She's 'is own flesh an' blood, ain't she?'

Ritz cowered against Ridley's outburst. 'All I was sayin' was, she may be 'is muvver, but surely the cash belongs to 'im?'

Ridley calmed down. 'Good point, Ritz. A very good point. 'Cos that's where we come in.' He leaned close to whisper directly into Ritz's ear. 'Yer see, my wife ought ter be able to advise 'er son on wot ter do wiv such a large amount of cash. Ter do that, she needs advice 'erself; she needs a man about the place. An' who better fer that than 'er own lovin' 'usband?'

Beattie's front room had never looked so good. She was now on night shifts, and every day, before she started work, she made a point of cleaning everything in sight. The linoleum was swept, washed, and polished, rugs beaten with a shovel in the back yard, fire grate freshened with stove paint, brass ornaments polished with Brasso, and any cobwebs removed with a long feather duster. On the day before the special occasion, she had even got Ed to help her put up clean white lace curtains at the windows, whilst Ma was given the job of polishing the cutlery, which used to adorn the Melfords' more formal dining table back home in Thornhill Road.

'You know, you don't have to go to all this trouble, Mum,' said Ed, as his mother laid the table with her best china. 'Aunt Sarah and Uncle Freddie are only coming to tea. They're not coming to inspect the place.'

'It matters to me,' replied Beattie, who was setting out linen napkins beside each tea plate on the table, something Ed hadn't seen her do in a long time.

'I 'ope all this is worf it,' said Ma, grumpily. She was getting just a bit fed up with all the fuss. 'Gord knows, I've used up all our week's food rations ter make the fruit cake!'

'It'll be worth it, Ma,' Beattie assured her.

Ma grunted, and disappeared into the kitchen.

After she had gone, Ed went to his mother, who was polishing the mirror over the fireplace. 'Come here, you!' he said, taking her hand and plonking her down on the sofa. 'You're getting yourself all worked up for nothing. You know that, don't you?'

'Do let me go, son,' Beattie said, trying to get up again. 'They'll be here soon.'

Ed pulled her back again, and sat beside her on the sofa. 'Relax, Mum,' he said, comforting her.

'I'm nervous, Ed,' she replied. 'I'm not sure this is a good idea.'

'But you invited them,' said Ed, holding her hand. 'At least Aunt Sarah replied to your letter.

You didn't think she ever would.'

'She waited nearly three weeks.'

'Better late than never.'

Beattie sighed. 'I *am* nervous.'

'Let me tell you something,' Ed said, putting his arm around her shoulder. 'Aunt Sarah is probably just as nervous about this meeting as you are. You've had a stormy relationship over the years, but now you're older it's worth the effort to find new ground. And in any case, you'll like Uncle Freddie. He's a very genuine man. It's hard to believe that, after all these years, you've never even met your own brother-in-law.'

Beattie leaned her head back on the sofa. 'What happens if it all goes terribly wrong?' she asked. 'The last time Sarah and I met, we were at each other's throats. I was absolutely awful to her.'

'That was a long time ago,' said Ed. 'Don't look back. Just think of a new beginning.'

'I'm trying to, son,' Beattie replied. 'God knows, I'm trying to.'

They were interrupted by a ring on the front doorbell. In a panic, Beattie sprang to her feet. 'Oh my God! They're here!'

Ed tried to calm her. 'I'll go and bring them in. Just take it easy, and try to enjoy yourself.'

'Enjoy myself!' Beattie took a deep breath.

Ed went to the front room door, then turned and called back to her, 'Remember. A new beginning.'

During the few seconds that Ed was gone, Beattie felt her stomach churn with anxiety. Although she had written that conciliatory letter to Sarah, she had never thought through the consequences of what might happen if she accepted her invitation to meet up. But then she tried to remember that since the last time they had met, she and her sister, Sarah, had changed. A little more than ten years ago, she, Beattie, had been a reckless young woman, with no thought for anyone but herself, a rebel who imagined that the world owed her something, something that she was not prepared to earn. And Sarah, what of her? She was now a married woman, and had settled for a way of life that, until their parents had died, no one would have thought possible.

Oh God, thought Beattie, I do so want to like Sarah. I do so want her to like me. But what if it doesn't happen like that?

Despite Ed's efforts to bring them back together, it could all end in disaster, and this would be the last time: they would probably die without ever meeting again. She tried to imagine what Sarah would be like when she walked through that door. Would she look older, be just as set in her ways, formal, unyielding, critical? Or would she have mellowed with the passing of time?

'Hello, Beattie.'

Beattie turned with a start. She was there. Her sister, Sarah, was standing in the doorway. And suddenly Beattie was only five or six years old again. 'Sarah,' she replied nervously, apprehensively. 'Thank you for coming.'

The two sisters warily approached each other. For a brief moment, they hesitated as though not knowing what to do next. Then, watched by Ed, Ma, and Freddie, they embraced, kissing each other gently on each cheek.

'Some people have all the luck,' said Beattie, nervously. 'Just look at you.' She stood back to look at Sarah. 'You're younger than the last time I saw you.'

Sarah, embarrassed, shook her head. 'Oh no,' she replied with a friendly smile. 'I can assure you I feel every day of *my* age.'

Behind Freddie at the door, Ma dabbed her eyes and blew her nose. It was all too much for her.

'Uncle Freddie,' said Ed. 'Come and meet Mum.'

As her brother-in-law approached, Beattie squeezed her eyelids together to try to avert her tears. 'Hello, Freddie,' she said, holding out her hand. What she saw was a greying middle-aged man with kindly eyes and a beaming smile that could melt anyone's heart. 'I'm pleased to meet you.'

''Ello, Beattie,' Freddie replied warmly. 'I'm pleased ter meet you too.' He ignored the hand she was offering him, and leaning gently forward, he kissed her on the cheek.

Beattie had really gone to town on the tea, which turned out to be more like a feast. Despite the rationing, she had managed to get some veal and ham pie, cold pork trotters, fresh bread with a small pat of *real* butter, a pint of whelks, some shrimps, and sugar with the tea instead of the usual saccharin tablets. She had also prepared the most delicious trifle, with apples, and tinned fruit, and the custard layer on top was made with powdered milk. Freddie and Ma got on like a house on fire, and they both tucked into the grub as though they hadn't eaten since the start of the war. Ed smoked all the way through the meal, for he was far too intent on observing how his mum and his aunt were getting on to eat. In fact, tea time turned out to be a real eye-opener, for everyone seemed determined to get on well with each other, all talking at the same time, recounting memories from their days in Thornhill Road, the Bunk, Mitford Road, and St Alban's Place. There was no doubt that looking back was helping to break the ice.

The turning point, however, came when Ed made a conscious decision to draw his mum and his aunt closer together. Until that moment, they seemed to have been nervous of having a one-to-one conversation, and had merely joined in the light-hearted banter around the table. Ed knew that the time had come to move the two women on to a more productive relationship, but to do that, he felt he needed to pick their brains about the past.

'It must have been peculiar living in that house in Thornhill Road,' he said provocatively. 'I mean, what I remember was that it was quite a barn of a place.'

Inevitably, Sarah took the bait. 'I don't know how you can say that, Ed,' she said firmly. 'It was a wonderful house. It was big, but it had an atmosphere all its own.'

'Atmosphere, yes,' replied Ed, mischievously, 'but freezing cold in winter and hot as hell in summer.'

Surprisingly, Beattie came to her sister's

defence. 'Oh, our house was never cold, Ed,' she chided. 'During the winter we had coal fires in nearly every room. It was so snug and warm. You were just too young to appreciate it.' At this point, she turned to Sarah, who was sitting alongside her. 'Sarah, d'you remember the time when we were both small kids, when Mother bathed us in front of the wood stove in the kitchen?'

'Oh yes,' replied Sarah, with a broad smile. 'I remember how you made such a mess, Mother's cats fled for their lives!'

Everyone joined in with their laughter.

'Sounds like your poor mum 'ad a 'ell of a time wiv yer!' said Ma, her mouth full of trifle. 'I'd've given yer boaf a clip round the bleedin' ear'ole!'

'We weren't that bad, Ma,' said Beattie.

'Oh yes we were!' said Sarah, lightly.

Now Freddie joined in. 'Wot about that time yer told me about, Sarah? You know, when you an' Beattie played merry 'ell wiv yer dad – 'idin' 'is cigars an' all that.'

Both Sarah and Beattie burst into laughter.

'It was wonderful!' cried Sarah. 'Beattie hid them under the rug in the drawing room.'

Beattie continued the story. 'And when Father came into the room, he trod on them! He was furious!'

She and Sarah roared with laughter.

Freddie turned to Ma at his side. 'Wot would yer do wiv kids like that, eh, Ma?' he asked.

'Strangle the little buggers!' Ma growled.

This only produced more laughter from around the table.

Ed waited for the laughter to settle down, then said, 'Sounds like you two had quite a childhood.'

For a second, neither his mother nor his aunt answered.

'It had its moments,' said Sarah, with a sideways glance at her sister.

Ed exchanged a bit of a grin with Freddie.

After tea, Ed's plan was complete. Packing Ma off to have her customary afternoon doze, he then enrolled Freddie to help him do the washing-up, which left his mother and his aunt free to have a chat alone together.

It was by now beginning to get dark, so Beattie went to the window and drew the blackout curtains.

'I must say, you've got a wonderful memory,' said Sarah, when Beattie came back to join her in front of the fire. 'I'd completely forgotten all about that bath Mother gave us. And that telling-off we got from Father about the cigars.'

'I can remember things that happened a long time ago,' Beattie replied, 'but I couldn't tell you a thing about last week. Must be a sign of old age.'

Sarah watched her carefully. 'You'll never age, Beattie,' she said kindly. 'Even when you reach a hundred.'

Beattie gave a dismissive laugh. 'A hundred!' she gasped. 'I can't imagine me at a hundred years old. In fact, I wouldn't want to live to that kind of age.'

'It's easy to say that now,' said Sarah. 'But when it comes to it, I fancy we might think differently.'

Beattie sighed deeply. 'Maybe,' she replied.

Even in those few quiet moments, it was clear that there was a special kind of atmosphere developing between them, quite unlike anything they had experienced before. Usually, five minutes in each other's company would have been turbulent and unyielding, but in some extraordinary ways, a calm had descended upon them.

'Thank you for coming, Sarah,' Beattie said, breaking the silence. 'I can't tell you how grateful I am.'

Sarah lowered her eyes guiltily. 'You don't have to thank me, Beattie,' she said. 'It's something I've wanted to do for a long time.'

Beattie was puzzled. 'Then why did it take you so long to answer?' she said.

Sarah thought hard. It wasn't easy to explain how she'd felt when she'd received Beattie's letter. It wasn't easy to tell her, after their last meeting so long ago, that she had dreaded ever coming into contact with her again. 'I wanted to be sure,' she replied. 'I wanted to be sure that this time we had a real chance of understanding each other.'

'Oh God,' sighed Beattie. 'I've hurt you so many times. I don't deserve to be forgiven.'

Sarah leaned forward on the sofa where she was sitting. 'It's not a question of being forgiven, Beattie,' she said. 'We've both made so many mistakes. I suppose it happens in families. Everyone's looking for something different. Everyone thinks theirs is the only way. You made up your mind long ago what you wanted from life. I did too.'

'I was wrong.'

'I was too.'

Beattie sat with her hands in her lap, back straight. 'I just wanted my independence,' she said painfully. 'I wanted to be free. I didn't want to do all the things that were expected of me. I thought the only real people were those who had to work to survive.'

Sarah leaned across and put her hand on Beattie's. 'It doesn't matter where or what you come from, Beattie,' she said, 'everyone has to work to survive. Where you went wrong, where we both went wrong, was that we judge people for what they seem to be, not for what they are. Sometimes we forget that, whatever class we come from, there is good and bad in all of us.' She rose up from the sofa, went to Beattie, and kneeled beside her chair. 'In your letter to me,' she continued, 'you wrote that, as a sister, you've been a failure. Well, if that's true, then I've been a failure too.'

'It's not the same, Sarah,' Beattie said. 'When I think of you and Lacey, and all the pain I caused you. Blood is supposed to be thicker than water, and yet I treated you worse than any trash in the streets. And I was so jealous of the way Ed adored you so much more than me...' With a wave of the hand, Sarah tried to dismiss this. But Beattie would have none of it. 'No,' she insisted, 'it's true. You gave him so much more than me. You told him about all the things in life he needed to know, things that I've turned my back on all my life.' She hesitated only long enough to compose herself. 'During these past few years

I've often asked myself why it was that I could never bring myself to get on with you. It took Ed to help me find the reason why. He told me that I need you, that I've always needed you.' Her eyes swelled with tears. 'He's right,' she said.

Sarah put her arms around Beattie, and hugged her. 'I need you too, Beattie,' she said. 'The only trouble is that I've always been too proud to admit it.' She held on tight to Beattie. 'I'm not afraid to admit it now,' she said.

Tears now also swelled in Sarah's eyes. It was the first time that had happened in a very long time.

CHAPTER 26

Sarah just couldn't make out why Freddie had decided to close the shop early that day. Half-day closing was, and always had been, on a Thursday, and the fact that this was only Tuesday worried her greatly.

'But where are we going, dear?' she asked, as she put on her thick winter coat and warm woollen beret. 'It always makes me nervous when you behave like this.'

From the moment they'd got up that morning, Freddie had behaved in a very mysterious way. He'd started by singing out loud as he shaved, which was most peculiar, because when he shaved he nearly always whistled. Then, at breakfast, he lit his pipe, which made Sarah's porridge taste like wallpaper paste. But it was the final straw when, the moment he put the 'CLOSED' sign on the shop door, he went immediately to the back parlour and combed his hair. Extraordinary! Sarah was convinced that he was about to go down with the flu or something.

But the plot thickened even deeper when, as they left the shop and Freddie locked up, a taxi was waiting for them at the kerb outside.

'Freddie?' Sarah asked, all at sixes and sevens. 'What's all this about? Where are we going?'

Freddie opened the taxi door for her. 'Step in, and you'll find out.'

A few minutes later, they were heading off along Upper Street, but before they reached the Angel, the taxi turned off right into Liverpool Road.

Sarah was now so bewildered, she was beginning to get worried. Closing his shop early, spending good money on a taxi – it was all beyond her. As they passed all the streets that were so familiar to her, she felt a deep sense of sadness to see great gaps in the rows of lovely terraced houses, which had been devastated during the relentless air raids. She wondered what had happened to the people who lived there, people that she must have passed in the street a hundred times when she was young, or stood next to in a queue at the greengrocer's. No, even her beloved Barnsbury had not escaped the savagery of the war. In one way, it was a blessing that her parents were not alive to see it all.

When they suddenly turned into Richmond Avenue, and pulled up outside the Melfords' old family house, she was totally confused.

'Freddie!' she pleaded. 'What are we doing here?'

Freddie ignored her pleas, helped her out of the taxi, and paid the driver. The taxi pulled away.

'Freddie,' she asked again, 'what are we doing here?'

Freddie had a smug look on his face. 'I told yer I was lookin' fer a place ter buy yer,' he said, turning his gaze towards the house. 'Well – *this* is it.'

Sarah clamped a hand to her mouth. She was shocked. 'Oh my God!' she gasped. Then she turned to look up at the house where she was born. 'You haven't – you can't!'

'Oh yes I can!' he boasted. 'An' I 'ave!'

'You – you've bought it?' she asked with incredulity.

'Well, not exactly,' he replied. 'I've just put the deposit down. But it's in a bit of a state. Nuffin's bin done to the place fer years. We won't be able to move in fer quite a time yet, I'm afraid.'

Sarah thought she was dreaming. Freddie took hold of her hand and gently led her through the open brick fence, where once the iron gates had been positioned with such grandeur. Only when they moved into the front garden, however, was the full extent of the negligence really noticeable. They had to step over a pile of rubble to get to the front door, for bomb blast from nearby Liverpool Road had caused considerable damage, which had not been attended to. There were cracked bricks and grey slates from the roof, broken glass, drain pipes dangling out from the walls, and bits of discarded and partly burned furniture scattered all over the place.

For Sarah, it was a deeply depressing sight, and thrilled though she was by what Freddie had done, she had a sinking feeling. 'It's – tragic to see it looking like this,' she said, her eyes scanning the outside of the building from top to bottom. 'It's such a beautiful house. It needs love and attention.' She turned to Freddie, and linked her arm with his. 'Oh, Freddie, it's heart-breaking.'

'Well, we 'ave ter fank the previous owners fer that.'

'What happened to that awful man I sold it to?' she asked. 'I can't even remember his name.'

''Aven't the faintest,' replied Freddie. 'The agent says it's 'ad six or seven occupants in the last few years alone.'

Sarah couldn't believe her ears. 'Six or seven!' she cried. 'What's the matter with people? Don't they recognise a beautiful home when they see one?'

Freddie put his arm around her. 'It's just a 'ouse ter most people, Sarah,' he said sympathetically. 'Ter *you*, it's a 'ome.'

He had great difficulty in opening the front door, for it had warped, and when he finally did succeed it very nearly came off its hinges.

Sarah stepped through the entrance, and despite the unbelievable mess she found there, she immediately sensed the atmosphere of her younger years. In her mind, she could smell her mother's cooking, and she could hear the sound of Beattie's roller skates down the passage leading out into the back garden. From the hall, she could see the drawing-room door half open, and somehow she expected at any moment to see her father coming out to meet her, with his usual cigar stuck firmly in the side of his lips. The place was most surely full of ghosts, she thought, but friendly ones.

''Fraid we can't go upstairs,' said Freddie. 'The stairs are a bit rickety, and so are the floorboards up in the bedrooms. But we'll soon put it all right. It's goin' ter take time, dear,' he warned, still holding her hand. 'We shan't be able to move in till next summer at the earliest.'

They strolled into the drawing room. It was a depressing sight, for, as the windows had been blown in by bomb blast, it was freezing cold, and there were broken tiles around the fireplace, and a terrible smell of decay everywhere. For a moment or so, they just stood in the middle of the room, staring all around them.

'Where are we going to find the money to do it all?' she asked apprehensively. 'It's going to cost a fortune.'

'We'll manage,' Freddie assured her, his arm around her shoulders. 'For obvious reasons, I got the place fer a snip. My old mate Charlie Stumper – 'e's a builder – 'e's promised to do it up for us. It'll take time, but we'll do it.'

'Why?' asked Sarah, turning to look at him.

'Why will it take time?'

'No,' said Sarah. 'Why did you do this for me?'

Freddie smiled. 'Because I knew that this is where yer 'art is. I knew that, no matter where we went, this is the one place you'd always fink about most. Did I do right, Mrs 'Amwell?'

Sarah sighed deeply then, after a quick, loving look around the room, replied, 'Yes, Mr Hamwell. You did right. My God, you did right!'

Beattie and Ed picked their way over the debris that was scattered all along the streets of Holborn. Fortunately, the tube was still working after the heavy air raid of the night before, so they'd been able to get out at Holborn tube station. However, the Kingsway route was temporarily closed off, as quite a bit of masonry had apparently tumbled down on to the entrance of the tram tunnel, so they had to take the long way round via High Holborn, Chancery Lane, and Fleet Street. Although things were not much better there, they were at least able to take a short cut to their destination, a solicitor's office in St Clement's Inn, just behind the Law Courts.

Mr Johnson, whom Beattie had first met many years before, was now the senior partner in the firm of Silkin, Silkin and Johnson. These days he sported just the suggestion of a moustache, which was all the current rage for men, who all wanted to look like Rhett Butler, played by Clark Gable in a massive new hit film *Gone With the Wind.* But time was catching up with even him, for wisps of grey were gradually appearing in that moustache, his sideburns, and even his eyebrows.

'May I first of all offer you my warm congratulations on your coming of age,' proclaimed the legal man, immaculately dressed in a dark three-piece pin-striped suit. Admiring the officer's uniform Ed was wearing, he added, 'If I may say so, your grandfather would have been proud of your commission.'

Ed acknowledged the compliment with a polite nod. 'Thank you, Mr Johnson.'

Whilst discreetly searching for his tortoiseshell spectacles, which were trapped somewhere beneath a pile of documents on his desk, Johnson began his customary recitation. 'As I'm sure your mother has already told you, on attaining the age of twenty-one, in his last will and testament, your grandfather, the late Lieutenant-Commander Lacey, made you one of the prime beneficiaries of his estate.' He finally recovered his spectacles, put them on, and picked up the original copy of the will he was referring to. 'However,' he said, viewing both Ed and his mother over the top of his spectacles, 'there is some good news for you in this bequest – and some bad.'

Ed exchanged a discreet, but puzzled look with his mother.

'Let us deal with the bad news first,' continued the legal man, turning over a page of the will. 'I gather that when my client first approached you back in...' he referred to some notes on his desk, '...September 1920, he indicated his intention to you that, on his demise, your son would inherit a part share of the sale of the Old Manor House, together with a cash lump sum of five thousand pounds. Is that correct?'

Beattie leaned forward in her chair opposite him, and answered, 'Yes it is.'

'Yes, indeed,' said Johnson, 'that was the amount specified in the Lieutenant-Commander's will. However,' he took off his spectacles, 'I'm afraid that part has been declared null and void.'

Beattie could feel her hackles rising. 'What on earth for?' she demanded.

'For the simple reason that, after death duties, there weren't enough funds left over.'

Beattie sighed, and sat back in her chair.

'Yes, it is unfortunate,' said the legal man, now switching his gaze back to Ed. 'But I'm afraid your grandfather was quite a chap. In his latter years, he was quite generous to – shall we say, one or two lady friends.'

'Like father, like son,' Beattie muttered under her breath.

'I beg your pardon?' asked Johnson.

'Nothing,' replied Beattie, with a wry smile.

'However,' continued the legal man, 'all is not lost. The good news is that on the sale of the Old Manor House back in 1931, a sum of five thousand pounds was realised from a purchaser in Norfolk.'

Beattie sat up again.

'But,' said Johnson, shrugging his shoulders apologetically, 'I'm sure you are aware that apart from yourself, Lieutenant, there were two other beneficiaries to your grandfather's will. In effect, that means that you are entitled to a one-third share of the sale of the Old Manor House, and that amounts to…' he put on his spectacles again, and read from some more notes, '…the grand sum of one thousand, six hundred and sixty-six pounds, six shillings, and six pence – give or take a penny or two.' He took off his spectacles again, and gave Ed an ingratiating smile. 'That was, of course, the gross amount. Naturally, we had to deduct our standard company fee.'

'Naturally,' said Beattie, cryptically.

Johnson smiled weakly. 'Which leaves an amount in your favour, including some modest interest, of one thousand, two hundred and thirty-one pounds, four shillings, and seven pence.' He searched around on his desk, found the cheque and held it out to Ed. 'Made out in your name, Lieutenant.'

Ed stared at the cheque for a moment, then

took it. Then, to the legal man's astonishment, he dropped it back on to the desk without even looking at it. 'No thank you, Mr Johnson,' he said politely but firmly.

Beattie sat up with a start. 'Ed!'

'It's no good, Mum,' he said, turning round in his chair to look directly at her. 'If I took that money, it would be a betrayal of everything I believe in. I don't want people leaving things to me. I want to earn my own way in life.'

Johnson couldn't believe what he was hearing. This was the first time in his experience that a beneficiary to a will had actually *refused* a bequest. 'But the Lieutenant-Commander was your own grandfather, sir,' he said.

'All the more reason for me not to take it,' replied Ed. 'I'm sorry, Mum,' he added, turning to Beattie.

Contrary to what Ed had expected, Beattie was smiling in admiration at him. 'You know, it's a funny thing,' she said. 'On the only occasion that I ever met your grandfather, I couldn't bear the sight of him. To me, he was nothing but a selfish, arrogant, grasping old goat.'

The legal man leaned back in his chair with disbelief.

'But there was one thing he said that has now made me think how alike you are. He said, "A person should find his own way in life. If you make it too easy for them, they lose their energy and ambition." You've never lost your energy nor your ambition, Ed. You never will.'

They smiled knowingly at each other.

'That's all very well,' said the exasperated legal

man, 'but would somebody please tell me what I am supposed to do with this cheque?'

Ed turned back to him. 'I'd like you to issue another one, please, Mr Johnson. Made out to my mother–'

'No.' Beattie's indignation was firm and adamant. 'If my son doesn't need it, then neither do I.'

The harassed Mr Johnson shook his head in despair. Suddenly, his overcrowded, musty office seemed to be desperate for some fresh air.

Having thoroughly enjoyed what they had done, Ed and his mother exchanged another warm, knowing look. They were in no doubt that the dutiful Mr Johnson would soon find some poor deserving soul to relieve him of that bequest.

Freddie hadn't cut this particular customer's hair before. But, whoever the man was, for his age, he had a beautiful head of thick, manageable pure white hair, so different from the wisps of barbed wire that Freddie had to tackle with momentous regularity. He certainly seemed like a nice enough little bloke, even if he did tend to talk the hind legs off a donkey. East Ender, that's what he was, Freddie decided. You could always tell a genuine cockney by his mischievous grin and his cheeky banter. Mile End, Freddie reckoned, or even Bow itself. But when his unfamiliar customer dropped a bombshell, Freddie couldn't have cared less where he came from.

'I'm a pal of Jack Ridley,' said Ritz. 'Or at least, I *was* until I stepped fru that door.' He carefully watched Freddie's reaction in the mirror in front of him. 'Guess yer've 'eard of *'im,* Mr 'Amwell. Am I right?'

Freddie's attitude towards the man changed at once. He had already finished cutting his hair, and was starting to lather his face ready for a shave. Swinging a glare at him in the mirror, he growled, 'Who *are* you?'

Ritz trod carefully. He didn't like the look of that cutthroat razor Freddie was brandishing. 'It don't matter who I am, mate,' he replied. 'It's what I come ter tell yer that counts.'

Freddie swung the barber's chair round so that Ritz was facing him. 'What about Ridley?'

''E wants somefin' – from your sister-in-law.'

Freddie hesitated a moment, then he went to the parlour door at the back of the shop, and called up the stairs. 'Sarah! Can yer come down 'ere, please. Quick as yer can.'

Sarah's voice called from the rooms upstairs, 'Be right with you!'

Freddie turned back to Ritz, who had got up from the chair and was using the towel around his neck to wipe the shaving foam off his face. Fortunately, there were no other customers in the shop so he was able to talk freely. 'I don't know what you're up to, mate,' Freddie warned, 'but this'd better be good.'

Ritz dropped the towel back on to the chair behind him. 'It's nuffin' good wot I 'ave ter tell yer, Mr 'Amwell,' he said provocatively, 'but it's somefin' yer need ter know.'

Sarah suddenly came into the shop. 'Yes, dear?' she asked. But when she saw him with a customer, she smiled brightly and said, 'Good morning, sir.'

'This "gentleman" 'as somefin' ter say to yer, Sarah.'

As she saw the look on both men's faces, her smile faded. 'What's the matter?' she asked with concern, switching her attention from Freddie to the customer.

Ritz took a step towards her. 'I'm an acquaintance of your bruvver-in-law, Mrs 'Amwell. I come 'ere ter warn you.'

Sarah stiffened.

'I've known 'im a long time,' Ritz continued. 'We've done – quite a few jobs tergevver.'

Sarah watched Freddie as he went to the shop door, pulled the blind, turned the 'CLOSED' sign round, and locked the door.

Ritz made sure he kept his distance from both of them. ''E wants somefin', Mrs 'Amwell,' he said, voice lowered as though Ridley was in the shop, 'an' 'e wants it bad. Not from you. From yer sister.'

'Get ter the point!' growled Freddie, simmering with mistrust.

''E wants ter get back wiv 'er – yer sister, I mean.'

'I'm aware of that,' replied Sarah, coldly.

'Yeah,' Ritz said quickly. 'But wot yer don't know is – *why*.' For one reckless moment, he dared to take a step towards her, but Freddie moved forward to stand beside his wife. 'It's not 'er 'e wants,' he said. 'It's the money.'

Sarah did a double take. 'Money?' she said. 'What money? My sister doesn't have a penny to her name.'

'Not 'er money, Mrs 'Amwell,' said Ritz, nervously. ''Er boy's.'

Sarah exchanged a puzzled, astonished glance with Freddie. 'I don't know what you're talking about,' she replied.

Ritz pressed on. 'Ed's 'is name, in't it?' he said. 'See, I know everyfin'. Twenty-one terday? Right? Got the key ter the door? Right?'

'My nephew has no more money than his mother,' insisted Sarah. 'I don't know what you're getting at, but you've got it all wrong.'

Ritz sized Sarah up. Ridley had often talked about her. She was the one with the brains, he'd always said, she's the one who's got it all going for her. If things had been different... 'Ten years ago, 'is grandfarver – 'is farver's farver that is – well, 'e died an' accordin' ter Jack, 'e left everyfin' 'e 'ad to 'is only grandchild. That's where Ed comes in, if I'm not mistaken.'

Sarah found it hard to take this in. Over the years she had had many a conversation with Ed about his mother, even his father, but never once had she ever heard him mention his paternal grandfather.

Ritz went to the coat stand and collected his jacket. 'From all Jack tells me,' he continued, 'that boy could've bin worf a fortune years ago. The only snag was that he couldn't lay 'is 'ands on it till 'e was – wait for it – twenty-one years of age. Savvy?'

Sarah covered her mouth with her hand. Suddenly she felt quite weak.

'I don't see the connection,' said Freddie, who was still brandishing that razor. 'If the money was left to the boy, 'ow could Ridley possibly get 'is 'ands on it?'

'Oh, 'e'd find a way, don't you worry about that. 'E's a slippery one, is our Jack.' He put on his jacket, then took his overcoat from the coat stand.

'Beattie wouldn't have anything to do with him,' insisted Sarah. 'She told me that herself.'

Ritz chuckled to himself. 'I'm afraid yer don't know 'ow persuasive 'e is, Mrs 'Amwell,' he said with a sigh. ''E wants me ter go an' chat 'er up, tell 'er wot a good bloke 'e is. He also wants me ter tell 'er that 'e's dyin' of cancer or somefin', an' that 'e's only got a while ter live.' He chuckled again, whilst struggling into his overcoat. 'I don't know 'ow your sister would take ter that kind of story, Mrs 'Amwell,' he said, 'if she was made ter fink it was true.'

Trying to take everything in, Sarah went to the row of customers' chairs and sat down. She was thinking about Beattie, and whether she could – or would – ever feel sorry enough for Ridley to take him back.

'I don't know who you are,' she said, looking across at Ritz, 'but if what you say is true, why are you telling us all this?'

Ritz took his trilby off the coat stand and plonked it on his head. 'I dunno really,' he replied. 'Maybe it's 'cos there ain't no honour amongst fieves no more.'

Beattie walked at a brisk pace down Hornsey Road, past the old Star bug-hutch cinema, where years before hordes of kids queued to get in to the Saturday morning blood-an'-thunder shows, and endless cowboy serials with Tom Mix and Gene Autry. It was a pleasant enough afternoon, for the winter drizzle, which had settled overnight and turned to ice, had very quickly melted the moment the sun had established itself.

On her way past Hornsey Road baths, she recognised one or two of her neighbours from Mitford Road, waiting with their bits of scrubbing soap and towels to pay twopence to have a public bath. So she hurried past, for if anyone recognised her, they would be bound to ask where she was going, and that was the last thing she wanted. Once past the police station, she felt safe, so by the time she had crossed the main Seven Sisters Road at the traffic lights, she felt confident enough not to have to rush.

As she walked, she wondered about all that had taken place in the offices of Silkin, Silkin and Johnson that morning. She thought of Ed, and how proud she had felt to know that she had brought a son into the world who had principles that he believed in and fought for. She wondered what sort of life was ahead for him, and what he would make of it, providing, of course, that he survived this nightmare of a war.

Like a lot of people who miss so much when they walk along a road staring at their feet, she didn't take in the terraced shops on either side of the road, many of their windows now boarded up after bomb blast, and roofs temporarily covered over with tarpaulins. Thankfully the back of Pakeman Street School appeared to be intact, although most of the windows were covered over with protective strips of sticky tape. She didn't slow down until she had almost reached the railway arch, which stretched high above the road, for her destination was very close.

The house, which was set on three floors, was like all the others in the terrace, in bad need of a coat of paint. Even here, several of the windows were boarded up, which must have meant that the interior was desperately short of natural daylight. Using her own key, Beattie let herself in at the front door. Then, after wiping her feet on the passage rug, she quietly made her way up the stairs. The room she was looking for was on the second-floor landing, and when she got there, she tapped as softly on the door as she could.

The door opened and a man peered out. His was a young, pleasant face, with a pasty complexion, blue eyes, and light brown hair that fell over one eye. As soon as he saw Beattie, his face lit up. Beattie went straight in.

When the door was closed, they kissed passionately, and then they embraced. The man was several years younger than Beattie, probably about thirty years old. He wasn't particularly good-looking, but he had an intensity that was more emotional than physical. 'Oh God, I've looked forward to seeing you,' he said breathlessly. 'I've missed you so much, Beattie.'

Beattie looked into his eyes and stroked his hair. 'Come off it, Chris,' she said with a teasing smile. 'It's only been a week.'

'Is it only that long?' he replied.

A few minutes later, they had undressed and were making love in the young man's modest single bed. It was fortunate that the boards up at the windows prevented not only daylight from streaming in, but also the prying eyes of neighbours on the other side of the road.

When they had finished, they lay side by side, snuggled up as tight as they could to one another. ‘How much longer do we have to go on like this?’ said Chris, his voice low and intimate. ‘I love you, and you love me. So why do we have to keep it such a secret?’

‘Because this is not the right time, Chris,’ she replied, her tone equally intimate. ‘One of these days, it will be. But not now, not just yet.’

CHAPTER 27

At his own request, Ed's twenty-first birthday was a very low-key affair, which consisted mainly of having a Sunday midday drink in the Hornsey Arms pub with some of his civvy pals, followed by a special meal at his Aunt Sarah and Uncle Freddie's place above the barber shop, to which his mum and Ma Briggs were also invited. As it happened, the occasion turned out to be tinged with sadness, for it also marked the conclusion of Ed's sick leave. In fact, as soon as the meal was over, he had to leave for Charing Cross Station, but the only person he allowed to go with him to see him off was Freddie. It was, inevitably, a poignant departure, and would have been absolutely unbearable if Ed hadn't remained so optimistic and so completely confident that it wouldn't be long before he was back home safe and sound again with his family.

After Ed and Freddie had left for the station, Sarah, Beattie, and Ma did the washing-up together in empty silence. Then Sarah suggested that Ma go into the bedroom to have her usual afternoon doze, an invitation which the old girl readily accepted. As there was an hour or so to pass until Freddie's return, Sarah asked Beattie if she would like to take a walk and get some fresh air, which would also help to take Beattie's mind off the fact that Ed would not be there when she and Ma got home that evening. Sarah knew that a casual stroll out in the cold winter frost would not only be an ideal way to clear their heads, but would also help them to build on their new-found relationship.

For a Sunday afternoon, there were a surprising number of people strolling along Upper Street. Some of them were young couples, holding each other's hands and getting to know each other, others were there to see how the clearing-up was going on after the recent heavy week of air raids. Most people were impressed to see that nearly all the rubble had been cleared away from the severely damaged Lloyds Bank building. In front of the site itself, a small group of people had even stopped to talk over what had happened, and to speculate about whether the bank would be totally demolished or rebuilt.

As the sisters turned into Liverpool Road, it seemed as though the years behind them were once again flashing before their eyes. This was their neck of the woods, where they had played together, walked together, and then moved on into their different lives.

'It's all changed so much since our day,' said Sarah. 'The war has made such a difference. Nobody has the heart to take care of their property; they never know from one day to the next whether the place will still be there when they step out of their shelters in the morning.'

'Oh, I don't know,' said Beattie, whose eyes were scanning the long rows of Georgian terraced houses. 'It all looks pretty much the same to me, a little worse for wear, perhaps, but that's all.'

About ten minutes later, they had reached as far as Richmond Avenue, but when Sarah turned the corner, Beattie came to a halt. 'Do we really want to go any further, Sarah?' she asked. 'I'm not sure I want to go back.'

Sarah returned to her. 'What are you afraid of, Beattie?'

'I'm not sure,' she replied. 'I don't think I'm afraid. But I do feel guilty.'

Sarah was puzzled. 'Guilty? About what?'

'The way I treated it,' replied Beattie, uneasily. 'The way I treated you, and all my family.'

Sarah smiled and put her arm around Beattie's waist. 'Trust me, Beattie,' she said affectionately. 'I brought you here deliberately. There's a very special reason why I want you to come back to the house.'

A few minutes later, to Beattie's absolute astonishment, Sarah used her own key to open the front door of the house. Sarah ushered Beattie in first.

As she came into the hall, Beattie felt a sudden cold chill. 'Oh God!' she cried, her voice echoing round the large empty space. 'It's hard to believe. This is home, *our* home.' She took a few steps further, looking up to the ceiling, then all round her. 'I never thought I'd ever be standing here again.' She crossed her arms and squeezed them tight. She felt pain and anguish. 'You're right, Sarah,' she said. 'I *am* afraid.'

'There's no need to be, Beattie,' said Sarah, strolling over to her, 'because from now on, this place is back in the family, where it belongs.'

Beattie turned with a start. Had she heard right?

'Freddie's put down a deposit on the place,' Sarah said. 'We're going to do it up bit by bit, and, if the house survives the air raids, we'll move back in a few months' time.'

Beattie's eyes were wide with astonishment and bewilderment. 'Oh, Sarah!' she breathed.

'And both Freddie and I want you to know,' Sarah said tenderly, 'that the door of this house will always be open to you and Ed. That's the way Mother and Father would have wanted it.'

Beattie, her eyes glistening with tears, threw her arms around her sister and they hugged each other.

They then strolled together into what was once the kitchen. Like the rest of the place, it was a depressing sight, for the old gas cooker was black and filthy, the Ascot heater broken and hanging from the wall, the stone sink had split in two and was lying in separate halves on the floor, there was no glass in the windows, and what was left of the linoleum was covered with huge scorch marks.

'It's hard to believe we used to have most of our meals in here,' Beattie said, trying to take it all in. 'Mother and Father must be turning in their graves.'

'Don't worry,' assured Sarah. 'It'll look different in a few months. All this dear old house needs now is some love.'

Sarah's remark triggered something in Beattie's mind. It was something she had been keeping from everyone for so long, but which she realised now had to come out into the open. Sadly, she had always found that there were very few people in life that she could trust, *really* trust. It was strange, but even during her young years, if ever she had something that was troubling her, or needed someone to take her side, there was only one person she could turn to. It was neither her mother nor her father, but her sister, Sarah. And so it was all over again. Her new-found relationship with Sarah was the opportunity she had been waiting for to discuss something so intimate that she could not talk about it with Ed, or even Ma Briggs.

'I need someone to love me too,' she said quite suddenly and unexpectedly. 'And I think I've found him.'

Sarah swung her a startled look. 'Beattie!' she said, beaming.

'I've been meeting someone for over a year,' Beattie continued. 'His name's Chris Wilkins. He's a schoolteacher. He wants me to marry him.'

Sarah was overjoyed. 'Oh – Beattie!' she gasped, throwing her arms around her and embracing her. 'How absolutely wonderful! We must meet him,' she said quickly, eagerly, pulling away from Beattie and looking at her. 'You must invite him over to tea. Freddie and I would love to meet him. He'll be absolutely thrilled. *I'm* thrilled! I'll help you, Beattie. I'll help you in any way I can. Oh, what's he like? After all you've been through, you deserve a good man to look after you–'

'There's a snag,' said Beattie, cutting straight through her sister's excited response. 'He's a good deal younger than me.'

Sarah stopped abruptly. For a brief moment, her joy was overtaken by concern. 'How much younger?' she asked, apprehensively.

'About fifteen years.'

Sarah breathed a sigh of relief. 'Oh, that's all,' she replied. 'For one moment I thought you were going to say he was still in his pram!'

They both laughed.

'I'm not that bad!' quipped Beattie. 'But there's another problem. He's been married before.'

'Oh.' Sarah bit her lip anxiously.

'They married when they were both only eighteen. They were too young. It never worked. They split up within a year and got a divorce soon after. He hasn't seen her since.'

Sarah thought about this carefully for a moment before asking, 'Does the fact that he's been married before – worry you?'

If Beattie had doubts, she wasn't showing them. 'No,' she said, shaking her head firmly. 'But I'd be untruthful to myself if I wasn't just a little uneasy that he'd spent at least part of his life with another woman. But then, with me–' she perched herself on the remains of a wooden trestle table – 'there *was* Edward Lacey. Not to mention Jack Ridley.'

Sarah shrugged her shoulders in agreement. 'The main point is, do you love this man?'

Beattie hesitated. 'More than I ever thought possible. It's ridiculous, isn't it,' she said, with a sigh, 'falling in love at my age?'

'Love can come at any age, Beattie,' replied Sarah. 'It's not the preserve of the young.'

Beattie smiled appreciatively. 'I wonder what

they would have thought about all this?' she said, her eyes scanning the rack and ruin of the poor old kitchen. 'Mum and Dad.'

Sarah came to her, put her arm around her waist, and joined her in a reflective contemplation. 'I think they're very proud of you, Beattie,' she said with great affection. 'Something tells me they're going to approve of their new son-in-law.'

'I was actually referring to you and me, Sarah,' said Beattie. 'Please don't ever let us part again. I couldn't bear it.'

The two of them held each other tight.

'Now we only have one small problem to deal with,' said Sarah, whose mind was already concentrating on a more pressing matter. 'What are we going to do about Jack Ridley?'

Throughout his life, Jack Ridley had seldom stayed in any one place long enough to unpack his clothes. Not that he had many clothes to worry about, for it seemed to be his style to live from hand to mouth. But in his humble opinion, things were about to look up. Once Ritz had done his bit with Beattie, he would be able to move back into the fold, and work on his next move, which would be how to get his hands on part, if not all, of the small fortune left to Ed by his grandfather.

Jack's latest 'abode' was a room above a bombed-out toy shop in Duckworth Mews, just off the Mile End Road in East London. It wasn't much of a place, but he had got the rent for a song from a bloke who was half pissed at the time, whom he had met in a pub called the Bow

Arms, just near the tube station. The room itself consisted of nothing more than a single bed, a table and two chairs, a gas ring to make a cup of char, and a cold tap and washbasin in the corner, which was, for some absurd reason, hidden behind a tatty cloth screen.

But for Ridley, the one great asset of the room was the second door, which was situated at the rear, and a very handy device for making a quick exit to the back yard below, if and when it should be required.

Today, Ridley was in a very happy mood. Ritz was due to report back to him about his meeting in Mitford Road with Beattie. He tried to imagine how Beattie would react when she heard how Ridley was embarking on the final years of his life, struck down by a deadly illness, with no one to look after him during the winter of his life. As he lay back on his bed, smoking his usual rolled fag, he grinned to himself, amazed at the sheer genius of his idea. The only flea in the ointment was, however, Ritz himself. Ridley had never fully trusted the little pile of pig dung, mainly because his brains were about as big as a peapod. He began to have doubts about how Ritz would handle the situation. Would Beattie believe his story? Would Ritz be so convincing that she wouldn't fail to welcome Ridley back with open arms? Or would Ritz make a complete bungle of the job, just like he always had done, especially when he'd got him, Ridley, involved with the Dillon boys. Even as he was contemplating all the worst possibilities, there was a thumping on the door downstairs, followed by a voice calling out to him. 'Ridley! Are you there? Open up!'

Ridley leaned up from his bed and rushed straight to the small window at the front of the room. Peering from behind the curtain, he could see Sarah looking up at him from the cobbled mews below. 'Open up, Ridley!' she called. 'I want to talk to you.'

Ridley was about to panic. What's *she* doing here? he thought to himself. Why isn't it Beattie down there? He cursed Ritz. What had he done? This wasn't what he expected at all.

'Come on, Ridley!' came Sarah again. 'I know you're up there. I need to talk to you. Open up!'

Ridley stood back from the window and thought hard. The last time he'd approached this woman, he'd warned her what would happen if she didn't speak up for him to Beattie. His whole attitude changed. This was good, this was very good. This is just what he wanted. Beattie's sister was there to help him. She had clearly decided that speaking up for him was far better than him ruining her own marriage. In one swift, impulsive movement, he rushed out of the room.

'Well now,' said Ridley, as he opened the front door downstairs. ''Ere's a pleasant surprise.'

'Are you going to let me in,' asked Sarah, 'or do I have to wait on the doorstep all day?'

Ridley grimaced, and let her in. 'Welcome to my 'umble abode!' he said. He liked this woman's nerve.

'Leave the door open, if you please,' she said firmly as she came in.

'Wot's up?' he asked cheekily. 'Don't yer trust me?'

'How did you guess?' she answered, tersely.

The passage was full of broken toys and old cardboard boxes. There was junk everywhere. As she followed him up a small flight of stairs, Sarah covered her mouth with her hand; the smell of cat's pee was overpowering.

'So?' asked Ridley, once they were inside his room. 'And wot do I owe for the pleasure of your company?'

'You owe me nothing,' replied Sarah. 'And I certainly owe you nothing.'

Ridley's smile disappeared. 'Who told yer where ter find me?' he demanded icily.

'That doesn't matter,' said Sarah. 'What does matter is the proposition you made me.'

Ridley's face lit up again. 'Ah!' he beamed. 'Now we're talkin'. Wot about a little snifter?'

'I didn't come to drink with you, Mr Ridley,' she replied. 'I came to ask you a few questions.'

'Fire away,' said Ridley, going across to the small cabinet at the side of his bed to pour a drink.

Sarah made sure that she kept her back as close to the main bedroom door as possible. She felt stifled by the smell of stale beer and rolled fag smoke. 'I want to know, if I speak on your behalf to my sister, what you intend to do if you go back to live with her again?'

Ridley was puzzled. *'Do?'* he asked, whilst pouring himself a glass of dark brown bitter from a quart bottle. 'I intend ter take up where I left off, ter look after me wife, and be a good 'usband to 'er.'

'Are you sure you'll be well enough to do that?'

Ridley swung a look at her. 'Wot's that s'pposed ter mean?' he growled.

Sarah shrugged her shoulders. 'I gather you're almost at death's door,' she replied.

'Ah!' said Ridley. 'So Beattie's 'eard, 'as she?'

Sarah was now on the attack. 'In all the years you've been married to my sister, you've never once treated her like a proper wife. So what makes you think you can do so now?'

'That's not fair, Sarah ol' gel,' replied Ridley, taking down a huge gulp of bitter. 'I've always been fond of my little missus.'

'Is that why you beat her?'

'Is that wot she told yer?'

Sarah squared up to him. 'It's what Ma Briggs told me, and plenty of those ghastly neighbours of yours in the Bunk.' She moved further into the room. 'Ma Briggs said there were times when my sister had so many bruises and black eyes that she was tempted to call in the police.'

Ridley was angry. 'That stupid ol' cow!' he barked, wiping the beer foam from his lips with the back of his hand. 'She was always tryin' ter make trouble, always takin' Beat's side whenever we disagreed about anyfin'!'

'What do you really want from my sister, Mr Ridley?' asked Sarah.

Ridley came across to her, and angrily slammed his glass down on the table. 'Are yer goin' ter speak to 'er for me,' he rasped, 'or would yer prefer me ter 'ave a little word wiv your 'usband?'

'I ask again,' insisted Sarah, refusing to be intimidated by him. 'What do you want from my sister? Or should I say – from her son?'

Ridley froze, and stared her out. Gradually, his face broke into a huge grin. 'Ah!' he replied. 'I see we talk the same language after all.' He picked up his glass of bitter again. ''E's goin' ter be a very rich boy, your nephew,' he said, strolling back to his bed, and perching on the side of it. 'I fink the least 'e can do is ter take care of 'is poor ol' stepfarver.'

'I don't think that's very likely, Jack.'

Ridley leaped up from the bed to see Beattie, who had entered the room from behind Sarah.

'I'm afraid you won't get much out of him,' said Beattie, joining Sarah. 'Or me.'

'Wot the 'ell's goin' on 'ere?' snapped Ridley, rushing straight across to confront her. 'Where's Ritz? Did 'e bring you 'ere?'

'No, Jack,' replied Beattie, with cool calm. 'Sarah and I came all on our own.' She stood side by side with her sister. 'We wanted to have a little chat with you.'

Ridley eyed them both with deep suspicion.

'I'm afraid Ed had quite a disappointment,' said Sarah. 'Isn't that so, Beattie?'

'That's right,' replied Beattie, who, like her sister, was directing her words straight at Ridley. 'You see, his grandfather turned out to be not quite as generous as we all first thought.'

'It appears the old chap was a bit of a philanderer,' said Sarah.

'He went through his money like a hot knife through butter,' said Beattie.

'Which means,' continued Sarah, 'that there was nothing left for a twenty-first birthday present for the stepson who you adore so much.'

'Sad – isn't it, Jack?' contributed Beattie. 'But you can still come back and live with me, if you like.'

'Provided, of course,' said Sarah, 'that you'll be well enough to live that long.'

The two sisters exchanged wry smiles.

Ridley looked from one to the other. 'Ritz!' he barked. ''E's put yer up ter this! Just wait till I get me 'ands on 'im. I'll kill the sod!'

'The saving grace in all of this, Mr Ridley,' replied Sarah, 'is that your friend appears to have a conscience. It's something you might consider yourself some time.'

'Get out of 'ere!' He rushed over to the door and pulled it wide open. 'Go on – boaf of yer! Out!'

'No, Jack,' said Beattie, going to a chair at the table, and calmly sitting there. 'You're the one that's leaving, not us.'

'You see, Mr Ridley,' said Sarah, continuing where Beattie had left off, 'my sister and I are tired of your constant intimidation. We want to see the back of you – once and for all.'

'And I want a divorce, Jack,' added Beattie. 'Since you've disappeared without trace for so long, I don't think the Courts will have too many problems granting it. Do you?'

'Do we make ourselves quite clear, Mr Ridley?' added Sarah.

Ridley's hand seemed to have frozen on the door knob. He still hadn't quite taken in what had hit him. He gently closed the door, went back to the bed, and perched there. Suddenly, he felt like a man drowning; his whole life was floating before him. Throughout his lifetime, he had mixed with criminals and nefarious characters of all types, and always he had somehow managed to cope with them. But this was the first time he had come up against two women who were using their brains against him rather than their fists. As he looked across at the two of them, he found it hard to believe that they had been distant with each other for so long. There seemed to be a bond, a union between them that was hard to define. But, physically strong as he was, they unnerved him. No, there was no going back now, he told himself. This was the end of the road for him, and he had no alternative but to go along with what they wanted. But, being Jack Ridley, he would not give up without one last attempt.

'And what would you say,' he said, looking as menacing as he could, 'if I told yer ter go ter 'ell?'

Sarah walked slowly across to him. 'I don't think you'd do that, Mr Ridley,' she said in a cool, businesslike voice.

'As I told you once before, Jack,' added Beattie, 'I'd hate to be the one who shops you.'

Perched uneasily on the edge of his bed, Ridley sat staring aimlessly at the linoleum on the floor beneath his feet.

'We want you to pack your things, Mr Ridley.'

Ridley looked up to see Sarah standing over him.

'If you ever try to approach either me or my sister again,' she said uncompromisingly, 'we'll make it our business to inform the police about your part in the murder of a police constable.'

Jack looked long and hard at her, and then at Beattie. It was the last time he would ever do so.

Ma Briggs didn't much care for the schoolteacher. Not that it was anything personal – his looks, his appearance, or his manner. No, nothing like that. It was the disruption he was about to cause to her life that she objected to. In fact, although she was overjoyed in one way for Beattie, the prospect of Beattie getting married again thoroughly depressed her, for it meant that she would most probably have to pack her bags and leave for an old people's home or something. At least, that's what she thought. But on the evening that Beattie first introduced her to her schoolteacher friend, Mr Wilkins, all was not what she had been dreading.

'We want you to come and live with us, Ma,' Beattie said, during five o'clock tea time.

'We're going to look for a place outside London,' said Chris, the schoolteacher. 'In the country somewhere, probably Surrey.'

'In the country?' replied the old girl in disbelief. 'Outside London?'

'As much as we love Mitford Road, Ma,' added Beattie, 'don't you think it would be nice to find somewhere away from the smells of city streets, with fresh air, and cows and sheep in fields?'

'I like the smell of city streets,' Ma snapped grumpily. 'An' I 'ate fresh air and cows and sheep.'

Beattie and Chris exchanged gentle laughs. 'But you like me,' said Beattie. 'And Ed.'

'I don't like yer,' replied the old girl. 'I love yer.

But I still don't like cows and sheep. Stupid ol' fresh air!'

The moment she had told Ma about Chris, Beattie knew she had a problem on her hands. The poor old girl was now at an age when she was thoroughly set in her ways. But Beattie was determined that after all Ma had done for her and Ed, she would never dump her in an old people's home.

'I'll tell you something, Ma,' said the quiet-spoken schoolteacher. 'I was born in the countryside, a little village in Norfolk, a place called Swaffham. It was so small, hardly anyone seemed to live there except me and my mum and dad and two brothers. It was so peaceful, so peaceful in fact that it bored the pants off me. Then, after I'd done my teacher's training, I was sent to a school in the East End. God, what a difference! Talk about rowdy. And all that traffic going down the Mile End Road and Stratford. But I loved it – at least, I did for the first few years. It was a novelty, so different from everything I'd ever known. But I tell you something, after a while the novelty wore off, and pretty soon I became just as bored living in London as I was in the country. In fact, I longed to get back home again. But I'm glad I came here. Otherwise, the only kind of life I'd have ever experienced would have been in a tiny village in Norfolk. And most of all–' he turned to Beattie, who was sitting at his side on the sofa – 'I'd never have met Beattie – or you.'

Ma, whose indomitable curlers were dangling down from the few hairs she had left on her head, listened to all the schoolteacher had to say with rapt attention. All the time he was talking, she was sucking her gums, for those elusive pearly whites of hers had still not been recovered. But she did hear everything he said, and it made her feel guilty.

'I didn't mean ter sound ungrateful, Beat,' she said. 'It's just that, well, I fink I'm too old ter change now, too old ter up me roots an' go dancin' around the cows and sheep in the country.'

'Listen to me, Ma,' said Beattie, stretching across for Ma's hand. 'As long as you live, you'll never be too old for anything. Of all the people I've ever known in my life, you're the one who adapts to change more than any other. I remember when me and Ed asked you to leave the Bunk, to come and live with us in this road. I remember how, from the first moment you arrived, you gave us all the drive and the energy to make this place what it is today. If you did it then, Ma,' she said, 'you can do it again.'

As usual with Ma when she had just been given what she always considered was a lecture from Beattie, she sat with her hands on her lap, staring into the coal fire. After what seemed to Beattie and Chris to be an interminable silence, the old girl finally looked straight at Chris. 'It's nuffin' personal, yer understand,' she said sheepishly.

Chris gave her a great big smile. 'I know that, Ma,' he said.

Shortly after, the old girl went to bed in her usual place down in the air-raid shelter. Now left alone, Beattie stretched out on the sofa, with her head resting on Chris's lap. She was miles away.

'Penny for your thoughts?' he asked, smoothing her forehead gently with his fingers.

Beattie thought for a moment before replying. 'Oh, I was just thinking how lucky I am.'

'Lucky?'

'To have Ma, to have Ed, to have my sister, Sarah, but most of all, to have you.'

'I'm pretty lucky too.' As he looked down into her eyes, he took off his thick-lensed spectacles, which had been the reason why he had been turned down for military service. Then he leaned his head down and kissed her tenderly on the lips.

Beattie sighed. 'I feel strange,' she said. 'As though I'm coming to the end of an era.'

'That's a funny thing to say,' he replied. 'I would have thought we're just starting one.'

'No, but you know what I mean,' she explained. 'The past and the future seem to be coming together all at once, coming together in the most wonderful way. God knows, Ma's ancient, but at least we've still got her. And Ed – oh, Chris, I can't wait for you to meet him. You two are going to get on like a house on fire. I just pray he survives this awful war. It's odd. All those years ago when he was first born, I'd have taken any opportunity to throw him straight into the Regent's Canal, but now–' She sighed despondently. 'If anything happened to him, I don't know what I'd do.'

'Nothing's going to happen to him, darling,' said Chris, reassuringly. 'After the war, he's going to come home, and he and me are going to make your life hell!'

Beattie laughed, because she wanted to believe him. 'I can't wait for you to meet my sister, Sarah, either,' she said. 'These past few weeks have been – extraordinary. It's as though the two of us have been born all over again. Every time I think about it, I find it so amazing that we never held on to each other. But in some strange way, it's not just about flesh and blood – it's something deeper than that. There are times when I'm alone, when I feel she's such a part of me, I know where she is, and what she's doing.' She moved her eyes, and gazed lovingly up at Chris. 'For the first time in my life,' she said, 'I feel I know her. And I think she knows me too.'

She sat up and faced him. 'I just hope we're never parted again.'

'You won't be,' he answered, confidently.

'How can you be so sure?'

Chris thought about it for a moment. 'Because you don't want to be,' he replied.

She fell into his arms, and they started to make love. But the wail of the air-raid siren soon put a stop to that.

CHAPTER 28

The aerial onslaught on London came to a climax on the night of 29 December 1940, when practically the whole city was ablaze. Street after street, office blocks, restaurants, railway stations, hospitals, churches – all were left either in a pile of rubble, or consumed with flames in an inferno. Although the Royal Air Force courageously diminished the fire power of the marauding Luftwaffe, during the first few months of the following year, other cities such as Plymouth, Portsmouth, Coventry, Manchester, Leeds, and Liverpool all came under attack. It was, of course, a concentrated effort by Reichsmarshal Goering and his Nazi hierarchy to undermine the morale of the British people, but that morale was far more determined and indomitable than they had anticipated. Despite the constant day and night air raids, life went on as near normal as was humanly possible. The fish and chip shops did a roaring trade, so did the pubs, and even though food supplies were short, the British housewife queued outside any shop that could offer even a suggestion of something palatable. Whale and horsemeat, spurned as cruel and barbaric in times of peace, were, despite their foul taste, a necessary replacement for other foods that were simply unobtainable. People were also constantly forced to clear up each morning after the bomb blasts of the night before, and when it was impossible to find any more glass for their windows in the hardware shops, they settled for timber boards, which often had a huge 'V' for Victory chalk-marked on them. Everywhere else, the 'BUSINESS AS USUAL' signs sprouted like mushrooms. If this was to be the People's War, then this is how they would fight it.

During the early spring of 1941, Beattie married her schoolteacher boyfriend, Chris Wilkins. She desperately wanted a white wedding, but as the vicar of the local church was a bit puritanical about divorced couples, she had to settle for a straightforward registry office ceremony in Islington Town Hall. Even so, part of her wish was granted, for, undaunted by the vicar, Sarah took it upon herself to make a wedding dress for her sister, made from a white synthetic taffeta material, which Freddie managed to get for her on the black market. Very few guests were invited for the occasion, as several eyebrows had already been raised when it was known that Beattie was marrying someone who was fifteen years younger than herself. Sadly, Ed couldn't be there either, for at the last moment, his compassionate leave had been cancelled owing to the fact that he was about to join his unit for an 'undisclosed destination'. Chris's family turned out to be a lovely bunch, and everyone on Beattie's side, including Aunt Dixie, Aunt Myra and Uncle Terry, got on splendidly with them. During the wedding reception afterwards, which was held in a large hired room above a furniture store in Lower

Holloway Road, Sarah and Freddie had a wonderful time chatting with Chris's mother and father, warm, charming people, who had apparently taken to their future daughter-in-law the moment they laid eyes on her.

Ma Briggs, however, was the big success of the evening. Despite her years, she did a tango with Chris's father, who was a bit of an expert in ballroom dancing, and they were applauded so loudly that the record of Victor Sylvester and his Ballroom Orchestra playing 'Green Eyes' was played so many times, the grooves were nearly worn out.

Just before Christmas, Sarah's first meeting with Chris had at first been a little uneasy, mainly because she had grown very protective towards her younger sister, and didn't want her to get hurt any more. In many ways, Sarah was still quite old-fashioned in her outlook on life, and on that first meeting with her future brother-in-law, she treated him with a certain amount of suspicion. It was therefore not until several weeks after the wedding that she really got to know, and like him.

It was almost closing time at the barber's shop when Chris turned up to have Freddie give him his usual haircut. He was the last customer of the day, so, as soon as he came in, Sarah lowered the door blind, and reversed the 'OPEN' sign to 'CLOSED'. Then she went out into the back parlour and made all three of them a cup of tea. By the time she came back, Freddie was just finishing off Chris's comb-and-scissors trim.

'I was just asking Freddie,' said Chris, as Sarah put his cup of tea at the side of the hairwash sink. 'You must have wondered why Beattie should've got mixed up with a younger bloke like me.'

'Those sort of matters are not our concern, Chris,' said Sarah, rather primly. 'They're personal to you and Beattie, not us.'

'I know,' said Chris. 'But you must have heard the tongues wag. I have. So has Beattie.'

Sarah put Freddie's cup on the ledge by the sink. 'If you love each other,' she said, 'what business is it of anyone else?'

'Precisely!' answered Chris. 'I tell Beattie that all the time. But she still worries about it. She also worries about the fact that she's too old to give me a family of our own. I can't seem to make her understand that, as much as I love children, I love her more. I told her that right from the start, long before we decided to get married.'

'There we are then!' said Freddie, removing the towel from around Chris's shoulders. Then he collected the hand mirror, and showed him the cut from all angles.

'Excellent! Thanks, Freddie!' Chris said, swivelling himself round in the barber's chair. 'You're an artist!'

Freddie laughed, collected his tea, and went across to join Sarah, who was sitting on one of the customers' chairs.

'In any case,' continued Chris, 'if we want children all that badly, we can always adopt them. But there are other things I want to do first.' He turned around briefly, and picked up his cup of tea. 'I want to make Beattie happy,' he said. 'She's very special to me.' He paused a moment. 'D'you know she's the only woman in my life I've ever cared for. I often tell her how much I love her, and I've never told anyone that before, not even my first wife – especially my first wife!'

Sarah and Freddie exchanged tactful smiles.

Chris sipped his tea. 'But truthfully, there's so much I want to do for her. I have so many plans. So has she. D'you know, when we're down the air-raid shelter sometimes, we plan all the things we're going to do after the war. We talk about everything, from where we want to live, the kind of school I'd like to end up teaching in, the kind of people we'd like to get to know, even the colour of the walls in our bedroom! Poor old Ma. She must be sick to death of listening to all our drivel by now. It's a good thing she sleeps soundly!'

They all laughed.

'I'm a lucky bloke, that's for sure!'

They were interrupted by a tapping sound on the shop door. Freddie put his tea down and went to see who it was. Beattie was peering in and waving through the window. Freddie opened the door for her.

'I thought he'd be lurking in here!' she said, going straight across and giving Chris a kiss. Then, ruffling his hair, she said, 'I hope you've paid my brother-in-law for that haircut?'

'It's all in the family!' quipped Freddie.

'Hello, Sarah dear,' Beattie said, giving her sister a kiss on the cheek. 'I hope my husband's been behaving himself?'

'He's been a model customer,' replied Sarah, with a smile. 'So where've you been?'

'To see Mr Ogden,' she said, 'the dentist down the road. He's making a new pair of dentures for Ma. They won't be ready for another week.'

'Oh God!' groaned Chris. 'She'll go out of her mind!'

'Poor Ma,' said Sarah. 'She does so hate to be without her teeth.'

'So would you if you didn't have any!' quipped Chris, to gales of laughter from the others.

'We have to go, Chris,' said Beattie, with some urgency. 'It'll be the siren any minute. I don't want to get caught out in the ack-ack.'

'Right,' said Chris, turning then to Freddie and Sarah. 'Thanks a lot then, Fred. And for the tea, Sarah.'

'Byebye Chris,' replied Sarah, kissing him lightly on the cheek.

'Come on then,' said Freddie. 'I'll see yer out.'

Freddie led Chris to the door, leaving Beattie alone for a moment with Sarah.

'Thanks for everything, Sarah,' said Beattie, embracing her sister. 'As usual.'

'Come and see us soon,' replied Sarah. 'We've got a lot of gossip to catch up with. And by the way, I think you've got a very nice husband.'

Beattie's face lit up. 'Oh, Sarah, d'you really think so?'

'He's madly in love with you. Did you know that?'

Beattie giggled. These days, she seemed so much younger than her age. 'I'm pretty mad about him too,' she confessed. 'But it means a lot to me that you like him. When we got married, I had my doubts.'

'Well just remember this,' said Sarah, putting her arm around Beattie's shoulder, and leading her towards the door. 'Whenever you feel you're at your lowest ebb, just think how much you've got to look forward to. A new husband, a wonderful son, and a promising new life. So make the most of it.'

They stopped at the door, and paused. Beattie was radiant, and beaming. 'The next time I see you, I want to hear all that gossip you keep promising me.'

'I won't forget.'

'Promise?'

'Promise.'

They embraced, then Beattie went out to join Chris, who was waiting with Freddie outside. After final farewells, Beattie and Chris made off at a brisk pace down St Alban's Place to catch their bus back home from Upper Street. It was now getting dark quite quickly, and along the main road people were hurrying to get home before the air-raid siren heralded the start of yet another night's bombing.

Freddie put his arm around Sarah's shoulders as they watched Beattie and Chris head off towards the end of the quiet side street. 'I fink she's done all right there, don't you?' said Freddie.

'So has he,' replied Sarah. 'I don't think I have to worry about Beattie any more. She's happy now.'

'Yes,' said Freddie. 'But all these plans 'e keeps

goin' on about, I wish 'e'd 'urry up an' get on wiv 'em.'

'Don't be silly, dear,' replied Sarah. 'They're still young. They've got all their lives ahead of them.'

Beattie and Chris stopped briefly, and waved back to Sarah and Freddie. And then they turned the corner, and were gone.

'Jairmany calling! Jairmany calling!'

Ma Briggs was clearly a glutton for punishment. When Beattie and Chris arrived back home, there she was, listening to the man with the sneer up his nose again, cursing and blinding, and ready to smash up the poor wireless set with her bare fists. Lord Haw-Haw's subject tonight was the great success of the German invasion of Greece, and the ultimate surrender of the ancient city of Salonika. But when he got on to the continuation of the London Blitz, and how the population was gradually weakening beneath the pressure of the superior German air power, Ma was fighting mad. 'Lyin' sod!' she yelled at the pseudo-aristocratic voice. 'We should string 'im up an' be done wiv it!'

'We've got to capture him first, Ma,' said Chris, who liked nothing better than to wind up the old girl. 'When they do, I think you should be given first chance to get at him. What do you say?'

'Stop it, Chris,' scolded Beattie. 'Things are bad enough as they are. When you think how they nearly burned down the whole of the city last December, it gives you the creeps when you listen to what he says.'

'Don't be frightened, Beattie,' Chris replied. Sometimes he took it for granted that her nerves were made of steel, but in fact, she was just as nervous and vulnerable as anyone else. 'Why don't we play a game of Monopoly?' he said. 'It'll help to calm our nerves.'

'Calm our nerves?' barked the old girl. 'Buyin' an' sellin' uvver people's property? It's enuff ter give yer a 'art attack.'

'I don't think we should, Chris,' said Beattie, anxiously. 'The siren went nearly half an hour ago. We should get down the shelter before they start coming over.'

'They usually come over within a few minutes of the siren,' replied Chris. 'I haven't heard a thing. I don't think it's going to be much tonight.' He went to the sideboard. 'Come on,' he said. 'Let's make it a short one, and I'll show you how I can buy Mayfair and Piccadilly Circus all in a few minutes.'

Whilst Chris was getting out the Monopoly board, money, and cards, Ma reluctantly turned off the wireless set, but not before raising two fingers to her 'Jairman' collaborator friend.

A few minutes later, all three of them were hunched over the Monopoly board, engaged in the crucial business of takeovers, bank loans, and the buying and selling of valuable property. To Chris's intense irritation, tonight, as on all nights, it was obvious that Ma was going to be the triumphant player, for she was cunning enough, and observant enough to know every single move before it was even contemplated. But although Beattie loved seeing Chris get rattled, her ears were constantly listening out for the familiar droning sound of enemy aircraft. But the encouraging sign was that there was, as yet, no ack-ack anti-aircraft fire, and so, without being too complacent, she carried on with the game. Even so, her mind was on other things. 'I hope it won't be long before we hear from Ed,' she said, quite out of the blue. 'I haven't heard anything from him since before the wedding.'

'I doubt you will,' said Chris. 'If Jerry's going to try an invasion here, every bloke in khaki's going to be sitting around waiting for him.'

'It's so unfair,' protested Beattie. 'He's only a boy, and he's already been involved in some of the worst fighting of the war. Thank God he survived Dunkirk, and then all this business in Greece. He should be given a break, and let the others do some of the dirty work.'

'Unfortunately, there aren't enough "others" to go round,' said Chris. 'If there was any justice in this world, I should be out there with them.'

Beattie turned on him. 'No, Chris!' she snapped. 'You can't help your eye problems. And in any case, you do your bit in the ARP. That's quite enough.'

'You don't 'ave ter worry about Ed,' said Ma, confidently. 'If anyone knows 'ow ter take care of 'imself, that one does. Hey!' She had suddenly advanced her car token around the board so that it had landed on a prize property. 'Park Lane!' she bellowed. 'I'll buy it!'

Chris clutched his forehead in frustration. 'Oh no!' he sighed. 'Not another one!'

'Be quiet!'

Chris and Ma suddenly looked up at Beattie, who could obviously hear something, for her eyes were turned upwards towards the ceiling.

'What is it?' asked Chris.

'Listen!'

After a few seconds, they could hear the approach of what sounded like a single aircraft, its engines droning monotonously. It came from the far distance, and seemed to take a long time to establish itself, but there was no doubt that it was there.

'Must be one of ours,' suggested Chris, whose eyes were also turned towards the ceiling. 'Can't hear any ack-ack.'

Even as he spoke, all hell broke loose as the air was lambasted by the deafening crack of anti-aircraft fire.

'Everyone under the table!' yelled Chris, as he leaped up, and quite literally yanked both Ma and Beattie off their chairs, and helped them under the table they had been playing on.

But Ma was not as agile as the others, and she had a job to squeeze herself under the table. 'Bloody 'Itler!' she yelled, furiously. 'I'll get yer fer this!'

As the barrage of ack-ack fire pounded the night sky, all three finally managed to huddle together beneath the table. But it was a nerve-racking experience, and Chris had to use his arms to protect and comfort the two women.

The barrage continued for quite a while, with the house being rocked to its very foundations by the deafening sounds, and the tinkling of shrapnel on the pavement outside. And then, quite suddenly, the guns stopped firing. What followed was an intense silence, with only the distant shouting of people along the road outside.

After a moment or so, the three heads beneath the table felt confident enough to look up. 'Sounds like it's all over,' said Ma, who hardly dared to speak.

'That plane,' whispered Beattie. 'What happened to it? Did they shoot it down?'

'Hard to say,' said Chris, who felt more confident than the others to speak in a normal voice. 'I certainly can't hear it.'

They waited a moment or so longer, until they finally decided that it was safe enough to emerge from their makeshift shelter.

'Oh God!' said Beattie. 'We should have gone down the shelter. It's too dangerous to stay in the house once the siren's gone.'

'Well, I don't know about you,' complained Ma, bitterly, as both Chris and Beattie helped her up on to her feet. 'I'm goin' straight down there now. It's way past my kip time…'

'Out! Out! Out! Out! Out!'

The terrifying yells that suddenly pierced the air were coming from the road outside.

'Oh Christ!' called Beattie. 'What now?'

'Down!' barked Chris. 'Down!'

But by the time all three of them had thrown themselves to the floor again, another voice was yelling, 'Para – chute…!'

The word had hardly been completed when there was a sudden deafening explosion, followed by a blinding blue flash. In one horrifying moment of unreality, as if in slow motion, the entire house came tumbling down, bricks and mortar, glass, plaster, furniture, and personal possessions. The thick black smoke was dense, and by the time it had settled, nothing could be seen but a pile of rubble.

In the unnatural silence that followed, there was only the distant sound of a dog barking.

It was nearly two o'clock in the morning when Sarah and Freddie reached the Royal Northern Hospital in Holloway Road. Had it not been for the police constables who had brought them in their car, the only way to get there would have been to walk. The knock on the front door of the barber shop had given them quite a shock. At first, they didn't hear it for they had taken shelter in their Morrison, which had been erected in the back parlour. As soon as they heard the news about Beattie, they got dressed quickly, and were given a lift.

The air raid was still in full swing as they made their way to the emergency wing of the hospital through the Manor Gardens entrance. The place was jam-packed with ambulances bringing casualties from bombed-out buildings all over the borough, and in the waiting area of the wing itself, there were so many seriously injured patients waiting to be attended to that there was hardly enough room to move.

The moment they arrived, they were immediately sent to a temporary emergency ward on the ground floor that had been set up to deal with bomb blast casualties. The sound of people groaning was soul-destroying, and it took all

Sarah's strength to take in what was going on.

'I think you should both come straight in,' said a harassed ward sister with a soft Irish voice. 'I'm afraid there's not much time.'

Sarah's heart sank, and Freddie had to keep a comforting arm around her for support. Before they reached the last bed at the end of the ward, Sarah asked the nurse if she knew what had happened to the other occupants of her sister's house. But there appeared to be no information, other than that the house itself had been right next door to the house where a parachute bomb had been dangling from a roof top, until it finally exploded.

Beattie was in a bed behind screens. Sarah had to steel herself to go in, but when she did, she was still horrified to see the state her younger sister was in. Swathed in bandages that were blotched with leaking blood, and with tubes coming out from all parts of her body, it was obvious that she was fighting for her life.

'She had an operation to try to save her lung,' said the nurse, softly. 'There was so much heavy debris on her, it just crushed her entire body.'

'Can she survive?' This was the only question that Sarah now wanted answering.

The nurse responded by lowering her eyes.

After the nurse had gone, Sarah went to the side of the bed and searched for Beattie's hand beneath the bedclothes. She took hold of it, and gently squeezed it. To her astonishment, Beattie responded by slowly opening her eyes. 'Beattie,' Sarah called. 'I'm here. It's Sarah, darling. You're not alone.'

Beattie's torn and scratched face tried hard to smile. Then she tried to open her mouth. She was thirsty. Sarah immediately found a glass of water on the cabinet at her side, and using a spoon, eased a few drops of water between her lips. 'Is that better, darling?' she asked.

Beattie's head nodded just enough to notice. 'Sa-rah.' Her voice was only just audible.

'Yes, Beattie,' answered Sarah, leaning as close as she could. 'I can hear you, my darling.'

'Fred-die?' she was trying to ask.

'Yes, he's here,' said Sarah. 'Freddie's here.'

Freddie came round to the other side of the bed, and leaned down over her. ''Ello, mate,' he said, his voice cracking. 'Don't worry, I'm 'ere. You're doin' fine, mate, just fine.'

Beattie tried a smile again. It was as if she knew about the game that was being played, and it somehow gave her at least a moment or so of renewed strength. 'For-give me – Sarah,' she said, fighting for breath. 'For-give me for all I did.'

Sarah was struggling to keep back tears. 'There's nothing to forgive, Beattie. Nothing.'

'You – were always so – strong. I was – weak.'

Sarah was shaking her head. 'No, Beattie, no.'

'I remember…' Beattie swallowed hard, then coughed. But she quickly controlled herself. 'I … remember,' she continued, 'when we – had our picture taken – together – hand in hand.' She closed her eyes, but continued to talk. 'I put my tongue out…' A faint smile came to her face.

'Yes, Beattie,' said Sarah, softly. 'I remember.'

'When we saw – the picture – we laughed. We both laughed.'

'I remember, Beattie,' said Sarah, again. 'And I remember how angry Father was because he was the one who took it. He said we were two of a kind.'

Beattie was still smiling. But then she went silent. For one terrible moment, Sarah thought she had gone. But she was relieved when Beattie half opened her eyes again.

'Ed – yours now.' As she spoke now, Beattie's words seemed to be totally unconnected to anything she had indicated before. 'Ed – my boy – yours now. He's – always – been yours.'

Tears were now swelling hard and fast into Sarah's eyes. As she looked down at the frail features of her younger sister, all she could think of were the wasted years, the angry years of distance between them, the missed opportunities, and the sharing of life and experience. Until just a few hours before, Beattie and her new young husband had all their life ahead of them. They were about to discover the joys of a true marriage together, to learn how to respect and grow old together. But now, all Sarah could see was a life slipping away, a life that had endured so much pain and suffering, so many failed hopes. 'No, Beattie,' she said, feeling the warmth of Beattie's blood as she held her hand. 'Ed belongs to you, he always has. He loves you. He'll always love you.'

Beattie tried to raise her head. 'Your boy – Sarah,' she struggled to say. 'I – took him – from you. Stand – by him. Guide him. Love him.' Her head flopped back on to the pillow. She was silent for a moment, then she only had barely enough strength to whisper. 'Sarah...'

Sarah leaned close, and put her ear to Beattie's mouth.

'My ... sister ... Sarah...'

Sarah felt Beattie's warm breath gush into her ear, then stop. At the same time, her hand quivered, and went limp. She was gone.

Sarah sat there for a moment or so, unable, and not wanting to move.

Freddie let go of Beattie's other hand. Then he came round to comfort Sarah. Tears were streaming down his cheeks.

'She asked me to forgive her,' said Sarah, numbed, and still caressing her sister's hand with her fingers. 'But there was nothing to forgive.' She took Beattie's hand out from beneath the bedclothes and gently kissed it. Then she stood, and took one last look at her face. Despite the gashes and the complexion that now seemed to be drained of all blood, she thought her younger sister looked just as lovely as she always had done. But she would remember her not as she was now, but as she was in the picture they had posed for together – side by side.

Sarah turned, and with Freddie's comforting arm to support her, slowly made her way out along the ward.

A week later, Beattie's son, Ed, arrived home on compassionate leave. Unfortunately, he had been too far away to get back home in time to attend the funerals of his mother, her husband, Chris, and Ma Briggs, all of whom had perished in the parachute bomb explosion that night. But he was determined to say his own personal farewell to his mother, by paying one last visit to what had once been his home.

Mitford Road had quite literally disappeared. The entire road had been obliterated by the bomb, leaving just a pile of rubble.

As Ed approached the utter devastation that had once been his home, the numb feeling in his stomach almost made him turn back. But something made him go on, and when he eventually reached the front brick wall of the house, which, amazingly, was still standing, he paused just long enough to contemplate what had really happened on the night of the explosion. Then he moved on and, climbing over the mass of half-burned timbers, broken roof tiles, crumbled plaster, and fallen masonry, he made his way up what was left of the passage stairs. He had gone only a short way when something caught his eye, gleaming in the bright glow of the April sun. He crouched down and started to retrieve the object from a pile of rubble that had once been part of Ma Briggs' room on the first floor. He finally succeeded, but it was only when he managed to clean off the mud from the object that he was able to recognise it.

It was a set of pearly white false teeth.

CHAPTER 29

August was a funny old month. No matter how hard it tried, it just couldn't make up its mind whether it was to be the height of summer, or a reminder that autumn was on the way. In the end, however, it made its decision known by having a very positive heatwave. For several days at least, London and the south-east took the full brunt of the soaring temperatures, which sent thousands of people flocking into the parks wherever, and whenever, they could. Now that the Spitfires and Hurricanes of the Royal Air Force had finally stemmed the tide of the Luftwaffe blitz on London, there was an easing of tensions on the streets, and just a hint that perhaps the tide of the war was beginning to turn. And the news that Prime Minister Churchill had met with President Roosevelt on board the cruiser HMS *Prince of Wales* somewhere at sea was also a sign that perhaps at last the people of the United States of America were about to stand shoulder to shoulder with their British counterparts in their epic struggle against the Nazi tyrants.

It was therefore significant that Sarah and Freddie should have chosen a day during the heatwave to move into their newly restored house in Thornhill Road. From the time they stepped out of the taxi ahead of the furniture removals van, the house was bathed in hot, brilliant sunshine, and even the pavement outside was like walking on hot coals.

As most of the iron railings in London had been confiscated to help make weapons for the war effort, there was still a gap in the brick wall, but at least the front garden had been cleared of all the rubble and rubbish that had been accumulating there over the years.

When they stopped at the front door, Freddie paused, and turned to face Sarah. 'I've been waitin' fer this day fer a very long time,' he said. Then he formally handed her the key.

Sarah took it, and embraced him. 'Thank you, my dear, dear Freddie,' she said, holding him tight. Then, with a sigh, she put the key in the lock. This time, the front door opened effortlessly.

Inside, everything had been transformed. Despite the fact that they had both visited the house several times whilst Freddie's builder mate and his team had worked on the seemingly endless restoration, it was the first time that Sarah had actually had the feeling of coming home. Everything she saw reminded her of the old days, when the Melford family scurried about the place, taking everything in its stride. At one moment, it was almost as though she could see her mother disappearing into the kitchen, and then calling back, 'Supper's on the table! If you don't come soon, don't blame me if it gets cold!' The sights and sounds may not have been there in reality, but they were certainly in Sarah's mind, and she hoped they always would be.

'I'm going to walk round ter the dairy ter see if I can get some milk,' said Freddie. 'The removal blokes are bound ter want a cuppa when they get 'ere.'

'If not,' called Sarah, 'I've got some powdered milk!'

'Right!' Freddie called, as he left. 'I'll be right back!'

Sarah was now alone. She looked around the hall, and even though the place was still bare whilst waiting for the furniture that would make it a home again, she was astonished what had been achieved since Freddie first brought her there on that surprise visit so many months before. Most of all, she was impressed how Freddie's mate, Charlie Stumper, had managed to get enough paint on the black market to brighten the place up, especially as there was such a shortage of all building materials during a time when so many of London's homes and businesses had been damaged or destroyed by bomb blast. Even in the drawing room, all the holes and cracks in the walls and ceilings had been freshly plastered, and the green and gold wallpaper she had chosen weeks before was now giving new life and elegance to the room.

Going up the stairs on her own, however, was turning out to be more of an ordeal than she had imagined. In her mind, she could hear voices calling to her, beckoning, urging her on. But there was nothing threatening in the voices, or menacing; ghosts they may have been, but they were embracing her, and gently reminding her of the past. She could hear her father saying, 'I want you and your mother to start looking around for a lodger,' and Beattie throwing one of her tantrums about her relationship with Edward Lacey: 'It's me 'e wants, yer know – not you. And d'yer know why? Because I give 'im wot you never could, because you're incapable of it!' Sarah tried to dismiss the voices by hurrying up the stairs. But they pursued her right up to the first landing. 'Do you realise I'm a grandmother?' came the slightly deep-throated sound of her mother's voice, floating along the empty first floor. 'It's like having a child all over again – like turning back the clock.'

Her mother and father's room was bathed in the bright glow of summer sunshine pouring through the freshly painted windows. She remembered when she and Beattie were very small, and how on Christmas morning, at crack of dawn, they always invaded the room, and begged their parents to let them open their presents before breakfast. Without being aware of the fact, she had a huge smile on her face. Further along the landing, she went into what had once been her own room, and again, pictures of her early days there came flooding back – favourite dolls, a miniature teddy bear, and books – books everywhere.

The most difficult part of her exploration was yet to come, for as she climbed the stairs to what was once Beattie's room, her mind was crowded with horrifying pictures of Mitford Road on that last evening of Beattie's life. She opened the door of the room, and immediately felt Beattie's presence there. She could almost hear her saying,

'It's good to be back, Sarah – despite everything.' And then she recalled those last few moments she had spent with Beattie in that wretched hospital bed. 'For–give me, Sarah. Forgive me…' Those words would haunt Sarah for the rest of her life.

She walked across to the far side of the room, and stooped down, looking to see if there was still something there that she remembered from long ago. To her astonishment, the wainscoting around the bottom of the wall still bore the initial 'B' that Beattie had carved into it with a coin when she was a rebellious adolescent. As Sarah got up again, the voices returned: 'Your sister has already decided on which course she wishes to take … take … take…' This time, her father's voice disturbed her. 'Beattie made a mistake,' said her mother, whose voice intermingled with all the others. 'I failed her … failed … failed… She gave you so much pain…'

'For-give me…'

Sarah shook the voices from her head, and, arms crossed, strolled to the window and looked out. But for a moment, she could see nothing, for Beattie's voice persisted. 'Ed – my boy – yours now… He's – always – been yours…'

Sarah closed her eyes. Hearing Beattie's quiet, gentle voice was tearing into her; the pain of losing her was more than she could bear.

'…Always … been … yours…' Finally with indescribable sweetness, Beattie's voice whispered, 'Sarah … my sister … Sarah…'

And then there were no more voices, only silence – and peace. At last, Sarah knew that she and her sister would never be parted again.

Even though her eyes were tightly closed, tears were struggling out of them. When she opened them again, she found herself trying to look at something in the front garden down below. With the back of her hand, she wiped away the tears, and focused on the tall, lanky figure who was standing down there, face turned up towards the window.

It was Beattie's boy. And now he was *her* boy. Sarah's boy. It was – Ed.

The publishers hope that this book has given you enjoyable reading. Large Print Books are especially designed to be as easy to see and hold as possible. If you wish a complete list of our books please ask at your local library or write directly to:

Magna Large Print Books
Magna House, Long Preston,
Skipton, North Yorkshire.
BD23 4ND